P9-BZT-965

"Pearson excels at writing novels that grip the imagination."
—*People*

PRAISE FOR *PARALLEL LIES:*

"Pearson (*No Witnesses*, etc.) has written another terrific thriller . . ."
—*Library Journal*

". . . Pearson remains near the top of the genre . . ."
—*Booklist*

". . . grabs, he twists, he tightens the screws until you're drained by a superior read."
—Clive Cussler

"Pearson works this man-on-the-run episode like a pro . . . you'll be rewarded with a bravura display of acceleration."
—*Kirkus Reviews*

PRAISE FOR *MIDDLE OF NOWHERE:*

"Excitement quotient: high; technology details: intriguing."
—*USA Today*

"Master plotter, reliable thrills from a pro."
—*Kirkus Reviews*

"Fast-paced read from beginning to end. Pearson is able to effortlessly intertwine several detailed plot lines while still keeping his story firmly robed in reality."
—*New York Post*

"Pearson uses clear, forthright prose that perfectly exposes the psychological doubts and fears of his characters and keeps the plot racing from scene to scene. Craftily, Pearson weaves his web."
—*Providence Sunday Journal*

"Pearson has the details of a murder investigation down cold."
—*San Francisco Chronicle*

PRAISE FOR *CHAIN OF EVIDENCE:*

"This is an impeccable, high-speed thriller."
—*Boston Sunday Globe*

"Pearson handles the complex plot with grace and speed, packing a potent blend of action and procedural information into his work. A must-read for thriller fans."
—*Chicago Tribune*

"The gadget man is back with a bag of new toys. You don't have to be a techno-nerd to get wired on this scary stuff."
—*New York Times Book Review*

"Pearson weaves psychology and suspense into this tale of high-tech clues and complex motives."
—*Playboy*

"Ridley Pearson is an unequivocal success. I'm hooked again."
—*Entertainment Weekly*

PRAISE FOR *NO WITNESSES:*

"Tough and intelligent."
—*Fort Worth Star Telegram*

"Up-to-the-nanosecond techno-thriller."
—*New York Times*

"Infused with astonishingly effective overtones."
—*Boston Globe*

"Good old-fashioned storytelling."
—*Washington Post Book World*

"A serious, well-researched, complex thriller."
—*Los Angeles Times*

PRAISE FOR *THE ANGEL MAKER:*

"Exceptionally gripping and full of amazing forensic lore: a top-flight offering from an author who has clearly found his groove."
—*Kirkus Reviews*

"A chilling thriller."
—Dell Publishing

PRAISE FOR *HARD FALL:*

"Pearson excels at novels that grip the imagination. *Hard Fall* is an adventure with all engines churning."
—*People* magazine

"Mesmerizing urgency."
—*Los Angeles Times Book Review*

"Nifty cat-and-mouse caper. Crisply written tale."
—*Chicago Tribune*

PRAISE FOR *UNDERCURRENTS:*

"Neatly constructed plot. Hair-raising denouement. Remarkable insight and understanding of the motivations of the criminal mind."
—*Publishers Weekly*

"*Undercurrents* is a roller-coaster ride in the dark."
—Book-of-the-Month Club

THE BODY OF DAVID HAYES

ALSO BY RIDLEY PEARSON

THE BODY OF DAVID HAYES

RIDLEY PEARSON

HYPERION   NEW YORK

THE BODY OF
DAVID HAYES

ONE

LOU BOLDT PICKED UP BITS and pieces of the assault over an uncooperative cell phone. Paramedics were still on the scene—a trailer park near Sea-Tac Airport—a promising report because it suggested the victim was still there as well. If he reached the site in time, Boldt meant to ride to the hospital in the back of the ambulance. He owed Danny Foreman that much.

The Crown Vic bumped through a pothole that would have knocked dentures out. Boldt's eyes shifted focus briefly to catch his reflection in the silver of the windshield. Boldt had crossed forty a few years back, tinges of gray gave a hint of it. He was in the best physical shape of his professional career thanks to Weight Watchers, a renewed interest in tennis, and a regimen of sit-ups and push-ups in front of CNN each morning. He scratched at his tie, seeing that he was wearing some of his dinner, a familiar tendency, and hit a second pothole because of the distraction. His head came up to catch a glimpse of a closed gas station. Plywood tombstones where the pumps should have been, the signs torn down, the neon beer ads gone from the windows.

He turned down a muddy lane, dodging the first of many emergency vehicles. The air hung heavy with mist, Seattle working its way out of a lazy fall and into the steady, cold drizzle of winter. Three to five months of it depending on El Niño or La Niña—Boldt couldn't keep straight which was which.

Beneath twin sliding glass windows on the butt end, the once white house trailer carried a broken, chrome script that Boldt reassembled in his head to read *EverHome*. It had come to rest in a patch of weedy lawn that needed cutting and was accessed by a poured concrete path, broken and heaved like calving icebergs. The emergency vehicles included a crime scene unit van, a King County Sheriff patrol car, and an ambulance with its hood up. Technically the scene was the Seattle Police Department's and therefore Boldt's, but Danny Foreman's career had landed him first in the Sheriff's Department, then SPD, and now BCI, Bureau of Criminal Investigation, what some states called the investigative arm of the state police. Boldt wasn't going to start pawing the dirt in a turf war. Danny Foreman was well liked, both despite and because of his unorthodox approach to law enforcement. To his detriment and to his favor he played it solo whenever possible; it had won him accolades and gotten him into trouble. The job was as much politics as it was raw talent, and Foreman lacked political skills, which to Boldt explained their mutual respect.

Foreman lay on a stretcher inside a thicket of blackberry bushes that grabbed at Boldt's pant legs. A balloonlike device had been inserted into Danny's mouth. A woman squeezed the bag while monitoring her sports watch. Fore-man, a dark-skinned African American, looked wiry and older than the early fifties Boldt knew him to be. Tired and beaten down. His nap was graying now and cut short, and a pattern of black moles spread beneath both eyes, lending him the masklike look of a raccoon. Could it possibly have been as long as all that?

Boldt was quickly caught up to date by a deputy sheriff and the paramedic, both interrupting each other to finish the other's sentence. The deputy sheriff knew the name Boldt and acted like a teenager in front of a rock star, trying to impress while fawning at the same time. Boldt had enough headlines to fill a scrapbook, but wasn't inclined to keep one. He had the highest case clearance per average in the history of the Seattle Police Department. He had rumors to defeat and stories to live up to, and none of it mattered a damn to him, which only served to provoke more of the same.

Foreman had apparently been hit by a projectile stun gun and "subsequent to that"—these people all spoke the same way, and though Boldt was probably supposed to as well, he'd never taken up the language—"the subject was administered a dose of an unknown drug with behavioral characteristics not dissimilar to those of Rohypnol." The date rape drug of choice, alternately known as roofies, ruf-fies, roche, R-2, rib, and rope, produced sedation, muscle relaxation, and amnesia in the victim, more commonly a coed found later with her panties down than a cop on a stakeout.

The ambulance on the scene was having engine trouble, and though a second ambulance had been dispatched, efforts were being made to get this one started. Boldt's chest tightened with anticipation as he learned that the combination of the medication and the stun gun had resulted in "respiratory depression." Foreman had nearly stopped breathing. He'd been unconscious for almost fifteen minutes.

"Look what the dog drug in," a blinking Foreman said suddenly, his voice slurred behind the drug.

His gaining consciousness sent the paramedic into high gear, shouting out numbers like a sports announcer.

"You took a stun dart," Boldt said. "Then they roped you."

"Feel like Jell-O. No bones, discounting the one I got for Emma, my nurse here."

"Keep it in your pants, Danny," the woman said, grinning, "or I'll search my bag for the hemostats."

"Emma and I went to high school together."

"We went to the *same* high school," Emma corrected for Boldt's sake. "Only Agent Foreman graduated twenty-eight years ahead of my class."

"Always technicalities with you," Foreman said.

"We met outside of work," Emma further explained. To Foreman she said, "And here I am with my hand on your heart."

"Wish our situations were reversed."

"It's the medication loosening his tongue," Emma said. "Next thing he'll be proposing. Good part is, he won't remember any of this."

"Seriously?" Boldt asked.

"Doubtful. He'll sleep soon, and when he wakes he'll have lost most of the last few hours."

"Good God."

"Bullshit," Foreman said. "I'm as clear as day."

"Starting when?" Behind him Boldt heard the ambulance's engine rev and a handful of half-assed cheers.

"I've got a vague recollection of thinking a dog had bit me, or a bee stung me. That's about it."

"A stakeout?" Boldt inquired. "A solo stakeout?"

"Budget cuts."

"Meaning you will, or will not share the identity of whomever it was you were watching in that trailer?"

"I'll need a kiss before I can answer that." Foreman added, "From her, not you."

"Fat chance," the medic said.

As they strapped Foreman into the stretcher, Boldt collected more bits and pieces: Foreman had gone off-radio while on duty, which had eventually caused his own people to go looking for him. BCI had called King County Sheriff, asking for a BOLO—Be On Lookout. A patrol unit had found Foreman's car—a brand-new Cadillac Escalade—which had eventually led to discovering Foreman out cold in the bushes. Boldt was told the house trailer held "a good deal of blood evidence."

While the EMTs loaded Foreman into the ambulance Boldt conducted a quick examination of the trailer. A tube-frame lawn chair in the center of the small living room looked to be the origin of most of the blood. The scarlet stains radiated out like the spokes of a wheel. Dirty dishes filled the sink and the television was on, tuned to a rerun of *Con Air*.

The gloved forensics guy told Boldt the only thing they'd touched was the mute button on the remote: "The volume was deafening." Boldt filed this away as important information.

Several pizza boxes were stacked on the counter, the

cardboard oil-stained, indicating age. In the back bedroom, a room about eight by ten feet, he took in the unmade bed and clothes on the floor.

"We seem to be missing a body," Boldt said.

KCSO CSU was stenciled across the back of the man's white paper coveralls, the crime scene unit of the King County Sheriff's Office.

Boldt repeated, "Do we have a body?"

The man turned around. He wore plastic safety glasses over a pinched face. "We're told we have an earlier ID made on the possible victim by the surveillance team. The mobile home's rented to one David Hayes. Male. Caucasian. Thirty-four. Our guy claims Hayes was observed inside this structure earlier this evening." Boldt experienced a small stab of anxiety; he knew the name, yet couldn't place it. Another unpleasant reminder of his being on the other side of forty.

"Your guy, or BCI's guy? Are you talking about Agent Foreman?"

"We are. We do BCI's forensics," the technician clarified. Boldt had forgotten about the arrangement between BCI and the Sheriff's Office. SPD had their own lab and field personnel.

The ambulance driver wouldn't let Boldt ride along, so he followed in the Crown Vic. Once at the hospital, while they awaited processing, Boldt found himself a sugar-and-cream tea and joined Foreman in the emergency room. No one seemed in any great hurry to help.

"A pro job by the look of it," Boldt said.

"Sounds like it."

"Who's David Hayes? And why is his name so familiar to me?"

"It's a case we're working."

"We? Are you sure about that, Danny? Because I may have squirreled things for you there, without meaning to. I called your Lieu on the way over here. He said they'd assigned CSU to *your* assault. He didn't know anything about any stakeout, anything about a bloody trailer. *You* put CSU into that trailer when they showed up, Danny, didn't you? This is *before* you lost your breath and went unconscious. Isn't that right?"

"Hayes was paroled from Geiger four days ago. Two years in medium, two in minimum."

"And someone wanted him more than you did. Why's that?"

"Seventeen million reasons."

The light finally went on in Boldt's head. "He's the guy—"

"That's right."

A wire fraud case involving his wife's bank, six or seven years earlier. Seventeen million intercepted electronically. Not a penny recovered. "A Christmas party," Boldt said.

"How's that?"

"I met the guy, Hayes, at a Christmas party. For Liz's bank." Sparks firing on top of sparks. "You were with us at the time."

"I was in my fifth year with Fraud. Yeah. Before Darlene's illness. Before everything. Like eighteen-hour shifts for me."

"It was wire fraud, right?"

"Fucking black hole is what it was." Police used the term to define an unsolvable case. "We collared Hayes— by luck, mostly. We never recovered the software he used, and we never found the money. More important, we never uncovered whose money it ~~was~~. We knew it was headed offshore, but it never got there. That meant someone had seventeen million bucks he was willing to lose rather than identify himself. That's what interested us."

Boldt considered this and offered unsolicited advice. "A cop pulling an unauthorized stakeout on a guy who helped steal seventeen million dollars is going to get asked some questions, Danny."

Foreman said nothing.

More of the case came back to Boldt. It had been a bad time for him and Liz. He remembered that especially. "So we put the bloodbath in the trailer down to the rightful owners of the seventeen mil coming after Hayes," Boldt speculated.

Foreman changed the subject.

"We couldn't prove the money ever left the bank. Bank figured it got deposited into some brokerage account, papered over by Hayes. Still inside the bank's system. There, but not there. A real whiz kid, our David Hayes. A real wunderkind," he said, with the animosity of a scorned investigator. Boldt knew the feeling. "He was twenty-seven at the time, and the bank had basically given him control over anything with a chip inside it. They even called him that: 'Chip.' His nickname."

"Did you write this up? The stakeout?" Boldt brought it back to the here and now.

"No one in BCI gives a shit about a cold case like this. Ask around. I guarantee you this isn't anywhere on SPD's radar either."

"Tell me you're not pulling a Lone Ranger, because you know that's how this is going to play."

"Do I want the money? Yes. For me personally? Come on! This is about closing a black hole, nothing more."

"And you think that's how it's going to play?" Boldt repeated. "What the hell were you thinking?"

"We connect the dots on this, Lou, it's going to prove me out."

"We?"

"You're investigating my assault, right? SPD is in on this now."

It almost sounded as if Foreman had planned it that way. Boldt wouldn't put it past him. "You took a dive in order to get a case reopened?"

"It's not like that."

Part of Boldt wanted to congratulate the man if this were the case. Any cop taking a hit, even a Lone Ranger, was certain to awaken the sleeping giant of the SPD bureaucracy. The other part of him didn't want to give Foreman that kind of credit, didn't want to see a friend misuse the system, didn't want to believe the assault had been anything but a surprise to Danny Foreman. Most of all, he didn't want to think that Danny had caused that bloodbath inside the trailer and then done damage to himself in order to cover it up.

"Remember, Lou, this was Liz's bank. Still is, right? Tell me they don't want their money back. Or maybe you don't remember. I promise you Liz remembers."

Boldt felt stung by the comment, and he wasn't sure why. He remembered plenty. Just seeing Foreman's face and hearing his voice triggered any number of memories. The cancer ward at University. Darlene Foreman's funeral. A wake for her, while Liz healed and grew stronger. A growing distance between them as Foreman stopped calling and stopped returning calls.

"What the hell happened to us?" Boldt asked.

"Liz lived," Foreman answered, as if he'd been waiting to say this for years. And perhaps he had. "Resentment. Envy. Hang any name on it you want—that's what happened. And I'm supposed to tell you I'm sorry, but I'm not. I *still* can't bear the thought of being around you two. Throws me right back into all my shit. Seeing you now, it's a good thing, don't get me wrong. But not with her. Not the two of you. Not together. I feel cheated, Lou, and my guess is it'll never go away."

"You want me to pass this off to someone?" Boldt wanted nothing to do with the case, nothing to do with old wounds like these.

"It isn't like that."

"I'd offer LaMoia but he's tied up in a seminar. Two weeks of counterterrorism."

"Heaven help the enemy. Nah. My guys'll take care of this in-house. I realize it falls within city limits, but cut us some slack and we'll save you the paperwork."

"That doesn't sit right with me. You're saying you don't want me to open this up?" Was Foreman playing him? Taking it away so that Boldt would reach all the harder for it? And why was he suckering into it?

"It's open now, isn't it? I know how you are. Leave it be, Lou. Be a pal and pass it off to my guys."

It still felt like an attempt at reverse psychology. The paperwork finally came through and Foreman was officially admitted. An X-ray orderly arrived to escort Foreman to the "photo booth." Boldt stayed seated in the uncomfortable chair, a three-week-old copy of *People* magazine dog-eared in the Plexiglas rack, Stephen King looking at him sideways.

Boldt called out, "I'll wait and see if you need a ride home."

Foreman trundled off, his walk giving away the lingering effect of the drugs. Boldt felt a knot in his throat, still stunned that friendship could go so far wrong, guilty for getting all the breaks while Danny Foreman had gotten none.

He hunkered down for a long wait, thinking to call Liz so she didn't wait up. *Liz lived.* Boldt heard the words echo around in his head. *Like it was some kind of crime.*

TWO

LIZ BOLDT FINISHED HER MORNING run with sex on her mind. It wasn't often she hungered for it like this, but she seized the moment, sprinting up the back steps and through the kitchen door. Her battle with lymphoma had taken some of the meat off her bones a few years earlier, but she'd filled out since and she knew her husband liked the way she looked in her running clothes. She hurried into the living room where she found Lou down on the carpet in front of a quiet television, grunting softly through a string of sit-ups. The possibility of their joining in the shower heightened her sense of urgency. The kids would be up in a matter of minutes. Lou had been out late on a call, and consequently he was running much later than usual.

"You got back late last night," she said. "What happened?"

"Yeah, after two. It was Danny Foreman. Someone took it to him pretty badly."

"Beat him up? Danny?"

"Drugged him. Knocked him out cold. Harborview released him and I drove him home. He'll mend."

"We haven't seen him in ages." She felt awful about it, especially given Darlene's death. But Foreman wasn't the only friend they'd "lost" to the shift of kids and parenting. Their social calendar, never too full to begin with, given the demanding hours of both the bank and the police department, rarely included dinner with friends outside the smallest of circles. Liz's promotion three years earlier to executive vice president of Information Technology, a division that prior to that promotion she'd known little about, had come only months after her remission from cancer and only a year and a half behind the birth of their second child.

"Yeah." Lou sat up and grabbed around his knees. "We talked about that a little. He's got issues."

"We should have had him over to dinner."

"Him and about a dozen others."

"No, I mean it," she said. "As close as I was to Darlene? All those months?"

Lou stood. Liz couldn't remember him looking this fit. He said, "Which, as it turns out, is why he wouldn't have accepted anyway."

"You're not serious?"

"Totally. He resents that you lived and Darlene didn't."

She felt a spike of heat as a wave of indignation and guilt clouded her thought. "He *said* that?"

"It wouldn't have been a pleasant dinner."

"I should say not."

"It isn't aimed at you personally—"

"No, not at all," she said sarcastically, cutting him off.

"It's us as a couple, apparently. Understandable, when you think about it."

"It's not understandable, and it's not excusable. If there's a problem there, it's entirely our fault for not working harder when it counted. Did we even see him after the service?"

"Of course we did. A bunch of times. But it obviously didn't work for him."

Liz wondered what other tragedies lay in their wake. Children caused some serious waves.

"Listen, I beat myself up over this last night, but I'm all right with it, I think. It's all yours."

"Thanks a lot," she said.

She offered to shower first and take over the breakfast duty, and he thanked her for it. She had to organize Sarah's tote, but that wouldn't take but a minute. She caught herself laying out how to juggle the next forty-five minutes in order to carry it off smoothly. No one in the family did well when the kids turned the morning into a zoo.

While Boldt showered she dressed, taking her time to get it right. Miles entered, sleepy-eyed, awakened by the sound of the shower. The same every morning. Liz slipped into autopilot. Dress them. Brush their hair while they brushed their teeth. Beds made. Breakfast going. A pot of English Breakfast for Lou, which seemed to surprise him. She could tell she'd be a few minutes late to work this morning. But what was, was. She had no desire to change it.

Over a hurried breakfast, they managed fragments of a conversation.

"Danny's case," she said, moving around the kitchen, now tidying up. "Anything interesting?"

"That wire fraud case. The seventeen million."

"*Our* case?" she said, surprised. "The bank?"

"You introduced us once. The guy they caught. Remember? It was a Christmas party I think. That guy."

"David Hayes," she said softly.

"He's out on parole."

The first butterfly wings fluttered in her chest. She moved toward the wall calendar, as if interested in the week ahead: a dinner date at Jazz Alley and a church board meeting for her, piano lessons for Miles and ballet for Sarah again next Monday. *Parole? Already? Was it possible?*

"You didn't know?"

Had she spoken her thoughts aloud? She cautioned herself: *Steady!*

"Absolutely not."

"I would have thought the bank would have been told. That you guys would all be up to speed. On the lookout, as it were."

"We will. I'm sure we are."

"Well, that's Danny's case. Sort of. Not really. It gets complicated."

"Yes, it does. It must," she said, heading for an open chair and sitting down with the kids. Some things were impossible to juggle.

□ □ □

A bald eagle with a wingspan of nearly six feet soared past Liz Boldt's twenty-ninth-floor office window at eye level. She took it as an omen, even though she didn't believe in such things. Liz's beliefs were rooted firmly in God. And though she preached to no one, not even her children, she prayed her way through her trials and celebrations. Every day offered her an opportunity to learn something about herself, sometimes strengthening, sometimes testing that faith. She lived to see joy in the eyes of her children, to hear laughter around the house. The smallest things in life proved of the greatest significance. Selfishness, which she now felt had predestined her to cancer and to her rediscovery of faith, was a thing of the past. She had wrestled that demon free, throwing herself into service. She thought of her responsibilities in terms of a pyramid, with God at the top, her children and husband next, her church, her job, her community . . .

Paroled. It felt like falling out of remission. She had little doubt of where this was headed, only how to handle it.

Her family, her job, even WestCorp's reputation and therefore possibly the upcoming merger, could all come tumbling down around her if she didn't manage this exactly right. The eagle represented something frightening: a phoenix, David Hayes, risen from his own ashes.

Her phone rang, and she answered it.

"Elizabeth Boldt."

"It's me."

Paralysis. Her breath caught in her throat like swallowing water too fast. She knew his voice instantly.

"Tommy's cabin. Five o'clock. Watch for anyone following. Coast to the side of the road. Open the hood like there's something wrong. Shut it if you're in the clear and climb back inside. You've got to do this, Liz. Please. I'm in serious trouble."

With the sound of the click, she too hung up the phone, her hand trembling, her mouth dry, a sickening feeling worming through her. Stunned, she sat motionless, steam wafting from the cup of decaf. Her eyes stung.

The phone purred a second time but she would not answer it. Feeling as if she might throw up, she hooked the trash can with her foot and dragged it closer. A bubble wedged in her throat.

Tears threatened behind a screaming in her ears. Fingernails on a blackboard. She forced prayer to replace her thought, her memories, relying on an invisible force that supported her.

It had started innocently enough. Not so innocent later. And after that a pale, quivering need, a hunger of addictive proportions. The wet slap of flesh and the teeth-gnawing cries of secreted pleasure. A crime, and she the perpetrator. Her husband, the cop.

Her office intercom chirped, snapping her to the present. She didn't answer it. Everyone, everything outside this office suddenly felt like a violation.

Anger stole through her, overcame her, because she knew above all else, that she would do exactly as he'd instructed.

Nothing would be allowed to come between the peace and happiness she and her husband and their family had found.

She would end this again, as she had ended it once before.

□ □ □

Six years earlier, in the same office, she had waited impatiently behind her desk, unable to get any work done before someone arrived, annoyed that these things took so long. It was suddenly as if, with her computer frozen, she had nothing to do. Though she knew this was untrue, that there was plenty on her desk that needed her attention, she couldn't bring herself to it, her excuse the unresponsive screen in front of her and the resident terror that her data might be lost. She brooded, like a spoiled little girl, angry at herself for pouting instead of getting something done.

Finally, a knock on her door, and she looked up in time to see him enter. A kid in his mid-twenties. A little pale, but with sweet, intelligent eyes and a habit of pursing his lips between words as he spoke, as if everything he said held some secret irony for him. Dark hair and strong shoulders. She took him for a rock climber, or one of the army of twenty-somethings that headed into the surrounding forests on weekends in search of extreme outdoor experiences.

"I'm David. I.T.," he said, referring to the bank's Information Technologies department.

"Liz Boldt." She held him in the same regard as she did a garage mechanic, or the guy who came to fix the refrigerator at home. "You want my chair?"

"I'd like to sit in it," he said. "I don't need to take it with me."

A wise guy, at that. She stood behind and to his left, wanting to see what it was he did to her machine, wanting to step in and move him away if he restored the spreadsheet she'd been working on, because it contained figures such bank employees should not see.

He typed at a speed she thought reserved for only the highest-paid executive secretaries. It seemed at times his left hand typed while his right worked the mouse, navigating through a dozen screens so quickly that she failed to identify a single one.

"Control panel?" she asked.

"Very good."

"You're fast."

"Typing, yes," he said. "Not in everything."

She thought him rude for the comment, but wasn't about to say so, wasn't about to piss off the one guy capable of getting her back to work.

"You were working a spreadsheet?"

"Yes."

"You'd like the data back?"

"If possible. Please."

"It's all ones and zeros—anything's possible."

If only that were true, she thought. She and Lou had been nearly as frozen, as malfunctioning, as her computer.

David Hayes stopped what he was doing and looked back at her. Again, she wondered if she had spoken some of her thoughts aloud. Was there any other explanation for that inquisitive expression of his? Had he asked her something, and she'd missed it?

He returned to his work at the keyboard, but in that penetrating look of his she experienced both terror and excitement. Terror, because she didn't know what she'd missed, excitement because from somewhere within her bubbled up a primitive urge born of flesh and nerve and the raw juices that pulsed through her. She dismissed this physical response as nothing more than an errant sensation, like being barefoot on a carpet and having a spark fly from fingertip to wall switch. A low-energy warmth flooded her entire body. She tried her best to ignore it.

He left a few minutes later, her data restored on the screen, but not before she'd made the mistake of calling out to him, "You're my hero!" This offering of hers created the opportunity for him to connect with another of those looks. This time, as the door closed behind him, she felt herself shudder toe to head, her body warming as if after a shot of liquor, and she knew she'd crossed some forbidden line.

□ □ □

Liz skipped out of work early to make the 5 P.M. deadline. She drove through the nightmarish traffic that had come to own Seattle, the sun already sinking toward the green of the islands and the jagged, gray silhouette of the Olympics. She called home and left a message saying that if traffic allowed she would stop by the market, a cheat because she could have spoken to Lou by calling his mobile. Little tricks she had once played so well but that now unraveled her. Her work schedule had become so unpredictable with the approaching bank merger that Lou had taken on picking up the kids from after-school care. She still picked up Miles on Mondays, his music night, because it also happened to be Sarah's ballet class and both locations fit perfectly into her later commute. But tonight there would be no time for the market.

She repeatedly questioned her coming here, as if practicing her own defense to Lou, knowing her keeping the date had nothing whatsoever to do with any feelings for David Hayes, long since over, but instead with something much more basic—protecting the family, preventing the past from contaminating the present. David was certainly capable of using their past as a weapon. So she came here out of fear, and she knew that was wrong. She had to preempt or co-opt any attempt on his part to compromise her, and she had to keep her guard up, for she knew David to be a notch smarter than most, and his wounded-hero charm disarming.

She pulled over, as directed, along a stretch of two-lane roadway bordered by a forest of cedar, pine, and fir. He'd chosen this time of day, no doubt, for the limited light of dusk's gray wash. It was as if, for these few minutes, a fog had descended, enveloping her. The ground was spongy beneath the tires. She overheated, a result of nerves, and put down her window. A tangy pine scent, loamy and dark, filled the car, reminding her of their own family cabin on a lake. She stepped out of the car in a moment of anxiousness, hoping to cool off. Her shoes sank into the muddy grass, and she leaped back behind the wheel and pulled the door shut.

"Hey, Lizzy." She jumped. "I wondered if you'd come."

David Hayes stood just outside her window. His black Irish face was swollen and discolored with orange bruises, his green eyes sparkling as she remembered. By the look of the way the gray T-shirt held to him, jail time had been spent in the prison gym. He limped around the front of the van—blue jeans and a brown leather belt—and slipped through the passenger door, pulling down the visor and setting both the makeup mirror and the van's rearview mirror to his liking. His eyes darted constantly between Liz, the windshield, and to both those mirrors, moving with the speed of a fly sensing the swatter.

A mathematician and programmer, David lived for calculation. She knew he already had a plan, that in his mind she was already a part of it. This she could not allow.

"It's good of you to come." He wore a single leather driving glove on his left hand. She made out a ring of medical adhesive tape on that same wrist.

"Was I offered a choice?" She stared a little too long at

his bruises and cuts, and realized too late that he might take this as interest.

"I don't remember forcing you." He inspected her in a way that had once made her warm all over. Now it rippled fear in the form of gooseflesh. "I heard about you getting sick and all. That it was hard on you. But it isn't true. You look incredible."

"Don't. You're in trouble. I can see that. But I can't help you, David."

"You can, actually. If you want. If you don't want . . . Then that's another thing."

Looking straight ahead, she reached for the ignition. "It was wrong of me to come here."

He reached across, his right hand clasping hers, preventing her from starting the van. His gloved hand remained in his lap. "Can we talk this out, please?" She felt his temper bubble. She'd seen it boil a few times. *Stand back.* "You came here so we could talk, right? If not, why else are you here?"

"I don't know." She felt angry, on the edge of tears, and this made her angrier still. "*Fear,* I think. Afraid you'll ruin my life."

"No. Never," he said. "Just the opposite. What I propose benefits us *both.* You for your reasons, me for mine."

That reasoning of his.

"Please get out of the car. You're scaring me."

"I'm not talking about running off together, about jumping into bed. We've done that, no matter that we feel differently about it. Message received. I'm talking about freeing us both."

She felt herself shudder. She *had* felt free until a few hours ago. Now she found her own eyes wandering to the driver's side rearview mirror, hoping someone might drive by. She could jump out, flag them down. David was sure to run if she tried such a thing. Wasn't he?

"I fucked up, Lizzy."

"Don't call me that. And don't use that language with me."

"Got the wrong people mad at me. I think they would have killed me except they want their money back."

"Please get out of the car."

"For Christ's sake, Lizzy. I'm missing two fingernails on my left hand, my head's caved in." He touched his head. "They would have killed me."

I wish they had.

"You're probably wishing they had."

"Nonsense."

"I need your help."

"Absolutely not. Cut a deal. They'll protect you. It's how it's done."

"From these people? I don't think so."

"Please get out of the car," she repeated, her eyes desperate for traffic now.

"They described my dog, Buck. You remember Buck? They described killing Buck."

"Please get out." She felt frantic. *Do something!*

He held the car keys in his right hand, fingers blindly counting through them as if they were prayer beads.

"My mother wrote me about Buck. She was looking after him for me. Said he'd gotten into some bad food or something. Poisoned, maybe."

"I'm sorry about Buck."

"It's not about Buck. It's about my mother. The point is they know where she lives. They can *get to her*. They *will* get to her if I don't cooperate. These people don't care about anything but that money."

"Then give them the money. And give *me* my keys, please."

"I can't give them the money, because I can't get into the bank."

She felt her heart pounding, grow painful.

"You see?"

"No. That is *not* on the table. Turn yourself in. Make a deal for protection if you turn over the money."

He scoffed. "You think anyone cares about that money other than the people after me? The bank was insured. The state got their conviction. It's *over*."

"The bank would welcome the money returned, believe me."

"You're missing the point. The point is that *these people* would welcome the money returned. A few minutes, Liz—" He caught himself before he completed his nickname for her. "A few minutes of your time. If the money transfers, my mother lives."

"Do not put this onto me."

"Okay . . . Okay . . . Then who would you suggest? Tony? Who else has access to I.T.? Or should I call Phillip and ask for a hall pass?" Percolating, the lid still on.

She extended her open hand, awaiting her keys. "You know exactly how to help your mother, David. It is not up to me."

He inhaled and threw himself back against the headrest. "Some money then? Maybe get my mother on a plane or something. I'm good for it." He smiled an ironic smile.

"I feel bad about your mother. Honestly, I do. But the solution is to cut a deal."

"The state won't want just the money—they're greedy—they'll want me to set up these other people, the people I stole it from. And, for the record, I did not know who they were. An account is all. A dummy account. But there is no way . . . there is absolutely *no way* I am *ever* going to be that stupid, believe me." His left hand, the one with the glove, shook involuntarily in his lap.

She felt her original intention slipping away to his reasoning. There was no way she would participate in this, but she'd done little if anything to discourage him. "I love my husband. I love my family." She appealed to the man she'd once known. "Don't put me in this position, David."

The keys dangled above her open palm. "I didn't know where else to turn. Think this through. I have. You'll see." The keys swung back and forth like a pendulum. "It's going to work out."

She snatched the keys back, though he willingly released them.

He said, "At least think about it."

"Do not call me."

"All I ask is that you think about it." He slipped out of the car, looked both ways, up and down the road, and quietly shut the door. He had disappeared into the trees by the time her trembling hand worked the key into the ignition.

□ □ □

Seeing her family around the kitchen table like something out of a Norman Rockwell painting made Liz despise herself all the more as she walked in. It seemed so long ago that she'd returned from her morning run eager for some playful sex in the shower.

"Sorry I'm late."

Lou was already out of his chair. "Help you with the bags?" His gleeful innocence caught her in the center of her chest, knocking the wind out of her.

"The shopping . . ." She stumbled. "I never got there. Got hung up at work."

"You called from your cell."

Ever the detective. Sometimes she hated him for it. But not now. She reserved that emotion for herself.

"Did I? It's possible. I ran out to a meeting with the caterers. Phillip seems to think that because I'm a woman I should be in charge of food and beverage on the big night."

"What big night?" Miles asked expectantly. At six years old, he was sensing his approaching birthday party. He had his father's nose for clues.

She set down her umbrella, hung up her coat in the hall closet, and left her purse by the toaster, plugging in her cell phone. Little rituals that began to settle her nerves. *Better now.*

"Daddy cook dinner," Sarah said.

"I can see that. It looks yummy."

It was meat loaf and green beans. She loved him for all his interests: jazz, anything culinary, film. He wasn't a microwave husband. He even made his pancakes from scratch.

He stood for her, caught her chair, and dragged it back. She winced a grin of appreciation vaguely in his direction, refusing to meet eyes, her heart ready to burst.

"Rough day, then." He sounded cautious all of a sudden. Perhaps he sensed it. She hoped not.

"Same old, same old. You? How's Danny?"

"Who's Danny?" Miles asked. "Is Danny coming to my party?"

"A friend of ours," Lou answered his son. "And no, he's not."

"Mommy and Daddy are talking," Liz informed the children.

"We can do this later," Lou announced. "What'd you do in school today, sport?"

First grade for Miles, preschool for Sarah. Lou had once worked an illegal adoption case and ever since she'd felt fragile about leaving the kids—even dropping them off at school. Columbine hadn't helped. David Hayes didn't help. If anything ever pulled the marriage apart, it would be the kids who would suffer the irreparable damage. She thought it possible, however unlikely, she might even lose them to Lou in a judgment. She had strikes against her. For all his flaws, his general inability to groom himself, his blind dedication to the job, a sense of focus that could so distract him he would miss entire conversations, a sour stomach, and poor digestion that could clear a room, despite it all, Lou came off the hero, the white knight. She shook her head to stop the thoughts, sensing herself becoming panicky, irrational.

"Nothing," Miles answered.

"Seven hours and you just *sat* there?"

"Dad."

"Well?"

And it went on like this as it did every night, the kind of mindless prattle so easily dismissed one night, so treasured on this particular evening, when mindlessness was what she craved. She sat there as an observer, watching them like watching a movie: Lou teasing, the children laughing, manners being reminded, him stealing glimpses of her and offering a smile, and she returning it and feeling traitorous. Then it was dishes, and Miles with a broom he could barely control and Sarah announcing for all she had to go potty. Lou sweeping the child up in his strong arms and warning her to hold it as he rushed her out of the room.

"Mommy," Miles said, pointing down. "Muddy shoes you leave in twos." The school was teaching him all sorts of expressions like this.

She looked down, her pulse quickening. Mud and grass clung to the sides of both shoes. *I ran out to a meeting with the caterers. Right.* And Sherlock Holmes flushing the toilet for Sarah.

At first she didn't remember having climbed out of the car, but then she recalled opening the hood and closing it, just as David had instructed.

She glanced toward the living room—where Lou would be coming from—wondering if he'd already caught the mud. If she tried to hide it now, would it just compound her problems? They both knew there was no place downtown she would pick up mud and grass like this. The catering was out of a fabulous restaurant called Wild Ginger. Lou had helped her pick it. No city parks between the bank and Wild Ginger. She heard the toilet gurgle.

She cupped her hand beneath the faucet, and splashed her blouse, jumping back, as if an accident. "Dang!" she hollered, brushing herself off. Her silk blouse went translucent and she made sure it stuck to her chest, for she knew if anything would divert Lou's attention away from her shoes, her wet blouse would. They passed in the doorway.

Lou said, "All by herself."

Liz said, "I splashed."

Lou said, "Lucky me."

She hated him for being so predictable, for him allowing her to take advantage like this.

"I'll change," she announced.

"I hope not," he said, turning her meaning. Lou Boldt loved word games. "Sweetheart?"

She hadn't realized she'd started crying until her vision blurred. She cleared her right eye with her fingertip. "Hormones again."

He looked at her oddly, as if he didn't know her but seemed to buy it just the same, and that hurt worse. "I'll start the bath."

"Thanks."

"For them," he teased.

"I know."

"You okay?"

"No," she said honestly.

"Okay," he said, backing away and slipping into the kitchen. "Take your time."

When they finally made it to bed, she realized it was horrible timing to start into this now. He was talking about how tired he was, having been up the night before with Danny Foreman. She had her head buried in a church periodical, a magazine with testimonies of healing, and she searched the pages for guidance, knowing she'd pick up something if she stayed with it. Finally, reading a piece on avoidance, she placed the magazine down.

She gathered her courage. "You feel like talking for a minute?"

He fought off a yawn and said yes. He meant no, but that he'd try.

"I didn't go to the caterer." A feeling of weight lifted

off her, the childish glee of watching a hot-air balloon rise into a blue sky.

"I know."

A moment of incredulity. "You *know*?"

"Birthday shopping, right? I was ready to cover for you, if you needed it. I'm thinking of getting him a sport coat. He keeps asking for a coat like mine. Tweed, maybe. For his recital. Can you imagine? A little button-down shirt and tie? Tell me that wouldn't be amazing."

"Amazing," she said, choking back a knot in her throat, reaching over and gently touching his hair. It wasn't going to happen. Not tonight. He closed his eyes and smiled, lost in that imagination of his. She scratched his scalp, like rubbing a cat. "I'll get the light," she said.

"Um," he answered, already on his way to sleep.

THREE

"IMPRESSIVE," DANNY FOREMAN CALLED OUT loudly as the paper target crept toward Liz. It hung from a clip attached to a belt drive, allowing the shooter to replace it with a fresh one and then electronically return it to a desired distance. Liz was shooting thirty feet. She wore eye and ear gear and a blue business suit with black pinstripes. The indoor firing range was too loud for them to try to carry on a conversation, but she pulled one ear off her headset and shouted above the percussion of reports.

"Hardly impressive! Nine in the magazine. I only hit the target with three of them." She pointed out the holes in the black-and-white bottle-shaped target. "You want a go?"

"No, thanks."

"You sure?"

He assented, pulling hearing protection and goggles off a peg on the wall and accepting the weapon, a slick little nine millimeter. "This doesn't strike me as you, Liz."

"Lou gave it to me a couple years ago. I protested, naturally. But I took a course so I'd know what I'm doing."

They had yet to say hello to each other, Liz bearing the burden of what Lou had told her about Danny's lingering resentment.

"And now, a renewed interest?" Danny Foreman ran the target out to thirty feet, raised the gun, sighted, and squeezed off a single shot. It struck the target low. He lowered the gun, studied it, raised it a second time and caused Liz to jerk back as he unloaded the magazine with eight incredibly fast consecutive shots. He left a tight pattern, very near the center circle of the target. "Sweet," he said, placing down the weapon.

His shooting seemed charged with emotion. Tension hung in the air along with the bitter tang of cordite.

"I'm truly sorry," Liz said.

Foreman tugged the headset off. "What's that?"

"Never mind."

They chased down a pair of fiberglass chairs in the waiting area in front of two vending machines and a trash can that smelled of burnt coffee grounds. The sign on the wall read NO SMOKING, but there were well-used ashtrays on each of the three round tables. The vinyl floor had been swabbed down with a lemon-scented disinfectant. Foreman offered to clean her gun for her, and she took him up on it, handing him a gray plastic kit of swabs and oil that Lou had given her along with the gun. Foreman's big hands wrapped around the metal like talons on prey.

Danny Foreman spoke with a warm, sonorous voice that Liz remembered well, a voice it felt nice to be around.

She said, "We've not seen much of each other, have we? I want you to know that Darlene's passing hit us both very hard. We miss her—miss you both, Danny—very much."

"I could have called. Should have," he said. "I got this notion it was better to start fresh—a new life, you know? Transferred over to BCI. Bought a little place over to Madison Park. Didn't change much of anything, though. I miss her badly, Liz."

She wasn't the best at such discussions. Even among her girlfriends, she preferred listening to talking, and when she did speak it was to express her true opinions, most of which were the last thing anyone wanted to hear.

"There's no set time for grieving. It's a process. But speaking as a friend, Lou and I would like to see more of you than we do."

"Darlene and I always enjoyed our time with the two of you."

"And . . . here we are."

His face screwed up tight. "Yeah, but it's business. We both know that's why you called me. Let me tell you something: It makes it all the more difficult for me."

In fact, she had called him to test the thickness of the ice, like tossing rocks and watching them skim across the frozen surface. Called him, to edge her boot down onto that ice and listen for the splintering cracks beneath her added weight. If she misjudged or misstepped, she knew the peril she faced. This meeting with Danny would determine how much she shared with Lou, believing it unfair to revisit that pain unless absolutely forced to. She avoided eye contact, focusing on his long fingers and the meticulous way he handled the weapon.

She said, "He wants me to get him some cash."

"Hayes, we're talking about. Just to make sure I get this right."

"Yes."

Foreman pulled out a notebook. "Contacted you how?"

She ran down the events, bending facts slightly to make it sound as if Hayes had contacted her due to her position in the bank.

"And the location of this face-to-face. How was that known to you?"

She paused too long trying to think something up. Foreman filled the gap.

"In case you forgot, Liz, I was the investigator on the original wire fraud. That put me in a . . . let's call it a unique position, that allowed me to collect *all sorts* of information about this case, some of it relevant at the time, some not."

The room dropped about twenty degrees. She realized now that calling Foreman had been a terrible mistake. "I'm sure that's true."

"Do we understand each other?"

"Yes, we do." The ice gave way and she clung to the ragged edges, half in, half out. Lou would have to be told.

"I can't see any reason to drag Lou through any of this," Foreman said like a mind reader.

"Well, we differ there. But that's between Lou and me."

"Let me clarify one point in particular, and I want you to think carefully before you answer this, because I'm going to consider it as a statement to law enforcement, just so we understand each other."

"If I can help in any way, then I want to. That's partly why I called you."

"Some people, Liz, they call us first because they think that helps remove them from suspicion. Not that you'd ever resort to such a tactic. I'm just saying, who called who doesn't matter much."

"And the point you want to clarify?"

"You were or were not involved *in any way* with the initial wire fraud?"

"Was not."

"There is no way this is ever coming back onto you? There is nothing out there that's going to blindside me, or anyone else associated with this investigation? *Discounting personal relationships* that you may or may not have had with employees of the bank. I'm not interested in that unless it carries weight with my investigation. And you're telling me it does not?"

"That's correct." The edges broke free and she bobbed up to her neck, the weight of her clothing pulling her down.

"Okay. Good. Then tell me about the meeting. Location, time, circumstances, duration, topics discussed, any items exchanged. You want to edit out the personal stuff, that's just fine."

"There was no personal stuff." She regained some internal strength, defiant in her defense.

"I'm just saying . . . what you tell me here, Liz, is going down in my notes. You understand? My notes can be subpoenaed, probably *will* be subpoenaed, so a person wants to think that through."

"I haven't thought any of this through. David said he needed my help. He said he was afraid for his mother." She'd told him all this already. "Then the money. I told him I couldn't do that."

"Next time you'll agree."

"I most certainly will not."

"You played it right, believe it or not. Convincing. But next time you'll agree to pay in exchange for him leaving you alone—which he won't. We'll make the drop, not you, and that'll be the end of it."

"It won't be the end of it. You just said so yourself."

"Your role in it, I'm talking about. It's complicated, Liz. We want that money. We want whoever that money belonged to. More than anything, we want to know how he did it—how he hid that money for so long." Foreman's eyes were unrelenting and cold. "This merger," he continued. "MTK buying out WestCorp. That's significant. Hayes switched lawyers within a week of that announcement. Did you know that?"

"How would I possibly know that?"

"His new team pressed hard for parole, and they got it. Attorney-client privilege . . . we'll never know who hired those new attorneys, but someone wanted Hayes sprung for a reason, and that reason is the merger."

"But we announced the merger nine months ago."

"And they've been lobbying for an early release ever since. Your systems fold into MTK's, or the other way around?"

"I see what you're driving at. All the hardware's in place, if that's what you're asking—and mind you this is *confidential information,* so put your pen down." Foreman did so. "We're in beta testing on the front-end system. Our accounts merge into their hardware. We throw the final switch at a reception, Sunday, nine P.M." *And I'm in charge of the catering*, she thought absurdly.

"Front end? What's that about?"

"Both brokerage and retail operate on a three-tier server system. Windows environment on the front end—the retail side, for our account executives, tellers, and the like. Not terribly secure but easy to use. A UNIX level that handles account management, wire transfers, the nuts and bolts— much more secure. And a pair of AS/400s—incredibly stable and secure IBM machines—on the very bottom of the stack for the account data—the balances."

"But you're only testing the front end?"

"The Windows environment is the last to be tested. It's the most likely to have bugs and glitches. The technicians have been through the lower-level servers for months now. We don't expect any surprises there." She asked, "Why the technical interest, Danny?"

"I've got to think like Hayes. I've got to put myself in his shoes. He said he needed you to pull this off."

"He did."

"And what makes you special? *Ignoring* any personal connection."

"My access."

"Security clearance?"

"Yes."

"You the only one with this clearance?"

"Hardly."

"How many others?"

She had called for the meeting and yet they were working his agenda. "I'm not sure."

"Not sure or won't tell?"

"You'll have to go above me for that. Sorry."

"We don't want to get into this, do we?" His eyes drilled into her. Whatever past they'd shared was briefly forgotten. "Me, explaining how it was that Hayes came to you before anyone else?" He waited. "It's a simple enough question, Liz."

"And I'm forbidden from answering it. I signed documents. What you're asking is something I cannot do—consequences be what they may."

Foreman set down the clean and reassembled weapon and pushed back from the table.

She filled the resulting silence. "My point in calling you was to let you know that an opportunity exists to make a deal with David."

"Your point in calling me," Foreman corrected, "was to find out how much I know."

"He's clearly terrified at the moment, and I would think you'd want to jump on that."

Foreman steamed, still not recovered from her refusal. "I'm on your side. Don't make me jump through hoops just to understand the way this works. Understanding it is one thing. Stopping him is another. And it'll be impossible if I don't know what he knows. And he worked there, Liz . . . at the bank. That puts me at a distinct disadvantage from the get-go. How can I protect the other people with this clearance rating if I don't know who they are?"

"You'll have to go above me."

"Goddamn it!" Foreman slapped the table. The gun jumped. So did Liz. "Sorry," he said, composing himself.

His display of temper rattled her; she didn't know this side of Danny Foreman. How on earth did this case get so personal for him? "Cut a deal with him, Danny. If you use me, use me to bring him that deal."

"I'll work on it."

"And do it quickly, because I'm going to lay this all out for Lou, and after that . . . You know Lou."

"Give me a day."

"Can't. I've got to tell him tonight."

"There are channels to go through."

"At the bank, too."

"Give me a break."

She offered him her own deal. "I'll explore permission to turn over what you need . . . our classified information . . . if you'll put together that deal."

"Once Lou is involved he won't let you within a mile of David Hayes. Don't kid yourself."

"So we'll both work quickly," Liz proposed. "There are still a few hours left in the day."

"I don't know about you, but my guys don't move that fast. This is the government, don't forget."

"Try."

"As if I have a choice," he said, and acknowledged with a sly grin that Liz had won the first round.

FOUR

UNACCUSTOMED TO SUCH THINGS, LIZ suffered a bout of depression as she rode an elevator toward the fifth floor of the Public Safety Building and her husband's office. Revisiting the Affair—capital A—was certain to disturb and disrupt Lou, was certain to strain and test their marriage, and just the thought of that made her skin clammy, her neck tense. She'd never once been called to the principal's office, but now she knew how it felt.

Like this old public building, there had been an earlier time when their marriage had shone in all its glory. Now the place existed in a ponderous state of absolute cheerlessness. She hoped their relationship was not destined to suffer a similar fate.

Required to check in with an attendant outside of Crimes Against Persons, Liz indirectly alerted Lou to her arrival and he was waiting for her as she was buzzed through the door. To her relief, he looked neither troubled nor angry, and just seeing him made her feel better.

"Hey, you," she said.

He said nothing, escorting her into his office and shutting the door. Seeing their children's artwork taped and tacked to the walls and corkboard alongside crime scene photos and photocopied memos twisted Liz into a knot. She wanted—*needed*—to keep this businesslike yet personal, honest and yet not too specific, keeping in mind his feelings above her own. He was certain to take this as being as much of a shock as she had when she'd received that first call from David. She remembered her own reaction as breathless and frightened, and wanted to remember to give him a chance to recover, regardless of what his steeled exterior revealed. As a cop, Lou Boldt could hide anything going on inside him.

She sat down, and to her great relief Lou turned a chair to face her, forgoing his regular chair behind the desk. "Hey there yourself," he finally said.

She kept in mind that he questioned people for a living. He turned them around on themselves to where they would confess to what they had no intention of revealing. Both a good listener and quick on his feet, Lou was not to be challenged. She schooled herself not to get competitive or defensive.

"We need to go back several years," she began, "to the embezzlement."

"Okay." But it wasn't okay and he knew that, for it also marked another event in their lives.

She plunged in. "In all this time, you've never asked me with whom I had the affair."

"You've never told me," he said, making a point of his impression of the proper order of things.

"I can't tell you how much I respected you for that. Appreciated your leaving that choice to me. I know it can't have been easy."

"None of this has ever been easy," Lou said, "for either of us. I wanted to know so I wouldn't keep guessing every time we attended a bank function. I didn't want to know because comparisons were inevitable, and I didn't want to carry my own inadequacies around, didn't want to face where I'd failed you, didn't want to judge you for your taste in lovers and hate you for it. For the record, I'm over that stuff now. It's history."

He had a tendency to speak like this, adopting phrases from his work—"for the record"—and subjecting her to them.

"It's David Hayes."

She watched as the news hit him, actually glad to see he couldn't carry this off with a stone face and calm exterior. He paled, nodded. "The embezzler. Danny Foreman's stakeout." He nodded again, pieces fitting together for him.

"He was with I.T. Back then. This is before I was promoted to oversee the department."

"Did you know anything about it at the time? The embezzlement?"

The similarity of this question to that of Danny Foreman bothered her.

She rehashed for him the known facts of the embezzlement—the wire fraud, the missing seventeen million, the belief that the money still resided somewhere on the bank's servers, and Danny Foreman's determination to intercept any attempt to retrieve the stolen funds and the software responsible for hiding it, and to identify the people whose money it had been. Her husband stayed with her, never interrupting, his ear turned slightly toward her, his eyes fixed as if she'd winded him.

"David contacted me at the office yesterday, and I went to see him."

Lou nodded. She wanted more from him than this, any expression of his internal emotions. Anything but talking to a robot.

She described the threats Hayes had received, the physical beating he'd taken, and her insistence he go to the authorities to make a deal. "I took all this to Danny Foreman today," she described. "We made a deal that I'd try to get permission to release some of the classified bank information to him if he'd work on a deal to get David and his mother relocated."

Boldt said calmly, "There's a saying in witness protection: The difference between deal and dead is one letter."

"Right, well . . . what I want to say is I'm embarrassed and ashamed by all of this, by everything that's happened, back then, now, the fact he contacted me. But I can't hide it, won't hide it. And I won't give anyone the chance to use that against me, against us."

"I know how hard this must have been for you. Coming here. Explaining this. But if you expect me to thank you—"

"I don't expect any such thing. Do I want you to *thank* me? No! But a reaction would be nice. Shout at me, scream at me, be angry with me. What are you feeling in there, and why won't you show me?"

"I'm thinking *you're* the one that needs protection."

"Not thinking," she complained. "Feeling. What are you *feeling*?"

Lou straightened up and waited for her eyes to meet his own. "I don't *feel* in this office. This is not a place for that. I work here. I process facts. I process death. I occasionally allow myself to feel when I get into my car and head home, but even then I turn the radio up real loud, put the windows down, and stay quiet about it. You feel for about the first six months on this job. That would be a while ago for me. After that you try *not* to let emotion overcome reason. Not that you're always successful. You're not.

"What am I feeling now?" he continued. "Hurt. Trapped. Concerned for you. Worried about Danny Foreman being involved because he's famous for what we call a Lone Ranger attitude and I don't want you caught up in that. At the same time I'm grateful to be included, I do thank you for that, and while I'd like to be feeling more, at least for your sake, I find myself instead trying to jump ahead and get this thing contained, because you're my wife and I don't want you in the middle of this."

"Trapped?"

"Did I say trapped?"

"You did."

"I don't know what I meant by that."

Despite his outward façade of complacency, she recognized his fixed stare. He was lost to thought. She felt this kind of information was better doled out in doses than dumped all at once as she had done, but she'd had little choice.

"So what do we do?" she asked.

"I talk to Danny. We sort this out."

"And me?"

"We handle it from here, Liz. If he contacts you again, then that's where you're involved again. But that'll be by phone only. You're not to make any kind of physical contact with him again."

Any kind of physical contact; she resented him including

that. "I wasn't the one who made contact. I thought I explained that."

"You went to see him," Lou reminded. "You cooperated. That wouldn't look good to a judge or jury."

"What are you talking about?"

"What if it comes down to his word against yours that you had nothing to do with the original crime?"

"We're past that. We're *way* past that. Don't you think that just might have come out in the original trial?"

"How is the bank going to feel about you taking a meeting in secret with a convicted embezzler? Was the bank notified?"

"It's none of their business!"

"It's exactly their business. It's none of your business, or shouldn't be."

She processed this and knew he was right, and this filled her with an added dread.

"I'll talk to Danny," Boldt said again.

She didn't want Lou comparing notes with Danny Foreman, but any thought of containing this was long gone.

"Who else has access to I.T. the way you do?"

"That's what Danny wants too."

"I'm not Danny."

"I do. Tony does, of course. Phillip—goes without saying."

"Maintenance?" he asked. "Programmers?"

"A dozen or more for the UNIX system, sure. Not the AS/400s. Tony's the only programmer we have who works with the AS/400s. Typically we outsource that work to IBM anyway. They're their own worlds, the AS/400s."

"So, in some ways, Tony LaRossa is more important to Hayes than you."

"Except that David has a past with me. He thinks he can use it to his advantage. He'd have to strong-arm Tony or try to bribe him, and neither of those is even a remote possibility."

"Either is a possibility," Lou said. "These people drugged Danny. You said they pulled a couple fingernails off Hayes. They killed a dog. Threatened an old lady. What makes Tony LaRossa immune?"

"Okay," she said. "So Tony's in the picture as well. I'll call him."

"No," Lou said sharply. "You're discounting the possibility that Tony was involved from the beginning."

"Tony? He's my director of I.T.!" She said this but felt a worming sensation overcome her. "Tony? We barbecue with Tony and Beth. The twins—"

". . . were an expensive adoption," Boldt interrupted, finishing her sentence for her. "The failed in-vitros must have run in the tens of thousands. Where'd Tony get that kind of money?"

"He makes a good living."

"He's worth a look."

"We all get favorable loan rates. Don't lump Tony in with David Hayes. He's not that kind of person."

"And *you* are? Stay clear of Tony, Liz. Not a word until we've had a chance to run some background."

"I didn't come here to turn the investigation over to you, Lou. I came here to be honest with you, to include you."

"Consider me now included."

"Not like this."

"What'd you expect? I'd let Danny run you?"

"No one's running me."

"Hayes is running you. Or trying to. Going to Danny

before coming to me . . . How am I supposed to *feel* about that?"

She hadn't considered his professional pride might be more wounded than his husband's pride. Then, realizing the two were impossibly intertwined, she resigned herself to the fact that she'd botched the whole thing from the start. Without thinking, she asked, "Are you alright with this?"

" 'Conflicted,' I think it's called." Sarcasm was misplaced in him, like a preacher swearing. "I obviously failed you as a husband. No matter how far in the past, that kills me. Your taking this to Danny before me also hurts and, I might add, makes it all the more difficult for us both. Unlike Danny, I put your safety first, the investigation second. Whether or not I can make that happen at this late date is anybody's guess, but it has to happen because I am not exposing you to this guy again."

"I won't have his mother's murder on my conscience, Lou. That might not make any sense to you, but I want you clear on this. I *will* be involved, at least to the extent David *thinks* I'm involved. I want to be cooperative, I want to work this out, yes, but as wife and husband, not informant and detective."

"I can't make any promises. At least not the one you're asking for. I'll need to make some calls."

She felt a victim again, much as she had after the meeting with David. Lou had boxed her into something she'd not seen coming, and she deeply resented the way he felt it was his right to make decisions for her.

"I'll try to do whatever you and Danny ask, Lou, but I will not be excluded from the decision-making process. You, or someone, is going to offer David a deal. I will bring him that deal, if necessary."

"We'll protect the mother if we can. Depending on where she lives."

"California, somewhere."

"That's more problematic, but not impossible. As I said, I need to make some calls."

She felt the principal had dismissed her, but she wasn't done. "As far as I'm concerned, the worst thing that can happen is that we allow this to drive a wedge between us."

"Which is why Danny and I are now in charge," Lou said. "Because that's *not* the worst. Truth be told, it doesn't even come close."

□ □ □

Alone now, Boldt wondered why her affair had to resurface, why Liz had to remind him that he should feel something more than his general sense of numbness allowed. Over the past six years, he'd figured out how to hide much of this behind a carefully erected wall. Now, despite all his emotional masonry, that wall had crumbled down around him. Around them both.

Boldt phoned Danny Foreman, prepared to feel impotent and the source of another's unspoken amusement. Cuckolded. He lacked a cohesive strategy but knew time was of the essence. Danny would already be working angles that he, Boldt, had yet to see. To wait too long was to be completely excluded. Liz had put herself in the center of this, and now Boldt needed to extricate her as quickly as possible.

Foreman didn't pick up at his office, nor did he answer his mobile. Boldt left a pair of messages, but he knew in advance that there was good reason for Foreman's silence.

Danny Foreman was already hard at work, and Boldt was playing catch-up.

□ □ □

It was an unspoken rule in the Boldt home that police business not be discussed, and so the collision of these two worlds caused repeated violations, begun the previous morning with the discussion of Danny Foreman's assault and continued now through the post-dinner kitchen cleanup. As Liz patrolled the table and countertops, Boldt parked himself in front of the sink and splashed his way through a pile of pots and dishes, most of which were on their way to the KitchenAid dishwasher to his right, a noisy, prehistoric contraption that needed replacement. The thing would outlive most dogs without ever failing, but its churning, swishing, and occasional grinding amounted to an invasion of privacy, as far as Boldt was concerned, so he didn't turn it on when the time came. Instead, he eavesdropped on his son, Miles, practicing piano.

"It's beautiful," Liz said, finishing off a countertop with a damp sponge. He sensed in her the desire to reestablish their lives as normal.

"It's astonishing," Boldt said. "His age . . . and as little training as he has had." He was wondering what came next and how he could work to separate Liz from the investigation.

"Chip off the old block," Liz said. "Off the old *bolt*," she corrected, amusing him. For a moment, even to him, they felt like husband and wife again.

"I don't have a tenth of that kind of talent."

"He got it listening to you. Watching you practice as much as you do."

"I'd love to take credit for *any* of that, believe me. But that's more your department . . . more divine intervention than learned behavior. He's special."

"You're both special," Liz said. "And Sarah, too."

The wall phone rang, interrupting the few moments of distraction away from the case. With the chiming of those tones, both husband and wife went silent, caught in a pregnant pause of indecision as to who should answer, and who should listen in. Boldt had never loved the phone, considering evening phone solicitation a crime on the level of a felony, and now had no desire to ever hear it ring again.

They both expected it to be Hayes, but it was Laura Towle, inviting them to a dinner with the school board member who represented their district. Boldt listened one-sided as Liz accepted. She knew that her husband supported her own passion to improve the early reading program. But the intrusion registered on both their faces as Liz hung up. David Hayes had stepped into their lives. There was no getting around it.

Not long after that they rounded up the kids and got them to bed. Familiar routines that settled Boldt's anxieties and reminded him how important this family life had become for him.

Twenty minutes after the kids went down Liz's cell phone rang, and this time her face collapsed as she answered. Boldt edged up next to her and she cocked the phone away from her head just far enough for Boldt to overhear.

Hayes made it short and sweet. She was to withdraw five thousand dollars in cash from the bank, deposit it into an aluminum briefcase sold by a Brookstone store in the small mall beneath the bank, and carry it with her out of the bank and onto the streets. Additional instructions were to come by cell phone then.

"They're willing to deal," Liz said, stretching the known facts. "The details aren't worked out, but they're sympathetic to your situation. They're willing to protect you and your mother. Let me work this out for you, David."

The long pause on the other end of the call seemed good reason for hope.

"Don't let me down, Lizzy. These guys . . . there's no deal that could possibly be good enough. Help me out here. Do this for me. Tomorrow, four P.M. sharp."

The line disconnected.

Twenty-five minutes later, at Boldt's beckoning, Danny Foreman knocked on the back door, and Boldt let him in. He was out of breath, his forehead sparkling, his eyes frantic, betraying a cluttered mind.

"Let me explain this," Foreman said, looking too big for the lovingly restored parlor chair that had once been Liz's great-aunt's. He sat forward, dispensing a sense of urgency that Boldt found contagious.

Boldt reviewed the Hayes phone call with Danny Foreman as if Liz weren't in the room, an attitude corrected after a series of glaring looks on her part. He built up to a point where he felt himself capable of negotiating Liz out of the money drop that Hayes had requested. It was then that Foreman jumped in with his own news.

"I've spoken to Paul Geiser. Any deal is predicated upon the recovery of the software or whatever means was used to hide the money as well as the identification and apprehension of whoever's money it was in the first place."

"But that's ridiculous," Liz blurted out. "That's not a deal. That's conscription. He's not a cop, for heaven's sake."

"Paul is just a prosecutor. He'd have to pull some serious strings to provide permanent relocation for Hayes and his mother. Witness protection like that is only done on the federal level." Boldt felt himself nodding along. The state could protect an important trial witness for a matter of weeks, or sometimes even months, but true relocation was a matter for the Justice Department. "If he can put a racketeering charge onto whoever's got a thumb on Hayes, then the U.S. Attorney's Office takes over and he says relocation is possible, not guaranteed, but possible. But that's the only way it's going to happen."

"It's too much," Liz said.

"You're speaking for him now, are you?"

"Lay off, Danny," Boldt said.

Foreman sat back and collected himself. "Paul asked if Liz would go along with us, at least far enough to obtain what he calls the 'cloaking' software—whatever means was used to hide the money. I told him I doubted it, given your involvement."

"You've got that right."

"Let's not jump to conclusions, okay?" Liz leveled a look at both men. "Did you tell this prosecutor about David and me, Danny?" Foreman looked as if she'd slapped him across the face. "He knows, Danny," she said, indicating Boldt. "I told you I wasn't going to hide any of this."

"He knows I have some juice on you, yes, because he asked how far we could push you."

"And you answered, how?" Boldt asked.

"I was clear that the degree of her involvement would probably be defined by you more than by her."

"But you said you had juice."

"I did, but Paul has no idea of the nature of that."

"He can guess," Liz said.

"No. If he guesses, it will have to do with internal politics, because that's the way Paul Geiser thinks." Foreman looked around the room, his eyes landing on the kids' books and toys. Boldt wondered if he was thinking that had Darlene lived, such clutter might be on the floor of his own living room. "I want her to make the drop."

"Absolutely not."

"To show goodwill. To show him she means business, that he can trust her."

"Hayes needs her and her security clearance in order to access these computers. That makes her a constant target of possible abduction. A drop like this . . . for all we know, it's a trap being laid to kidnap her."

Liz interjected, "Then why wouldn't he have simply taken me when we met earlier? He had a terrific opportunity. No, it's not the way David operates. He's not going to kidnap anyone. If he can't get me to do this for him, he'll think of something else."

"We do not want to lose contact with him," Foreman pressed. "Liz is that contact."

"So we'll give him what he wants," Boldt said.

Liz asked, "Will someone please tell me what we're all agreeing to?"

"Give us a chance to set it up," Boldt told Foreman, who looked as surprised as Liz that he had acquiesced. Boldt told them exactly what he had in mind.

FIVE

"THE WOMEN'S REST ROOM DOWN the hall will have a yellow sign out front saying it's being cleaned," Danny Foreman told Liz over the phone in a calm, melodious voice. "Go in there now."

She walked out her office door and down the hall, telling her assistant that she'd be right back. She doubted that. The wall clock read 3:40. She was scheduled to pick up the five thousand in cash at 4:00. This was it. A day of clock-watching over, actually *doing something* felt a bit surreal.

Stepping inside, she was met by a woman she recognized. This woman locked the door behind her and whispered "Clear" into the echoing tile room.

It took Liz a moment to identify Detective Bobbie Gaynes because of the dark blue coveralls. Gaynes was the first woman to ever make Homicide. She wore her dark hair cut short, and the cleaning-company coveralls fit her loosely.

Gaynes spoke softly. "Your every movement will be tracked by Special Ops, Mrs. B." Everyone on the Crimes Against Persons unit called her this. "Just as the Lieu prob-

ably told you, I need you to follow my instructions closely
and do exactly as I say. Me and the girls urge you to ask
questions whenever you're unclear. We'll repeat or explain
ourselves as necessary, though time is of the essence.
Okay? We want to get this right the first time. Okay?" She
waited hardly a second. "Good."

Liz found it hard to breathe.

Lou had explained the operation to her, but it had
seemed at the time that little would be expected of her.
Now, even that little bit felt like too much.

Gaynes continued, "This here is Gina." The woman
stood about five feet, and had to be a size two. She had
Italian coloring, a sweet smile, and a firm handshake. "If
you ever seen *Cats* up on Fifth, you seen Gina's handiwork." In front of Gina, on the countertop between two
sinks, a series of open fishing tackle boxes offered a wealth
of cosmetics, from eyebrow pencils and blushes to hair-
pieces and bras.

A woman with dark hair, average height, stood next to
Gina, her blouse unbuttoned and hanging open. She looked
familiar, though Liz felt certain they'd never met. No introduction was made. This woman remained firmly fixed
on Gina.

"Your bra size, Mrs. B.?" Gina asked, the familiarity of
her addressing Liz this way unsettling, as if she, too, were
a part of CAP.

"Thirty-two A," Liz answered, embarrassed by what
two nursing children, chemotherapy, and drastic weight loss
had done to her breasts.

The other woman peeled her blouse off and removed
her bra, leaving her naked from the waist up. Gina posi-

tioned Liz to face the mirror while she worked on this other woman's face. Gaynes and Gina wrapped the stand-in's chest to flatten her high breasts.

Gina explained, "Believe it or not, and I'm sure you will, it's the first thing a guy'll notice—the chest."

"What the . . . ?"

Gaynes interrupted, "Gina's done all our S.O. work for the past couple years. Best in the business." Special Ops was a prestigious though dangerous posting.

The woman who had not yet been introduced by name redressed herself. Only then did Liz realize this person wore the *exact* same clothes as she.

"Is this what I think it is?" Liz asked.

Gina asked Liz for the brand and color of the lipstick she wore. The cosmetologist then directed Gaynes to one of the tackle boxes, all the while using small pieces of foam rubber dabbed and coated in various bases and blushes to build the coloring onto the woman's cheeks and brow. She worked incredibly fast, her hands nearly a blur.

Gaynes reported, "Two minutes."

Gina explained, "We don't want you to spend more than five minutes in here, because after that it can raise eyebrows. Speaking of which . . ." She grabbed up an electric razor and zipped it along the other woman's brow, then turned to a pair of tweezers.

"Officer Malone here is going to take your place," Gaynes said. "It's a bit of a tricky deal, so you're going to want to play this heads-up. If we blow it, either something happens to you or to Officer Malone here—not that she doesn't know the score. It's just that we want to give this the best shot." Gaynes unzipped the coveralls and handled a police radio apparently clipped to her belt. "One minute," she announced. The thing spit back at her. A man's voice, but not Lou's.

Malone looked at Liz for the first time and Liz gasped aloud at this woman's similarity.

"Pretty fucking good, huh?" Gaynes said, slipping into her more familiar self.

Backing up, she gained just enough distance to where she could see the woman clearly; the hastily applied makeup blended perfectly into the surface of this woman's skin, shallowing her cheeks, stretching her chin, transforming her looks. Gina put finishing touches to the hair— clearly a wig that had been chosen ahead of time.

Gaynes said, "Malone's with Washington State Bureau of Criminal Investigation, on loan . . . it's a shared operation, Mrs. B."

"Pleased to meet you," Malone said, stretching out her hand.

Liz Boldt's hand shook of its own accord as she stepped forward and greeted the nearly perfect reflection of herself. Malone's hand was hot; Liz's was bone cold.

"Okay," Gaynes said, "party's over, girls. Time's up."

□ □ □

Gaynes quickly briefed Liz on how to execute the substitution as Malone zipped herself back into a pair of house-cleaning coveralls and Gina placed a dark scarf over the stand-in's head.

"The good thing," Gina said calmly as she pulled the scarf forward to hide as much of the face as possible, "is that no one pays any attention at all to the help. We're invisible. It's straight to the elevators for us."

For Liz, who was to return to her office for exactly five minutes, their behavior took on the feel of choreography, and she envied them their cool. Her role was to be fleeting, with Malone carrying the brunt of the load, and yet she still felt light-headed with anticipation.

Back in her office, she shut the door and paced, watching the time and wondering how it could slow so drastically. Only childbirth produced a slower clock than this. The phone rang, but she let her assistant pick up. When Lou was announced, Liz snatched it up.

"Thank goodness," she said.

"Are you okay?"

"No."

"Can you go through with this?"

"Yes."

"Gaynes briefed you."

"Yes."

"Three steps," he said.

"I understand."

"The most important of which—"

"Is turning around and hiding," she interrupted. "I got that."

"The black raincoat," he said. "Turn around once you're in there."

"Small steps."

"Exactly."

"I've got it," she said.

"Scared?"

"You bet."

"That's good."

"How can you say that?"

"There will be a diversion once you're out. You get to that door—"

"She told me."

"A plainclothes will be waiting for you on the other side."

"I wish I were there now."

"We can call this off," he said, his expectant voice clearly preferring this choice.

"No. I want you to catch him. I want this over." They had discussed this. Once the money was delivered, Hayes was guilty of extortion. At that point they had the pressure to negotiate a deal to get Liz out of the middle and Hayes to cooperate. If all went well, a matter of hours and she and Lou could begin the process of rebuilding.

"Time's up," he said.

"Everyone keeps saying that."

"At any given moment, there's one of us within three or four steps of you."

"It's her I'm worried about . . . this Malone girl. What if he harms her? How am I supposed to live with that?"

"No matter what, you stay inside the bank. Gaynes explained that?"

"Time's up," she said, impatient now to have it over with. She added, "She explained it, Lou. Twice. I've got it."

"Be safe," he said.

He hung up before she had the chance to tell him that she loved him. Maybe he'd sensed it coming, she thought. Maybe he couldn't handle that right now.

□ □ □

The building's lobby contained WestCorp's flagship branch. It looked like a downtown men's club with teller windows elaborately decorated in dark wood paneling, reproduction partner desks, green banker desktop lights, brass and smoked glass chandeliers, and a rich green carpet with borders of twisting gold braids. The phones purred, they did not ring. Voices traveled only a few feet.

Wearing her black, full-length raincoat and carrying the aluminum briefcase she'd purchased in the WestCorp Center's small mall only minutes before, Liz entered the branch office as nervous as on her wedding day, keenly aware of the elaborate charade and her role as a participant. To anyone else, the bank's main floor appeared no different than on any other business day, but to her the abundance of familiar faces made this seem more like the staging of a Christmas play. She immediately identified no fewer than five familiar faces from Crimes Against Persons: two behind desks, posing as bank officers; one up a ladder affixing to the wall a bright orange banner offering low-interest car loans; two others just behind the bank tellers, pretending to be busy with paperwork. Seeing their faces calmed her.

She approached the teller line, cordoned off by stainless steel stands and retractable belts. She hesitated a little too long at the small sign atop the stanchion. "Next?" A young Asian guy in his twenties standing in the third window over. Liz felt a jolt of panic. "I can help you," the young man encouraged. In all, it took her a little under five minutes to get the cash, withdrawn from their home equity line. She tried not to be bothered by the feeling of a dozen eyes boring into her. Behind her, a maintenance man moved aside two orange cones from in front of the revolving doors, removing the CLOSED FOR REPAIR sign. She identified him as Detective Frank McNamara.

The pounding of her heart, the dry mouth, the stinging eyes accounted for the panic she fought to control, along with the rhythmic surge of blood in her ears and the coarse sound of her breathing. She stepped inside the revolving door, hoisting the briefcase and pushing on the bar with both hands. The lumbering carousel began to spin, the glass tinted ahead of her, its surface mirrored behind—a new feature. This had been McNamara's handiwork. The Mylar-mirrored glass would hide her.

She recalled Lou's instructions vividly: Clutch the briefcase to her chest, turn toward the center of the revolving door, and compress herself, taking tiny footsteps, careful not to jam the door's motion.

No one had warned her how confined this space would feel, how it would shrink around her, removing all the air. Two steps into it, she sagged, and thought she might pass out.

□ □ □

As a Crimes Against Persons lieutenant, Boldt's participation in this, or any Special Ops surveillance, even one involving his wife, was strictly in an advisory role. Boldt was ready for undercover street work if necessary, dressed in blue jeans, a black sweatshirt advertising a Paris jazz club, and a British driving cap pulled down low on his brow. The disguise was finished off with a pair of black-framed fashion glasses. He looked nerdy by design—a forty-year-old loner who sat on park benches feeding the pigeons.

In the front of his thoughts lay the possibility that the money drop was nothing more than a clever cover for the opportunity to abduct his wife. Never mind the Special Ops switch—Malone for Liz—Boldt was not going to have any abduction on his conscience.

Pahwan Riz, a thirty-five-year-old Malaysian American whose mother was a full-blooded Englishwoman, had skin the color of a leather couch, mercurial green eyes that squinted naturally in a constant suspicion, and a lilting, singsong voice that belied his intensity. Riz commanded this special operation, and ran his unit like a military man. Under normal circumstances Boldt celebrated Riz's formalities, admired a man who had fought racial prejudice in order to reach the coveted position of commander of a twenty-five-person team that was regularly at high risk. S.O. offered officers the likelihood of live ammunition combat and, as such, drew its water from a dark well. Because it was made up of those willing, even eager, to put themselves into the line of fire, S.O.'s direction of the operation came as a mixed blessing.

Boldt occupied the cracked vinyl passenger seat of a former steam-cleaning van confiscated years before in a drug bust. It served as the communications command vehicle, mobile headquarters for Riz and his black-clad squad of commandos.

With the van parked on the third level of a parking garage across the street from the bank, both Boldt and the wheel man, a guy named Travis, brandished binoculars, trained onto the bank building's exterior. Behind them, on the other side of a black curtain, where a bank of television monitors flickered in the dim light, came the sputtering and spitting sound of radio traffic orchestrated by a dull-voiced, unexcitable woman dispatcher who sat next to Riz.

"Reece!" Boldt called out using the universally accepted but incorrect pronunciation of the commander's last name as the bank's revolving door moved for the first time.

"We saw it," Riz confirmed.

The revolving door spun like a giant paddle wheel. Riz called out commands and the dispatcher repeated them. A big guy on the sidewalk sucked on a cigarette and turned toward the revolving doors just as a woman wearing a black raincoat and carrying an aluminum briefcase stepped out from those doors and into pedestrian traffic. Even knowing what to look for, Boldt missed the switch, never saw his wife's black raincoat tucked into the apex of that spinning wedge of the revolving doors.

"Phase two," Riz said calmly.

A woman dressed as Liz Boldt, looking like Liz Boldt, and carrying an aluminum briefcase like the one Liz Boldt was supposed to be carrying, headed down the sidewalk as instructed. Boldt hoisted the binoculars. Even under magnification Malone passed for Liz.

Boldt popped open his door and said, "I'm on channel one-six, and I've got my cell. Keep me in the loop."

"Lieutenant!" Riz complained, too loudly for the small confines of the panel van. He stopped Boldt. "I remind you: We have an operation in place. You cannot, must not, visit your wife inside that bank. Not yet. It could be watched."

"I know that, Reece." The guy made it sound like Boldt had never been on a surveillance. He eased the van's door shut, inexplicably drawn to protect this woman pretending to be his wife.

Once out on the street, Boldt quickly spotted the woman

in the black raincoat walking west down the hill on Madison.

Boldt wore a cell phone ear bud in his right ear—a common sight on the streets now and one that made such clandestine surveillance easier than before. In Boldt's case, the ear bud wire was plugged into a portable police-band radio tucked under his jacket.

In his ear, the dispatcher's voice inquired, "LTB?" Boldt's radio handle. He acknowledged. The dispatcher then rattled off a request that Boldt switch sides of the street. Riz didn't want anyone from the team directly behind Malone. Boldt obeyed the request, crossing with a group of southbound pedestrians, tension surging through him in long waves. He was thinking that Malone's walk was all wrong, lacking both Liz's elegance and the subtle but stirring sway of her hips. Malone's efficient stride was all about training, athleticism, and preparation. At a moment's notice, Malone was ready to either drop to the sidewalk like a sack of cement or sprint in the opposite direction. Under that controlled movement was a body like a cat's.

Malone continued west on Madison, down toward the waterfront now directly ahead of her. The street's dead end into the north/south sidewalk that fronted Elliott Bay would somewhat contain her, and Boldt thought Hayes too smart to corner himself like that. So what the hell was he up to? Then he realized that Riz was being forced to reduce the number of personnel he sent into the area, for fear that in large numbers even the undercover officers might be spotted. Riz cut back from eight undercover officers to four on foot, holding the others in positions two blocks away, across the deserted stretch of parking tarmac beneath the elevated lanes of Alaskan Way. An unmarked van of SWAT-like S.O. operatives was moved into position across from the Seattle Aquarium. It was here, the aquarium, a series of restaurants, an IMAX theater, that Riz initially focused his personnel.

Boldt understood Riz's reluctance to accept that Hayes would make things easy for them by directing "Liz" to a ferry or a boat—fully contained and so easily tracked and followed—a criminal's nightmare. But with the middle stretch of waterfront buildings soon to be under the umbrella of Riz's well-orchestrated team, Boldt played the contrarian. Riz did finally direct a few of his people toward the ferry docks, but by the time he thought to do so, Boldt was already several hundred yards ahead of not only the closest operative but Malone as well, for she had stopped and stared out to sea for seven long minutes, presumably under the direction of Hayes, as she now carried Liz's cell phone. Her pause caused a momentary paralysis for Special Ops, finding themselves unable to predict her next move.

Boldt, by playing against the grain, ended up at the ferries well ahead of the mark, and ahead of Special Ops also, the only one already in place when Malone made her unexpected move south.

South, to the ferries.

□ □ □

The Washington State Department of Transportation—WSDOT—operates the busiest ferry system in North America, handling nearly seventy thousand passengers per day. Piers 50 and 52 of the Seattle Terminal, a sprawling landscape of parking lots and docks, present managers with a logistical challenge similar to that of running a small airport. In constant motion, teams of dockworkers and sailors and maintenance personnel, food service people and housecleaners, attempt to keep a fleet of thirty-one ships on a reliable schedule. The two terminals operate under a surprising calm, the result of a well-practiced routine.

Boldt faced a decision as he read from the electronic sign that listed scheduled departures. Slip 3 offered a Bainbridge Island ferry departing at 4:40, and with a short crossing time of thirty-five minutes. Right or wrong, Boldt had to commit. Boarding *ahead* of "Liz"—Malone—was something he doubted Hayes would anticipate. Police reacted, they *followed* a surveillance mark, they didn't arrive ahead of the mark.

Hopeful that Riz might yet sneak one or more of his undercover operatives onboard, Boldt believed Hayes would be looking to identify those behind Malone. He doubted Hayes would recognize him, especially given the jeans, the glasses, and the hat pulled down over his brow, but he nonetheless stopped at a tourist stand and bought two Orca whale Beanie Babies for the kids. With the white shopping bag in hand, marking him a tourist, he felt even better disguised.

Head down, bunched in with a dozen commuters, Boldt boarded the gray-and-white ferry, *Puyallup*. Filled to capacity, as she was to be at this hour, *Puyallup* carried 2,500 passengers and more than 200 vehicles. The teeming masses of commuters contributed to Boldt's camouflage.

He bought a *Times* from a vending machine in the main cabin and headed to a window seat with a view of the boarding areas.

As the dispatcher barked orders, Boldt realized Riz and

his team were now scrambling to deploy undercover officers onto the ferry.

Hayes orchestrated Malone's arrival at the pier to within a few scant minutes of the *Puyallup*'s departure, leaving her one of the last passengers to board. Interpreting what he heard in his ear, Boldt saw a single undercover bike patrol officer board the ferry behind her. Boldt searched his memory for a name: Hendersen, a lanky surfer dude, blond, in his early thirties. He wore colorful Spandex bearing Lance Armstrong's signature and the U.S. Postal Service logo, a black helmet that was pointed in front and back, a red backpack with a dozen zippers, and a pair of stereo headphones connected to a jogger's portable CD player that strapped to his chest. The CD player was in fact a police radio. The space-age riding glasses he wore concealed a microphone allowing two-way conversation. Hendersen bobbed his head constantly, as if he were listening to music.

The ferry left the pier smoothly. Malone, deeply into the role of Liz Boldt, arrived on the passenger deck, the aluminum briefcase in hand, among a cluster of the last passengers to board. Seconds behind her, Hendersen appeared, easily spotted by his helmet.

Malone walked the length of the ship and out through the forward doors to the bow deck, Liz's cell phone held tightly to her ear.

Boldt reached inside his jacket and turned down the radio's volume, distracted by the clatter of dispatch. With ten staircases and three decks, an elevator, and twenty-five hundred passengers, the *Puyallup* seemed an easy place to lose somebody. Once Hayes manipulated her below deck, it would require but a matter of seconds to stash Malone into a vehicle. Smuggling her off the ship would prove more difficult, but he put nothing past Hayes given what he'd seen so far: an organized, patient personality.

Boldt reached Hendersen and introduced himself without looking directly at the man. They divided the ship in two between them, Hendersen taking the outside deck, Boldt remaining inside.

They would pass responsibility for her back and forth between them via the radio. If she moved up or down levels, whoever was following her at the time was to stay with her because radio contact could be problematic given all the steel.

Boldt added in a whisper, well aware of the many passengers surrounding them both, "If she heads *downstairs* to the vehicles, get word to me somehow, because that's the deal."

"Got it."

They split up, both aware of the difficulty of having only a two-man surveillance team. Boldt watched Hendersen head outside only yards behind Malone, the two visible through the passenger deck's large windows. Like watching a silent movie.

Boldt noticed the horizon shift as the ferry corrected course. The dispatcher came onto the radio, announcing that personnel would be deployed on the ground at the Bainbridge Island ferry terminal in the event Malone disappeared onboard or later disembarked. The island's law enforcement quickly proved itself ill prepared for a spontaneous undercover operation. An officer was currently racing home to change into civilian clothes and to switch cars with his wife. Boldt asked that this man and his car be available to him in the event Malone left the ferry. Hendersen could follow on bike, if necessary. It wasn't a great plan, but it was all they had.

Malone completed a full circle of the outside deck, and Boldt called off Hendersen with a simple command sent over the radio. Bainbridge Island drew closer. The sun sank lower, finally slipping behind the dramatic mountain range and delivering a thickening twilight. Boldt took over, following Malone to the ship's stern, where she reentered the enclosed passenger deck. Boldt stopped outside rather than enter behind her. He glanced over the rail at the ship's bubbling wake and the ruffled feathers of a group of hungry white seagulls riding the wind. Facing away, out to sea, he called over the radio to Hendersen and made a second handoff.

"Stairs!" came Hendersen's blunt reply. "Ascending. Repeat: ascending." Boldt reentered in time to catch a glimpse of Hendersen's colorful bike uniform disappearing through a metal exit door.

The ferry sounded its loud horn. Boldt felt a jolt with the unexpected sound. Dusk settled, softening edges, blurring the horizon, running color to gray. Boldt reached the upper level with its small cabin and larger deck. Malone's back was turned to him as she passed outside.

Hendersen and Boldt met eyes, exchanging a look as Hendersen retreated down the stairs and Boldt took over.

Malone, Liz's phone pressed to her ear, nodded faintly as she listened.

A family of four headed past Boldt, down the stairs, leaving only him and one other man, who sat alone with his back to Boldt. Outside, Malone joined a line of others pressed against the stern rail. A chill wind blew.

It took Boldt a change of angles to spot the black wire

leading from the seated man's ear—the same kind of hands-free cell phone wire that he himself wore. Talking to whom? he wondered. *Malone?*

Boldt edged closer, excitement pounding inside his chest. *Ten feet . . . Five feet . . .*

On the edge of his peripheral vision, Boldt saw Malone's movement as she glanced back over her shoulder at him. Boldt paused, instinctively knowing something was wrong.

The seated man turned, and Boldt saw his face. Not David Hayes, but a man in his sixties with poor skin.

Malone threw the briefcase off the side of the ferry with all her strength. Its brushed aluminum spun in lazy loops as it tumbled and then disappeared, out of sight.

Boldt stood paralyzed. The ferry was nowhere near landfall. Five thousand dollars in marked bills had just been tossed overboard. No matter how tempted, he could not give Malone away—could not compromise her. Instead, he casually reached inside his jacket pocket and tripped the button to speak to Riz's dispatcher.

A moment later came the response: A helicopter would be dispatched, though it wouldn't be airborne for at least thirty minutes. Boldt was to secure a GPS location from the ferry's captain ASAP.

A trickle of dread swept through Boldt as he sensed a much bigger plan at work, wondering if that plan still called for the abduction of Malone, a.k.a. Liz Boldt.

Hendersen had caught Boldt's radio communication and waited on the main passenger deck.

Malone remained outside in the bitter wind, cradling Liz's cell phone in her palm as if it held answers.

Boldt hurried across the deck, jumping a chain that forbade him from doing so, and climbed the steep ladder. He pounded on the heavy door to the pilothouse, displaying his credentials and shield through the thick glass window.

A moment later he was inside, relaying the ferry's latitude and longitude to Riz and company. He checked the ship's radar, surprised it picked up no boats in the immediate area. No vessels of any kind. He'd been absolutely convinced that some kind of small craft was out there retrieving the money.

Boldt engaged one of the deck officers, throwing a string of questions at him.

The man, small but with a thick neck and jutting jaw, replied in a tight, high voice. "The WSDOT website offers ferry-cam-dot-com. Vessel watch. Live video of the terminals. GPS locating of the ferries."

"GPS?" Boldt asked. The Global Positioning System's satellite technology allowed pinpoint location. Given the exact time Malone had thrown that briefcase, a person could evidently visit a website that indicated the ferry's precise location.

"On the Web," Boldt mumbled, realizing that Hayes could know exactly where that briefcase had been tossed overboard. Or had the briefcase bought from Brookstone had a transmitter already embedded in it? Had anyone checked for that? He didn't think so.

Boldt scrambled down the steep steel steps leading from the pilothouse and crossed to the upper sundeck, realizing that Hayes could already be heading for the cash. He grabbed for the radio, yanking it from his pocket, dispensing with policy.

Boldt asked to speak to Riz. When the C.O. came onto the radio, Boldt said, "Tell me Liz is okay."

"She's in a back office with one of our girls," Riz said. "We're sure?"

"Positive, Lieutenant. Your wife's been on the phone with him off and on for the last ten minutes, Malone listening in to those calls and performing as he says."

Two guys in their twenties came through the door and into the upper deck area engaged in a heated baseball debate, the only two words that Boldt heard being "sacrifice fly."

And then all at once, he had it. *The briefcase would never be retrieved. Sacrifice fly.* Hayes had tested Liz, directing her to withdraw the money and toss it on command, and she had passed that test. But there was something larger at work as well.

"Oh, shit," said the lieutenant, known for never swearing. "We've been scammed, Reece. He dug a hole and we fell into it. Seal the building!" Boldt hesitated only a second, knowing the trouble he was about to cause if he turned out to be wrong about this. "David Hayes is inside the bank."

SI**X**

BOLDT BELIEVED THAT HAYES HAD used the money drop not only to distract police but to access the bank's powerful AS/400 servers, described by Liz as the "heart of the data system." But with the office building currently locked down, and everyone inside the building being funneled out a single exit, proffering ID and subjected to random searches, Boldt's theory showed signs of collapse. David Hayes was nowhere to be seen.

An acne-ridden young man named Pendleton Hartsmith joined a florid-cheeked Irishman, Douglas Witte, who headed the bank's security department. The pair sat with Boldt in a small conference room typically reserved for loan review. It smelled of carpet glue.

Witte explained that access to WestCorp's offices required a credit-card-sized ID card, like the one Liz carried. Each and every access was recorded by time, date, employee, and location of entry or egress. The UNIX servers and the AS/400s each required additional clearance for access.

"Following nine-eleven," Witte explained, "we installed

palm scanners on our two hardware plants, the suites that
house our major servers. Access is limited to a very select
group of executives."

Including Liz, Boldt thought. "And can we determine if
that security has been breached?"

Witte said, "It hasn't. It's the first thing we checked
when you called for this lockdown. The AS/400s are pris-
tine."

Witte popped a stick of gum into his mouth and offered
some to the others. Hartsmith took a stick. Boldt passed.

"Cameras show anything?"

"Your guys have already requested our pictures," Witte
said. "We're making dubs, as I understand."

"I see a possible conflict," Hartsmith said. That won
both men's attention. "We're all digital here, Lieutenant.
Security clearance, video surveillance, it's all digitized information, and all of it is stored on one of the four UNIX
servers."

Witte jumped in and explained. "That's what I meant by
making a dub. Our video surveillance is stored electronically to disk. Think TiVo. We can review it straight off the
disks or dub it down to half-inch tape, or DVD, as we're
doing for you."

"And if someone got into these servers," Boldt said,
leading Hartsmith on.

"That's my point. You look at it that way, it's a pretty
fallible system."

Boldt could see Hayes having entered the building, and
then the processing suites, but convincing the computer-
controlled security system otherwise. Boldt suddenly wondered if that had already happened, if Hayes had come,
gotten his money, and gone.

"Can you put a guard, a human being, one of your security guys, on the doors to these processing rooms? Can we not rely on the technology so much?"

"It would cost. I'd have to check."

"Check," Boldt said. "And if you're refused, let me know right away."

He looked for cracks in his reasoning, absolutely certain that Hayes used the money drop as a diversion, but stumped to prove it. Witte pulled himself out of a chair and left the small conference room. Hartsmith's intelligent eyes stared off into space, deep in thought.

"It's problematic," Hartsmith said. "A computer controlling its own security. But then again, it's integrated. A closed system. You can't get into the system to mess with it, because it guards its own door."

"But if you do get through that door . . ." Boldt could *see* Liz being forced to gain Hayes access to the servers, could feel her terror. Increasingly, it seemed to Boldt that if Hayes could not get her to cooperate, his only choice would be to kidnap her or someone else at the bank with the proper security clearance.

"Then we're toast. Yes. You erase any record of your visit, and you dump any video that captured you. It's brilliant, really, except that it's putting the cart before the horse."

"But how do we know absolutely?"

"There is no absolute way. But if you're asking if I think someone raided the AS/400s today, I'd put a good piece of change on that not having happened."

Boldt understood then that both Foreman and Liz were right: Hayes needed Liz for her palm print to gain access. Once inside the server suites, with access to the mainframes, he could not only steal his money back but erase any record he'd ever been in the building, clear himself of any charges, and he could do it using the very same computers that were supposed to catch him. Perhaps today, using Liz to make the money drop, to distract bank security and the police, was nothing more than a dry run, a chance for him to inspect the place, to get a lay of the land and refine his plan. If so, they'd pick him up on the security video.

Boldt caught up to Liz still being held in a small room off the bank's branch offices located on the ground floor. He asked her to assemble a list of all WestCorp employees and executives with security clearance to the server suites. He intended to interview them all. He then called in the best eyes on his squad, unwilling to wait for video dubs from the bank surveillance cameras. Within the hour, he had six officers in front of televisions, carefully screening the jerky imagery—still images shot every four seconds and stored to video. At shortly after 11 P.M., one of the officers spotted David Hayes.

"Elvis is in the building," the woman announced to her colleagues, a little punch-drunk from the hours of tedious viewing.

Boldt was telephoned and awakened at home.

Thirty minutes later, Boldt found himself waiting for Danny Foreman outside the First Hill brownstone belonging to one Thedona Rembrandt Wilson. He'd left two messages for Foreman, as well as sending a page, and felt confident that rain or shine, Danny Foreman would meet him there, given the gravity of the find. He tried Foreman's cell phone one last time and finally elected to make the interview alone. He'd left Liz at home, with the kids, but not before placing a team of uniformed patrol officers, one on foot, one in the cruiser, to watch his own house. Boldt remained convinced Hayes intended to abduct her. He wasn't about to leave her unwatched and unguarded.

Thedona Wilson, an African American woman with good bone structure and large hands, required Boldt not only to show his identification but to pass his credentials through her chained front door, allowing her to make a call downtown. By the time she admitted Boldt and showed him into the living room, she was dressed in a white satin robe tied tightly around the waist and was sipping herbal tea. She offered nothing to Boldt, viewing him with skepticism, until Boldt placed some photocopied images in front of her and happened to mention that Elizabeth Boldt was his wife. At that point she did, in fact, offer Boldt tea or coffee, but he declined, too edgy and high-strung, interested only in making some progress on the case.

"These images, captured on security video, show this man, the one in the hat, at your desk, do they not?"

"Yes, sir, they do."

"Do you remember this man?"

"I'm a customer service representative, Mr. Boldt. I'm supposed to remember faces, make conversation, and cross-sell. This man here was in his late twenties, early thirties. Polite. Handsome. Soft-spoken."

Boldt shifted uncomfortably, not wanting to hear Hayes described in any of these ways. "You leave your desk at one point. Then he leaves with you . . ." Boldt shuffled the freeze-frame images.

"To his safe-deposit box."

"Safe deposit," Boldt echoed, yanking his notebook from his blazer's inside pocket.

"That's all I know. Don't remember the box number. In

the two hundreds I think—two-oh-six? Two-oh-eight? Or is that an area code?" She tugged her robe to ensure it stayed tightly closed at her chest. "It'll be in the log."

"A name?"

"Brindle? Binder?" She searched her memory.

Boldt felt all the blood settle out of him, like someone had pulled a cork. "Brimmer," Boldt said.

She snapped her long fingers, cracking the air. "Brimmer! First initial, E. A funny name, Everest? Everett?"

"E. Brimmer," Boldt said, this time dryly. "Not Hayes? You're sure it was Brimmer?"

"He doesn't gain access without signing in, without me comparing that signature card, and I'm telling you, it was Brimmer for sure."

The signature card would allow an expert to compare handwriting. If it came back Hayes, as he was certain it would, then it would serve as probable cause for them to obtain a warrant and to drill the safe-deposit box. Boldt assumed this effort would prove fruitless: He suspected Hayes had kept the "cloaking" software—which he'd used to keep the seventeen million hidden in WestCorp's system—in the safe-deposit box. He had it now, and with it, the ability to recover the money. Given use of the pseudonym, Brimmer, bank officers had failed to identify the box as registered to Hayes.

Boldt told Ms. Wilson he'd meet her at the bank at 8 A.M., Monday, and that together they would examine the safe-deposit logbook. An exercise in futility, he knew.

"That name, Brimmer," she said. "Why the long face, Lieutenant?"

"It's nothing," Boldt answered, lying well. In fact, it was Liz's maiden name: Elizabeth Brimmer. *E. Brimmer*, a false identity Hayes had established, no doubt, years ago while still a bank employee. While still infatuated. *In love?* Boldt wondered. That name, that safe-deposit box, connected Hayes to Liz, and Liz to the past, and Boldt's memory to that shared past as well.

Suddenly, he felt sick to his stomach.

SEVEN

"THE STRUGGLE IS NOT IN solving this case," Boldt told Liz, who was still half asleep. "Because to tell the truth, I don't care about the embezzlement, this seventeen million dollars. The struggle is to protect you and to save our marriage, it's retaining or maintaining respect for each other, making it out the other side in one piece."

"I didn't know he'd used my maiden name."

"It borders on worship, that kind of thing. I'm thinking he probably had a shrine to you in his jail cell."

"Stop it."

"I'm serious."

"What if he did? So what? You don't see any shrine on this end, do you?"

"I'm telling you, the battle I face right now is forgiveness. Finding forgiveness. That and protecting you. This money? I could care less!"

"I'm sorry," she said, pulling up the bedcovers, experiencing a chill.

"I woke you up. It was stupid of me."

"Don't be ridiculous!" she called out, as he crossed the

bedroom to the bathroom door. "And don't walk away from me."

He turned, one foot, half of him, into the sanctuary of excusable privacy.

"You have every right to be upset," she said.

"Don't do that," he said. "Don't manipulate me like that."

"I am *not* manipulating you. I mean every word of that."

"It doesn't help things."

"It's honesty. It's what I'm thinking. It has to help."

"I'm just telling you: I don't care about the money."

"Neither do I."

"I care about you."

"That's important to me. To us."

"I hate the images I have in my head. The two of you together. I'm resentful I even have them."

"Understandable."

"Don't patronize," he cautioned.

"Is there a script I'm supposed to follow?" she asked. "I'm saying what comes to my head, Lou. What comes to my heart. Don't condition that. Let me speak."

"So speak."

"You're mad at me," she said. "I accept that."

"There you go again."

"I'm not going anywhere," she fired back bitterly. "Are *you*? Is that what this is about? You're the only one who's walked out on this marriage, Lou. I didn't."

"This again?"

"Yes, I suppose so: this again. And again, and again. And I hate it as much as you do—*for the record*. I'd like nothing more than to rewind and erase the tape, forget it ever happened. But we can't, right? We're stuck with it.

We're both going to have to live with it, maybe forever. I appreciate your efforts at forgiveness, but you don't just jump there all at once. It's a *process,* not a destination."

His mouth opened twice, and he even raised his hand as if about to speak. But then he pounded a fist against the doorjamb, his jaw muscles knotted. He choked out, "I don't want this."

"Well, I've got news for you: Neither do I."

"I'm going to go sleep with Miles."

"All I'm going to say is that if you start that kind of thing, it's hard to undo it."

"So what do you want from me?" he asked, frustrated.

She considered this deeply and finally waited for eye contact before delivering her response. "Time," she said.

Boldt slept in their shared bed that night, and through the weekend, though fitfully, if at all. Mercifully, work saved him from his insomnia in the wee hours of Monday morning.

The alert came from his pager at a few minutes before four. The code was for an assault, the address not one he recognized. But he knew damn well that even the dumbest dispatcher would not page a lieutenant unless the reported crime was of incredible importance to either the department as a whole or the lieutenant personally. Sergeants and their squads kept on-call hours, but not lieutenants.

He hung up the bedside phone.

Liz spoke through a dry throat. "Sweetheart?"

"It's Danny Foreman," Boldt said.

"What's he want at this hour?"

"Not the call," Boldt answered, correcting her. "The victim. Robbery/assault. Someone beat him up pretty badly and robbed him. I gotta go."

"Is he going to be okay?"

"I think so. Get back to sleep if you can."

"I'm up," she said. "You call me when you can."

"Maybe I just had to get that off my chest Friday night," he said.

"Meaning?"

"I feel better for having said what I said. I feel more like a team all of a sudden. Us, I mean."

"Music to my ears," she said.

"Speaking of which . . ."

"I'll pick up Miles, yes," she said. "I'll get them both and be home around six."

"I'll get the team back here to watch the house as soon as I can."

"Okay."

He was dressed now, standing at the closet safe, fetching his gun. He slipped the blazer on, tugged on his shirt-sleeves. She called him over and scratched out a stain.

"Can't take me anywhere," he said.

"Oh, I don't know about that."

He hesitated a moment, but he leaned over then and kissed her on the lips, a little peck, but a kiss nonetheless, and she felt like a high school girl who didn't want to wash her face for a week.

☐ ☐ ☐

A mile down Martin Luther King Boulevard, Boldt turned right and worked his way into the middle-class, mostly black, neighborhood. Foreman's house was a modest one-and-a-half-story clapboard.

Inside the front door, Boldt met with the familiar smell

of a crime scene: male sweat. He walked through the house and descended steep stairs into the dank cellar.

It was dark and bitter down here, a tomb with stale air that carried on it the rusty tang of fresh blood. Clusters of halogen lights on aluminum tripods, stenciled "SPD," blinded the man who remained in the wooden chair at their center.

Foreman sat slumped forward, doing his best to hide the pain.

The smell of solvent stung Boldt's sinuses. Acetone. It didn't make sense that SID, the department's Scientific Identification Division, would "fume" for prints down here with rescue crews still in attendance. "Glue?"

"Duct tape *and* Superglue," answered the female half of the two personnel working on Foreman. "Wrists and ankles to each other, and the chair to the floor."

Foreman's left hand was missing two fingernails, accounting for the pool of blood on that side of the floor.

"Twice in a week," Boldt said.

Foreman didn't react.

The rescue woman informed him that Foreman had been given a sedative to help with the pain.

The basement space was small, with little room for more than a heating system, a hot-water tank, and a beat-up washing machine. Add to that two light stands, the chair and the man at their center, the two Search and Rescue personnel attempting to free Foreman, and a pair of EMTs standing by half tucked under the wooden staircase, and it was approaching claustrophobic.

Foreman's lip was split, and his right eye swollen. Boldt pulled out a handkerchief and gently wiped the man's face clean. Foreman lifted his head and the two met eyes, and Boldt felt pain tingle clear through him.

"Bastards," Foreman managed to mutter.

"Who?"

"No fucking clue."

One of the EMTs piped up that the small spot on the right side of Foreman's neck "was consistent" with an injection.

"They got you again." Rohypnol, the "date rape" paralysis drug. *Truth serum*, Boldt thought.

Foreman merely rolled his eyes. He appeared ready to pass out.

Boldt made a quick study of the basement, disappointed to see so many people and so much equipment. The scene was now contaminated beyond recovery.

The young woman said he could try his wrists now, but it might hurt. Danny Foreman tore a four-inch strip of his own flesh away, he pulled so hard. His face grimaced and his eyes shone, but he did not cry out. An EMT shot forward and went to work bandaging the wounds. Boldt saw more blood now. It was everywhere. Sprayed around like a kid with a garden hose.

Boldt took in some of the odds and ends piled on a dusty shelf. A faded Frisbee. Well-worn work gloves. A pair of hiking boots. A waffle iron with a cracked black cord. Two or three cardboard boxes that Boldt knew without looking contained Darlene's things: clothes and accessories and maybe some photo albums; a hospital bracelet cut off a limp wrist three years earlier.

Seeing the damage to the skin, the rescue woman told Foreman they were going to give the solvent a few minutes longer on the ankles.

Foreman gushed through a string of expletives, still under the influence.

The rescue worker called for Boldt's attention and pointed out what appeared to be the carcass of a dead bug, a housefly or larva, to the left of Foreman's chair. When that bug rolled lightly a few inches across the floor, Boldt identified it as cigar or cigarette ash.

"Any of you smoke down here?" Boldt stepped carefully toward the evidence. No answers. "I'm going to ask all of you but this woman to leave now." He instructed them on how to leave in single file, being careful to set their feet down slowly and gently and only in a clear area of the floor.

Boldt knelt down and eased the small worm of gray ash into a three-by-five manila envelope that he kept on his person for evidence collection. Foreman tried to speak, but ended up drooling and spitting instead. "Fuck!" he finally managed to moan, throwing his head around like a blind man at the piano.

Other than the pulled nails, Foreman's hands showed no signs of struggle, no indication he'd fought back. A moment later, the rescue worker had Foreman's ankles free and asked Boldt's permission to summon her partner and the EMTs in order to get Foreman into the waiting ambulance. Boldt acquiesced, again trying to minimize the crime scene contamination.

Once Foreman was gone, Boldt searched the house, now joined by the timely arrival of his own department's Scientific Identification Division.

"Better late than never," Boldt told the anemic thirty-year-old wearing the blue windbreaker marked with his department's acronym. The guy had thin, bluish lips and the pale skin of a cadaver. Boldt had never seen him before.

"The only espresso was a twenty-four-hour drive-thru on the other side of Broadway. And believe me, you do not want to see me before my first espresso."

"I believe you," Boldt said, leading the man into the bedroom, guarded by a uniformed patrol officer.

The bedroom was undisturbed, except for the closet. There Boldt saw a number of shoes swept aside, a hinged shoe rack swung out of the way, and an empty wall safe hanging open with no sign of tampering.

Boldt said, "The combination probably came sometime around the second fingernail."

"How's that?" Captain Espresso had not seen Foreman's left hand.

"It's nothing," Boldt replied. "Develop prints if you can, inside the safe and out, and keep alert for cigar or cigarette ash anywhere in the house. Check all the trash cans, the sinks, the perimeter outside. I'd love an extinguished butt if we can find it."

"Got it," the SID man replied.

"This guy's in the family. On the job. You understand that?"

"I got it, Lieutenant. We're all over this."

"Tell Bernie Lofgrin I'm lead."

"You, Lieutenant?"

"My squad." Boldt would have to put this off on someone; lieutenants didn't run cases. "But I want Bernie calling me."

"Got it."

"And try eating some red meat," Boldt said. On his way out of the small bedroom Boldt thought he heard the guy mumble "Fuck you" under his breath, but didn't return to challenge him. He deserved it.

Danny Foreman had not deserved it, however, and Boldt resolved to bring somebody in for gluing wrists together and using vise-grip pliers to extract fingernails. And also to learn whatever it was that his former friend and colleague, Danny Foreman, wasn't telling him.

EIGHT

LIZ SKIPPED HER RUN, GOT the kids up and fed, and dropped
them off at school with little fanfare, one of their better
mornings. At work now, she felt the presence of her cell
phone weighing on her purse, hoping it might ring, that she
might hear from Lou about Danny Foreman being a "victim" and what that meant to the investigation. Still caught
up in the events of Friday, culminating in the discovery
that Hayes had used her maiden name on his safe-deposit
box, she felt hypersensitive to her surroundings and the
goings-on within the bank. Asked to turn over the list of
names of bank employees with security clearance to the
UNIX and AS/400 servers, Liz also felt obligated to personally notify all five of them of this development, not so
much as a warning but as a courtesy, one colleague to
another.

She spoke to Phillip in person, clearing both her release
of the names and letting him know that she intended to
make the calls herself. His reaction was positive, though
guarded. As WestCorp's CEO, he wanted his employees
and his computer systems protected, but he reminded Liz

no less than three times of the impending merger and how any negative publicity could affect the company's stock price. With equity markets tanking, many a merger had been put off or canceled outright. WestCorp could ill afford any such setback this late in the game.

Liz's first warning was to go out to Tony LaRossa, her director of Information Technology, seemingly a target for Hayes since Tony knew the bank's computer systems inside and out and was one of a select few who could program an IBM AS/400. She decided to see Tony in person as well, using her security pass to allow her access to the twenty-fifth floor. The elevator doors slid open and she stepped through to the quiet chaos of the busiest division in the company: hers. With the technical transfer of the merger only days away, her people were basically working around the clock. And they showed it.

"Two-five," as Liz's I.T. team referred to this floor—never "twenty-five"—was of an open floor plan: eleven office cubicles with walkways between them. All but two were currently occupied. To her right, a meeting was under way in the larger of two corner conference rooms. To her left, the entire north end was now screened off by a wall of thick shatterproof, bullet-resistant glass and the buffed steel girders to support it. This dividing wall had been erected after the fact, post–9/11, and offered but a single door, accessed by one of the now infamous electronic palm-scanners. Inside this glassed-in room there was also a door accessing a second server. To her left was Tony's private office, one of two executive offices on this floor.

Liz approached Tony's secretary, a sweet-faced Hispanic woman who favored a good deal of makeup. "Can he see me?" She barely hesitated, already moving toward his office door.

"He could if he were here," the secretary responded.

Liz checked her watch and then the wall clock: 9:20. Tony LaRossa was typically the first to arrive and the last to leave.

Liz teased, "He's not allowed to be sick this week. Call the CDC." But then the more dreaded conclusion seeped into her consciousness. "When you say he's not here, since when?"

"Not here, since all morning."

"You've called home? Spoken to Beth?"

"Called home, of course. No answer. And his cell. Voice mail. He missed a very important conference call with MTK. No one ever heard from him, which was when I heard about it. And believe me, I *heard* about it."

Liz clarified, "Beth didn't answer the home phone?"

"No, ma'am."

"The twins," she said. "The twins must be sick." Beth and Tony had adopted Russian twins less than six months earlier.

"You all right, Mrs. Boldt?"

"Fine," Liz said. "Concerned is all."

"I'm sure he's all right."

"No answer on his cell phone?"

"No."

"You paged him?"

"I did. Twice now."

Liz couldn't help but wonder if the money drop had not been more than just a distraction away from the bank. Had David, or whomever, used it to abduct Tony LaRossa at the same time? Liz scribbled out her cell phone number on a yellow Post-it and passed it to the secretary. "I want to know the moment you hear from him. Okay? And have Tony call this same number as well. I want to be the first to speak to him after you."

"Sure thing." The secretary picked up on Liz's jumpy nerves and interrupted her departure. "What's going on, Mrs. Boldt?"

She avoided giving an answer, understanding then how practiced Lou had to have become to endure bad news without the slightest indication, how he must have learned to quash his own emotions, to keep himself out of it, and this went a long way to explain him to her. It struck her as odd that she was still learning things about him, that it had taken hardship to open her eyes.

She crossed the room to Tommy Ling's cubicle. She'd had a lot of dealings with Tommy over the past year because his bailiwick was computer/security integration. Tommy's Chinese American heritage put him a third-generation American, with not a twinge of Asian accent. He wore a sumptuous dark green wool suit and a shiny black tie against a gunpowder gray shirt with an English spread collar. He looked to be in his early twenties, but she knew from his employment records that he was pushing forty.

"Tommy," she said, "you can set it up to have the system alert you when Tony enters the building, can't you?"

"If you say to."

"I'm saying to." She wrote down her office extension and cell phone number, to save him having to look them up. "The *moment* he enters. Okay?"

"Is there anything wrong?"

She considered how to answer. "I have some really good

news for him, for the whole department, and I want him to be the first to hear."

The answer clearly satisfied, even pleased, Ling.

She returned to the executive floor before trying to reach Lou. By now her heart was working a little harder than normal, her chest warm, her face flushed. She peeled off the gray suit jacket hoping to cool off, the phone pinched at her shoulder.

"It's Tony," she told her husband, without introductions. "He'd be right at the top of my list, in terms of people with access to the system."

"What about him?" She heard concern in his voice; she knew she was speaking too quickly, but couldn't control herself.

"He's not in."

"So?"

"You know what they call him on Two-five? The Rooster, because he's up before everyone else. It's nine-thirty, Lou!"

"Liz, I'm going to say something, and I don't want to hurt your feelings, but when you get excited or nervous you beat around the bush, and you're doing that now, and that's getting me nervous and excited. So please just take a second to settle down and tell me what it is you want me to come away with from this call."

The reprimand and Lou's instinct toward professionalism had their desired effect. She felt her frustration sink and her thoughts clarify. She also felt a little ticked off at him for being so blunt, but knew she deserved it. "He's not answering any of his phones. More puzzling, Beth isn't picking up at home. Tony has already missed an important conference call and a meeting. That's not like him."

She knew to allow Lou time to think.

"An emergency with the twins?" Boldt suggested.

"I know," Liz said. "That's what I thought, too. But his cell phone *and* his pager? His secretary can't find him. Tony LaRossa? He's the most wired-in guy there is."

"Okay."

"Okay, *what*?" she asked, feeling the heat return.

"I agree it's significant. I can send a patrol unit out to their house. Make inquiries. But more than likely they're just broken down in a tunnel or on a bridge—somewhere that interferes with reception. Hospitals require you to shut off phones and pagers, which brings us back to the twins. Or maybe it's batteries. It happens. There's usually a pretty simple explanation for things like this."

Either he was trying to calm her or he believed this, she didn't know which. She told him about having asked Tommy Ling to watch the system for Tony's use of his access card.

"That's good thinking," Lou said. "You must be married to a cop."

"You'll send somebody?"

"I'm on it." He paused and then said, "That's what you wanted all along, wasn't it, me to send a unit over there?"

Her breath caught. *Busted,* she thought. She said, "I'm getting Miles and Sarah, don't forget."

"Don't change the subject on me. You just worked me."

"Thanks for this." She hung up before giving him a chance to vent.

At 9:55 A.M. her office phone sounded the intercom tone and she picked up.

Tommy Ling said frantically, "Main entrance!"

"Tony's here?"

"He's had a heart attack or something. You'd better get down there."

There were times Liz marveled at the speed and ease of elevators, but this was not one of them. She arrived on the ground floor to a sea of security shirts bent over a pair of legs she assumed to be Tony's, a throng of employees lined up trying to get in, and chaotic shouting of nearly everyone involved.

She pushed her way through the attendants, enough to first identify and then get a better look at Tony LaRossa. His face was a pale color she'd never seen before, his lips a faint blue. He was either unconscious or dead. He'd made it through one of the two metal detectors, and had collapsed. A black nylon webbed briefcase lay unzipped and opened on the security inspection table. It was common practice for security to search every bag. It appeared that Tony had collapsed in the middle of just such a search.

She established that an ambulance had been called, verified by the sudden distant whine of a siren that grew progressively louder. One of the attendants got Tony's feet elevated as a woman began CPR on his chest. A male guard pinched off Tony's nose and administered mouth-to-mouth, a handkerchief placed over Tony's lips. A low, steady voice counted, "One-two-three-four . . ." and Liz felt her chest swell and her eyes challenged by tears as this team of trained people tried to save him. Tony's life seemed to be passing before her eyes, and she silently whispered prayers that Tony not be harmed. She removed all fear, all claims that the images before her could in any way harm him. She fought this her way, while they fought theirs, giving no thought to calling Lou or to anything outside the sphere of this immediate need.

The EMTs swarmed inside with their equipment and wheeled stretcher, and took over the CPR without missing a beat. It looked to Liz so rehearsed and choreographed, and she realized that there were people in this world who did nothing but save other people. Or try to. She marveled at how strange it must be to rise every morning and put on a gray-striped shirt and know you will see death and injury before the sun sets.

"What happened, Dilly?" she managed to ask the guard she knew only by his first name. She saw him twice a day, every day. Dilly was middle-forties and beer-bellied, with an easy disposition.

"Mr. LaRossa. Same as always: got the green light, stepped up to be checked, but tripped the mag going through." He indicated the metal detector. "And, I don't know, just something came over him, like. He pulls out his cell phone. No big deal, but something hammered him. He just stared at it, tried to pass it off, and keeled over. Dropped like a stone. Three of us here, not one of us got to him in time to catch him. Went down hard. Thunked his head pretty good."

"That's the cell phone?" she asked, stepping so easily into the role of inquisitor, understanding the rush that Lou felt doing this. A blue Nokia sat on the scratched vinyl-topped table that security used for searches. Liz stepped up to the open briefcase. Papers. Pens. Several small computer disks. A laptop. A Palm Pilot device. A second cell phone: a small Motorola flip.

Liz glanced back and forth between the two cell phones. *Two,* not one. Before she even placed the call to Lou, she knew this addition to be of significance to Tony's heart attack. She knew it all had to do with David and his determination to get at this money. *Tony LaRossa?* she thought in stunned disbelief.

She caught Lou on his way back to work. He'd followed the Foreman crime scene with a meeting at the bank looking over safe-deposit logs. Speaking to Lou over the phone, she said, "We have to find Beth and the kids. Something terrible has happened."

NINE

LIZ CAME THROUGH THE LAROSSAS' front door timidly, knowing she was on Lou's turf, and feeling strange about it. Her job, her "assignment," was to get Beth to talk. Lou had offered to drive Beth to the hospital, but all she would say was that Tony had told her to stay here.

In all their years together, Liz and Lou had never crossed over like this—Lou investigating the bank; Liz walking into one of his crime scenes. That was how it felt to her: a crime scene; not Beth and Tony's house, where she and Lou had attended a christening reception only a few months earlier. She thought of this living room the way it had been then: loud voices, laughter, beer and the smell of cigarettes on a passing suit. Kids running around in their Sunday best. Elton John on the stereo. Beth's tight dresses that reminded Liz of Sophia Loren in an old film—much too low at the neck, tailored at the waist to cling to her swaying hips, too retro to qualify as retro, as if she shopped the Salvation Army. But Tony wasn't much for fashion either, so that visiting them left Liz feeling as if she'd stepped into an old black-and-white television show. The LaRossas had never left the late sixties.

Beth and Lou occupied the room's love seat, a plush white, fuzzy carpet spongy beneath Liz's shoes. She saw several patrolmen gathered in the kitchen. The twins were not in sight, though a distant crying pulled Liz's attention toward the second floor. "Who's with the twins?" Liz asked.

"They're upstairs with Mary," Beth said to Liz. Judging by Lou's relieved expression, Liz had extricated the first words of significance.

"They're both okay?" Liz asked.

"Fine," Beth said. Dazed, she told Liz, "Tony said to stay right here."

Beth had been run over by the events. Her reddish, shoulder-length hair, usually worn with a severe flip and needing gobs of hairspray, hung lifeless and tangled. Her large brown eyes that typically animated her speech dimmed in a squinted, gloomy sadness. Her high cheekbones looked sunken, and her plucked eyebrows, always arched too high, lay flat behind a scowl. But nothing limited the beauty of her Italian skin. It possessed an almost artificial luminescence that knocked ten years off her thirty-eight.

Liz couldn't tell how long she'd been in her clothes—a white turtleneck and casual black pants with an elastic waist. It might have been all night. She had that weary look about her.

On a nod from Lou, Liz said, "You understand that Tony collapsed, Beth? At the bank. We'd like to get you to the hospital."

"They said not to go anywhere. That they'd call when it was okay to leave."

"Who?" Boldt asked.

"There were two of them," Beth said in a tight whisper, her eyes locked in a stare as she relived events. "Stayed with us all night. Tony was supposed to do something at the bank for them. They said they were staying with us until it was done. Then, later, one of them got a call on his cell phone, and they just up and left. In a hurry. Told me not to leave the house, not to use the phone until Tony came home."

Liz asked, "What was Tony asked to do for them, Beth?"

She shook her head back and forth, a child not supposed to reveal a secret. "They gave him a phone and a disk. That's all I know about it."

Boldt wrote on the pad, faster than Beth was supplying answers, and then tore the piece of notepaper loose and, leaning across toward Liz, left a laundry list of questions sitting in front of her.

Descriptions?
Timing?
Exactly what happened?
Demands?
Two cell phones?

Liz thought there might be something to the order he'd written them in. She felt privileged to be included and wanted to do this right. She and Beth could not be considered best friends, but Beth had, on several occasions, unloaded onto her about her fertility problems, talking extremely personally and graphically. Every relationship was viewed differently by those involved. Lou took her affair with David much more seriously than she ever had; Beth might believe them far closer friends than she did, so Liz proceeded, combining sympathy with a forced intimacy.

She asked Beth what "they" looked like, and when Beth stammered and began sliding back toward emotion rather than reason, Liz salvaged her by prodding with descriptions of her own: tall, fat, loud, dark?

"There were two of them," Beth repeated, her eyes darting between Lou and Liz.

Lou said softly, "We know they told you to say nothing about it, Beth. Tony's going to get better, and when he does, he could be in some trouble here, and no one wants to see that happen."

"They *made* him do it!" Beth shouted loudly. One of the patrolmen poked his head out from the kitchen and then retreated. "They told him they'd hurt the twins if they didn't get a call within the hour. Then, when they did get the call, I don't think it was what they expected. They panicked and took off. They must have heard he'd collapsed." She added cautiously: "I'm afraid to leave. They told me not to leave."

Liz asked again if Beth could describe them.

Beth explained once again that there were two of them, both wearing nice suits. Good-looking men whom she'd initially taken to be FBI agents or cops. They'd arrived at the back door the night before, just after dinner. "Tony was careful. Wouldn't let them into the house. But then when they mentioned the embezzlement investigation and that they'd rather talk in private, he let them in."

Liz repeated, "Two men. Dark suits. Good-looking."

"The man who spoke . . . the one on the left . . . didn't have much of an accent. But the other one . . . once they were inside the door . . . I knew something was wrong."

"What kind of accent?" Liz asked.

"Thick. I don't know. Italian? Russian? Not French, not Spanish."

She glanced at Lou's list. Description and timing taken care of, she moved on, asking Beth what happened.

Beth wormed her fingers as she spoke. "They were polite at first. I had no idea . . ." She was interrupted by a muted peal of joy from the upstairs. The twins were clearly enjoying themselves, oblivious to their mother's contained terror a floor below. Beth looked up toward them, her face bunching as tears threatened.

Lou asked, "What did they say they were doing here?"

"All I remember is that all at once they were pushing Tony. The other one pulled me, turned me, and covered my mouth. It happened so quickly." She rubbed her wrists where Liz could see thin but deep red bruises. "They had the twins then. I don't remember how, exactly. Tony and I . . . we did exactly as they asked. I stayed with the children in the living room. The one who couldn't speak so well watched us while the other one took Tony into the kitchen. There was talking but I couldn't hear."

"For how long?" Lou asked.

"Five minutes? Ten? Everything slows down, you know? Did you know that? Slows down to where it *feels* like forever. All I wanted was them gone. To leave us alone. It seemed like forever."

Liz asked, "You don't know what they said to Tony?" She saw immediately that this question frustrated Lou, and she resolved that before asking anything more, she would wait for a signal from him.

"The one who could speak . . . it was something to do with the bank. Tony came in and told me to do whatever the man asked, that all he had to do was go to the office for a few minutes. Everything was going to be okay as long as we did what they asked. They'd stay at the house until they confirmed Tony had done whatever it was they were asking him to do."

"You said they panicked and took off," Lou said. "When was this?"

"I couldn't tell you," Beth said.

Liz reminded her that Lou wanted to get Beth to the hospital, if possible.

"I'm not going *anywhere,*" Beth said. "I'm not leaving the children, and I'm not going without them, and I'm not taking them with me. You see? I'm staying."

"It's over," Lou said.

"No!" she replied sharply. "Just because you say it's over doesn't mean it's over."

"No, of course not," Lou said, shooting Liz a quick look, which she took to mean she should continue.

"You don't know for sure what they asked Tony to do?" she asked.

"Just something at the bank. That's all. That they would hurt him—us—if he didn't do this . . ." She looked up at Lou and burst into tears. "I did what they told me to do."

Liz moved over to comfort her. "Of course you did, Beth. It's not your fault."

Lou excused himself and walked into the kitchen. A lot of male voices in there, but Liz couldn't make out what was said.

Liz said gently, "We need to get you down to the hospital, Beth. That's why Lou asked me here. Mary's with the twins. The police can protect them better here, but Tony needs you right now. These men wanted something from Tony, wanted him to do something—we think we know what it might have been."

Beth jerked her head up to meet Liz's eyes, some of the brightness returned.

"Tony's security clearance allows him a great deal of access at the bank," Liz said. She knew another possibility existed, but didn't mention it: that Tony had been part of the earlier embezzlement, that everything that had happened here this morning connected directly to the past, just as what had been happening to her also connected to her past.

"Tony's a good man," Beth mumbled. "You've seen him with the twins."

"He needs you, Beth. We've got to get you down to the hospital. Why don't I check with Mary and make sure everything's okay?" Mary was Tony's older sister and the mother of five. "If she's got it under control, we'll let Lou take you to see Tony. Okay?"

Beth nodded, though appeared off in another realm. Lou signaled a patrolwoman, who came over and sat across from Beth. Liz hurried upstairs, knowing in advance that Mary had everything under control. Finding it so, she returned to the living room and won Lou's attention through the kitchen door.

She told him somewhat loudly so Beth could hear, "Beth has agreed to go see Tony with you. I told her there'd be plenty of officers here while Mary looks after the twins."

"Absolutely," Boldt said.

Beth stood up from the couch, and the patrolwoman hooked an arm to steady her.

Liz said, "Let's get you freshened up, and Lou will drive you over there." She felt nearly desperate to get back to the bank and keep her people on point, in Tony's absence. Like it or not, the merger quickly approached, and her team was directly responsible for a smooth transition. She contained her impatience, willing to give this a few more minutes.

Not long thereafter she pulled the Boldt minivan back into the bank's subterranean parking garage and her reserved spot. She shut off the engine and collected her purse. Climbing out of the van, she was immediately jolted by the ringing of her cell phone, and she scrambled to answer it.

Occupied as she was, her left hand holding her purse while her right hand dug down into a pocket for the phone, she jerked back but did not scream as a hand clapped over her mouth. *Broad daylight,* was her first inexplicable thought. The garage glowed beneath a gloomy twilight of tube lighting. By the time her panicked brain registered anything beyond the time of day, she'd been catapulted through the van's open sliding door, a bag placed over her head and a wide piece of tape slapped around her head, holding it to a headrest while wedging open her mouth. She heard the tinkle of keys along with the contents of her purse spill. She heard her cell phone beep and the familiar sound of the van's seat belt warning buzzer, but the engine did not start. In the course of events her arms were yanked and taped together behind the seat, although her wrists did not touch. All this in a matter of ten to fifteen seconds.

By the time someone pinched at her eyes and pulled the

fabric away, her head was swooning toward unconsciousness. She heard a sound she assumed to be the glove box, followed by another familiar sound she couldn't place. She struggled, attempting to whip her head side to side. Her initial fear was rape—these were men, and she was a woman, and she'd been immobilized and her hands taped apart. Her ankles were bound too, now that she thought to try to move them. But sitting up? In the backseat of a car? When the first of the two eyeholes was cut away and she saw the front seat of the van empty, she braced herself, expecting to be groped or molested. Instead, her vision was temporarily blocked as a hairy wrist crossed its path and a second eyehole was cut from the fabric. Then she heard a metallic click, thinking first and foremost of Lou's Leatherman all-in-one tool, a gift she'd given him not too many Christmases ago, but a gift she'd never seen him use since.

They're going to cut me. The thought threw her into a sudden frenzy. She feared anything to do with fire, drowning, or cutting. She'd have rather gotten struck by a train or hit head-on by a truck than any of those three.

The van's door slid shut, silencing her surroundings. Only a small hum penetrated the vehicle. She tugged at her arms, but to no avail, then quit altogether as she tired and took in more of her surroundings. The sounds she'd heard had been the operation of the van's VCR and a videotape being inserted into a deck that hid in the console between the front seats. She knew this because the tiny television screen that folded down from the ceiling shone a bright blue, a bold white arrow pointing to the right.

When the first of the sordid images filled that small screen, she thought this some kind of perverse, sick joke—someone tying her up and forcing her to watch pornography. Terror again stole through her as she imagined some stranger sitting directly behind her in the third seat, watching the video as he contemplated where to start with her.

But then the woman, naked and on all fours, her blurry bare backside toward the camera, slowly turned around, a man's chest and shoulders seen behind her. All at once the background looked far too familiar, logs, a lamp, a clock. All at once Liz couldn't breathe, choked, the tape and hood pressing so tightly into her open mouth. She screamed, but barely heard her own voice. She squinted her eyes shut as that face on the screen slipped first into profile and then turned toward the camera's hidden lens. But she looked again, driven by a defiant curiosity. The bare breasts and shoulders so familiar. The hair. The line of the neck. The curve of the hips.

A face, all her own.

□ □ □

For all her endless hours in this vehicle as driver, Liz realized she had never once sat in these backseats. The minivan's VCR typically ran nothing more offensive than *Peter Pan* or *The Wizard of Oz,* something to occupy the kids in bumper-to-bumper traffic, or for the nearly two-hour drive up to their cabin. Liz looked away but found her blurry eyes wandering back to the small screen in a wave of self-loathing. The video was date- and time-stamped in the upper right-hand corner, a date she would have done anything to erase from her life.

The camera angle, possibly shot from inside the cabin's closet, offered an unobstructed view of the bed, where Liz, sporting a haircut she would never have again, a haircut that also dated the event, once again turned to face the camera. The contact of skin, the silent motions captured in grainy black-and-white, the pursed lips and agonized faces all added up to an unattractive, disgusting carnal dance that debased her.

From outside the parked van, one saw only the flashing blue light from the screen playing out on a woman's face wet with tears, and a gaping mouth held open by silver tape. As the woman struggled to be free, the van rocked side to side, as if driven by a strong wind. Inside, atop the stained carpet floor, lay her daughter's second favorite doll, a coloring book, and a plastic bag of crushed Goldfish crackers.

She felt half dead as she watched, amazed at the familiarity of the whore on the tape. Strange coincidences. Even the birthmark on the outside flank of her right buttock looked just like her own. "My little Martian," her husband called it.

It couldn't possibly be she who had done these things, her heart told her, but of course her eyes proved otherwise. Back and forth she went, wife, mother, sinner, slut.

Slowly, in timing with her efforts to free her wrists, she came to understand the effect this videotape might have on her own and her husband's careers. Their lives. More important, their children if the tape ever went public. What kind of looks would the children endure from their teachers, the parents of their friends? How would it affect her own relationship with her children, *for the rest of their lives?* She attempted to measure the fallout if the tape were sent to Phillip, the date confirming a connection to David Hayes at the time of the embezzlement. *The Seattle Times.* Posted on the Internet. Her world shrank.

Her cell phone rang from the front seat, where it had been dumped from her purse. With one mighty effort the tape tore and her hands came free, and only then did she see that one edge had been cleanly cut, only then did she connect this with the sounds she had heard just before she'd been closed inside. The Leatherman tool. They had wanted her to free herself.

She tore the tape from her mouth and slipped off the hood, slammed the retractable video screen up into its locked position, and lunged for the phone. She fell to her knees, her ankles still taped.

"Help me!" she hollered into the phone before her mind registered that this tape must never be revealed to anyone. Any kind of help was the last thing she wanted.

A deep male voice that nearly hid the rich, Eastern European accent said, "Next time you are asked to do something, we will expect you to do it yourself, not send a replacement. Cooperate, and you can be the last person to ever see this tape. Be ready to act at a moment's notice." Disconnected.

Standing away from the van, listening carefully, one could hear, along with the whine of passing traffic, a woman's painful sobbing from within. A woman stretched thin between the past and the present, a woman faced with the reality of self-loathing and the disintegration of all things good, of all things held dear and sacred. Bared before her eyes. Destroyed.

TEN

BOLDT MUMBLED THROUGH AN APOLOGY, embarrassed, humiliated, even, that Miles had not been picked up from his piano lesson and was awaiting a ride. Like every aspect of private education, admission to concert pianist Bruce Lavin's afternoon session had required an application, referrals, a waiting list, and a substantial deposit. Six months later, Miles had finally been "asked to join."

"A confusion on our end," Boldt said, sucking up to Lavin and feeling like a sycophant. He realized how stupid this explanation sounded.

"I don't run a babysitting service," Lavin clarified. "The schedule here is—"

Boldt interrupted, "—very tight. I know." Lavin had nearly beaten this mantra into parents. *Preparation and punctuality* were his credo. As long as his students practiced and showed up on time, Lavin kept them in the program. "I'm on my way."

"If it should happen again . . ."

"It won't," Boldt assured the man. The cost of the course, paid in full and up front, was nonrefundable if a child was let go. Expulsions could not be appealed, but the child could reapply for future sessions.

Boldt tried Liz at the office, and then on the cell, ready to give her a piece of his mind. But when she failed to answer either phone, his anger quickly shifted to concern. He hadn't seen her, hadn't heard from her since their meeting out at Beth LaRossa's house, earlier in the day.

Having assigned it himself, he knew that the security duty amounted to a single, unmarked car watching either the bank or their home, depending on her location. By mutual consent, she wasn't to be followed unless she requested it, and she was asked to make that request if her movement involved contact with Hayes. Otherwise, Boldt and Liz had agreed she should be allowed to "have a life."

Boldt was informed that "the Sienna was observed leaving the garage about twenty minutes after its return from the LaRossa residence." That put her leaving work late morning or early afternoon.

"No contact prior or since?"

"No contact, Lieutenant."

He tried both lines again, and then on a hunch he tried home, but to the same result. A cop with Boldt's experience didn't panic; it had been programmed out of him, but a groundswell of internal dialogue ran as background chatter in his thoughts—several voices inside him competing for airtime. Prioritizing his responsibilities, he hurried to the Crown Vic and challenged traffic to reach Miles before Lavin reconsidered and expelled him from the program.

He inched the car up to First Hill, staying on small streets with stop signs every block, trying to avoid the congestion of traffic lights, but he and a few hundred other drivers all had the same idea, and the going remained bumper-to-bumper. When his cell phone rang, he prepared to berate Liz.

He answered, "Yeah?" hoping to project his anger so she couldn't miss the subtext.

"Lieutenant?"

His expectations flattened, he barked, "What is it?"

"Call for you. Something about your daughter."

He called the number. A cat did a somersault in his chest.

Mindy Crawford answered—Sarah's ballet teacher. He knew what was coming and cut in immediately, interrupting her introduction of herself.

"We messed up our pickups today," he said. "My fault."

The woman paused, perhaps surprised by his prescience. "I could drop her by your house," Ms. Crawford offered, "but I've another class to teach first. It would be a little after seven, if that's all right."

The ballet school was the other end of the world from Madrona, where Boldt was heading. He and Miles could try to make it, but her offer sounded like a better idea. He told her so.

"No problem," she said so cheerfully as to instill guilt in Boldt. It *was* a problem, a big problem for the Boldt family. He tempered some of his anger with calls first to SPD's Metro, and then King County Sheriff's Traffic Patrol, to make certain Liz hadn't been in a traffic accident. Then he called LaMoia. Sergeant John LaMoia, who had mentored under Boldt for a good part of his Homicide career, who had stepped in as squad sergeant behind Boldt after Boldt's promotion to lieutenant, was a man who knew few bounds but got the job done.

"Yo," LaMoia answered.

Boldt asked how the terrorism seminar was going, unable to jump right in with a request to find his wife.

"I've seen shit you wouldn't believe! Bombs the size of cigarette packs and briefcase gadgets that can zero every computer in a building. This is the ultimate techno-romp, Sarge." LaMoia continued to call Boldt by his former rank. "If these rag-heads get their mitts on half this shit, we got big problems."

"Danny Foreman said if you're our line of defense, heaven help the enemy."

"Got that right." LaMoia understood when to rescue Boldt from his own misgivings. "Talk to me about Foreskin." LaMoia had nicknames for everyone.

"I've got some problems of my own," Boldt said, grateful for the bridge LaMoia offered him. "One I could use your help on."

"Go."

Boldt explained his situation—Miles needing to be picked up, and the greater need of finding Liz. He didn't go into details on Liz's current situation or the case in general because LaMoia would have picked up most of it already. The ferry surveillance had involved too many people not to get talked up in the department.

"I can cut out of here in ten. I'll hit all the hot spots, though I can't exactly see Mrs. B. in a fern bar."

"I was thinking you could check with Danny Foreman. You should know he's fresh out of the hospital himself. Make up some excuse that you screwed up surveillance on my wife and don't want me finding out, and wondered if he knew her ten-twenty."

"Me screwing up. That would fit. That's good cover."

It was generous of him; LaMoia was no screwup. But

his reputation as a rogue player would make just about anything he said believable. Ironically, Foreman, of all people, a class-A Lone Ranger, would understand his situation.

Clearly deeply concerned, a different LaMoia asked, "How worried are we here, Sarge?"

"There's no doubt in my mind that she's in play. Their first mark, a guy named LaRossa, a friend of ours through the bank, keeled over of a heart attack this morning and is in Intensive Care. The way it plays for me is that the tune-up that Hayes took—this is the night we found Foreman lying in the bushes outside that trailer—was to win some cooperation from him. He ends up accessing a safe-deposit box, where he'd probably hid the software that had cloaked the embezzled money. That software gets passed to La-Rossa by whoever's now running Hayes, because LaRossa can get to the bank's computers. LaRossa didn't get the job done for them, so Liz moves to the top of their list. She, too, has access to the bank computers. And now she's missing."

"That sounds like something worth a little more than a chat with Foreskin."

"Danny's lead on this—at least in his mind he is—and he's more than a little crazy with it. It's all tied up with Darlene for him. I wouldn't be surprised if *he* was running Liz in some covert op that only he knows about."

"Peachy."

"That's why I think we look there first."

"Got it." LaMoia hesitated before asking the obvious. "And if that's not happening?"

"Let me get the kids home. Get them safe. You check with Danny. Then we'll worry about the next phase, if there is one." Boldt emphasized, "Lean on him, John. We don't want to waste resources and energy if Danny's hiding something from us."

"Me and Foreskin, we got some history, Sarge. Don't worry about a thing."

口 口 口

Bruce Lavin met Boldt out on the curb, Miles in tow. As Miles climbed in the back and buckled himself in, the piano teacher came around and stepped up to Boldt's window. Boldt prepared himself to be lectured, something he didn't need right then.

"We need to talk." Lavin spoke in a whisper, an urgency, his body language punctuating his words. He was a small man with wild, curly hair and piercing eyes. His voice crackled like the sound of a cheap radio.

"Is there a problem?" Boldt spun around to look at Miles so his son could feel the depth of his concern. Miles had been endlessly briefed about the level of privilege these lessons represented.

"Quite the contrary," Lavin said, his edgy voice still hushed. "Your son, Lieutenant . . . your boy . . . is perhaps the most musically gifted child I've *ever taught,* and believe me," said the teacher, "I've taught plenty. He needs testing—mathematically, musically. If he is what I think he is, although I'd be honored to work with him, you can and should do better."

Boldt felt a father's pride engulf him. *A child prodigy.* He'd seen the same aptitude at home, which had inspired these lessons in the first place. He'd been so prepared for Lavin's abuse about bad parenting that this complete reversal caught him off guard. His throat constricted and he choked out, "You can arrange the testing?"

"Of course."

"I'll have to speak to my wife. Is it expensive?"

"Wickedly. As is Juilliard," the man said, an impish grin satisfying his sense of humor. "And that may be where he's headed someday."

"Sorry about the pickup," Boldt said. "We must have gotten our wires crossed."

Lavin patted him on the arm—a shocking gesture from what Boldt knew of him—waved good-bye into the back-seat, and walked back into the house.

Boldt sat motionless, the tingling sensation only now receding, well aware that this was one of those moments in life he would never forget—a minute-long conversation through a car window. An entirely new world unfolding before him: his son, a musical wizard.

He couldn't wait to tell Liz.

□ □ □

By midnight, Boldt, LaMoia, Bobbie Gaynes, and Daphne Matthews had all made calls, had driven the streets, had checked with Liz's friends. LaMoia reported that he'd spoken to Danny Foreman, who had professed to know nothing of Liz's whereabouts. "But the way he said it, Sarge. He may not be lying, but he isn't solid. Something's up with him." Boldt had the same feeling about Foreman, though there wasn't much to be done about it. Initiating anything like a formal complaint would require a good deal more than suspicion and bad feelings.

The Boldt kitchen served as the command center, with Boldt acting as both dispatcher and babysitter.

Memories of her imposed themselves, an involuntary reaction to her absence: making a vegetable face for the kids, cucumber eyes, orange mouth. Driving Miles and Sarah amid fits of laughter; to school, to church. Arriving to bed playful and daring. A woman who attacked life, sometimes to the detriment of her popularity. A woman unafraid. Tested, by cancer, by faith, by degrees. Her resolute composure inspired him like wind to a sailor. Not long ago she had suggested that should he want to retire from policing and take up his jazz piano full-time, she would support such a decision even if it meant downscaling their lifestyle. A partner, in full.

Matthews and Boldt shared a volatile history as coworkers who had, for a single night, been much more. The lingering sensations of that night had carried forward years into their relationship. With Matthews now testing a live-in arrangement with LaMoia—no two more opposite people existed on earth, in Boldt's opinion—new lines had been drawn. The teasing and subtle flirtation was gone for now, and that somehow didn't feel right. Boldt considered her his closest female friend after Liz, a person he could share himself with honestly. There was no end to his appreciation for her and what she gave back to him. But the spark that existed there now flickered instead of glowed.

Matthews stopped by the house, running out of ideas of where to find Liz. A blue Gore-Tex rain jacket, tight jeans, and a crisp white shirt. Her hair damp, but not stringy. A little more fatigue around her eyes than her office hour cosmetics allowed. She stood just inside the kitchen door, having turned down a chair, not wanting to stay. Boldt knew this had more to do with the current state of their friendship—tested by her decision to be with LaMoia—than it did her schedule. They knew each other a little too well.

When she brought up the unmentionable, he thought it so appropriate to come from her. Only she could ask him such a thing.

Daphne asked, "Have you tried her doctor—the hospital?"

"I'm still hoping Foreman knows where she is."

"Lou? Have you checked? Have you called?"

"Is that the psychologist or the friend asking?"

She fired back, "Is that the detective or the husband asking?" her skill at twisting things around second only to her ability to keep a straight face.

"I have not."

"Listen, Lou—"

"Don't!" he said sharply. "She would have told me. That's not something she would hide."

"You have to turn cell phones off in hospitals," she explained, repeating an argument he'd given Liz earlier that same day. Emotional mirrors. "Things drag out and take twice as long as you thought."

"She and I went over the arrangements for picking up the kids twice. This is not something she would have forgotten to do. It's not that it's just unlike her; it's impossible."

"Maybe the first place you should have called was her doctor."

He checked his watch to see that only a few minutes had passed since his last check. He'd never learned how to wait well. He assigned other people to wait in place of him;

he ordered people to wait for him; but he did not wait himself.

"Now it's midnight, and you're not going to reach her doctor even if you tried. And you *know* that," she said, interpreting his expression.

Busted.

"You did this *intentionally,* didn't you? Waited like this?"

"She turns her phone off when she's praying, too," he said. "She could have gone to a reading room, a library, any place quiet."

"And you believe that." Daphne made it a statement, just to sting him.

When a pair of headlights bumped into the driveway at 12:15, and they both identified Liz's minivan, Daphne offered to leave by the front door, her car parked out on the curb. She said, "I'll call off the others," already moving for the front door. "She won't be thrilled to discover you called out the bloodhounds. I'll make sure it's zipped up on our end, and left between the two of you to handle as you want." She'd reached the front door, talking softly for the benefit of the sleeping kids. Daphne could juggle a dozen balls at once while riding a unicycle.

"I owe you," he called out.

"Shut up." She closed the front door quietly behind her.

Boldt was about to charge out back when he thought better of it, schooling himself to show concern, not anger. Waiting up for her was fine—expected even. Attacking her was unforgivable.

Five long minutes passed and Liz had still not appeared. Boldt finally succumbed and headed outside. On the back steps, he stopped abruptly as the garage door pushed open and Liz staggered out.

As drunk as a skid-row bum.

□ □ □

Liz sputtered as she walked unsteadily forward, unable to enunciate, barely able to walk. "If I don't pee in about five seconds . . ." She looked up, took in Boldt as if just now noticing him, and cocked her head, saying, "Oh, shit." She crushed a hydrangea on her way to hoisting her skirt and running her panties down to her ankles. She squatted right there and urinated in the garden, then rocked forward, falling onto her knees, and vomited.

He'd nursed her through the evils of chemotherapy, the drain of radiation, the indignities brought on by childbirth, but he'd never seen her stone-cold drunk. Inside the back door he got her out of her suit coat and shirt, both messed with vomit, and left them at the top of the stairs for the basement laundry. He undressed her in the bedroom and placed her sitting up in the tub with a warm shower running. She never said a word, resigned to a dull, stupefied embarrassment. She threw up again in the tub, and yet again into the toilet after he made her drink a full glass of water. When the water finally stayed down, he got three more glasses into her as well, shunning the aspirin that would have helped a good deal but went against her convictions.

She passed out in bed as her head hit the pillow. Boldt stayed awake another forty minutes, adrenalized, making sure she slept on her side in case she vomited in her sleep. He drifted off some time past three.

□ □ □

When Boldt awoke to Miles shaking him at 7 A.M., Liz was already gone from the house, having fled the humiliation.

Flipping pancakes, washing faces, changing clothes, making sandwiches, Boldt worked himself into an angry lather. Isolation. Desertion. Betrayal? Was this about David Hayes? Thirty minutes late for work by the time he'd dropped the kids, he felt he deserved an explanation, believed it up to her to call.

He snatched up the receiver with every incoming call, barking into the phone while expecting to hear Liz's apologetic voice. Over the past twelve hours, burdened by little sleep and challenged by an emotional abyss, Boldt had traveled through concern, worry, anger and into the depths of infuriation. It now spilled out of his pores as an acrid smell and registered in his bloodshot eyes as venom. Quickly moving silhouettes slipped by the glass wall of his office like shadow puppets, his squad desperately avoiding him.

And then the call came.

ELEVEN

LIZ PICKED A SPOT FAMILIAR to her, one where she felt safe, comfortable, and emotionally protected, a place where she had come to meditate and pray during her convalescence. The weather-worn bench in Golden Gardens Park aimed toward the Sound, offering a wide-angle view of green water, lush islands, and a steel-wool sky that moved inland swiftly overhead.

Boldt came around and sat down next to her.

"Thank you," she began, knowing what she had to do, and grateful he would do this on her terms. "I know you're busy."

"I don't need an apology as much as an explanation."

She heard him holding back as he always did, afraid to expose himself, to speak too quickly and later regret what he said. The trouble was that in trying to play it safe, he didn't play at all.

The sea breeze blew some stray strands of hair off her face. That wet wind felt surprisingly good to her.

He looked out into the gray. "You and this bench."

"Yes." She gathered her strength, knowing she wouldn't

find a way to cozy up to this. She had to inch to the edge and then jump. The only way. "There's a tape."

The sounds were the wind and her husband's breathing. "Go on."

She looked up into the gray wash of sky. "I'm on the tape. With David. It's video, and it's awful."

"Awful."

He would drag it out of her of course, because he couldn't help himself. Twenty years of questioning people.

"They surprised me in the van. In the underground parking. They taped me to a seat and made me watch."

He turned and touched her, and she felt a jolt of electricity with the contact. "Are you all right?"

She felt a wash of relief come with his concern. In a rush she described the terror in the van, the fact they'd cut the tape to allow her to fight her way free.

"They?"

"Two of them. But don't do this, please. Don't interrogate me. Please, don't. I need a husband, not a detective right now."

He pulled closer to her on the bench. She despised herself for everything she'd done to him and the marriage. Briefly, she wished she'd died from her illness and spared them both all of this.

"It's how I think," he said.

"Two of them. It happened quickly." She told it all to him again, hoping he wouldn't make her go through it for a third time.

"And where's the tape now?"

"In the van. I haven't touched it. I don't want you to see it, Lou."

"I don't want to see it," he said. "But I do want to run it through the lab for fingerprints."

"No. Someone will play it, and I couldn't bear that."

He put his right hand on her leg and threw his left arm around her and pulled her to him. From behind they looked like a pair of lovers, but that was not how it felt to her as she shook in his hold. He said, "Bernie will handle this however I want it handled. Not to worry."

"I feel awful."

"I understand that, but we can and will protect this. The point is that I need to know as much about this tape as possible. Bernie can work magic with things like this. Trust me to handle this discreetly. I'll do what I have to do and nothing more."

"They knew it wasn't me with the money." She couldn't remember if she'd told him about the cell phone call that came after. Her brain wasn't functioning correctly. "Said I had to do it myself next time—that no one would see the tape if I did as they said. I'm to be ready 'at a moment's notice.' "

"Who has your cell number?" asked the detective. "Hayes does. We know that. But who else, outside your circle of friends?"

Her recall of the events inside the van suddenly included the beeping of her cell phone as they had that hood in place over her head. She told him she thought they'd switched her phone off and back on again, the chimes familiar to her. He said that would explain them knowing her number— some cell phones displayed their numbers on start-up.

"It also seems to put Hayes in the clear," he said. "For all we know, Hayes doesn't know about the tape himself."

"How can that possibly be true? Of course he knows about it: He *made* it."

"That's an assumption," he corrected. "We don't have the luxury of assumptions."

She released a contemptuous laugh. "I can't do this. I can't play Watson. I'm on that tape, Lou. Someone *has* that tape. And if I cooperate with them, if I help them get this money, that's breaking all sorts of laws. I'm a sworn executive of the bank. I cannot do what they ask. And yet if I don't—" She mulled this over for the umpteenth time. "Do you realize what happens if that tape gets out? The date's on it. I told you that, didn't I? David *must* have been involved in the embezzlement by then. Every way you look at this, it's bad. I don't see a way out of it. Damned if I do, damned if I don't."

"If it's not Hayes extorting you, then we need to know who it is. That's where we start, and we don't get ahead of ourselves. No one has asked you to do anything. Not yet. By the time they do, maybe we know who they are. You'd be surprised how things can turn around, even in something like this. The challenge for you and me is to stay above it. Our feelings, our emotions, work against us. They're probably counting on that. They're probably counting on it dividing us. We can't let that happen."

He sounded so detached, as if he'd already let go of the pain associated with her sordid past.

"I hear the detective speaking, but I'm wondering about the husband."

"He's out of the office," Lou said.

"Can you compartmentalize so easily?"

"Who said it was easy?"

"There's more," she said, bringing herself to a place she'd been unable to face alone.

"More." It came out of him as a gasp, a blow to the chest.

"You'll find out anyway," she said. "Better we discuss it now. But please, please remember that this never had anything to do with inadequacy. Don't jump to that conclusion, okay? It was revenge, I think, for all the time I never got. We've talked about this before. It was my short-comings, not yours."

"Takes two," he said.

"I know it does. And that's generous of you to say. No . . . what I have to tell you involves the date."

"The date."

"Yes." Here she was, about to explain something even she didn't fully understand. Dangerous territory. She took a deep breath. "When all this happened . . . back *then* . . . We talked through it. I agreed to call it off."

"I remember."

He clearly didn't want memories forced on him, but she didn't know how else to approach this.

He said, "We picked up, and we started again."

"It wasn't over," she blurted out. "There was one more time—only one—about three months after our agreement. He called, and . . . I don't know. One of those mistakes for all time. I know by the date that this was the time he videoed. I don't know why he did it. Why *I* did it."

"You're better off if you let it go," he advised, and now she understood just how angry he was, knew he was boiling inside. She couldn't broach this issue with him feeling this way.

"I can't do this right now," he said, as if reading her thoughts.

She'd dreaded this moment ever since committing the act—and she'd known all along this moment would someday come, as it now had. She'd wounded him; she'd invalidated the sense of trust that had taken so many years to rebuild. She felt awful, and yet she felt a selfish relief that she feared he sensed and would only make matters worse.

The truth, like a razor, could cut painlessly at first. She feared what would happen between them as he started to bleed.

It rained all of a sudden. One minute a fine mist and then torrential. The two of them on that bench, unable to move and run for shelter.

The rain on his face looked like tears to her. Maybe a combination, she thought, paralyzed by the pain she'd inflicted. She understood now that she would continue to suffer for her actions, as she had for nearly six years. But suffer together, not alone. A part of her had hoped sharing this might mitigate some of that internal pain, but she'd lied to herself about that as well. Pain couldn't be shared. Pain was a very private thing.

□ □ □

They drove in the dead of night, two people uncomfortable with the silence as well as the expectation to fill it. She wore the evidence of an impossibly long day in the form of bloodshot eyes and redistributed makeup. He carried the deadened countenance of a man poisoned by grief. The steady sloshing of the wipers worked like background music. She wanted to be home in bed, the victim of a temporary, eight-hour suicide, her brain all but used up.

"I miss them already," she said. They had left the kids off an hour ago.

"They're safer there."

"I know that, but it doesn't make me miss them any less."

He said, "After what happened to Beth and Tony, we don't have a choice."

He kept telling her things she already knew. She let it go. "Did you see their faces?" she asked. Tears and confusion, a hopeful pleading that Mama and Daddy were not going to drive away and leave them.

"They were laughing and playing by the time we were out of the drive. Count on it. They love Kathy. And knowing my sister, she'll spoil them rotten. It's a match made in heaven." Lou's sister, unable to have children of her own, doted on Sarah and Miles as if they were royalty. Liz didn't think it the best for anyone.

"We need to think about getting him tested," he said. "His music aptitude. It's something we need to think about. When to do it, what it means to him, to us, in terms of some home schooling. And there's the cost, of course."

"I can't do this now," she said honestly. "I can't pretend all's well like this. Between us, I mean."

"What would you rather talk about? Broken promises? If we don't pretend it's normal, it's never going to be."

She turned toward the car's rain-streaked side window studying the bars of silver and black, like a cage. "This is coming apart on us, Lou."

"Uh-huh."

They worked through another few minutes of silence.

Lou reached for the radio at one point but apparently thought better of it. He pulled the car off the highway into a service station close to the on-ramp to buy himself a cup of tea and her a bottle of water.

"I didn't mean to go back to him and I should have told you right away. I know that." She waited to say this until he was closing his door to head inside.

"Uh-huh," he said after the door was shut.

Back on the highway, he told her, "I'm ready when you're ready."

"I know that," she said.

"Doesn't have to be now."

"It can't be now. Not when I'm this tired. And you . . . you look sick with grief."

He didn't respond.

"Please don't give up, okay? Don't shut me out. So much has changed. So much good has come into our lives. That's worth fighting for." She waited for him to say something. Anything. When he did not, she said, "I think I'd like it better if you yelled at me or something, got angry, if you let out whatever's inside of you. How can you be so calm?"

"I am not calm."

"Then show it. *Do* something. *Say* something."

"I need to hear it from you," he said. "Whatever excuses you have, I need to hear them. Just confessing it isn't enough. I have to understand it."

"He tricked me. He used sympathy. He probably did it just to make the tape. He played me—that's how you would put it—and I gave in. I regretted it at the time, and I regret it now."

She saw anger pass across his face with the oncoming headlights.

"So you got drunk rather than tell me."

The bars of the cage bent with the speed of the car. She cried privately, not allowing him to see. He dug out a handkerchief, offered it across the seat to her and she rejected it, angry that he would attempt such a gesture.

He said, "You came home and made love with me and pretended it hadn't happened? How could you have done that?"

"I don't know," she answered honestly. Slap, slap, went the wipers. "For what it's worth, with him it was never 'making love.' It was sex. An escape. Nothing more."

"That's not worth anything. Not to me," Lou said, "though I'm certainly glad you made that important distinction."

Mile markers slipped past, the distance between them growing.

"I miss them already," she said.

"Yeah. Me too."

TWELVE

BOLDT'S DASHBOARD CLOCK REGISTERED 7:04, the colon between the numbers flashing as it counted off the seconds in the evening darkness that enveloped the car's interior. Less than twenty-four hours earlier he and Liz had dropped off the kids, and now the events of this day occupied him as he navigated around the streets clogged with traffic, inventing a route that might speed his arrival to what he had been told was a bloodied cabin and possible crime scene.

He had not slept well, if at all that prior night, laboring under the strain of their discussion in the car, wondering about their future, feeling betrayed by their past. The early morning, derailed without the routine of the kids, had presented them with too much time together, too much opportunity to speak, and nothing to discuss. They settled on a truce of silence, each reading a different section of the morning paper, or in Boldt's case, pretending to read.

Work that day had been paint-by-numbers: one of the only times he welcomed a lieutenant's paperwork, the administrative meetings, the indulgence of actually reading the group e-mails. Anything to occupy him without discussion, without human contact. He had swum around the fifth floor like a fish in the wrong school.

Now a call from Danny Foreman summoned him to a cabin in the woods, a cabin that Foreman claimed to know about because Liz herself had provided its location. Boldt's head spun with possibilities.

Earlier, he'd been thrown into turmoil over a call he'd received from Dr. Bernie Lofgrin, the civilian director of the police department's crime lab.

"You got a minute?" Lofgrin had asked.

"I'm signing off on overtime vouchers and desperate for distraction," Boldt said. Not that he would have ever put off a call from Bernie, who was both a close friend, a fellow jazz enthusiast, and the sole source of all things evidentiary. Among several dozen active cases, the lab was currently working both the Foreman crime scene evidence and Liz's videotape for Boldt, and the call could have concerned either or both. Boldt had been eager to learn about one, extremely reluctant to hear about the other.

"The tape's a second-generation copy."

"Dubbed from the original," Boldt clarified.

"Correct. And not to worry about content. For viewing I digitally obscured a central panel allowing only a half inch border to show. I sampled the first thirty seconds of sound for bandwidth and signal. Also supports the determination of it being second generation. Those half-inch borders don't reveal any live action, only the setting, a darkly paneled or log room, and a time-and-date stamp. I suspect the location is a bedroom, and I'm not asking questions. I'm the only one who handled the tape and it remains in my possession. No case number has been assigned, which means you owe the taxpayers for about an hour of my time."

Boldt thanked him, knowing when Bernie needed to hear it. The man had taken several key steps to protecting the tape.

"I developed four good latent prints and six partials off the videocassette itself. Ran them through ALPS," he said, meaning the computerized comparison, automated latent print system, "and struck out with known felons, convicted or otherwise. No hits."

The bubble of Boldt's building optimism burst. He'd hoped against hope that some of the prints would come back for David Hayes, a registered felon and ex-con. The letdown was severe. "Well, I don't mind saying that's a disappointment."

"So I ran it through WSW," the Washington State Workers database that included all day care instructors, public school teachers, most health care personnel, all firemen, policemen, politicians, their spouses, and in some cases their children's prints as well, "and I nailed down two. Then on to the State INS database," Immigration and Naturalization Service, "and a hit for one of the partials, but I've got to caution you, it would never hold in court in case that's a consideration. You got a pencil?"

Boldt assured him he was already taking notes—something Bernie always wanted to hear.

"The partial comes back one Malina Alekseevich— that's a male name, by the way: Malina. I double-checked. But as I've said, we ain't gonna prove it's him anyway." Like many in the department, Bernie slipped into street speak whenever a situation called for it.

"Did INS happen—"

Bernie cut him off, interrupting. "Employment is listed as a driver for S&G Imports."

"Never heard of them."

"Your department, not mine, I'm happy to say."

"And the two positives from WSW?" Boldt asked. He assumed one of these two identities would prove to be Liz, although in reconstructing events Boldt knew she claimed to have never handled the tape. If her prints were on it, that would need explaining—yet another uncomfortable discussion between husband and wife. The deeper he involved himself, the worse it got.

"Daniel Foreman and Paul Geiser."

Lost in thought, recalling the conversation now, Boldt nearly drove off the road. *Danny Foreman and Paul Geiser.* Foreman he understood. The tape could have once been in Foreman's possession. But a prosecuting attorney's prints? How was that to be explained? Added to this was that the request Boldt had received to drive out to the log cabin, a possible crime scene, had come from Foreman. Things were getting interesting.

His cell phone emitted a single beep, indicating a text message. One eye on the road, one eye on the phone, Boldt read the message as it scrolled across the phone's tiny screen:

From: B. Lofgrin: Cig. ash IDed from Foreman
CS: Proletarskie (Russian). More 2 come-BL

It didn't surprise him that Bernie was working late; the man kept all hours depending on the lab's workload. He assumed Bernie had become excited by the discovery of Foreman's prints on the video and then went back and pushed his crew to work the Foreman crime scene. Nor did it surprise him that Bernie had not telephoned him. His friend would assume Boldt was home with the family, and would not have wanted to disturb him. Sending a text message allowed Boldt to make the choice to read it or not, think about it or not. Boldt was certain he'd find a carbon copy on his office e-mail in the morning, hopefully along with the "more to come" information. The point that Bernie seemed eager to make, and one that required Boldt to read between the lines, was the connection between a Russian with temporary immigration papers identified by a partial fingerprint left on the videocassette, and a Russian brand of cigarette found in the form of ash at the Foreman torture. As the pieces both began to take shape and to fit into place, Boldt found himself excited, his senses heightened. The Russian seemed a promising lead to follow, someone to interview and look at closely, no matter that the evidence remained circumstantial. But it was Foreman's role, as victim, as another person found to have handled that video, as the man who had called Boldt out on a misty, dark evening, that currently intrigued him. Suspicion worked its web. Boldt had to weigh how much to give Foreman and how much to withhold, how much to explore and how much to place aside. Pieces fitting was one thing. The picture those pieces were a part of, the story they told, quite another.

Boldt drove into the dense woods that led to the cabin. He pulled the car forward and parked alongside Danny Foreman's sparkling new Escalade, wondering why anyone would dump so much money into a luxury vehicle. He could see there was someone inside the cabin, and he assumed it to be Foreman, but despite the presence of the man's car, he wasn't taking any chances. There were too many fingernails lying on the ground in this case for him to be careless. Too many questions now surrounding both Foreman and Geiser.

Boldt reached the edge of the trees and worked his way around back, the blood pressure building in his chest and surging past his ears as a low whine. He paused along the way to allow his ears to stretch and his eyes to scan.

The backyard was small. Ankle-high field grass and weeds ran up to a poured concrete patio that housed a rusted barbecue grill and twin beach chairs that had seen better days. A frayed patio umbrella listed above the chairs, anchored in a stack of rock and brick. A can of charcoal starter caught his eye. Concrete steps led up to a back door that had been left open an inch. Not taking his eyes off the door, he withdrew his weapon, crossed the spongy back-yard, and eased the door fully open. Using the jamb as cover, he called out.

"Danny?"

"In here."

It was Foreman's voice.

"I'm at the back," Boldt announced, playing it safe, not wanting to walk into a trap. *Let him come to me.*

Foreman entered the kitchen casually. He looked tired. He wore a disposable glove on his right hand but not on his left because of the two heavily bandaged fingers. "Hey."

"Hey," Boldt echoed, returning his gun to his belt holster.

Foreman led the way through the tiny kitchen. "Guy used this place as his hang. Belongs to a friend. When Liz mentioned it, I knew exactly where she meant. We did some surveillance out here back during the embezzlement."

Some surveillance. "What kind of surveillance, Danny?"

"Meaning?"

Boldt didn't answer. Like an emcee, Foreman swept his left arm out, indicating the room before them. The cabin's central room was contaminated with spilled blood. Boldt slipped on gloves and squatted and touched a droplet on the floor. It was tacky, not wet, but not dry. *Less than four hours old.*

"Another one," Boldt said, noticing the two fingernails on the cabin floor next to the leg of a blood-covered wooden chair to which the victim had been taped with duct tape. All of this came into his mind effortlessly. He didn't merely surmise the crime scene, he *saw* it as an eerie black-and-white moving image. A man in the chair struggling. Gagged, blindfolded. Another man in front of him, a pair of vise-grip pliers in hand. Boldt shook this image out of his head and continued to collect information.

"I don't know about that," Foreman said. "It certainly looks like another one. Hayes, then me, now this. Similar. But I don't know . . . something's not right. It's almost like me and Hayes were clinical, you know? Whereas this one . . . this looks emotional. Angry. The guy doing the deed lost it and got all wild like."

Boldt took in the carnage. "I don't know. At your scene we found blood on the ceiling as well. The walls."

"Yeah, but look at this place!"

Boldt recalled that Bernie Lofgrin's Scientific Identification Division had determined that Foreman had probably been beaten using a plastic bag filled with wet sand—this theory supported by forensic evidence recovered at the scene. At some point the bag had torn open, spraying sand into the bloody mix and matching the splatter patterns.

Boldt carefully dodged the chair and examined some blood splatter on the far wall. He didn't see any sand mixed in. Foreman had been here longer, had a head start.

Boldt said, "You'd think a person could maybe narrow this down by method. Rohypnol, duct tape, fingernails. That's got to be a signature crime. I ran it by Matthews and didn't get very far. I think I'll try OC this time." Organized Crime.

"We got to ask ourselves," Foreman said, "if this *vic*— and I'm assuming it to be David Hayes—got up and walked away or was hauled out of here in a Hefty lawn bag; 'cause one thing that ain't part of the original signature is the lack of a body. I was in that chair, Lou, and I'm telling you there's no way you get yourself out of this and go for a stroll."

But there had been no body at the trailer either. It seemed odd that Foreman would overlook the obvious.

Boldt circled the bloody chair and again watched his theory play out briefly as film. Hayes, or whoever had occupied that chair, was taking a beating, his head snapping left and right. Boldt studied the splatter patterns on the ceiling that supported this determination. The blood was dense immediately above the chair and more sporadic and separated farther out from this epicenter. All this made sense to him. Some of it did not, however.

"What do you think?" Foreman asked, as if the two were regarding a painting in a museum.

"I've got some questions."

"What kind of questions?" Foreman clearly didn't like the sound of that. He wanted this cut-and-dried. He wanted his assumption—that Hayes had probably been killed in this chair—front and center.

"Questions for SID."

"I'm first officer," Foreman declared. "It won't be SID, it'll be our guys."

The State Bureau of Criminal Investigation outsourced their field detection and lab work to King County Sheriff's. The lab had a good reputation, but Boldt didn't personally know anyone there, and it was the personal relationships that got investigations cleared.

Foreman repeated, "What kind of questions?"

Boldt doubted then that Foreman had read the preliminaries from the two other such beatings—including his own. He wasn't sure he wanted to give something away for nothing. There were answers he needed as well.

Boldt wandered into the doorway of the adjacent bedroom and suddenly felt breathless, his chest tight, his imagination besieged by images. It was a twin bed, pulled off the wall, a nightstand shoved into the corner. It faced a closet with louvered panels on the folding doors. Boldt looked away just as quickly.

He asked, "How'd you manage getting the camera into the closet?"

"What?" Foreman answered.

"The video. It's why they beat you, wasn't it, Danny? That video? Pulled your nails and drugged you until you coughed up the combination and location of the safe. You had the video in the safe. *Six years* you kept that thing. Why? Just tell me you didn't drag it out at night and slip it into the VCR, Danny. Tell me that's not why your prints were on it." Boldt felt sick, a combination of this bedroom, the smell of blood and vomit, and other images now swarming his brain. He didn't need to see the video.

Foreman let himself down into a wooden chair just outside the bedroom door. "I obtained the warrant through an Assistant U.S. Attorney at the time. I lured Hayes away from the cabin with an anonymous call. The hope was for data capture—to record his keystrokes. In all, three cameras were installed, each covering an area that included a phone jack because we assumed he was doing this online. Tech Services did it for me, under the protection of Special Operations."

"You were with us at the time," Boldt said. Seattle Police.

"Correct. He used a laptop. Moved around. We couldn't predict what room he'd use. I had *no idea,* Lou. I went fishing, and I caught the wrong fish. If it hadn't been relevant—"

"It *wasn't* relevant!"

"A bank officer? It was very much relevant. For two or three days, she was a primary suspect. Your *wife* I'm talking about. The only thing that saved her, the only *one* who saved her . . . you're looking at him. I kept the tape to myself, explored what needed exploring, and never surfaced her name. We went through the treatments together," he said, meaning their wives' cancer treatment, "and it just got harder and harder to look you in the eye. And then Darlene slipping and Liz recovering. Uglier and uglier."

"What were Paul Geiser's prints doing on the video?" Boldt asked, trying to keep their personal history out of this, but seeing clearly how entangled it all was. "Get your story straight, Danny. That way you only have to tell it once."

"To hell with you!" Foreman shouted.

"You should have destroyed the tape."

"You mean I should have told you about it, don't you?"

"That's *not* what I said."

"A bank exec is sleeping with my embezzler—my *suspect*—and I'm supposed to destroy that evidence? Would *you* have destroyed that evidence?"

"Six years," Boldt said, his throat dry. "Yes, I would have."

"The tape wasn't the only thing in my safe. Every scrap of information pertaining to this case was in there with it, most of it burned to disk. All of it gone now. Destroyed? I don't know. This is the first I've heard about the tape resurfacing." A pause as Foreman added it up. "So they got to Liz again. That's what you're telling me."

In fact, Boldt was telling him more than he wanted to, the result of allowing his emotions to play into this. "Was it the only tape? Of them?"

"Yes."

"And Geiser's prints?"

"I can't answer that," Foreman said. "News to me. My *guess* would be that all the tapes at some point crossed his desk. I don't have a specific memory of Liz's tape being grouped with the others. I do remember clearly the first time I saw it, and the realization—the need—to protect you, if possible. My memory is that I got this tape out of the group. But they were numbered at the time, you know? And I can see me keeping tabs on it, but including it, so nothing fishy surfaced—a tape being noticed missing—and maybe it was in the stack that crossed Paul's desk. Early on, as inventory was being matched against the warrant. Something like that."

Boldt didn't like the explanation—it felt to him as if Foreman were making this up on the fly—but he accepted it for the time being.

"I feel a little sick," Boldt said.

"Probably the air. It stinks in here."

"You must have surveillance notes putting Liz with Hayes last week." He wondered if they'd met here at the cabin. Was Foreman aiming to involve Liz?

"No. I wasn't watching this place."

Was this credible? Boldt wondered. A location under surveillance six years earlier and Foreman doesn't chase it down when the man's released from prison?

"I sat on the rental—the mobile home—thinking he might make a move. Got stung instead."

"They got you twice, and now they appear to have gotten Hayes twice. Why risk that?" Boldt asked. "Why not do what had to be done the first time?"

"They weren't going to torture me out in the damn woods," Foreman complained. "And these guys are smart: They don't put kidnapping on the rap sheet. Assault. Maybe second-degree manslaughter. But it's in the victim's home. It's breaking and entering. Robbery. Light stuff compared with kidnapping."

That argument wasn't quite right, but Boldt didn't push it. "They got Hayes that first time. We know that by the blood type at the scene. Why risk, why bother with a second event?" This stuck in Boldt's craw. These people seemed smart—as Danny had just said. Even Liz's assault in the van looked more like robbery. They were carefully avoiding the charges that drew mandatory time and a maximum-security facility. So why risk a second attack on Hayes? Especially given that he might be being watched.

Boldt gestured at the torture scene. "Did you see this go down, Danny?"

"Of course not."

"But Liz had told you about the cabin. You were watching the cabin. You said so."

"That's you talking, not me." He added, "I was suckered away from here. Anonymous call saying I should take a meeting in town. That Hayes was thinking of turning. I ended up stuck in a traffic jam on the 520. I'd been over in Bellevue. Missed the meet entirely. Fuck me."

Boldt felt a measure of pride at having successfully distracted Danny Foreman away from asking again about the forensic evidence that Boldt found inconsistent at the scene. Veteran cops rarely snuck something past one another, and Boldt had done just that by focusing Foreman on himself—a subject most people found irresistible.

"You know what happens when I call in the lab techs?" Foreman asked. "They're going to go *room by room*," he said, "dusting, developing prints."

Boldt felt a spike of heat travel up his spine.

"Thing about latents," Foreman said. "They can't be dated. They could be from yesterday, or they may be *six years old*, and they all look the same."

Boldt paced back to the doorway and glanced into the bedroom again. This time the film that played in his head had his naked wife grabbing headboards, touching the bedside lamp, pressing her sweating palm on the wall. With her prints in the WSW database, it would be only a matter of time until she'd be placed in the cabin and questioned. A matter of time until she'd have to detail the affair with Hayes.

He felt himself shrink and recoil. Would Foreman now suggest or offer to destroy evidence and wipe down the cabin? Where was this going? What was it Foreman wanted?

"I need her to go along with whatever they ask her to do," Foreman said.

There it was, words hanging between them, as if stopped in space and floating. Boldt's response determined their power or impotence.

"I need her safe," Boldt said.

"You walk out of here now, and there's no record of your having been here. What forensics finds or doesn't find is a product of what there is to find in the first place. But when the prelims on this cabin come back clean for Liz, you'll know why. She gets another call, and I'm the first one you contact. She gets asked to do something for these people and she does it. No more substitutions, coach. If they were gonna snatch her up, they'd have done it. Clearly, she's of more use to them on the outside. They aren't going to harm her, they're going to *use* her. And you're going to let them."

The message didn't surprise Boldt, but Foreman's edgy, demanding tone did. The ordeal that Foreman had gone through had taken its toll. Boldt had no idea what it was like to have fingernails pulled, no idea what that did to a person.

"It's seventeen million dollars, Danny. WestCorp was insured. They're not out a cent. I know they'd love to prevent something similar from happening again, but the only person who seems to really give a damn about closing this case is you. As for me . . . my concern is for Liz, and only Liz. I want her out. I want her disconnected. Neither of us needs to relive this. All it can do is hurt us. What you're asking is impossible. It's the *one thing* I'm working against: her involvement. As to my condoning the destruction of evidence—I can't do that either. Her prints or not, the cabin needs to be gone over by the technicians. We need every scrap of evidence there is. And I'll tell you why," he said. "Because this crime scene—whatever happened here, whoever it happened to—is wrong. Can I put my finger on it? No, I can't. Not yet. But it's wrong. You don't do this twice to the same guy. I just don't see professionals doing that. That's why I need the technicians. That's why I'm going to stay right here with you until they arrive. Liz's prints can and will be explained, no matter the outcome. Does anyone think she possesses the strength to tie David Hayes into a chair? Even with Rohypnol? Not a chance. She *will not participate* beyond serving as a comm center. They want to call her, fine. Beyond that, it's surrogates, undercover officers, and that's that."

"You're going to make this decision for her?" Foreman asked. "Without her?"

"You tried to blackmail me a minute ago, Danny. Extort me. For what? A six-year-old case that no one cares about? Look in the mirror. There are reasons the original investigating officer doesn't get the lead when a case resurfaces. You embody those reasons. You're burned out, Danny. You blame that case for Darlene's illness, even for her death, for all I know. You're hanging on to this one and it's going to take you with it. Let it go, man! Pass it off to someone less personally attached."

"Is that what you're going to do?" Foreman asked, his voice steady and calm, but belying an undercurrent of raw energy that raised Boldt's hackles. "Practice what you preach, soldier."

Boldt felt a severe stab of pain in the center of his chest and nearly buckled over with it. He was *living* this case, something every detective knew not to do. It caught up to you, this kind of thing.

"You okay?"

Foreman's voice sounded distant to Boldt. He hadn't realized he'd gone blind in one eye until the condition cleared like a window shade lifting.

"Lou?"

"Fine," Boldt lied. But he could see clearly again out of both eyes. His hearing returned to normal, losing that echo. He realized they were like two high school kids who entered into a brawl as opponents, but rose from the pile bloody and shaking hands. "I can't do what you ask. I've got to say no to the evidence tampering, and no to Liz doing anything for Hayes or whoever's behind this. I'll take what comes my way is, I guess, what I'm saying to you. You want to play hardball, that's up to you."

"It's not up to me," said Foreman. "Never has been. If there's a body out there, I want to find it. Fast. Yes. Because maybe it leads us to who did this *ahead* of whatever they have planned for Liz."

"They?"

"Whatever. If Hayes survived, or if he gave up whatever's necessary to get that money back, then there's only one person this is gonna come back on, Lou, and that's Liz. Slice it, dice it, I don't care. It's going to be Liz. She has access, and she has history. Who would you come after?"

Boldt knew he was right, though wanted to talk himself out of it. This being Wednesday evening, the bank reception celebrating the merger was now just a few days away. The embezzled money had to be wired out ahead of that deadline or be lost. It seemed hard to imagine that by Monday morning everything would be back to normal.

"There's stuff I've got to do," he said. "So who makes the call? It's Wednesday night, Danny." He held this leverage over Foreman—SID processed evidence at all hours. Foreman's private lab likely did not. It was to both their benefits if Boldt made the call, if SPD did the work.

"So make the call."

Boldt saw a flicker of thought register in Foreman's eyes. Just a flicker, but enough to sense he'd been had. Danny Foreman knew he'd never have his evidence in time unless SPD's lab handled the crime scene. He had purposefully manipulated Boldt into making the offer to involve SPD's lab. The involvement of the lab would mean Boldt, or one of his squad, would inherit the paperwork, the meetings, the explanations, the press, the analysis. Danny Foreman had just encumbered Boldt, leaving himself free to pursue the money trail. More to the point, Foreman knew Boldt would not walk away from any crime scene.

"I don't like being run, Danny."

"I suckered into a phony tip or I'd have been here to prevent this. At the very least, to witness it. How do you think I feel?"

"So who did that to you? Not me."

"Come Sunday night, you and Liz are gonna see there's only one way to play this. She walks into that bank. She does what he asks—*they* ask—and we follow that money to the scumbag who's causing all this trouble. You aren't there yet, but you'll get there, Lou. I know you will."

"I wouldn't count on it."

"That tape ever gets seen, it'll sure as hell end her career, and it won't help yours any."

"We'll land on our feet."

"And I'll be there to catch you."

"Sure you will, Danny."

Boldt raised his phone and called Bernie Lofgrin directly, ready to involve the lab.

He sensed he was making a huge mistake.

THIRTEEN

BOLDT FOUND TRUE POLICE WORK electrifying. Now that he carried a lieutenant's shield, such moments came rarely and so when encountered proved all the more meaningful. For him detection was a mathematical process, and therefore very much related to his music, which he thought of as a mathematical language. As a detective you connected A to B and B to C and therefore A to C, and around and around it went, simple algebra and geometry applied to everyday problem-solving.

The problem had been to approach his interview of Malina Alekseevich with more than a hunch and a whim. For Boldt, several disparate pieces of evidence came together in the men's room midway into his morning routine at work.

Standing at the urinal, going about his business, he heard the distinct *click* of the door's deadbolt being thrown and glanced over his shoulder to see a woman locking the lavatory door.

"Wrong door," Boldt called out, his right hand fishing to return himself to his shorts. "This is the men's room."

When the woman told him she needed two minutes of his time, and called him by rank, Boldt hurriedly zipped himself up. In all his years of policing, he'd never been ambushed in a men's room.

She was a handsome woman in her early thirties, strong-bodied and big-chested. She wore her blond-tinted hair as bangs in front and cropped at her shoulders, lending her coif the look of a helmet. He searched for a name to go with that pleasant face but couldn't find it. He washed his hands as she moved over to him and spoke quickly and softly.

"Sorry for the cloak-and-dagger, but I couldn't think how else to ensure privacy."

He apologized for having forgotten her name.

"Olson," she replied. "Maddie Olson. Organized Crime."

Boldt was glad for the moment it took him to yank a couple of paper towels from the box and dry his hands, for it gave him time to think. He'd put the request through to OC earlier this same morning, attempting to establish the torture scenes as signature crimes, hoping OC might have someone on file who liked to pull fingernails. And now here was Olson, delivering information in a quirky, and exceptionally unusual way. He did not question her motives, except to know that if she'd gone to these lengths, she must require an enormous amount of secrecy.

He realized too that she was right about her choice of methods. Any detective from OC visiting a Homicide lieutenant was going to be noticed, even if they took a minute together in a conference room. The safest way was to force an encounter outside the offices, but Boldt went from his car to his office to his car and home. He didn't offer a person like Olson much chance to corral him.

"Okay, I'm listening," he said.

"Your inquiry this morning: Rohypnol, duct tape, and fingernail extraction. You're not going to get anything out of OC on that."

"I'm not," he said, trying to follow her.

"No. You'll nudge us again in another few days and we still won't have an answer for you."

"I don't have a few days."

"I know that. I'm in the cubicle next to Marcel. I overheard your request."

Marcel Malvone, on OC nearly as long as Boldt had been Homicide. Boldt had taken the request to Malvone directly, knowing that penetrating OC's hierarchy could be difficult at best.

Olson glanced quickly toward the men's room door, as if expecting an interruption. She then turned on the water in the sink to increase the background noise.

Boldt felt his palms sweat. He dried them on a fresh paper towel.

"The thing about OC," she said. "We're worse than Internal Investigations half the time. We live by the covenant *no one can protect you better than you can protect yourself*. It's not so much about misinformation as it is disinformation. When someone pushes a hot button we make sure that information is lost."

"I pushed a hot button," Boldt said, working with what she was telling him.

"No one's going to give you this. If I'm proved wrong, so much the better. But when I overheard your time constraints, I decided to act. Maybe you repay the favor someday."

"Will if I can."

"That signature you're looking for would come back for a CI," civilian informant, "that's currently working a case for us. No way anyone's going to give him up for you and yours."

"No one but you."

"But me," she confessed. "My sister's stepson." Here it comes, Boldt thought. Olson had the favor ready at hand. "He's on the buying end of a drug deal in the backseat of a car when the skel riding passenger decides to pull a piece and blow away a corner dealer. Car's pulled over and everyone in the car is charged with manslaughter except the shooter, who wins himself a capital murder charge. My nephew's a good kid. Wrong place, wrong time. Drugs. He deserves a bad rap, maybe some time, but not the manslaughter."

Boldt actually knew of the case. He promised to look into it, to do his best.

"That's all I ask."

"Done."

"This CI is planted deep. It's a joint effort in-house with Special Ops. U.S. Attorney's Office and INS are even in on it. But this signature you described . . . I know for a fact he's into manicures," she said, meaning the extraction of fingernails. "The Rope, that's news to me." She meant the use of Rohypnol. "So maybe it just skews to him but isn't him. I can't say. That will be Malvone's justification in not sharing him with you—if you ever bring it back onto us. The Rope is not part of his gig, not on his sheet. They can withhold him from you for this reason. But the tape and the manicures—that's him, for sure."

"The case?"

"These guys are into *everything*, Lieutenant. We're talking fraud, smuggling, black market retail. Money exchange. Money laundering. Anything and everything to do with a buck. No drugs, no prostitution, nothing for Narcotics or Vice. But racketeering? Shit, Lieutenant, this guy—the boss, I'm talking about, not the CI—when they wrote the definition for racketeering, they had him in mind. They run a fucking empire. This guy is the fucking Brando of the Russian immigrant community. And he's Dangerous, capital D. That would be another reason they wouldn't steer you into this: It's a fucking one-way street to the graveyard to mess with these people. Our guy, our plant, he's a gold mine. Constantly funneling information. Reliable, bankable, good information. Compromising him would be a serious setback. We're picking up foreign networks, massive laundering. The mother lode. That's how I know you'll never get him out of us."

A crashing sound as someone banged into the door expecting it to open. This was followed by a sharp knocking. "What the fuck?!" came the complaint.

"A name?" Boldt asked, his heart dancing in his chest. *The Russian community,* she'd said. Russian cigarettes from the ash found at Foreman's torture. A Russian name on a partial print from Bernie Lofgrin. Click, click, click, went the pieces. He loved this job.

She lowered her voice so that even Boldt could barely hear her above the rush of water into the stained sink. "Yasmani Svengrad. The Sturgeon General."

"*Sturgeon* General," Boldt clarified the irregularity.

"He imports caviar. Or did . . ."

"Let me guess," Boldt said. "S&G Imports."

She leaned back, impressed. "Well . . . yeah."

More banging on the door. Boldt shouted for the guy to cool it. He said to Olson, "Your CI. He's called Malina Alekseevich."

Her lips parted in surprise. She had nice teeth.

"How'd you know that?"

"He's sloppy," Boldt answered.

He told her to take a stall and lock the door. He'd knock on the bathroom door when the coast was clear.

Boldt then unlocked the main door to a disgruntled detective who quickly changed his attitude in the presence of a lieutenant. Boldt hovered by the water fountain in the hall until this detective left the men's room. Boldt knocked, and Olson slipped into the hall, walking quickly away, never looking back.

The mother lode, she'd said. And that was how Boldt thought of it.

□ □ □

Most of Seattle's former canneries and icehouses, the brick boathouses and sail-making workshops, had long since been razed and replaced with co-op housing, restaurants, or tourist traps. A few structures remained, some rusted, some crumbling, the majority along the northern shore of Lake Union's ship canal, the last salty smell and briny taste of a history that would never return. Computer chips had replaced tins of smoked salmon; software, for soft-shelled crabs. Boldt rode in the passenger seat of John LaMoia's Jetta as LaMoia turned down an alley. The southernmost boundary of Ballard was a seawall containing the canal and the seagull-white-stained wooden pilings supporting it. The empty lanes of litter-encrusted blacktop running between vacant buildings were reminiscent of the tumbleweeded streets of the Old West. The wind that rose off the water whispered like sirens in Boldt's ear.

"That's the place." LaMoia pointed out a set of barely legible numerals above a rust-red door on the side of a corrugated-steel building with a tin roof.

Boldt removed his department-issue Glock, a weapon that had replaced the Beretta 9mm two years earlier. He checked out the gun, an uncharacteristic act.

LaMoia had spent the ride over going on and on about his terrorism seminar, part of a continuing education course, once again expressing his concern over the devices believed to be in terrorists' hands. Nearing the end of the course, he had one last session late afternoon that he described as a "field trip" to watch demonstrations of some of the explosives and triggering devices. "But the weirdest weapon puts out something called Electromagnetic Pulse, EMP." LaMoia's enthusiasm could make anything sound interesting.

"You tried to explain this before," Boldt interrupted. He was interested in technology only if it fit his own needs—he didn't need to try to understand everything that was out there. He dumped water on LaMoia's flames before suffering an explanation of EMP. Thankfully the water rolled off LaMoia's back.

"Liz was sleeping with this guy David Hayes," Boldt said. "Six years ago, when it all fell apart on me? That was Hayes. There's a videotape. A sex tape. This guy, Svengrad, may have it. So if that comes up in the discussion, that's why. I don't want you looking surprised."

LaMoia sighed, glancing away uncomfortably.

"You're allowed to be surprised now."

"I am."

"It would be nice to keep it off the Internet, off the evening news, out of the bank's next board meeting."

"I imagine it would."

"And you might think that's why we're here."

"I might."

"It isn't. We're here to bring Alekseevich in for questioning. We have a partial—never mind that it's inadmissible."

"Doesn't bother me."

"We not only have a Russian brand of cigarette but, as it turns out, S&G, Svengrad's company, has the exclusive import contract for the entire West Coast. What we want, what we need, is to put a pack of those cigarettes into Alekseevich's pocket. That, and the partial, give him to us."

"He might come voluntarily."

"Right," Boldt said with a snort. "That's a strong possibility."

"If things go south in there?"

"No matter how badly this goes, we talk our way out. We walk out. The people behind this—and maybe that's Svengrad—have gone to great lengths to avoid class A felony charges. That speaks volumes, I think. They're not going to hassle two cops. They're extremely careful. We do our job. We grab up Alekseevich if he's in there, and we leave."

"Not my style," LaMoia said. "I'd rather shoot it out."

Despite the various burdens weighing on Boldt's shoulders he found room to laugh.

"You're a bundle of laughs, Sarge."

"That's what they say."

"No . . . that's not what they say."

Boldt flashed him a look. "Then what *do* they say?"

"I think I'd like to keep my job." With that, LaMoia popped open the door and headed toward the building.

As they approached through a light drizzle, Boldt said, "Seventeen million reasons for lying to us, don't forget."

"You think?" LaMoia asked, wondering if the embezzlement trail led to this rusting building.

"We'll find out soon enough."

LaMoia knocked and they entered a small office area containing a pair of ancient gunmetal-gray steel desks loosely shaped into an L, a woman receptionist in her late forties with big hair and red nails, some whiteboards on the wall scribbled with colorful reminders, and four large color posters, all showing busty women with pink tongues. Caviar ads, but oddly targeting readers of *Playboy*. The receptionist called through on the telephone. Boldt could hear an extension ring out back.

"Silicon Valley," LaMoia said, pointing to one of the girly posters, a nearly naked black woman barely out of her teens working a jackhammer on a city street. The implants grafted to her chest accounted for LaMoia's comment. She wore a yellow hard hat that bore the American flag. The words above her read: "If it smells fishy . . ." The jackhammer aimed into the seam of a superimposed can of caviar, beneath which it read: ". . . you're in the right place—Svengrad, Beluga Negro."

They were admitted into a cool warehouse that smelled

sour with fish. Their escort was a well-dressed, darkly com-
plected man in his early thirties with a fairly thick accent.
Not Alekseevich, according to the sheet in Boldt's inside
coat pocket.

Steel mesh shelving was crowded with carefully arranged cardboard boxes. The shiny gray concrete floor was
marked with bright yellow lane lines courtesy of OSHA,
while overhead mercury vapor lights lent human skin a
sickly green tinge. To Boldt's disappointment, the warehouse was quiet, void of human activity.

"It isn't every day we get a visit from Seattle's finest,"
their escort said.

He had the right lingo and had done a good job of
wearing down the edges of his accent, all of which told
Boldt he'd probably been in the States for some time. The
nice suit was somewhat unexpected though not surprising,
given Beth LaRossa's description of the two who had pressured her husband. The man led them across the warehouse
floor to a glass box of an office from where a muffled
recording of a soprano's voice carried. Boldt liked opera.

Their escort opened the door for them but did not enter
himself.

The office reminded Boldt of his own—a space within
a space, and little more. It was a place of business, heaped
with paperwork. The man behind the desk was broad-
shouldered with pinprick black eyes, a barroom nose, and
a salt-and-pepper beard, carefully trimmed. He too wore a
dark, tailored suit, but a pair of more workmanlike, rubber-
soled black shoes revealed themselves from below the
large, leather-top desk, a piece of furniture incongruously
out of place. Boldt knew better than to automatically as-

sume this man was Svengrad. A manager perhaps. An employee.

Fan lines edged his eyes as he rose and introduced himself. "General Yasmani Svengrad." He made no offer for them to sit down, and remained standing himself. "Let me guess," he said. "You've lost something."

Boldt picked up a trace of British in his speech. The man sucked air between his two front teeth—either a tic or an attempt to fight a painful tooth. Boldt felt taken aback and slightly intimidated, not an easy feat. Svengrad was a perfectly proportioned, enormous man. He stood six foot four or five, with hands like baseball mitts. But where some men looked big, Svengrad's proportions confused the eye. A trompe l'oeil of a man, like someone from *Alice in Wonderland*.

But it was more than the personage. Prior to coming here, Boldt had taken what little had been passed him in the men's room and had dug first into S&G Imports and then into its notorious owner, quickly reading up on the man courtesy of the Internet. The picture that unfolded explained OC's desire to turn an employee as a state's witness and catalog the steady flow of information that resulted. Yasmani Svengrad would not fall easily.

A decorated naval officer, Svengrad had proved himself a shrewd politician as well. With the collapse of the former Soviet Union, Svengrad had unexpectedly transferred to oversee naval operations in the Caspian Sea, considered an undesirable posting without political clout. It was only later his true motivations had been recognized. As the senior military officer in charge of the Caspian, he had seized control of its waters and filled a power void as management of the Caspian slipped from Mother Russia's firm grasp.

With no fewer than five newly formed governments claiming rights to the Caspian and her all-important sturgeon, Svengrad brutalized his way to dominance, quickly owning the Caspian's lucrative, multimillion-dollar caviar business. Svengrad's friends back in Moscow allowed this, even encouraged it, as poachers nearly ended the caviar trade by slaughtering immature fish for their famous eggs and pushing the sturgeon toward extinction. No doubt, Svengrad made sure his friends in Moscow both ate and lived well for allowing a monopoly that continued to this day. From what he'd read, Boldt considered Svengrad both a man of vision and one unafraid of using force to get what he wanted. Many a poacher vessel had been "lost at sea" during the early years of Svengrad's power grab.

He'd settled in the United States seven years earlier and had been granted citizenship not twelve months ago, a discovery that made Boldt suspect either the intervention of diplomats or the exchange of hard cash. Svengrad had nonetheless never personally been arrested, had never spent a single night in so much as a drunk tank. Most such "Teflon thugs" found themselves targets of federal or state undercover investigations at some point, and as far as Boldt could determine, Svengrad's time had now come.

Boldt played it carefully. They came without a warrant, and he kept this firmly in mind—if asked to leave they would be obliged to do so. "Lost something? We're just a pair of public servants doing a favor for INS."

"A Seattle Police Department lieutenant and sergeant doing a favor for INS?" So the man knew how to read. He handed back the credentials, still not offering them chairs.

"You don't think our captain, doing a favor for the feds, is going to send a *detective* to see you, do you?" He could see that Svengrad actually considered this, though not for long.

"How long do we keep this up?" Svengrad asked.

Boldt threw his hands out in an inquisitive gesture that asked, *How should I know*?

"If you have business here, state it," Svengrad said. "Or should I play along? What can I do for INS, gentlemen?" He asked this in a schoolgirl voice that instead of comical, Boldt found threatening. "Remind me: Don't you need a subpoena, a writ, a warrant? Should I call a lawyer?"

"Why so jumpy?"

"We're here informally," LaMoia said, jumping into the fray.

"You are at that," said the man wearing the designer suit as he looked them over. "Do you press those yourself, or send them out?"

LaMoia's infamous blue jeans finally took a direct hit; if Boldt hadn't been working to understand, and possibly undermine Svengrad, he might have celebrated the moment.

Boldt calmly removed Malina Alekseevich's INS sheet and placed it in front of Svengrad. "You're listed as the employer of record."

"As I should be," Svengrad said, not batting an eyelash. "Were that I was."

Boldt thought he was actually doing OC a favor by making Alekseevich into a suspect, and therefore above consideration as a double agent. Never mind that entities like OC and Special Operations and the INS liked to run control on their civilian informants; Boldt didn't see much harm coming of this.

Svengrad continued, "Malina's a hard worker. A good

man. He might even have avoided being laid off if Fish and Wildlife had played fair."

"Laid off?" LaMoia inquired.

Boldt paled. *Played fair? Fish and Wildlife?* Depending on when Alekseevich had indeed been laid off his job, they had little or no way to connect Svengrad to the tortures of Hayes and Foreman, even if Alekseevich were responsible. Svengrad would simply claim that, unemployed, Alekseevich had resorted to his old ways. More's the pity. Boldt quickly looked for a bridge that might keep himself and LaMoia in the room long enough to stir the pot. He didn't see anything obvious.

"He *drives* for us, or did, before layoffs," Svengrad answered LaMoia. "He has not gone and gotten a parking ticket or something, has he?" The man grinned smugly. "Date of termination—because that's the next thing you're going to ask, yes? Ninety-three days. You may ask the Fish and Wildlife Department." He met Boldt's surprise. "Not INS, Fish and Wildlife. They will tell same date."

"Ninety-two days," Boldt said, misquoting him. "You track all employees with such enthusiasm, or is Alekseevich special to you?"

"Ninety-*three* days, Lieutenant. We, our caviar, is under a lockdown. Forbidden from making business. Big mix-up on government's part. And yes, I *do* keep track. Certainly. When this affects one's livelihood, one keeps count of such things."

"A lockdown," Boldt repeated, spinning on his heels to look once again at the quiet warehouse behind them. Svengrad's explanation fit the human emptiness of the place.

Svengrad flipped through a Rolodex and fixed on a card. "We have the same address—for the home of Alekseevich—

as does INS." He handed Boldt back the sheet of paper. "Have a nice day, Lieutenant."

"You said we were missing something," Boldt said.

"My mistake. Fedor will show you out."

"Something, or some*one*?"

Most people shrank some from a cop's gaze. Not this man. Svengrad fixed his attention onto Boldt and asked, "You like dirty movies, Lieutenant?"

It wasn't often that Boldt had to contain himself from striking out at a man.

Svengrad said, "I find them quite a turn-on myself. The home movies on the Internet are the best. Crude lighting. The women always trying too hard to look sexy. The men trying to look hard. Much better than cheap porn, don't you think? Gives reality TV a new meaning." He added, "But to answer your question, no: some*thing*, not someone."

Boldt asked, "Do you get these films off the Internet, or do you have the *originals*?"

"I have my sources," Svengrad said. "Mature women are the best, don't you think? They know what they want— what it takes for them—and they aren't afraid to say so."

Boldt's stomach squirted some bile into his esophagus. He coughed through the burning and swallowed it down. He'd have bloody stool if he continued to keep this tension inside: ulcers the size of golf balls.

"Where would I get such a home movie?"

LaMoia shifted on his heels, uncomfortable. He whispered, "Sarge."

Boldt did not so much as look in his direction. "John," Boldt said, still eye-to-eye with Svengrad. "Ask the guy out there for a cigarette, would you please?"

LaMoia withdrew from the room, though reluctantly. Once he was on the other side of the glass his attention remained on Svengrad and Boldt, as did the attention of Svengrad's man.

"You like caviar?" Svengrad asked Boldt, ignoring Boldt's inquiry. He swept his arm to encompass the warehouse.

"No," Boldt confessed. "I never acquired the taste."

"Too bad. Your wife, where do her tastes lie?"

"I will not now, nor at any time, discuss my family," Boldt said. "And neither will you. To misjudge me in this regard would be a terrible error on your part."

"I thought we were already discussing your family," Svengrad said. "Or at least home videos." Boldt kept the death stare on him. "No matter," the other said. "Even if I wanted to, I could not give your wife our best Beluga Negro. This is because of some very good forgeries of my company's labels. These have caused the . . . interruption in my business."

"The feds can be a real bother sometimes," Boldt said.

"Indeed they can."

"Counterfeit caviar?" Boldt asked. "Seriously?"

"Paddlefish eggs," the general answered. "Gravely serious. We never heard about it until your Fish and Wildlife service discovered them bearing our label. Paddlefish, at four dollars an ounce, mixed in with our eighty-dollar Beluga. Like cutting cocaine with powdered milk."

"I wouldn't know," Boldt said. "About either."

"I am the victim here. But because I am Russian, I must be big mafia guy." His attempt to come off as an innocent bordered on comical.

"Paddlefish eggs."

"Bearing my label. Perhaps, when this small problem is resolved, we can work out an arrangement that is mutually satisfying."

"The most I can do is look into it."

"Don't underestimate yourself. The right motivation, it's amazing what a man can do."

"This late in the week," Boldt reminded, "I'm unlikely to make much headway."

"What a shame. For a moment there I thought we had a real connection."

A knock on the glass window where LaMoia held a pack of cigarettes to the glass. *Proletarskie.*

The general saw this as well. "Russian brand. We import them along with half a dozen others."

"Alekseevich smokes this brand," Boldt said.

"Malina smoke? I do not think so. Too athletic."

"Sell a lot of this brand, do you?"

"Enough to justify importing it," Svengrad replied. "The kids at the raves. The colleges. They love Russian cigarettes. Much stronger. They make Camels look like Virginia Slims."

"How many cartons, cases, a week?"

"You bring a warrant, I'll gladly turn over this information. Otherwise, no reason to let my competitors know my numbers."

"I'm not your competitor," Boldt said.

"Sure you are."

Boldt understood the general's tactics then: gun and run. He struck an area of Boldt's vulnerability, the video, and then came back with his own needs—the lockdown of his caviar—and then got defensive when his cigarettes came into play. Boldt might have enjoyed this more had Liz not been directly involved.

"You like birds, Lieutenant?"

"The winged variety?" Boldt asked, wondering what came next.

"The magpie will watch the same bird nest for hours. Must seem like forever, a brain that small. Patient like a saint. The mother bird leaves that nest, even for a moment, and the magpie eats her eggs. Right there in the nest."

Boldt felt a warmth run through him, like he'd peed in his pants. He pictured the yellow yolk spread around the bird's nest the same way the blood had been spilled around the cabin. Svengrad made sure his message was received. "You like art, Lieutenant?"

"Some."

"I collect WPA-era charcoals. It's a seller's market right now. Smart time to watch for forgeries." Svengrad sat on the word—an elephant on an egg. "The limitation of imitation," he said. "It's good of you to have stopped by."

Dismissed, Boldt thought he meant to say.

◻ ◻ ◻

Back in the Jetta, Boldt loosened his tie.

LaMoia said, "It's not so much the salty taste that bothers me, but the way they pop between your teeth."

"Smelling like low tide doesn't help," Boldt said.

"So what happened after I was excused?"

"I had to do that."

"I understand," LaMoia said, but his voice betrayed him.

"He wasn't going to threaten me in front of someone."

"And did he?"

"Not exactly, no. He wanted to cut a deal: his import business back for the video of Liz and Hayes."

"Damn," LaMoia said. He pulled the Jetta out onto wet streets. The sky this time of year was worse than a leaking faucet.

"His caviar business is important to him. We can assume that's where the seventeen million came from in the first place: some undeclared profits."

"You think it was his money?"

"I think it was. But his main message was a story about magpies."

"What-pies?"

"Birds. He took the long way around to explain to me that the Hayes crime scene, the cabin, is a cheap imitation. His guys turned their backs, and somebody took Hayes."

"You buy that?"

"There's a second interpretation. This may just be me being paranoid."

LaMoia waited.

"Liz and I drove the kids out to Kathy's—my sister's—in the middle of the night, Tuesday night. We literally took them out of our nest. Maybe I blew it. Maybe we were followed. Maybe he's warning me not to try to move them again or he'll take action the next time. Maybe he doesn't know where they are and he's looking for me to panic and lead him to them. We both know the Russians have a reputation of working the family when the going gets tough." Boldt recalled an unsolved child murder, and the suspicion of Russian involvement.

"Holy shit," LaMoia breathed.

"That's why I'm likely to make a call asking about the possibility of lifting this lockdown. And I'm going to talk to Bernie about cross-comparing every single piece of evidence from that cabin against Danny Foreman's crime scene. I think what just happened in there was that Yasmani Svengrad confessed to us that Alekseevich is our guy, but that he didn't do Hayes at the cabin. My bet is, Svengrad wants Hayes as badly as, or worse than, we do."

"The merger. The deadline."

"That's it," Boldt said, but his main thought was that this still put Liz squarely in the center.

FOURTEEN

LIZ COULDN'T SPEND TIME IN the house with the kids gone. She'd left for work earlier than usual, wrung out by waiting for the phone to ring and by the eerie silence of an empty home. Lou called with an invitation to lunch. It hit her hard because they were both too busy for such extravagances, which meant this had to be of the utmost importance. It also occurred to her that she was probably the last person in the world her husband wanted to sit down to lunch with, and this both broke her heart and made her all the more curious and fearful of his reasons.

Somewhat typical of Lou, he chose Bateman's, a semi-underground lunch joint that made the freshest turkey sandwiches in the city but at the expense of atmosphere. She walked to the cafeteria, despite a light mist in the air that others might have called rain, not only aware of, but glad for, the man and woman in trench coats who followed behind her. Bobbie Gaynes and Mark Heiman were both familiar faces to her—and yet seeing them surprised her, for they were among the very best of Lou's detectives. By assigning these two to watch her, Lou sent her a message, intended or not, of just how serious he took the threat to her safety. As the three of them reached the restaurant, Gaynes peeled off and crossed the street, entering a mystery bookshop from where she would watch Bateman's and any activity on the street. Heiman followed inside and ate at a table nearby, a cell phone/walkie-talkie on the table in plain view.

But not too nearby. Lou wanted his privacy. After moving through the line, they took a table well away from Heiman, so the detective couldn't overhear.

Liz worked on a bowl of chili, picking out chunks of meat and setting them on the plate. Lou deconstructed a turkey and cranberry on wheat and dug into it with a plastic fork. It struck her that neither of them could simply eat what had been served.

He spoke in the practiced voice of a man used to talking in the third row of a courtroom while the trial was under way. "You and I have barely had five minutes to catch up." His tone suggested apology and so she braced for more bad news. *Not the kids,* she thought, presuming he would not wait for a lunch meeting if whatever it was had to do with them. Lou pushed some cranberry jelly onto a piece of white meat and ate the combination. He washed it down with hot tea.

"We don't know how it all fits together, or for that matter, even *if* it all fits together, but there are some things you need to know." He told her about the blood evidence at the cabin, and how forensics would be the clincher, but that he couldn't say exactly what had gone on out there. He warned her that if her latent fingerprints surfaced, they would have to deal with it, that such a discovery might signal the end of their keeping the affair secret, and that he wanted her prepared for that eventuality.

"The tape?"

"Danny Foreman shot that tape of you two."

She calmly set down the spoon. Either the chili had landed on an empty stomach, or this news was about to make her sick.

"It's a surveillance tape that he suppressed," Lou explained. "He didn't think it relevant at the time, which is cop speak for his not wanting to get you in trouble." He told her the lab had discovered both Paul Geiser's and Danny Foreman's prints on the outside of the cassette. "And another partial that belonged to an INS green card holder—a Russian." He covered the difficulty of connecting a partial print legally to an individual, but how the discovery of a Russian cigarette ash at the Foreman assault had helped confirm suspicions and led them to a distributor. This, without naming names. "What you need to know, Liz, is that this man, this importer, he plays rough. The Russian mafia is famous for coming after one's family as a means of pressure."

"The LaRossas," she said.

"Yes. The Russian . . . I saw him late yesterday . . . told me this tale—the story's unimportant—that may mean that he, they, I'm not sure, followed us out to Kathy's. May know where Miles and Sarah are." He lowered his head.

She felt made of stone. Frozen, both from motion and in terms of cold. She knew exactly what he was telling her, and yet her mother's sense of protection tried to reinterpret whatever it was so that it wouldn't come out the way it had sounded. The way he meant it. She finally said, "I want to hear the story."

"It's not important," he repeated.

"I . . . want . . . to . . . hear . . . the . . . story."

"I screwed up, Liz. I'm sorry. I did everything I could to avoid being followed."

She understood then that he took this as a failure on his part. She wanted to forgive him, placing little importance on how it had happened, but then reconsidered and felt angry he'd let them be followed. It felt so wonderfully good to deflect the blame for some of this onto him—even if only briefly. But within seconds she felt awful about gloating over his shame, knowing these problems had nothing to do with him and everything to do with her own past, and this realization and the combined guilt ate into her all the more deeply. She pushed the chili aside distastefully. "The story," she said again.

He took a moment to explain the tale of the magpie waiting for the empty nest. "We can't be sure," he added quickly, "that it has *anything* to do with the kids. It could very well have been his way of denying responsibility for what happened to Hayes at the cabin. We know Danny Foreman was lured away from the cabin. It's not inconceivable that this man I'm talking about . . . his guys were lured away as well, or even followed Foreman when they should have stayed on Hayes. It's not clear. I want to emphasize that."

"We've got to get them out."

Lou had the audacity to shake his head no. "That's not an option."

She'd never felt this kind of cold, even through her illness, never anything close to this sense of removal and distance. "Why? Kathy can take them somewhere. Boise. Reno. Someplace far away."

"If they're being watched, it'll do no good, only take them farther from us. Look, they may simply know our kids are gone and be using this to trick us into leading them to Miles and Sarah."

"This *can't* be," she said too loudly. Heiman turned his head slightly, and then thought better and returned to his sandwich. Liz suddenly felt as if eyes from everywhere were upon them. It felt claustrophobic to her. Oppressive.

"We . . . don't . . . know," Lou said firmly. "We can't jump to conclusions. It does no one any good. But at the same time, we have to be *wise* about this. We have to rethink *everything*."

Not really listening to him, she said, "We—you—could send police cars. A whole phalanx of them. Middle of the night. Get them out of there. Use dummy cars like they do with the president. They can't follow them all."

"Then it's Kathy they go after," he said, meeting eyes with her. His were filled with pain. "Or your parents. Or you. Or me, even. Maybe they wait six months, a year— and then go after the kids. The point being, if this was meant as a threat—and we don't know that for sure—then there's no way to beat it. You don't beat these people, Liz. Not at their game."

"This is *not* a game."

"You know what I meant."

"There must be a way."

"For the time being, we cooperate."

He stunned her with this announcement. Her eyes searched the various tables, the people working the sandwich line, wondering if *they* were watching them right now.

"Are you saying the money's tied to these people?"

"We don't know that either."

"You're just a wealth of information, aren't you?"

"It's fluid," he said.

She disliked that term. He used it all the time.

He said, "We work on a couple of different assumptions. One is that they may know that Miles and Sarah are with Kathy. The other is that it may have been their money—this Russian's money. It makes some sense because his business is in trouble with the government right now, and he's probably cash shy. It makes that seventeen million all the more tempting. He hires Hayes's new lawyers, gets him out on parole, and puts him to work."

"What have I done?" she asked, a desperate sadness permeating her.

"You can't beat them at their game," he said in that Lou way that suggested he'd already thought this through to where he was now ahead of it. She knew this about him, loved him for it—always looking around the next corner, but could hardly see clear to understand what he meant.

"We beat them, we make it safe, by either playing along or putting the whole lot of them in jail. We've already taken certain steps, and there's more I have planned, but in the meantime, no matter what, you play along. That was the message I took away from there. That's something I won't even share with my own team. If you get a call, when you get a call, you call me first and we decide how to play it. Whether or not, and how I include our guys, I don't know yet."

"That doesn't sound right."

"It's not right," he said. "But it's necessary."

"I just go back to work now? Just another day at the job?"

"You have a reception to plan."

She couldn't believe he'd said that. Her expression told him so.

"There's a second interpretation to the story about the magpie, an interpretation that is further confused, or maybe supported, by physical evidence."

"I don't see how you can be so *calm* about this," she blurted out.

"Either Danny Foreman or a DPA—a deputy prosecuting attorney—named Paul Geiser could have been partnered with Hayes, could be behind the crime scene we found. They're the magpie, stealing Hayes out of the nest and away from the Russians."

"And David? Is there a body yet?"

Lou didn't answer that. "It's incredibly important that should you hear from either Foreman or Geiser, *regardless* what either may tell you, you must come to me first—even if he makes a convincing argument to the contrary. Don't believe anyone but me, Liz."

She nodded, confused, unsure whether David Hayes being alive or dead benefited her family more. Amazed to be in a position to even *think* such a thought.

Lou reached across the table and took her hands in his. To her surprise, his were colder than her own.

FIFTEEN

DEPUTY PROSECUTING ATTORNEY PAUL GEISER'S OFFICE reminded Boldt of a librarian's or research assistant's with its untidy stacks of papers covering every horizontal surface, the dust, the unsavory smell of old food. He knew Geiser by reputation: a courtroom bully; opinionated to a flaw; outspoken. He'd languished in the prosecuting attorney's office significantly longer than even the prosecuting attorney himself, destined to never be recruited by the U.S. Attorney's Office, the proper career track, because his mouth had made him more enemies than it had won friends. The question on Boldt's mind was whether Geiser could help him learn more about the federal case against Yasmani Svengrad, and what, if anything, Geiser knew about Liz's affair with Hayes, given his prints on the tape. If Boldt were going to attempt to sting the very investigation he found himself a part of—this in order to protect his family from Svengrad—he had to know all the players, their roles, and their weaknesses.

A man who probably sweated in his sleep, Geiser wore a sheen of perspiration, as if he'd showered too quickly after a run. He was said to be an expert in the martial arts, and this rumor was now confirmed by a group of photographs on the wall, one of which, a triptych, showed him breaking a small concrete brick in two with his bare hand gripped in a fist. He was said to play the bars for the young impressionable women new to jurisprudence, scoring more often than not, considering himself a real ladies' man, though Boldt doubted real ladies ever looked his way.

"Lieutenant." Geiser's voice sounded sadly misplaced—a nasal-prone adolescent stuck in a forty-year-old's well-conditioned body, a voice useful in court no doubt, but lost on conversation.

"You mind?" Boldt asked, indicating Geiser's door.

Judging by his eyes, Geiser did mind, though he nodded. Boldt shut the door, moved a pile of papers aside without asking, and took a seat. By moving that pile, he wanted Geiser to understand he was taking charge. As a rule, attorneys believed they could win any argument. Boldt was here to prove that wrong.

"You're familiar with David Hayes," Boldt began.

"I convicted him. What's this about?"

"Are you aware we found blood evidence in a cabin north of the city that we believe will come back positive for Hayes?"

"Yes, I am. Have you found a body yet? No?"

Boldt fought the urges that rushed to the surface, forcing an artificial calm in their place, believing it a mistake to confront Geiser on his prints being lifted from the videotape, because according to Foreman, Geiser didn't know the content of the video. There was no sense in bringing his attention to it. Boldt toed a tentative line between exploration and revelation.

"I could use a favor," he said, beginning to walk that line. Attorneys loved negotiation.

"What kind of favor?"

Geiser wore frameless glasses, a thin length of silver wire hooking behind each ear. He'd lost two front teeth—to the martial arts perhaps—their unnatural white giving his ironic smile a glint that drew Boldt's eye. Boldt did not find him handsome, but saw how some might. He had an intensity about him. The type of man who might go unnoticed when entering a room and yet would later commandeer the conversation at the dinner table; not exactly charming, but not feckless either.

"You must have associates, within the USAO for instance, with whom you're on good terms." Boldt knew Geiser's failure to reach the U.S. Attorney's Office had to weigh heavily on the man, and tried to say this in a tone that did not imply he was taking a shot at him.

"Go on."

"I need a case looked into. Quietly, if at all possible. There's a situation—it could help us both—that apparently involves a federal ruling in favor of a position held by Fish and Wildlife."

"You must know a few people over there yourself," Geiser said. Not to be fooled, Boldt thought. "We've both been in this work a long time, eh, Lieutenant?"

"Yes, of course I do. But an inquiry coming from me is completely different than one from you."

"Not necessarily. It depends on the request."

"Yasmani Svengrad," Boldt said, watching intently for a tic or other reaction, trying to drop it like a bomb so that Geiser couldn't protect himself, knowing full well that experienced attorneys taught themselves to never visually react to *any* news, no matter the surprise.

"The Sturgeon General." Geiser disappointed Boldt with his placid expression. "You *are* in the shit if you're messing with Svengrad."

"I'm not messing with anyone. I'm exploring the strengths and merits of a federal injunction preventing Svengrad from importing and selling caviar."

"So the question that needs to be asked is why would you, a Seattle police lieutenant of some note, care what happens to the alleged don of this city's Russian mafia?"

Boldt opened the bomb bay doors and dropped number two. "I think Svengrad may be the one whose seventeen million went missing."

This won only a protracted stare from Geiser. "How certain are you?"

"Entirely speculative. But if I . . . if *we,* you and I . . . could use the lifting of that injunction as a carrot, something to bring to the table, I have a feeling we might win more than we lose."

"IRS wants him on tax fraud. The injunction is nothing but a stall while they sharpen their pencils."

"Then you're familiar with the case?"

"That Internal Revenue is investigating S&G and Svengrad, yes. But don't ask me in public, because I'll deny it. As to this other possibility you've just now surfaced, no. That's news to me."

"Interested?"

"Interested enough to keep listening."

"Do you know Svengrad?"

"By reputation." Geiser clearly felt Boldt's accusatory

tone. "One of his guys surfaced as our primary in the Radley Trevor case."

Boldt, along with everyone else in Seattle law enforcement, knew the Radley Trevor case. A twelve-year-old boy found buried alive, presumably held hostage for ransom. Boldt remembered now the whispers of Russian mob during the course of that investigation. His chest seized with the thought of his own children.

"Do you believe it possible that the seventeen million was his?"

"Anything's possible, Lieutenant. The IRS plays it close to the vest, but let's assume their case revolves around laundering or offshore accounts—that would dovetail nicely with your theory. We know for a fact that David Hayes intercepted at least one wire transfer from a dummy account at WestCorp intended for a Bahamian bank. That would fit what you're suggesting."

"I'm under the impression that if we get the injunction lifted Svengrad will provide information concerning several assaults we're working. Might possibly even hand over a suspect." This wasn't Boldt's impression at all, but instead that if the injunction were lifted, if Liz cooperated in transferring the seventeen million, then his family would be spared bloodshed. Until he found a way around this, a solution that might keep Liz out of it, he pursued the obvious.

"I'm not sure how that helps the prosecuting attorney's office exactly," Geiser said. "My interest is . . . ?"

"We prosecute a man responsible for tearing the fingernails off of at least two individuals, and quite possibly for holding the LaRossa family hostage."

"Your wife is going to help them, isn't she, Lieutenant?" Geiser dropped a bomb of his own. "Svengrad's turning the

screws, is he? Since when does a Homicide lieutenant rec-
ommend aborting a multidepartmental federal investigation
in order to apprehend a subordinate, some thug who
slapped a few people around?"

"Since one of those he slapped around was a state investigator."

"Danny Foreman and I discussed running your wife,
Lieutenant. He detailed to me the contact made by Hayes,
both by phone and in person, and we agreed that your wife
remained our best bet of busting open this case. Now you
show up in my office, just after our primary suspect dis-
appears in a pool of blood, looking to help a mobster who
may be behind the whole case? What exactly is my reaction
supposed to be?"

Boldt experienced the rare sensation of being pushed
back onto his heels. He was usually the one doing the pushing, not the other way around. "My wife's cooperation is
not out of the question at this point."

"If Svengrad got to you, Lieutenant, the right and proper
course of action is to seek protection. I can help with that,
as can the USAO. What you do not want to attempt is to
manage this yourself. *Physician, heal thyself.* Don't believe
it. That's a mistake. If you came here seeking my help, if
you're concerned about confidentiality, I can assure you
that as of this moment I can and will consider you a client."

Boldt realized he had to push back now. "When's the
last time you spoke to David Hayes?"

"An individual *identifying himself* as Hayes telephoned
me night before last. He said he wanted to cut a deal and
suggested we should meet. Why?"

This matched with what Foreman had told Boldt. "And
did you meet up with him?"

"It wasn't Hayes. I couldn't confirm it was Hayes calling me. In light of these assaults, I thought it a more prudent course of action *not* to take too many risks. I reached the rendezvous, but then left ahead of time. Left quickly. I never met with Hayes."

"Danny Foreman received a similar call. Are you aware of that?"

"I am. You look puzzled."

"Hayes makes pleas to both you and Foreman and within hours is bludgeoned or tortured, perhaps to death. Is there, was there, wire surveillance in place on that cabin?"

"I'm unaware of any. But Foreman is certainly in a position to have bypassed me and gone directly to an Assistant U.S. Attorney. My federal colleagues are far more facile when it comes to granting surveillance."

"If not a wiretap . . ." Boldt said, intentionally not completing his thought.

"Yes, I see," Geiser said. "Then either Foreman or I would have been the source of such information to whoever did the punishing. One of us leaks that Hayes wants to cut a deal, and someone—let's say Svengrad—steps in and teaches him a lesson in loyalty."

"Or kills him," Boldt said.

"Or that."

"Which makes that person party to capital murder." Nothing had gone as Boldt had foreseen or hoped. He wasn't any closer to lifting the injunction against Svengrad, and instead of pinning down Geiser he felt as if he were coming away partially trusting the man. His detective's sense told him it was time to check both Foreman's and Geiser's alibis for the night Hayes had been assaulted.

"So if you passed on the offer to meet Hayes, that left you where two nights ago?"

"Are you accusing me of something, Lieutenant?" Geiser seemed genuinely amused. "I'm offering to protect you, and you're accusing me? Of what? Bludgeoning David Hayes? I'm a black belt, Lieutenant. If I wanted to hurt or kill David Hayes—or anyone else for that matter—I would never make such a mess of it. You just bit the hand that was feeding you. I'm going to ask you to leave now. I will keep what we discussed, in terms of you and your wife, in confidence, but I warn you again: Do *not* take on Yasmani Svengrad by yourself. In all likelihood, that's what David Hayes seemed to have tried, does it not? And just look what it got him."

"We don't know what it got him."

"Not yet we don't. And if Svengrad doesn't want us to, then we never will."

□ □ □

Boldt and Liz were just sitting down to reheated gourmet dinners from the Whole Foods in the U District when the home phone rang. Neither knew when or even if the call to Liz was coming, so each ringing of the phone brought its own sense of dread. Boldt answered.

"Lieutenant? Sergeant Szumowski. Front desk."

"Yes."

"Sorry to bother you with this, but I just got me a caller asking for your mobile or home number. When I refused to give them out, this individual made me write down a message for you, word for word. You want the message?"

"Read it to me, please."

"Okay. Here goes." Szumowski cleared his throat as if auditioning for a part. " 'Has your wife watched any good movies lately? If so, you might want to let me have your numbers when I call back.' " He waited through a good deal of silence. "Lieutenant?"

"Did you get a caller-ID, Sergeant?" By agreement with the phone company, every call that came into SPD showed its caller-ID, even if the line owner subscribed to call-blocking. But not every caller-ID number was written down.

"I did, yes."

"Run that number and get back to me the moment you have a location."

"Yes, sir." Szumowski paused. "As to that other thing, sir. How should I handle that? Giving out your numbers and all."

"If he calls back before you get back to me, then yes, give him my mobile." Boldt recited it for the man, sparing him the need to look it up in the SPD directory.

"Right back at you, Lieutenant." Szumowski hung up.

"Lou?"

"Looks like I'm going out," Boldt told Liz. "I'll ask Gaynes to come inside with you. That'll still leave the cruiser and Heiman's unmarked out front."

"I don't need babysitting."

"Not up for discussion," Boldt said, and the air froze between them.

A moment later the wall phone rang, and Boldt answered. He scribbled down the physical address for the phone that had made the strange call. A bar in Fremont, only a few minutes by car from the Boldt home. He now knew where the call had come from; the caller didn't know he knew. He felt a flutter in his chest.

"They may have made their first mistake," Boldt told Liz, who appeared frightened. But then he saw it not as fright, but doubt—a keen and penetrating doubt—and as he replayed this statement in his own head, even he found the sound of it foolish.

□ □ □

Fire codes required all commercial businesses to provide a minimum of two points of egress. No cop in his right mind walked through the front door of a establishment like Tanker's Tavern when looking for a possible suspect. Even in blue jeans and a dark windbreaker, as he was currently dressed, Boldt knew he stuck out, indelibly marked *cop*. Not to mention that whoever had called for him had the advantage of knowing what he looked like. Boldt entered the bar's back door off an alley marked by dented Dumpsters and stacks of beer bottles awaiting recycling. The door opened onto a narrow hallway offering a men's room and women's room, marked TANKED and TANK TOPS, a battered pay phone, and an empty cigarette vending machine missing a front leg. Someone had key-scratched the words BLACK LUNG across the glass of the vending machine.

Boldt moved furtively down this narrow hall, alert for someone to spring out from the men's room unexpectedly, attempting to grab him up. The miles he wore as lines around his eyes accounted for years of experience, qualities that could never be taught at the police academy or in college classrooms. They eventually instilled themselves as instinct, a kind of sixth sense of knowing when danger loomed. Boldt was not big on belief in a sixth sense, and yet he possessed the unusual ability to "see" crime scenes through the eyes of the victim, a faculty that he kept to himself, knowing others would not understand. He moved ahead with heightened senses, smelling the stale beer, disinfectant, and cigarette smoke, hearing the background grind of rock and roll behind loud conversation, seeing the spinning overhead fans in a kind of slow motion, the flickering television screen playing a football game, the bartender patrolling his narrow aisle between the regimented bottles and the cronies on stools, bent on elbows glued to the wooden bar that separated them from their spirits.

Mixed into this clamor, the faint but distinguishable ring of a telephone, a sound that Boldt's brain elected to single out and bring to the forefront of his consciousness. Why, he wasn't sure.

He stood with his back to a corner, the barroom now open before him. Pinball and a video game in a small room to his left, circular tables, mostly full, in front of him. Glassy-eyed men drinking beer. Women of every type, from fully available and advertising, to withdrawn and hurt, relationships forming and disintegrating before him.

From the din a word so incongruous in this setting that at first he fully ignored it, believing his brain was playing tricks on him, or perhaps not hearing at all. Not feeling. The events of late had numbed him, like a limb falling asleep and tingling without the ability to feel or stand. "Boldt?" a male voice called. Still his brain refused to process the information correctly. "Boldt?" Again.

He turned toward that voice. The bartender, his mustache and curly hair reflected in the mirror behind the bottles. He held a phone's receiver, standing at the end of the bar, by a waitress with more cleavage showing than necessary, a tray filled with empties in her hand.

Boldt wondered if by identifying himself, he marked himself for abduction and a "manicure," or if the call were actually a call meant for him. Then it slammed home: He'd been led here like a dog in heat, the caller to the police department knowledgeable enough to know how Boldt would proceed, that he would request the caller-ID information and investigate. And if not, what then? he wondered, believing a second or third call would have been placed, and eventually contact would have been made. But the caller had wanted this on neutral ground, someplace Boldt could not easily or quickly trace, and that implied either a substantial conversation or a threat that one wouldn't want recorded. The first name to pop into his head was Svengrad's, the Sturgeon General. When he accepted the phone and heard the metallic, distorted sound of voice synthesis, he felt caught off-guard. The caller was using a voice-altering device, readily available from Radio Shack, that made his voice sound inhuman, like a robot.

"Well done, Lieutenant," the Darth Vader voice said. It sounded vaguely comical, and had the circumstances been different, he might have experienced it as such. As it was, he suffered under the realization he'd been sucker-punched.

Not Svengrad, Boldt decided immediately. He couldn't see the Russian wanting to obscure his identity— Svengrad's power and authority came out of his personage. Why hide it?

Boldt resented his being so predictable, so easily baited.

"Why the cloak-and-dagger?"

"You have forty-five minutes to retrieve the software carried by Tony LaRossa when he collapsed in the bank lobby. I need your cell phone number. I'll contact you."

"I don't think so." Boldt hung up the call. The bartender flashed him an expression that asked if he was done with the phone. Boldt held up a finger, begging more time. He asked if this bar phone was used a lot by customers. The bartender replied that the one in the hall hadn't worked in over a year.

"Anyone make a call from here about an hour ago?" Boldt asked.

"I don't pay much attention."

"You paid attention to me," Boldt said.

"I don't know you."

"Know most of your customers, do you?"

"Part of the job."

Boldt said, "Including the guy who used this phone about an hour ago?"

The bartender offered a smug look. Boldt flashed his shield, and the man's composure wavered. He pulled out a twenty, and then another, and laid them both on the bar.

"Put it away," the man said, somewhat apologetically. "I came on thirty minutes ago. I have no idea who used the phone an hour ago."

"Someone we can check with?" Boldt inquired.

"Listen, it's so damn busy in here between five and seven, there's no way anyone's going to be able to help you."

"I don't believe that."

"Okay, listen . . ." The bartender stood within inches of the bar and leaned toward Boldt. "Truth is, officer, the hall phone is kinda wired into the house line. It don't ring there; it rings here. But customers dial out on the hall phone."

"And the house pockets the money from the pay phone."

"Something like that. Hey, I'm not the owner."

"So unless you were in the hall, you wouldn't know who used the phone."

"That's about it."

The phone rang. The bartender reached for the receiver, but Boldt held him off. "This is for me." Boldt yanked up the receiver. "Boldt."

That same synthetic voice said, "Your wife has nice hands. You hang up again, she's wearing gloves for the next six months, and her little pussy dance is on the evening news."

"I don't talk to robots," Boldt said. Inside, he decided he'd gone too far. He wasn't sure what had possessed him to hang up the first time, to feign a lack of cooperation, except that it went so against his nature. This was, he decided, the call Liz had been expecting, except that the first step was apparently to collect the coveted software. Boldt had read two department e-mails on the analysis of the LaRossa disk. The first expressed optimism that the password cryptography on the disk could be "cracked." The second explained in some detail the sophistication of the security protecting the software contained on the disk, and how it was never going to be compromised.

The bartender overheard Boldt's comment, twisted his face, and walked away to service a customer.

"Forty-five minutes. Your cell number."

Boldt repeated his cell number into the phone.

"You do this alone, or it all comes back on you and yours. Tomorrow, next week, next month—listen, you'd better keep looking over your shoulder if you bring others in on it, or do anything but what I say."

"You don't know me very well," Boldt said, again won-dering why his mouth got ahead of his brain.

The line went dead. Boldt hung up the receiver. The guy was smart, and that worried him.

He called Pahwan Riz, the Special Operations com-mander, before he even reached the Crown Vic. Hell if he was doing this alone. He could smell a trap a mile away.

□ □ □

Discovering himself the target of a surveillance operation left Boldt with mixed feelings. He couldn't remember ever having been on the receiving end of such attentions, and he found it off-putting. The arrangements were made hast-ily, primarily because of the time restrictions imposed by his anonymous caller, but the brilliance of some of these guys never ceased to amaze him, and by the time he bumped the Crown Vic into the restricted parking garage attached to the Public Safety Building, the operation was already well under way.

Suspecting, but not quite willing to believe, that who-ever had called him might have civilians paid off within the department—spies—he obeyed Pahwan Riz's chore-ography to the letter. The Crown Vic was already equipped with GPS transmission equipment because, like patrol cruisers, it carried a Mobile Data Terminal on the dash— the equivalent of a built-in laptop computer that allowed text to be sent to and from the car. Limousine services and some taxis, parcel delivery and express delivery vans, all carried similar equipment—and all contained the satellite tracking device allowing dispatchers to locate any vehicle at a moment's notice.

The trick was to get some of this same equipment—a small GPS and a voice-recording device—onto Boldt without him being descended upon by technicians. Riz's solution was to leave the equipment in a men's room stall, and to direct Boldt to visit the rest room upon his arrival at SPD, which he did. From the bathroom, now wearing the two devices, he proceeded directly to Property and signed out for the bright red disk that had been in the possession of Tony LaRossa as he'd collapsed from his heart attack. He took the man's bank ID access card as well, already foreseeing its future use. With Boldt being lieutenant in charge of Crimes Against Persons, there wasn't anything the Property sergeant was going to deny him. He signed the requisite forms, accepted the plastic bags bearing the chain of possession, all carefully detailed in indelible marker, and returned to the Crown Vic at a slow jog, moving a few uniformed officers out of his way while checking his watch on the fly. Ten minutes in which to reach the exit of I-5 north.

Whoever had planned this for him had timed it to within seconds. He knew immediately that the drop was to be just as perfectly timed, that he would be pushed right to the limit to accommodate the demands.

As it was, he hit the street with the pedal down, built-in grill and window lights pulsing the blinding blue light, clearing traffic.

Eight minutes to go. It would be a miracle, but he just might make it.

Several miles above him, in the cold black void of space, satellites tracked his every turn, and Pahwan Riz—in the steam-cleaning van, with a team of four unmarked vehicles—followed at a distance, never letting Boldt out of his sight.

SIXTEEN

THE KNOCK ON THE BACK door sounded like a gunshot as it banged off the walls of the kitchen and ran through Liz like a jolt of electricity.

"It's okay," said Bobbie Gaynes, a wire in her ear leading from a walkie-talkie. "It's Officer Foreman, BCI. I'll get the door. You sit tight."

Liz had made them both some Red Zinger tea, and she noticed the steam in the light of a lamp as it swirled and tried to follow Gaynes, dissipating a few inches from the cup. She felt this way too—her energy fading the longer Lou stayed away. First the kids, then Lou. She felt as if all the love in this home had lost its way. She blew on her own tea and took a sip and returned the mug to the coaster, noticing that it shook slightly in her grip and wondering how much more of this she could endure.

She heard Danny Foreman's sonorous voice interspersed with the female chimes of Gaynes's and, a moment later, the back door thump shut. Foreman entered the living room asking if she had a minute. He carried what looked like a silver Palm Pilot in hand, and kept it in his lap as he sat down. He looked tired and worn. He glanced over at Gaynes's mug of tea, grabbed hold, and drank from it, savoring the taste. She found his brazenness disturbing and thought it some kind of sign, a signal that she should have interpreted more clearly.

"Where to start?" he asked, peering over the mug as he took a second noisy sip.

"Lou's not here," she said.

"I'm up to speed on that."

"I'm not. Not exactly."

"He's busy."

"Well, that certainly clarifies things."

"It's to our benefit he's occupied."

"Is it?"

"What I'm about to tell you is strictly confidential. I can only assume that a banker knows all about confidentiality, and I can only hope that despite what I presume to be your loyalty and devotion to your husband, you *keep* this confidential."

"Message received." She made no agreement, extremely careful of her word selection. Lou had warned her to expect such a meeting; how he anticipated such things was beyond her, but she was glad for it now.

"It affects us all, Liz, and is not to be taken lightly."

"Do you think I'm taking *any* of this lightly?"

Foreman returned an unsympathetic stare.

"I know how painful the past is for you, Danny. We're alike in that way, I think. We're both stuck. And I'll tell you something, I'm not going to help you, or Lou, or anyone with this investigation for the sake of the investigation. I want to get unstuck. That's all I care about. So if you're

looking for a helping hand, you've picked the wrong time
for me."

"Paul Geiser and I were behind the disappearance of
David Hayes." He threw it out and let it wrap itself around
her until she found it hard to breathe. He continued, "We
had to get him off the radar of a major player, a guy you
don't need to know about. But it had to be done. Hayes
wanted to cut a deal to turn state's witness—and if you, or
Lou, or anyone else questions Paul, I guarantee you he'll
pull a Sergeant Schultz on you. He'll deny any knowledge
of any of this, as well he should. Hayes has agreed to
recover the missing money and to implicate the man whose
money it was. We're assuming that you've been compromised either by Hayes or this bigger player, and I don't
need you to answer that either way, but the reason Lou is
not being included in on this is just that: because we believe you've been compromised. Lou is so by-the-book that
we didn't trust he'd agree to let you run this software for
Hayes. I'm here to plead with you to do just that. In a very
short time Hayes will have the software necessary to pull
this off. Once he does, we can assign a government account
as the destination account. You can wire that money over
to the government instead of risking it disappearing again.
Do so, and it's done. Hayes gets his plea, the player goes
away, and your life gets back to normal." He paused to let
her absorb the scenario. "Sunday night, before the reception, you will receive the instructions either here at your
home or on your cell. You follow them to the letter, and
it's over."

Liz wasn't sure what to make of Danny Foreman. She
felt a wild pounding in her chest, like she'd run, or swum

underwater a great distance, and only now stopped for a breath.

"We faked a bloody crime scene," Foreman said.

"And called Lou out to it."

"Had to be convincing. If it convinced Lou, and I think it did, then we've established a perimeter of protection."

"And you're telling me this because . . ." She fished for the logic behind it, then answered the question herself. "Because regardless of the destination account number I'm given, you want the money wired back to this government account you set up."

"That's it exactly."

"Would you have let Darlene do something like this?"

"If it put you at risk I wouldn't ask you to do this. You must know that, Liz."

She snorted involuntarily. "I don't believe that. I believe you'd do anything necessary to get at this money, whatever your motivation."

She watched his nostrils flare, saw the effort involved in holding himself in check. He could ill afford to allow his emotions to show, to raise his voice with her. This reserve in him had the odd effect in her of reversing her own sense of helplessness. He *needed* her. They all *needed* her. She and her access to the AS/400s were the key to the investigation. Danny Foreman would have tried every way possible to circumvent her participation and thereby risk Lou's involvement. This was a desperate man in the midst of a desperate act. Liz had seen this situation a hundred times as an executive and had taken advantage of her position more often than not. Only as Foreman contained himself, did she regain her strength.

"Hayes believed you could be trusted. Maybe he was wrong."

"You can do better than that, Danny."

"What are you willing to do about this, Liz? How much are you willing to risk?"

His question cut her to the quick. Scandal. Embarrassment. Her job. Her family. She found it her turn to cover what she felt inside, and quickly realized the game of give and take that was under way. A tingling sensation raced up the back of her neck as she realized the power she held over this man, and also what was at stake: the survival of her marriage and her family.

"I don't know to whom you're referring. David?"

"It doesn't matter who we're talking about," Foreman said. "It's what we call 'the juice' that counts. What it is they have. The tape." She felt herself blush. Danny Foreman had certainly viewed the tape, as it had once been in his possession. He'd seen her naked. Doing things. Somehow she'd blocked out this truth, and the sudden realization shook her, even frightened her in a weird kind of way. He had "the juice" on her too. How was he looking at her now? Without her clothes? Engaged? She felt sick to her stomach.

"Thing is," Foreman continued, "would Lou risk his career to save you? I think he would." As he said this she saw through cracks in the veneer. Danny Foreman resented Lou, whether because Danny had lost his own wife to cancer, or because Lou had achieved that rare reputation in law enforcement of being one of the best and a decent man at the same time. Danny's own career had suffered following Darlene's death.

Liz said, "Lou would never bend the rules, even for me, and you know it. That's what bothers you, isn't it? You can't get to him."

"This isn't about Lou. It's about you. You can handle it. You can put these people away. Paul Geiser and I are your answer, your only way out of this. I promise you. Think through whatever it is that Lou's telling you, and you'll come back to this time and time again. David Hayes is working for us, and as long as he's working for us, we control it. Not Lou, not even Hayes himself."

"And so you fool Lou with the cabin torture to . . . What? Keep the straight arrow out of your game?"

"It's all about leaks," Foreman said. "It's hard enough to contain something like this with three people."

"Do you actually think I won't tell Lou?"

"I think you'll do what you have to. Lou is a cop, a good cop, Liz. You give him this kind of information, he's going to run with it. Will he let you do this? Finish this? I doubt that. But if you do it without him—if you divert the funds into this government account, then it's over. The player's name is Yasmani Svengrad, Liz. A hard-core criminal who rolls over anyone and anything in his way. He's a heartless son of a bitch. Just ask Beth LaRossa. You think you can work with him? What happens if you do? When you're done getting him his money, do you think it will end then? You think that tape will get destroyed, that he'll forget all about it? He'll *own* you *and* Lou. He'll know your weak spot because it worked once. Plus he'll have evidence against you for helping him and he'll *use* it against you to do another transfer, another wire, establish a fraudulent account. You roll a rock like that downhill and you will *never* stop it. But I can stop it for you. Me, Liz. Not Lou."

"Do you think I can do anything without half of SPD knowing about it? How many layers did you have to pass through to see me tonight? They've built a wall around me. I'm not doing anything, going anywhere, without Lou knowing it. And Lou won't have it. Even if I *wanted* to, Danny." She tried to make it sound as if she did want to, but this was far from the truth. Lou had something going. She knew him well enough to know this. "Damned if I do, damned if I don't," she muttered, more to herself than anything.

He checked that Palm Pilot in his lap, slipped a folded piece of paper out of his shirt pocket. His cell phone number, he explained. Hayes was putting this together as they spoke. If he or Hayes contacted her, the account number given would be the government account. If anyone else directed her what to do, she was to call Foreman immediately.

Danny's offer sounded tempting despite everything Lou had warned her about. Hide the money from the thugs; put everyone in jail. Wasn't that what Lou wanted?

"Remember to call me," Foreman said and let himself out.

SEVENTEEN

BOLDT PULLED INTO THE WEDGE of white hash marks separating the northbound lane of I-5 from the NE 45th Street exit ramp leading into the U District, believing whoever was behind this was ingenious for his choice of locations. The highway traffic to his left moved at sixty miles an hour or better, the exit traffic to his right only slightly slower given that it was a multiple-lane ramp. The SPD car following him was forced to drive past, remaining on I-5. By the same token, whoever was behind this could also drive right past, Boldt never the wiser. He thought it more promising that his mystery man was parked with a good view of his position, monitoring him, interpreting the degree to which he was willing to cooperate. If this person wanted him off the highway, he could direct him to exit right. If he wanted him back on the highway, that was possible too.

Boldt waited.

He answered his purring cell phone with a steady voice despite the way he felt inside. Pahwan Riz spoke his rank. "Lieutenant."

"I'm assuming you lost visual," Boldt said. "That's okay, Reece."

"Affirmative. Give us about three minutes, we'll have someone break down in the opposite lane."

"Too obvious."

"Let me do my job."

"My terms. That was the agreement."

"Which is why I'm doing the service of calling you," Riz explained. A commander, Riz was not used to taking orders.

"You'll have to do better than a breakdown in the opposing lane, that's all I'm saying. They'll spot that in a heartbeat." His own heart beat somewhat frantically. Boldt longed for a cup of tea. It never failed to settle his nerves.

"We've got you on radar," Riz said, meaning the Global Positioning System. "We'll stay with that for the moment, circle the wagons, and let you come to us." Boldt found this acceptable. Riz would establish perimeter surveillance positions and wait for Boldt either to drive past one of his people or to provide the team the color of a car or a description of the individual who showed up to receive the encrypted computer disk.

Boldt's cell phone beeped in his ear, indicating call waiting—an incoming call. He told Riz to sit tight and answered this second call, placing Riz on hold in the process. The synthesized voice named another location. "I-5 south. The Boeing Access Road exit. Pull into the wedge between the highway and the exit lane and await instructions. You have seven minutes." The line went dead.

An unreasonably short amount of time. Boldt jerked the wheel right, getting off the exit in order to cross and return in the southbound lanes. Once onto the highway, he'd have to invoke his siren and dashboard bubble flasher if he were to make it on time. He switched the phone call back to Riz. "I'm heading south toward Boeing Field."

"We've got you," Riz said. Again, Boldt believed he meant they could see him on the GPS system.

"Visual?" Boldt asked.

"Negative. Will have any minute. I'm signing off for now. Hang in there, Lieutenant." The phone clicked and Riz was gone.

Somewhere, somehow, this man who ran him intended for Boldt to pass the disk or make a drop. But with Riz's team lurking a short distance away, it seemed unlikely a runner could get very far without becoming a target of the same surveillance. Boldt brought the Crown Vic up to eighty-five miles per hour on his way toward the bridge. Even in light traffic, he'd have to slow somewhat when he reached the narrowing stretch of highway that ran through the city. He wondered how the drop would be engineered, confident in the abilities of Riz's team.

Boldt understood better than anyone the precarious situation he was in. He had to control Hayes's software in order to ensure the recovery and transfer of the money, if he were to safeguard his family. He still hadn't settled on a way to allow Liz to help Svengrad, but no matter what, this software was the key. His inclusion of Special Operations was mandated by the fact that someone wanted him to make that drop in the first place. If Svengrad or Hayes were behind this plan, then why not just have Boldt remove the software from the property room and hand it over to his wife? Why bother with this elaborate and risky scheme? The first answer that came to Boldt was that Svengrad or

Hayes had determined a way to get the money out of the bank without Liz's involvement. He/they needed the software, but not Liz. This didn't make a lot of sense, since Svengrad had taken an enormous risk by pressuring Boldt for his wife's involvement. And if not Svengrad or Hayes, then who, and why? Boldt couldn't make the drop without knowing this, and he couldn't know this without Special Operations.

The second thought that came to him was this elaborate plan was simply a way for Svengrad to protect Boldt from being seen as cooperating, a way to tangle up the investigation. Handing the software to Liz would signal the endgame, would give investigators a head start on surveillance of every kind. Boldt's cooperation in that event might be construed as a criminal act. At some point Boldt would answer for that. A shiver ran through him as it occurred to him that Svengrad had wanted to protect him merely because he was a police lieutenant, a Homicide lieutenant at that, and a good cop to have in your pocket. Had this drop been orchestrated merely to make Boldt look less culpable than he really was? This idea hit him hard—that he was now seen as an asset by the Russian mob, a turned cop worth preserving.

He slowed and stopped the car in the triangle of paint that separated the highway from the exit ramp. He wiped his brow with a Starbucks napkin. Raindrops on the windshield grew in size. Boldt switched on the wipers. A semi-truck rolled by, the concussion of its wake rocking Boldt's car. He pulled ahead a few feet and angled the car slightly, pointing in toward the highway traffic.

His mobile phone rang. The caller-ID read OUT OF

AREA. No number to trace. He answered the call, but the reception made it impossible to hear.

"Wait!" he shouted into the phone, afraid he might miss an instruction, his eyes fixed on the flickering small black bars indicating reception. He hurried out of the car, into the rain, running up a slight embankment, his head aimed up, looking hopefully at the phone's signal indicator as it moved from one bar to two and then three. He clamped it to his ear and said, "Is this any better?"

"Don't fuck with me," the eerie electronic voice warned.

"I'm not," Boldt shouted.

"Webster's," the voice said. "It's a bar just south of northeast Forty-fifth on Brooklyn."

"I'll find it."

"Leave your phone on. And come alone." The line died.

Boldt was still looking up into the wet night sky, eyes searching for a cell tower's blinking red light when something winked at him through the rain. *Binoculars?*

Boldt moved his head, trying to force that wink to appear a second time. And there it was! Another wink of light from a spot slightly above the overpass. Some spy looking down, perched in a tree beyond? he wondered. But then he saw it again. Not a person at all. A camera lens mounted high atop an aluminum light post. A *traffic cam*.

He was being watched, but from a distance. Cell phone in hand, he wanted badly to make a call but thought better of it, not knowing if in the rain and the dark that camera could see him or not, but not wanting to test it. He headed back to the car at a run, slipping once on the wet grass, smearing his knee down into the muddy incline, and jumping back up. He hurried toward the car realizing the traffic camera, if accessible from the Internet, which he was guessing would prove to be the case, allowed those running him to look for ground surveillance while at the same time confirming Boldt did exactly as he was told. Big Brother, and in the hands of the wrong people.

Back in the car, yanking the wheel to make the exit ramp so he could reverse directions and return to the very exit where he'd been parked only ten minutes earlier, Boldt pulled the phone to his ear to report his situation. But the idea that the person on the other end of these calls might not be Svengrad or Hayes stayed with him, and for a moment he resisted connecting with Riz. The idea of a third party, an unknown, instilled fear. On some level, Boldt believed he could fight the enemies he could see—but was he putting the kids or Liz even further at risk if this proved to be an unknown? He took a moment to think.

As he drove, he typed the bar's name into the Mobile Data Terminal to confirm its existence. After a long hesitation the computer's tiny screen returned:

> *DO YOU MEAN: "Web-Stirs, 1100 NE 45th Street" ??? (Y)es (N)o ?*

Boldt pushed Y, and the terminal offered to compute the quickest course, but Boldt declined, well aware that I-5 was the fastest way there.

Web-Stirs, he realized, was an Internet bar, and now he raced to conclusions. Weighing risks, he nonetheless called Pahwan Riz and caught him up to date on the traffic camera and his next destination being an Internet café. Before Boldt was off the phone Riz had confirmed that the traffic camera he'd seen was one of about fifty viewable live on the state's highway website. Whoever had arranged this was able to watch Boldt move place to place in the comfort of his living room. It made him feel all the more like a pawn and brought his blood pressure considerably higher.

"I'm not liking this," Riz said. "An *Internet* café. Get it?"

Boldt was no techno-wizard unless it related to the crime lab, an area where few could outdo him. "No."

"Ingenious."

"How so?"

"David Hayes? Web-Stirs an Internet café? That means a small office network hub, a router. Simple stuff. For a guy who could probably hack the Pentagon, kid's stuff."

"He'll hack the computer network at the bar," Boldt said, feeling his way through this.

"He has long since hacked the network. He's established drive sharing on one or more of the machines. This guy is *good,*" Riz said with a distant respect. "What he's going to do is direct you to a particular machine. You'll insert the disk, and the rest will be history, he'll take it from there. He'll enter the correct password that we could never determine, copy the disk, reformat it, destroying all its contents. Brilliant."

"Can we stop praising him and start figuring out some way to prevent this?"

"No," Riz answered. "Not unless you simply refuse to show up."

"That's not an option."

"I'm aware of that."

"He's got us?" Boldt asked.

"He's got us," Riz confirmed. "You're about to turn over the software to him."

The Crown Vic screamed over the bridge through the

pouring rain, Boldt bothered not only by what he heard, but by something else, something intangible, indefinable, like a moving shadow. *Highways?* he wondered. *Cars? Websites?* Something in the back of his mind that he couldn't quite pull forward.

Riz, on the other hand, proved prescient, and for the first time a tingle of suspicion entered Boldt's thought that a police insider like Riz could mastermind all of this from behind the scenes, no one ever the wiser. Make it all seem like the work of someone else while this person manipulated events for his own personal wealth.

This thought churning inside him, Boldt parked and walked a wet block to Web-Stirs, a glass and tile, ultra hip, ultra modern interior with colorful graphics and odd shapes hanging from the ceiling that Boldt assumed were meant to be art. A twenty-something bartender with slicked-back hair and black-framed nerd eyeglasses served food-coloring-hued mixed drinks in exotic plastic stemware. James Bond on a budget. The beer looked like a dark amber. The crowd was a surprising mix of women and men— Boldt had expected all men for no reason other than his own prejudices. The women showed their navels above their pants' waists, as provocative as the waitresses, one of whose buttocks cleavage showed when she bent to retrieve a fallen napkin.

His phone rang again and, for a second or two, Boldt debated what Riz had said, debated not answering it, or walking out of the bar altogether. But it was not to be. He answered the call, stuck the phone to his ear, and was dictated a simple instruction. "Machine in the corner, when it comes open. Insert the disk into the drive bay and walk away."

An Asian girl occupied the machine at the moment. Boldt wondered if the caller knew that, and what it meant if he did. Boldt scanned the room's ceiling for security cameras and spotted two in opposite corners, wondering if a hacker could gain access to these as well. His world felt smaller and more claustrophobic everywhere he went, people watching. The girl looked over her shoulder at him and smiled, and he wondered if she were a plant or an innocent. Then he wondered if there were any innocents anywhere, taken in again by the sexual, casual dress of these kids—from his angle it was nearly impossible not to look directly down the shirt of this Asian girl. He turned and walked toward the bar, keeping a fuzzy eye on her in the smoked-glass mirror behind the bar.

"Get you something?" the bartender asked.

"Hot tea to go?"

"Two doors down." The owner was not stupid enough to go up against the coffeehouses.

"Something soft," Boldt said.

The guy ran off a list of pop drinks and bubbling waters. Boldt requested a ginger ale. The Asian girl spun out of the chair. Impossibly tight pants wrapped around a firm body. She headed in Boldt's direction. He felt ancient in this company. He wondered if she were a messenger, a spy, a twenty-something prostitute. She walked right at him, her young nipples showing darkly through the T-shirt, the not-so-gentle sway of her hips emphasized by the low cut of the corduroy pants, the straight-cut black bangs so classic and timeless.

"Lieutenant Boldt?" she asked.

He felt a spike of heat, deciding someone had sent her, perhaps believing Boldt in need of a computer coach. He doubted immediately they'd ever trace the twenty or fifty he believed he'd find in her pocket to a suspect. At every turn the person behind this proved himself clever, and that pointed increasingly away from Svengrad and toward Hayes in Boldt's mind. No way he had died in that cabin horror.

She said, "I'm Ming Lee, a junior at the U. Your lecture series: The application of the physical sciences to the detection of crime . . . I made criminalistics my major."

Boldt felt catapulted into another realm. This bursting package of primal youth, a person he felt sure connected to the case, nothing but a secret admirer.

"What are you doing at Web's?" she inquired. Then she blushed, glanced around, and said in a forced whisper that proved just as loud as her normal voice, "Are you undercover or something? *Oh, my God!* How totally cool is that?" She stepped closer and again he looked away, for as short as she was, his aerial view left little to the imagination. "Did I just blow this, or what?"

"Nothing so dramatic as that," Boldt lied. "I live near here and our home computer went down. That's all. Missing some e-mail."

"You gonna have a drink?" she asked, and he expected that the next thing out of her mouth was going to be her coming on to him and he didn't know what to make of that. So-called badgers came in every age, every ethnicity, but usually went for the young, hard, and handsome men in uniform.

"Nonalcoholic," he said. "I'm on duty." Immediately regretting the pat response.

"I thought you said your home computer went down . . ." Then she blushed again. *"Oh, my God,"* she repeated, covering her mouth. "I'm so sorry." Now more convinced than ever she'd interrupted an undercover op. "Can I sit with you?"

"I think not," Boldt said.

"I won't say a word."

"Better not," Boldt said. "We can discuss this at the next lecture."

"*After* the next lecture?" she pressed, and there was no mistaking that look in any woman's eyes, even a woman this young. He felt his face flush and his groin stir.

"Another time," he said. "Good to meet you, Ming." He stepped past her, leaving a whole other world behind him and wondering why a collision like this would present itself just now. Other than during his occasional teasing with Matthews, no woman had openly flirted with him in at least a decade, certainly not a child. The repartee with Matthews had ground to a halt once she'd attached herself to LaMoia. The implied interest of this *girl* nearly derailed his thought long enough for him to forget himself. But he moved to the computer terminal in the corner, sat down on the warm stool, reminded once again of his eager student, and leaned to slip the disk into the machine.

Within seconds the disk drive began to whir. With it, in Boldt's mind, a resurrection. Yes, David Hayes was very much alive.

□ □ □

Driving home twenty minutes later, the disk coming out of the machine blank, as Riz had anticipated, and Boldt momentarily blank along with it, Boldt crossed I-5 in the Crown Vic, catching sight of the painted triangle where he'd been pulled over and waiting for a call only an hour before. He yanked the wheel, hit the emergency flashers, and pulled over in traffic on westbound NE 45th.

"Command," Riz answered the phone.

"The Forty-fifth Street exit off I-5 north," Boldt said, without further introduction. "Is there a traffic cam that watches that location as well?" As Riz checked, Boldt ended the call and crossed the busy street and peered over a low rail at the interchange in question, his mind whirring. He had briefly held suspicions that Riz, or another SPD officer, was involved in this. It was certainly not beyond the realm of Yasmani Svengrad to "turn" a cop through extortion or threat, or to entice a cop with the smell of that kind of big money. Now, watching the highway traffic stream past, Boldt's phone rang and it was Riz.

"Affirmative," Riz said. "They had you in plain sight for both stops."

They discussed the possibility that Hayes might have been able to access Web-Stir's video security cameras, and Riz confirmed this possibility, "depending on the firmware they're using."

Working on the notion that the obvious is always the solution to a certain level of crime, and rarely the solution to sophisticated crime, Boldt placed a call to his department's traffic division. He felt like a spider carefully laying out his web while knowing all along his predatory victory amounted to little more than haphazard chance. The fly had to be in the room for the web to be effective.

Boldt requested any and all reports of breakdowns or accidents for late afternoon into the early evening hours of Wednesday on highway 520—the day Hayes had apparently been tortured—and Foreman had allegedly been stuck in traffic on state highway 520. A few minutes later he received the report. He disconnected the call and hurried back to the Crown Vic.

His phone purred as he climbed back inside behind the wheel.

"It's me." Liz.

"Hey."

"Everything okay?"

"In a manner of speaking. He . . . or someone else, has the software now. He did it smart, and we're not going to trace it."

"He?"

"We believe it's Hayes. There's only one thing left they need now."

"Access," she said. *Her.*

"Yes."

"That's why I'm calling," she said. She detailed Foreman's visit, leaving out nothing, including the Palm Pilot. "They made it look like torture and then they hid him. Danny's convinced they can bring in whoever's money it is, and then that's that. He suspected I'd tell you, but needs it kept confidential. Says Geiser will deny knowledge of any of it."

"SID found tooth chips, an excessive amount of blood, and pieces of two fingernails at that crime scene," Boldt told her. "That doesn't fit with what you're telling me."

"They wanted it to look right?"

"Maybe," Boldt allowed. Foreman and Geiser would both know the details of the other tortures. It suddenly explained to Boldt why he'd felt so uneasy about the Hayes crime scene—the lack of cigarette ash and shoeprints among the missing pieces.

"The thing is," Liz said, "if I am involved, if I do make

this wire transfer for someone, and I send the money to an account Danny specifies, where's that leave us if Danny doesn't catch Svengrad? The tape? The kids? You said these people are not to be toyed with."

"That's right," Boldt said, his head throbbing as he tried to set this straight in his thought. Once the tape went public, their lives—quite possibly their children's lives—would never be the same.

"I'll think of something."

"Danny was off, Lou. Wasn't himself."

"Pressuring you couldn't have been easy. It was right of you to tell me." Boldt figured Geiser had put him up to it. Paul Geiser was pulling the strings now. "Thank you for that."

"You don't sound convinced."

"You're going to get the call," he said. "We have to prepare for that."

"There's not much to prepare for. I wait and see what it is they ask me to do."

"There's a call I need you to make," Boldt said. "It'll have to be from your cell phone."

"What's going on, Lou?"

"Not now," he said, imagining his home line tapped. "Call me back from your cell phone." He took a moment to sign off politely and cradled the mobile phone in a cup holder.

He no longer trusted his own people.

□ □ □

There had been a time when rousting LaMoia, morning, noon, or night, would have been easy. Here was a cop who seemed to approach the job, each day, with youthful enthusiasm. The tougher the work, the better. The more risky, the better. But home life had changed all that, and Boldt resented Daphne Matthews taking that part of LaMoia from the job. Now LaMoia wanted to be home with Daphne and Margaret, a toddler who seemed destined to be swallowed by the state's child protection laws despite the loving care she was receiving from Matthews, who'd been assigned temporary guardianship. Only a state government could consider over fourteen months of daily care "temporary." But LaMoia felt the pressure, along with Matthews, of the child possibly being taken away, and the result was a man who never wanted to leave his loft condominium.

Boldt finally laid out his suspicions to LaMoia in a desperate act he'd hoped to avoid. It wasn't his way to voice those suspicions until he had more to go on than hunches. But none of this was going "his way," and so he resorted to outright manipulation, knowing LaMoia wouldn't be able to resist.

"Two visits in the same day. To what do I owe the pleasure?" Dressed in blue jeans and a plaid flannel shirt, Paul Geiser looked nothing like the attorney who occupied the small office in the Justice Building. He'd become so predictable in his gray suits, white shirts, and conservative ties, that this alter ego at the front door surprised Boldt. Geiser looked at them over a pair of dime-store reading glasses perched on the end of his nose.

He admitted Boldt and LaMoia with no reference to the late evening hour, no questions on why the surprise visit. "Beer? Coffee? Tea for you, Lieutenant?" He motioned for them to follow him when they failed to answer. Geiser might have lost the suit but not the swagger of confidence that epitomized prosecuting attorneys.

The room smelled of airplane glue, a potent odor that took Boldt back to his youth. "Models?"

"Close," Geiser said, impressed that Boldt had picked this up at such a distance.

The trio passed through another door and into a leather-and-mahogany paneled library that belonged in a faux English manor, not in this clapboard two-story with aluminum windows. The built-in stacks ran floor to ceiling, a trick chair unfolded into a small ladder in the far corner. But all of it looked purchased from a catalog instead of inherited. It was a would-be world in the heart of middle-class suburbia.

A dark leather globe stood in a stand next to the reproduction desk. Newsprint had been laid down to cover the desk, atop which a green glass bottle rested on its side. The first pieces of a ship's hull could be seen inside it. A set of long tweezers lay at rest, accompanied by a magnifying glass, spools of thread, a small pile of dark wood the size of toothpicks, a razor knife, and a stack of wood-sticked cotton swabs.

"Who is she?" Boldt asked, easing into an uncomfortable leather captain's chair facing the desk. LaMoia fit himself into the other, looking all around.

"The *Francis and Elizabeth*. Seventeen forty-two, Rotterdam and Deal to Philadelphia."

"Impressive," LaMoia said, unconvincingly.

Geiser picked up the magnifying glass and studied the beginnings of the ship inside the bottle, then set it down and addressed his visitors. "I apologize for continuing this, but I can't stop in the middle. I have glue drying." He scooted the reading glasses back up his nose, picked up a pair of forceps, and displaying impossibly steady hands, delivered a structural element to the side of the tiny ship's hull.

"Our glue's drying too, Paul. And we can't stop in the middle either."

"So talk," Geiser said, never taking his eyes off the model.

Questioning a DPA about his personal involvement on a case was dangerous ground and Boldt knew it.

"We need to know where he's being kept."

"Who?" Eyes on the model.

"We need to know now," Boldt said. "We can't do the dance. Not tonight."

"How can we even dance if you won't share the music? I don't know what you're talking about, Lieutenant."

There was no forcing the man, so Boldt thought he might try to break him down a piece at a time. This had not been entirely unexpected. LaMoia was in attendance primarily as a witness. It occurred to Boldt that Geiser had figured that out already, and if so, he was already on notice that Boldt's visit was formal.

"What did you leave out about the proposed meet with Hayes?"

"I told you: It failed to materialize," Geiser said. "Am I supposed to waste your time?"

A legitimate reply, but not to Boldt's satisfaction. "You said something came up."

LaMoia said, "You didn't even watch the bridge? Like from a distance, or a building, or something?"

"I did go to the bridge, in fact. I parked where I was told to park. But when Foreman informed me he was stuck in traffic, I got the hell out of there."

Boldt asked, "Do you happen to remember if Danny

told you where he was when he let you know he wasn't going to make it?"

"You want me to provide an alibi for Danny Foreman?" Incredulous, Geiser carefully wiped the tips of the forceps with a cotton ball and solvent. He placed them down and looked up at Boldt for the first time. "Or perhaps you want an alibi for me as well, eh, Lieutenant?"

Boldt felt himself flush with heat. He told Geiser what the man knew already. "SID is processing the cabin."

"Good for them." Geiser went back to his model.

Boldt repeated, "Did Foreman mention where he was when he was stuck in traffic?"

"He was on highway five-twenty, I think. Construction backup. Rush hour. A breakdown in the opposing lane. Same old, same old."

This roughly matched what Boldt had been told. In another witness Boldt would have questioned the degree of accuracy, the level of detail, but attorneys guarded their facts. "The Pine Street overpass? Your choice, or the voice that called you?"

Geiser hesitated, either to attend to his model, or because he was considering how to answer, and this bothered Boldt. The *man* bothered Boldt. The resolute calm.

"Are you laying traps for me, Lieutenant? Do you not trust me?"

That didn't answer the question, but for Boldt to press a DPA, treating him like a suspect, would be a mistake.

Geiser sat up and pushed back from the desk admiring his handiwork, the model still a long way from looking like much. "Listen, can't you people check this kind of thing?" Looking between the two cops, he said, "I'm sure

Foreman mentioned construction and something about a car in the breakdown lane. Somebody'll have that, right?"

Foreman had mentioned traffic problems to Boldt as well, and Boldt had already made the call, but Geiser didn't need to know that. Boldt stuck his neck out as far as he dared. "An attorney and an investigator . . . working together . . . could make a whole hell of a lot of trouble if they wanted."

"One hell of a team," LaMoia said.

"Now wait just a goddamned minute," Geiser said, not taking any time to catch on to the suggestion.

LaMoia said, "They could sequester a state witness for instance."

Boldt added, "Covering their tracks by leaving a bloody crime scene behind but with the body missing."

Geiser's narrowing eyes tracked back and forth between the two. "Give me a break. Do you have any idea of the hoops we'd have to jump through to pull that off? Do you honestly believe the U.S. Attorney's Office or my own office would condone *misleading* an investigation in order to sequester a witness?" He could see on the men's faces he wasn't gaining ground. "We start down that road and when would we ever mend that fence? Huh? You tell me. SPD would never cooperate with our office again. Not ever. And who could blame you? Listen, I'm not saying we might not try something like that. It's pretty ingenious, you ask me. Damn good ruse. But it would be in concert with you guys—*someone* in your department would catch wind of it well before it ever went down. You've got to see that, right?"

It made sense to Boldt, but he was loath to admit it. Horrified even to think that his captain, Sheila Hill, or some other gold badge would cut a deal with the attorneys and leave him in the wind. But his wife was involved, and that might account for any number of things. A sense of near panic filled him. Was his own department running him around in circles while they had plans of their own?

He found himself believing Geiser, and it bothered him. He said, "I need to know if something like that is in play."

"I imagine you do."

"Do you believe Danny Foreman was stuck in traffic at the time he called you?"

"Well, now we're getting to the heart of it, aren't we, Lieutenant? The hell of it is, there's no way I can know that, is there?"

"Would you know if Hayes had cut a deal for protection?"

"I should. It should go through my office. Absolutely."

"But it wouldn't have to."

"It could just as easily go through the U.S. Attorney. Maybe more likely, you think about it. The USAO can negotiate with Treasury for witness protection. I can't offer that."

"Danny Foreman told my wife that you and he had Hayes under protection and that you'd deny it 'til hell freezes over."

"Well, he's right on one account, isn't he?" Geiser said. He scooted his chair up to the desk again and met eyes with Boldt. "You'd better move before your glue dries, gentlemen. You can find your way out."

❑ ❑ ❑

Paul Geiser was in the middle of a tricky bit of business on his model when his kitchen doorbell rang only minutes after Boldt's departure. Angry that Boldt would play the "oh, I forgot something" technique on a seasoned attorney, Geiser hurried through the house to the kitchen's back door, ready to give Boldt a mouthful. His glue was indeed drying. He yanked open the door, already mid-sentence. "This is the oldest game in the book—" but cut himself off, not recognizing the two men in the suits who faced him. FBI, by the look of them. *Treasury*, he thought, reminded again of the discussion of witness protection. Boldt had been followed, or the house had been watched. Fucking feds were full of such tricks.

Seeing two strangers at his back door was jarring; he had expected Boldt and LaMoia. In those few seconds it took his facile mind to clear the slate and begin again, one of the two stepped through the door and hit him with two open palms squarely in the center of his chest. *Not federal agents after all*. The impact not only threw him across the kitchen like a puppet, it froze his lungs and vocal cords in a nerve-deadening spasm.

One of them spoke to the other, his words clouded by an unfamiliar accent. Only then did he fully register what was going on. Only then did his thought finally catch up to real time, the specter of Boldt and LaMoia fading like the orb left behind by a camera's flash.

Thugs, goons, a dozen different names. Geiser called them "apes" around the office. One was dropping the blinds while the other was shoving a damp and smelly kitchen rag down Geiser's throat, pulling him by the hair and standing him up while wrestling his arms behind him. If his feeling had returned sooner, he might have fought them both, given his training.

The interrogation was conducted by mobile phone so that Geiser never saw his questioner—a walkie-talkie feature that allowed use of a speakerphone so that it didn't need to be held to Geiser's ear, and so the two men could follow instructions where necessary as well. The advantages of modern technology. His back ached from the way they'd bound his torso to the chair, sitting up so perfectly straight, hands out in front of him, also taped to the arms of the chair. They'd moved him into the basement by simply throwing him down the stairs, part intimidation, partly a way to keep him physically stunned. They knew their work well.

When he answered questions incorrectly, the big one shoved the musty kitchen rag back into his mouth as the smaller guy pulled a Leatherman out of a belt case and worked the polished metal multi-tool device into a pair of pliers.

"Please . . . no," Geiser gagged, tape wrapped around his head holding the rag in his mouth. His words came out as only deep grunts, nearly indistinguishable, except in volume, from the cries of pain that followed.

"Where is he?" the voice asked over the phone's thin speaker.

Geiser shook his head. He had no idea.

"Nyet," the ape said for the sake of the interrogator, which caused Geiser to loosen his bowels.

The voice on the other end of the phone wanted answers he didn't have. He understood the frustration of such a position from his years of working as a trial attorney. There were times he'd wanted to use these same methods on some of his unforthcoming witnesses. Wild with desperation— that ape stepping closer, the pliers extended like a prosthesis designed with only one purpose in mind—Paul Geiser understood that it promised to be a long night.

EIGHTEEN

WHEN BOLDT DROPPED LAMOIA OFF at his building, John offered his round-the-clock services, an expression of fraternity that implied there would be no overtime filed for, nothing on the books if Boldt wanted it that way. This reaching out by his former partner, a man Boldt had personally trained to follow in his path, meant the world to him.

"I may take you up on that."

"Do it. And I can safely volunteer Matthews as well." Boldt found it amusing that John still referred to Daphne by her last name.

He was about to pull away from the curb when a woman's figure stepped out of a doorway and headed directly for his car. Boldt couldn't imagine prostitutes working this neighborhood, but he prepared his shield to display and drive her off to another corner.

The woman opened Boldt's passenger door, and he had dropped his credentials wallet onto the seat and had his gun in hand by the time he recognized her.

"Maddie Olson," she reminded him. "We met in the men's room."

"If I were the paranoid type," Boldt said, "I'd say you were lying in wait for me."

"Word gets around," she said. "Drive please."

Boldt pulled the Crown Vic into traffic and started taking random turns through an old part of town where traffic was moderate. "You're not serious," he said, when she failed to instigate conversation, "about knowing I'd show up."

"Sure I am. I knew you had snatched up LaMoia. I'm telling you, there're no secrets."

"Geiser," he guessed.

". . . is in the Emergency Room at Swedish Med Center, Central district."

"I was with him an hour ago."

"Our guy, the same guy you're never going to speak to—"

"Alekseevich," Boldt supplied.

"—got word to us that the shit was flying. Geiser had been scheduled for a manicure. Foreman's up next, if they can find him."

"Damn." Boldt was not surprised to hear Foreman's name. He'd just fed it to Geiser himself.

"You don't sound surprised," she said.

"Two nights ago Danny Foreman led me to a crime scene." He went on to explain the blood in the cabin. "It made me suspicious of him."

"Because?"

"Danny had missed an important meet. Claimed he was stuck in traffic. Gave me the same excuse that he gave Geiser. I made some calls. Followed up on those calls just now. We look for patterns, right? I had one I thought worth pursuing, and come to find out, the highway where Danny was stuck in construction traffic while watching a car get towed turns out to be an area watched by a traffic cam. We live and die by the details. Danny tried too hard, said he'd seen a broken-down car to both me and Geiser. Too much information. When Geiser gave me that, my antenna went up."

"Reporting what he saw on the traffic cam allowed him to pretend to be somewhere he was not?"

"By the look of it, yes."

"And where was he, in fact?"

"This is all just speculation," he cautioned, "but my guess is he was doing a damn good job of imitating your Mr. Alekseevich so we'd take the bait. Meanwhile, I thought he was sequestering our primary suspect for the U.S. Attorney's Office. That is . . . that's the direction I was going until what you just told me."

"And now?"

"If they hit Geiser they don't have what they need. Maybe Danny tortured Hayes for information and then dumped the body."

"It will pan out. The Geiser manicure. Foreman being next."

"And you're telling me this because . . . ?"

"My sister's kid."

"I made a call about that," he said defensively, thinking she was accusing him of not having acted.

"I *know* you did," she said. "What goes around . . ." she added.

"I guess so," said Boldt.

"The next corner is fine," she said, pointing.

Boldt slowed the car for a red light, glad for the extra minute or two. "You said Geiser is in Emergency. What about Danny?"

"We rolled a car to Geiser's following the tip. Probably should have kept it off the radio in hindsight, because chances are they were scanning and knew we were coming. Found him in the basement in a bad way. Very fresh. Foreman's off our radar so far."

"Are you so sure?" Her words had sparked an interesting idea in him.

"We haven't found him," she repeated, missing Boldt's meaning, and Boldt was in no hurry to correct matters.

"I need you to arrange a meeting for me."

"Alekseevich? No can do."

"Pretty please, with caviar on top?"

"I'd love to help out, Lieutenant. But I get off the bus here."

"Five minutes. Ten, max."

"Not possible."

"Then tell your people this. Sunday night, one way or another, I'm delivering Svengrad on the front steps, so they better stop your guy from crossing into Canada or boarding a flight because we're all going to need him if we're going to make the charges stick."

"They'll go ballistic, I give them that." She sounded a little desperate now herself. "We've been building a case for the better part of a year now. You cannot do this, Lieutenant."

"I'm not asking permission, Detective. I'm trying to give you a heads-up."

"And if I can get you the meet with Alekseevich?" she asked. "Where's that put all this?"

"Now you're listening," he said. Pulling the car to the curb as she'd directed, Boldt knew he'd won the meeting. "Your name never comes up in any of this."

"I don't know whether to kiss you or throw a punch," she said, popping her door open.

He made sure she had his cell phone number, and then headed back into traffic, confident he'd led her away from her own very good idea, and wondering if he could now turn it to his favor.

口 口 口

Liz was half out of her mind with impatience and the claustrophobic sense of being watched and guarded. Lou's last-minute request before he'd left had nearly floored her, but she knew to trust his judgment and instincts—when it came to planning, few were his equal.

To her surprise, the third shop she phoned was open late on Friday nights, the effeminate male voice on the other end trying to cross-sell all kinds of extras she didn't need. She made this call in secret, as Lou had suggested, from the kitchen's portable but in the bathroom with the water running, while Bobbie Gaynes babysat her in the living room, leafing through magazines and constantly adjusting the ear bud that linked her with dispatch. Liz had heard Lou talk about such operations dozens of times over the course of their marriage, but being the centerpiece of such a thing proved exhausting despite her doing nearly nothing and going nowhere. The nervous energy alone drained her of physical strength and threatened paranoia. Pickup and delivery of a costume was arranged. She reviewed the arrangements twice, making sure there were no misunderstandings. Lou had given her specific orders, and she meant to carry them out.

"Everyone okay in there, Mrs. B.?" It was Gaynes knocking lightly on the bathroom door.

"Out in a minute. There's another upstairs," Liz added.

"It's not like that," Gaynes said. She didn't need a toilet; she needed her charge back in her chair in the living room. Cops were territorial animals.

Liz willed her mobile phone to ring—to engage her, give her something to do other than worry. She would not have expected being so eager to be involved, so ready for it. At that point in time, if someone had asked her to clean fish she would have done it. Anything to relieve the stress of waiting.

She kicked herself a moment later for not thinking the way Lou thought, for not realizing her environment and how to handle herself. She left the bathroom and, by her way of thinking, did a pretty fine job of returning the kitchen's portable phone to its wall cradle. But a moment later she looked back to see Gaynes striking a pose in the doorway shared between the kitchen and living room, one shoulder on the jamb, one leg crossed before the other.

"No," Gaynes said into the portable phone. "Just checking if you're open." She hung up the call with the press of a button. She had pushed *redial*. She had realized what Liz was up to in the bathroom and had gone straight to work upon the phone's return.

"What's up with the costume shop, Mrs. B.?"

"I think you'd better come over here and sit down," Liz said. "This may take some explaining."

□ □ □

"I didn't think you'd take me up on my offer so soon," LaMoia said from the passenger seat. Less than thirty minutes had elapsed since Boldt had dropped him off. "I just barely wolfed dinner." LaMoia carefully picked at a thick brownie, nibbling off tiny amounts and savoring each bite.

Boldt couldn't remember when he'd last eaten. He currently had the remains of a hot tea warming the cup holder. Boldt caught LaMoia up on the surprise visit by Maddie Olson, but did not mention her by name or division within the department, referring to her only as a "female officer."

"Best kind," LaMoia said, his teeth black with chocolate.

"It presents two very different scenarios," Boldt said, driving faster than he normally did, and knowing that John recognized this but was too cool to acknowledge it. "Either Foreman stung us by faking the torture and stashing Hayes for the U.S. Attorney's Office, or he actually tortured Hayes himself and put it off on others."

LaMoia reacted sarcastically, one of the only emotional responses he allowed himself. "Oh, well, that second one's certainly a dandy. Pissed at the system, he decides to take the money for himself?"

"It might account for Svengrad going after Geiser and him."

"Why do I sense we're not out for an evening drive?" LaMoia asked, popping the last bit of brownie into his mouth and rolling his eyes as he chewed. Boldt had just run a red light. "These things might come from a box," he said, licking his fingers, "but Matthews has it down. The trick is undercooking them."

"The Martha Stewart of Homicide."

LaMoia, adding a southern twang, said, "And damn proud of it."

Boldt explained, "First thing I did was try the Sheriff's Office, looking for Danny, because this cop mentioned having Danny on our radar, and I think without meaning to, reminded me that all the MDTs," Mobile Data Terminals, "track real-time location of the cars, same as ours do."

"And you got a fix for his new ride? The Escalade?"

"Not exactly."

"You're driving as if you did."

Boldt suppressed a grin. The first faint acknowledgment from John. It was worth cherishing. "I've got a fix, but it wasn't courtesy of the Sheriff's Office."

"Is this supposed to be twenty questions or something?" He eyed Boldt's tea, still smacking his lips. "You mind if I have a swig of that?"

"Finish it," Boldt said. LaMoia knew perfectly well that Boldt did mind sharing both drink and food. This was LaMoia's attempt at being polite while he got what he wanted. "Sheriff's Office only keeps real-time information, and they currently have nothing on their screens for Fore-man's Escalade. Means the engine's turned off. They'll call me if that changes."

"We call them 'motors,' Sarge," LaMoia corrected, "but I'll forgive you this time. Motors, because they're engines that move you." John was a gear-head of the first order. Boldt should have known better than to wander into his territory.

"Do you want to hear this?"

LaMoia, not wearing his seat belt, had slumped back in the seat, as if tempted by a nap despite Boldt's erratic driv-ing. The man had some Old West mannerisms like this—

the town sheriff tipped back in the spoke chair outside the jail—that he wore effortlessly, and that fit him well. He reminded Boldt of the best of Steve McQueen. As if Boldt had already briefed him, LaMoia said, "I'm way ahead of you. The new Escalades offer an On-Sat service package that gives you twenty-four-hour road assistance, electronic mapping, live operators." He paused for dramatic effect. "GPS, twenty-four-seven. You're about to tell me On-Sat maintains GPS data for some specified amount of time; I'm guessing between six and twenty-four hours. That way they know where you've been, and this helps their operators look good when you ask for a nice restaurant or motel nearby." He gave Boldt a smirk. "Voilà! The wheres and whens of Danny Foreskin's comings-and-goings over the past whatever-amount-of-time." He looked over at Boldt ponderously, and when Boldt failed to contradict him, slid further down in the seat, saying, "Wake me when we get there, Daddy. I need to close my eyes a sec."

Boldt felt as if he'd had his pocket picked. "The location is nearby. Southeast, in SoDo. Foreman's Escalade has been in this area three times in the past twenty-four hours. It's not a firm address, but it's got to mean something."

"When you're right, you're right," LaMoia said. "I stole your thunder. Didn't I, Sarge?" His eyes remained closed.

"Yes, you did."

"Good."

"Why's that good?" Boldt asked, after a long period of reflection to consider this.

"Because then you're probably pissed off at me," he said. "Am I right?"

"Mildly irritated."

"And if you're pissed off at me, then your juices are

flowing, and we're going to need our juices flowing by the time we get there."

"And what about *your* juices?"

"Sarge? This is *me* we're talking about."

"One of these days, John . . ."

"Yeah, I know." A stifled yawn, well practiced. "I know."

LaMoia asked about the Escalade's current location according to On-Sat. Boldt said it was last recorded at the edge of a rail freight yard nearly directly west of their present location.

"And why aren't we looking there first?"

"Because that, if anything, would give us Foreman, and we want Hayes."

"Why are we so anxious to get to Hayes, Sarge?"

This was the question Boldt could not allow himself to answer, for it would reveal too much of his upcoming plan. In his own unique way, LaMoia had wormed into the heart of the matter, drilling for the truth and ripping Boldt open in the process. There was little these two men had not shared over the past decade, and Boldt's silence suggested a line not to cross for LaMoia, and the man was briefly but clearly hurt.

LaMoia placed a call from his cell phone, interrupting himself to ask Boldt for the address where they were headed, which Boldt then supplied begrudgingly, wondering what he was up to. He spoke to a woman, judging by the way he flirted, and she apparently did everything he asked, because he kept continually thanking her. He disconnected the call, clipped the cell phone back to his waist, and sighed.

"Sometimes I wish I wasn't so smart."

"Oh, yeah," Boldt said, "there's a problem." Now LaMoia would make him drag it out of him. Unlike Bernie Lofgrin, who had to bore you to death explaining everything in excruciating detail, LaMoia never volunteered his information, his little game.

Southeast of SoDo was a no-man's-land of brick and cinderblock, chain link and rusted signs, a DMZ-like stretch between the city and Boeing Field. Sidewalks sprouted weeds; broken windows called attention to themselves. For a while gangs had used the area, moving in and then driven out, like livestock crossing neighbors' property lines. Mom-and-Pop shops, burger houses, delivery businesses, and car repair had started the process that would lead the former warehouse and light industrial space into offices and retail storefronts. The unstoppable evolution of neglected urban space under pressure. Even an unpredictable economy couldn't stop the city from growing—the bacterium had grown immune to antibiotics.

"Okay, I give up," Boldt said. "Why are you so smart?"

"There's a building within a block of where the On-Sat put Foreman's car that's on BCI's impound list." Law enforcement agencies, SPD included, took possession of assets in narcotics raids and RICO convictions, often to offset taxpayers for a particularly expensive or time-consuming investigation. Vehicles, boats, homes, commercial properties were all impounded. Most of the time these were put on the auction block and the proceeds returned to the public coffers once the court case settled. On occasion, a vehicle or boat would be impounded and later put into service by the agency of possession. Real estate in particular typically lagged in the process, sometimes staying on the books a year or two before auction. Locked and chained and standing vacant, they dotted the urban landscape, tracked by some bureaucratic auditor. On occasion, as appeared to be the case now, an arresting agent later came to believe the car, or boat, or commercial real estate in fact belonged to him or her as long as no one was using it. LaMoia's discovery of such a property within walking distance from the various locations where Foreman's parked Escalade had been tracked suggested anything but coincidence.

LaMoia checked an address written in pen on the back of his hand and indicated a turn to Boldt. A moment later they parked and climbed out. "Place was a print shop. Supermarket coupons, some counterfeit lottery tickets, sports tickets. Went on BCI's impound list a year ago September."

They faced a sturdy steel door. Looking up through a rusted steel fire escape, Boldt said, "I asked both the On-Sat people and BCI to call me if they saw Foreman on the move, especially returning to this neighborhood. Who knows if they'll oblige us."

"So we stay ready to be surprised," LaMoia said. "You want to take it alone, have me play sentry, or do we do this together?"

"Together. We'll call for backup if we manage to get inside."

"I saw you looking at the fire escape," LaMoia said.

"Yes, you did."

"You want me up there?"

"We take the dime tour first, aware of the fact that Svengrad may have already gotten to Foreman. If so, Svengrad's people may have arrived ahead of us, or could even be on their way right now."

"They got to him once. I don't see that happening a second time. Foreskin's got more sense than that."

"Danny's playing Lone Ranger. That makes him vulnerable to all sorts of mistakes. If I'm Svengrad, I want to know where Foreman is at all times. That is, if Danny isn't working for Svengrad. Seventeen million can go a lot of ways."

"Point taken."

They walked along the front of the building and then down an alley where they spotted a distinct architectural division that designated a change in structures. A second fire escape led down here in the alley.

LaMoia said, "I could maybe get up there . . . you see that third-floor window?" Several panes of glass in the window were broken out. "Maybe I can get back down to the first floor from inside." The impounded print shop had occupied the entire first floor and the basement, according to John's information.

"We don't have a warrant. And good luck getting one when it's a BCI-impound property without involving BCI. Just go ahead and imagine that nightmare. Foreman's working an investigation, and we're interfering. That's how the prosecuting attorney's office *and* BCI are going to view this, especially if Foreman ends up making BCI look bad."

"We've got a BCI agent gone missing, and an informant telling you he may have met foul play."

"That informant's not on the books and is never going to put herself there."

"But that right there is probable cause to enter a place our missing guy may have visited several times in the past twenty-four hours." LaMoia added, "I'll tell you what: The Sturgeon General sure as shit is not waiting around for a warrant. If Foreman or Hayes is inside this building, we gotta get swinging on some ropes here, Sarge."

After hours, Boldt thought. Not the greatest time to go hunting down a search-and-seizure. "Mahoney could expedite this for us," Boldt said. DPA Lehla Mahoney and Boldt had forged a good working relationship over the past few years, and she'd proven willing to go out on a limb for him. He took a moment to call her while LaMoia began his ascent of the fire escape toward the broken window, an act that required them both to push a Dumpster beneath the fire escape to give LaMoia a leg up.

Boldt had to leave a callback number on Mahoney's service, but to his surprise she returned the call within a minute. LaMoia had reached the second floor. Boldt detailed their situation, and the attorney listened closely, interrupting with a number of interrogatives along the way. In conclusion she said she'd try to get Boldt a paper bag warrant—a verbal warrant from an on-duty judge known to be slightly to the left of Ralph Nader. Boldt warned her that he and LaMoia considered time a factor and were therefore going to kick it, counting on Mahoney to come through. She didn't like that the initial information came from an informant working for the U.S. Attorney's Office through SPD's Organized Crimes unit, seeing that a possible obstacle, and warned Boldt they might not get their warrant.

"Yes," Boldt said, "but at least I called. That's got to count for something."

"Not much," Mahoney replied. In fact, officers could and did kick doors based on probable cause without ever applying for the proper paperwork. Boldt knew that maybe sixty percent of the time evidence collected in such raids actually made it to court. He didn't want to lose evidence, but he didn't want to leave Foreman or Hayes inside this building another minute, and so he made a hasty and difficult decision to give LaMoia a thumbs-up from his place below the man in the alley. Part of his reasoning should have included that they weren't even sure they could reach the impounded property from that broken window, and that argument might have held up if it had been anyone but LaMoia climbing that fire escape. But as Boldt gave the signal, he moved immediately back toward the building's locked front door, knowing that at any minute LaMoia would appear there, a shit-eating grin on his face, a wisecrack ready on his lips.

"Welcome to the Hyatt. May I check your reservation?" LaMoia asked.

"I knew you'd have something cute. You just can't leave it alone, can you?"

"I have a reputation to live up to," LaMoia said.

Boldt stepped through into a vast, empty space that smelled of cat urine and feces. A poured concrete floor stained from spilled ink, papered with litter. It was dark. Both detectives used small Maglites to light their way.

The central space looked to be about the size of a basketball court but beneath a low ceiling. Boldt experienced an immediate sense of dread, an early-warning sign he'd come to trust over the years and felt inclined to do so now. This "sense" usually proved to be no sense at all, but his picking up on evidence subliminally, evidence that didn't jump out at first. When Boldt stopped walking to take in the vastness of the space, LaMoia knew better than to challenge him, or even speak. Boldt trusted the man to put the wisecracks away and knew it would be so. Despite all his antics, LaMoia was a serious cop on the inside. LaMoia squatted, also looking around, sweeping his own flashlight across the floor.

LaMoia's light stopped moving, illuminating a wedge-shaped cone of concrete. "Is that what you're looking for?" His light held on two thin hash marks, black, like skid marks from a bike tire. Not one, but two of them, and nearly parallel.

"Good work, John."

The men followed the irregular black lines across the floor. Fat to narrow. Long to short. Boldt discerned the direction of movement from their shape and pattern. "Heel marks," he said, following them across the cavernous space. A body being dragged. Boldt's temperature increased and he worked to control his breathing, to fight the adrenaline that wanted to own him. The deeper they moved into this room, the darker, the more dependent they were on the small flashlights. Boldt knew they could be following the markings of a machine being dragged across the print shop or a cart with black rubber tires or a hand truck. But he believed otherwise. *A body,* his internal voice cautioned. *The body of David Hayes,* his first thought.

"This is SPD turf, and that gives us jurisdiction to investigate that busted window. We're cool, Sarge. This isn't coming back on us." LaMoia said all this for himself, knowing instinctively as did Boldt that they were on to something, and not wanting to face that they could lose by technicality whatever lay at the end of these skid marks. But both men had experienced such loss enough times to know the truth. They'd taken a gamble. The admissibility of whatever they might discover here remained in question.

They followed the skid marks around a wall to a missing door and a wide set of steel and concrete stairs leading down. Reflexively, LaMoia grabbed for his handgun, checked the weapon for operability, and gripped it along with the flashlight, both hands extended before him. Boldt remained half a step back, avoiding any line of fire, but did not take up his weapon. He checked it once, hooking his sport coat behind its bulge, so that he could withdraw it at a moment's notice, and only then if LaMoia needed backup. John LaMoia was a crack shot. If anything moved down here without fair notice, Boldt knew the outcome.

The bottom of the stairs presented them with a closed door, and LaMoia tugged it open, standing to one side to screen himself. A pitch-black space faced them, slowly illuminated by their flashlights. This basement level was crowded with discarded printing presses, stacks of white plastic, five-gallon drums, junk of every shape and size, all stacked together without logic or organization. The floor failed to yield the telltale skid marks of a body being dragged, and so the two split up, Boldt heading to the right, LaMoia to the left. Using hand signals they communicated a rendezvous point at the far end of a space that remained so dark that the light they carried died in blackness before reaching a distant wall. The operating theory was that it had to end somewhere, and when it did, they would find each other. Meanwhile, Boldt kept glancing over his shoulder to keep track of LaMoia's ever-dimming light.

The junk was piled in heaps that created a few aisles to Boldt's left, and the larger aisle that he continued to walk. He squared a corner, discovering a side wall, and felt tempted to call out to LaMoia when, at that same instant, he felt a vibration travel up his legs, resonate through his body, and he guessed that a vehicle had either just passed by the building or had parked alongside.

Boldt's skin prickled as he hurried his pace, checking a number of side storage rooms. He had his weapon out now, in hand, and wasn't sure when that had happened. He reminded himself that he had a Kevlar vest in the trunk of the Crown Vic and that Miles was almost seven and Sarah just four and that they deserved to have a daddy well into their childhoods. He also reminded himself that he had applied for the lieutenant's shield to raise his pay, but that Liz saw it as a means to keep him out of situations like this, and he struggled with the irony that Liz herself had put him into this situation. It seemed it was always at moments such as these that memories and considerations tried to overrun his thoughts, an involuntary invitation of images that challenged his ability to stay focused and made the job all the more difficult. As a young cop, such images never plagued you; experience had its downside.

The fourth door that Boldt tried failed to open, and his flashlight revealed a shiny new hasp and padlock at head height. He whistled once, and LaMoia whistled back, and at the same instant a muffled voice came from the other side of the door, and Boldt felt his bowels rumble. When it came to victims, Homicide cops rarely dealt in the living.

The muffled cries continued from the other side of the door.

"You feel the shake and bake?" LaMoia asked in a forced whisper, coming up behind Boldt.

"I did," Boldt said, snapping on a pair of latex gloves before tugging on the lock.

"Visitors?"

"We knew it was a possibility." Boldt added, "It could be our own guys trying to catch up to us and update us on Foreman's status."

LaMoia nonchalantly located a section of pipe amid the debris as they talked, leveraged the lock and hasp, and split the wooden doorjamb as the screws pulled loose and the hasp gave way. Still locked to itself, the hardware hung from the door. Boldt twisted the doorknob and eased the door open an eighth of an inch, aware there could be trip wires rigged to an explosive or incendiary device. If the work of Foreman, as an investigator he knew to destroy evidence and leave a few surprises for visitors. LaMoia leaned in close as Boldt held the door, and without a word of instruction searched the open space carefully with his flashlight held to the crack.

"Nada," he said.

Boldt pushed the door open another two inches, and LaMoia reached inside this time, his fingers gently inspecting the gap. He shook his head. "No."

Both men paused as they heard the unmistakable sound of someone entering the building upstairs.

LaMoia whispered, "You *did* lock the door behind you, right, Sarge?"

Boldt nodded. "Whoever's up there had the key."

"Not our guys," LaMoia said, trying it out as a joke, or releasing tension, or both. The flip remark bothered Boldt, who pushed and held the door open another three inches, allowing LaMoia's head to fit through. LaMoia sized up the room's interior, still looking for booby traps.

"It's Hayes," he said softly. "Looks in decent shape."

"The door?"

"Clear," LaMoia said, tapping Boldt's hand and swinging it open further.

Boldt glanced only briefly to confirm it was Hayes. The man was gagged and bound to a metal chair in a room filled with cluttered shelves. His left hand had been roughly bandaged and his mouth and face looked bruised and swollen.

"What about our friends?" LaMoia asked.

"Exits?" Boldt asked. He slipped past LaMoia, leaving him to guard the room. He freed Hayes but did not untie the man's mouth, unsure whether the man would keep silent.

He heard footfalls overhead and guessed there were at least two of them. He didn't need or want a confrontation where the prize was a man capable of delivering seventeen million dollars. Those kinds of stakes made men stupid, and stupid men did stupid things.

"I passed one, yeah," LaMoia informed him, "though I can't vouch for it."

"Let's go." Boldt pulled Hayes out of the chair by the arm. The man stumbled under cramped legs, and LaMoia stepped inside and took the other arm. The room smelled of excrement and urine, and Boldt realized Hayes had fouled himself long before.

"Motherfucker," LaMoia said, getting a close whiff as the man came out of the chair.

They guided Hayes through the door, his weight hanging between them like that of an invalid. Boldt saw the first sweep of light on the stairs and motioned LaMoia to lead them. They turned and hurried down an aisle created between the stacks of industrial junk. Boldt could feel the pressure of whoever was back there, knowing they drew closer with every step. He shook his hand vigorously, pointing ahead, trying to pick up their speed, and LaMoia responded by carrying more than his fair share of the weight.

LaMoia steered left at the end of the long aisle.

Boldt checked behind him to see through the tangle of metal what appeared to be two lights. They'd reached the bottom of the stairs and now faced the same indecision that he and LaMoia had faced only minutes before. One light went left, and one right, in a mirror image. Boldt looked ahead hoping for an exit sign, but couldn't see more than a few feet. LaMoia trained his light toward the concrete floor, as did Boldt, all three of their heads aimed down in order to overstep obstacles and avoid making noise.

The visitor on the left turned the same corner that Boldt had, and when he called out, it was in what sounded like Russian, and Boldt felt his legs suddenly move that much faster. He didn't consider himself scared of anyone; he'd spent too many years on the job for that—they were usually afraid of *him*—and yet the sound of that particular language, associated with all means and methods of violence, turned his blood cold and he experienced a pang of fear. LaMoia, no coward to anyone or anything, picked up his pace as well. Perhaps it resulted from the burden of Hayes carried between them, and their vulnerability, but whatever the motivation, they moved in unison. Even Hayes seemed to find his feet with the first echo of that foreign tongue. The three reached a rusted steel door bearing an emergency warning not to open it, and Boldt wondered if it was to be their luck that the one thing that still worked in this building was the emergency exit alarm built into the box attached to the door.

No matter what, their attempt to open this door promised to make noise: Old, rusty steel didn't move quietly. Presently subterranean, they had to hope the stairwell—that presumably led up into an alley—was not also piled with debris, either blocking the door or preventing them from climbing out once through.

LaMoia checked with Boldt in the dim light, his right

hand on the door's panic bar. He was looking for permission from Boldt, and with the moment of truth at hand, Boldt wondered if this was indeed the best course of action. Without a doubt, their departure would attract attention. To do so unnecessarily seemed a ridiculous risk to take. But as the light to the right flickered and died, far closer to their aisle than Boldt had imagined, he gave the nod and LaMoia shoved on the tarnished panic bar.

The door came open with a horror-movie groan of metal on metal, not merely calling attention, but shouting. LaMoia swung it open, and it stuck. He let go of Hayes, threw a shoulder into it, and won enough room for them to pass. The shouting from behind also rose in Russian, followed immediately by hurried footfalls. Boldt, the last to pass through, braced himself for the sting of a bullet, or the pain of a club to his head.

LaMoia awaited him with a bent and battered discarded trash can that looked like an oversized crushed beer can. He rudely knocked Boldt out of the way and braced the can beneath the door's outside handle, wedging the door shut.

They hurried up the stairs, the first loud bang on the door and the agonized sound of the trash can's tin bending. Boldt didn't like the idea of running from thugs, and he knew without asking that LaMoia felt the same. The thing to do was ditch Hayes and stand their ground and make arrests based on breaking-and-entering. But if these two were backed by two more, if SPD backup failed to arrive quickly, with seventeen million on the line, things could get dicey.

"So?" LaMoia asked hopefully, nowhere near as out of breath as Boldt felt.

"We can't," Boldt said.

Hayes got his feet under him and no longer needed

much assistance. His mouth remained gagged, silver tape holding the gag in place. Bug-eyed he shouted to communicate but neither Boldt nor LaMoia was interested.

"Where to?" LaMoia asked.

"The Slumberjack," Boldt proposed, naming a run-of-the-mill motel that SPD used occasionally.

"Lucky you," LaMoia said, forcibly taking hold of Hayes now by his collar and throwing him ahead to keep him moving. "Free HBO and the taxpayer pays."

"It's not exactly how it's going to work, John," Boldt informed his sergeant, his mind already playing through his and Liz's needs over the next forty-eight hours. "I'm paying for this one. Let's keep it between the three of us. Foreman's got to have access to anything we're doing, either officially or through his pals. We can't risk that." These lies came so effortlessly now, he nearly believed them himself. He wondered if they made it past LaMoia as well.

Hayes appeared nonplussed at the mention of Foreman's name, leaving Boldt to wonder who had been responsible for the man's abduction. That, or Foreman had thought to use Rohypnol to erase the man's memory of the event, and to further tie the abduction to the earlier tortures. Boldt had slipped the name into the explanation hoping for a response, and felt the wind knocked out of him when it failed to register.

Hurrying toward the Crown Vic, Boldt dragged along this man who'd had sex with his wife, his only real wish to find a legitimate excuse to kick Hayes squarely in the balls. Start kicking and never stop.

NINETEEN

BOLDT'S CELL PHONE, PLUGGED IN and recharging, cut a shrill tone through the bedroom's darkness at exactly 2 A.M. Liz stopped snoring and sat up as if hearing a fire alarm, still in a dream state. "The kids?" she asked Boldt, who was already out of bed. Then she remembered the state of affairs, sank back to her pillow, and said, "Oh," as she realized it was only another of his late-night summonses. Another part of the same nightmare.

A woman's voice said into Boldt's ear, "He'll talk to you and your guy, but *only* you and your guy. No wires. No tricks. Half hour from now—two-thirty. He'll give you ten minutes, tops. Nothing on the record." She named the location—the Pink Lady—a strip joint on First Avenue. "If there's no objection, we'll see you there."

After some struggle, he identified the voice as that of Maddie Olson. He said, "No objection." Both he and LaMoia could reach the club within fifteen minutes. She disconnected the call without ceremony.

Boldt dialed John. He felt tempted to go it alone, but LaMoia was street-smart, willing to play tough off the books, and handy to have around as backup. He had to consider the possibility, however remote, that Olson was leading him into a trap.

Matthews answered and passed the phone to LaMoia, and from somewhere inside Boldt came the need to look across through the gray haze of a dark bedroom and see his wife's head on the pillow. The sight pleased him, and it occurred to him that he didn't harbor any hatred or resentment for her affair with Hayes, at least not at that moment. He worried over the videotape, and what it would do to Miles and Sarah if their teachers, and the parents of their friends, saw pieces of it on the evening news. There were no secrets for anyone in public service, especially a veteran Homicide cop whom so many would love to see knocked off his pedestal. But something about dragging Hayes from that abandoned building, about placing him in the motel under the watchful eye of Bobbie Gaynes, had lessened the mystique surrounding the man. Bloodied and beaten down, Hayes had struck him as a sad excuse, a pitiful kid gone bad.

"But, Sarge," LaMoia whined, "a downtown strip joint? How about someplace a little less distracting?"

Boldt marveled that even just wakened, LaMoia not only had his sarcasm intact, but was willing to say such a thing in front of Matthews.

"Fifteen minutes." Boldt hung up without dignifying that with a response.

The Pink Lady seethed neon lighting and loud music, a sweet-and-sour smell of male excitement and cheap cologne mixed with the tang of salt-rimmed margaritas. It was nineteen-year-old girls, not women, in negligees serving drinks, and another up onstage, naked and with a shaved pubis, rubbing herself against a stainless steel pole and try-ing to look anything but pained to be there.

Maddie Olson wore a tailored black leather coat and a turtleneck that flattered her. Her jeans hugged her bottom, the seam running up her crack, and Boldt was surprised when LaMoia didn't trip on a small step, because he hadn't taken his eyes off their hostess. They were led to a red leather corner booth with a large Formica table anchored to the floor. Alekseevich looked about nineteen himself. He wore a nice suit, probably paid for by Svengrad, dark gray, but he'd lost the tie for the after-hours entertainment. He wore a gold chain around his furry neck that, if real, was worth sev-eral months of Boldt's salary. He held a Proletarskie—the smoking gun—and had large hands with clean nails but several cuts and bruises. His razor couldn't keep up; there was a shadow across his cheeks and down his neck. He used gel in his short hair and a tooth whitener. But it was the outright contempt in his blue eyes that struck Boldt first. He looked disgusted to be in their company.

"Thanks," Boldt said, adopting an unusual opening to this particular chess match.

Alekseevich's face softened some. Just a kid under there somewhere.

"You like baseball?" Boldt asked.

"Football. Soccer," he corrected himself, having used the European term first. "MLS," he said. "I follow Colo-rado, but Seattle's trying to get an expansion team."

"My boy plays soccer," Boldt said.

"And piano," Alekseevich said, turning Boldt's stomach. "Pretty good, your boy."

Stepping in to cover Boldt's shock at this knowledge of

his son, LaMoia asked, "Who holds your passport, Malina? You or the detective, here?"

The man's face burned.

LaMoia said, "The lieutenant has a little tit for tat. You understand tit for tat? Not tit for twat. You gotta pull your mind out of the gutter for a moment, maybe stop letting your eyes drift over my shoulder at Beaver Cleaver, because you're going to want to pay attention here."

Alekseevich tried to look bored and disinterested, but LaMoia had gotten to him. Boldt said, "I need some information from you. There's not time to verify it, so I'll have to take your word. If I get your word, if I like the information, then I'm going to give you a heads-up that will save everyone a lot of trouble. If I read you wrong, you don't get the information."

The man checked his watch. "Seven minutes."

LaMoia said, "Go on, be like that, tough guy." He shook his head. "Pulling fingernails off people who can't fight back. The shit does not work like that here. The lieutenant here has some good juice to give you, and you keep playing like you don't give a fuck, then we're outta here, and that's that."

"You're the tough one, is that it? Good cop, bad cop?" Again, Alekseevich feigned boredom.

"You don't even want to go there," LaMoia said, leveling a gaze on the man that could have frozen water. "Tonight, we're both bad." With LaMoia you got what you saw, and at that moment he was all testosterone and adrenaline.

Alekseevich offered a mock shiver.

LaMoia had the last word with a subtle grin that maybe

only Boldt understood, but one that left no doubt that if he let the two go at it out back, LaMoia would prevail. A street fighter with an absurd amount of confidence and a tolerance for pain, LaMoia was not to be messed with. Alekseevich directed his attention away from LaMoia and focused on Boldt, and yet he held the unsure expression of a little old lady on the sidewalk gravely concerned about the approaching mutt, unleashed and with its ears back.

A waitress showed up to take their orders. She wore a sheer, translucent nightgown tied around her waist with a purple ribbon. Her breasts were high and small, her nipples dark as chocolate, and her pubic hair shaved low and narrow, like a Mohawk. LaMoia took it all in, since her chest was at his head height due to the raised booth. He ordered a domestic beer. The girl took the rest of the order—for Boldt, a ginger ale, for Olson an iced tea—and then reminded LaMoia that she and all the wait staff were available for lap dances. She made it sound like a bank teller reminding a customer of home loans. Alekseevich tried to win her attention, but she was impressed by LaMoia and didn't give the Russian the time of day. Boldt loved the look on the Russian's face as the girl went to get the drinks.

"So," Alekseevich said to Boldt, "you were saying?"

"No. I was asking," Boldt corrected. "A certain individual—and to humor me, let's just say that individual is you, and that I can prove it—assaulted a man named David Hayes, and later, a state Bureau of Criminal Investigation officer by the name of Foreman. Tonight we got word that a man named Paul Geiser lost a few fingernails, and that Foreman was on the list again as well."

Alekseevich shook his head in denial and looked to Olson for help. "What is this?" His indignant tone fell falsely flat.

Olson said, "This is you talking to them. This is me buying you a break, and risking my assignment to do it. You're supposed to be the wise guy, right? So wise up."

"I'm not asking if you did those assaults," Boldt said. "I know you did. What Detective Olson knows is that regardless of your arrangement with other law enforcement, I now have enough evidence to arrest you for those crimes."

Alekseevich tried to look as if this didn't surprise him or upset him, but an actor he wasn't.

"What I need to know is if you did David Hayes night before last. And I urge you to think real clearly on this matter. In terms of your discussions with Foreman and Geiser, I want it verbatim if possible. Word for word," Boldt explained, in case his vocabulary went over the other's head. "What I'm *offering* you, and Detective Olson and her colleagues, is the chance to keep this little charade of yours going. This snitching of yours for the government." Olson looked troubled. Boldt said, "I have two options. One, as I mentioned, is to arrest you. The second, less ideal for you, is to tell Svengrad who his mole is and let him discuss this with you directly."

The waitress returned with the drinks and practically put her breast into LaMoia's face while leaning over the table. Boldt waited for her to leave. The ginger ale smelled of dishwasher soap and tasted flat. He pushed it aside.

"It lays out pretty simple," Boldt continued. "So why don't you start talking right now."

"Five minutes," LaMoia said, turning Alekseevich's own arrogance back onto him.

The room's shifting neon lights threw red across their

table. Alekseevich's skin took on a crimson tone, nearly matching the leather.

Boldt looked at his watch and said, "Four minutes." He then met eyes with the Russian. "You've got a lot of ground to cover."

Alekseevich looked over at Olson as if maybe she could fix this. Boldt hated to burn her goodwill, as it had gotten him to this point, but for him it came to Liz against Alekseevich, and that made it no contest. Olson sat back in the red leather, heaved a sigh of disgust, and said, "Start talking."

"Call them," Alekseevich instructed Olson.

She looked across at Boldt, her anger building. Boldt shook his head. She told the man next to her, "I can't."

"Call them," he repeated.

"This meeting isn't happening," Boldt reminded. "Not in her world, not in ours. So how can she make a call? She'd have to acknowledge arranging the meeting, and she's not willing to do that. Neither are we. By the time she places the call, we're out of here, and you're left with either arrest or Svengrad."

Alekseevich's blue eyes jumped between the three, his indifference losing some of its starch.

"Care for an extension?" LaMoia asked.

Boldt pulled out his detective's notebook and a pen, in an act of overt confidence.

Alekseevich began his debriefing, "I do what I am told. I am immune as long as I give report."

"Immunity," Olson provided for Boldt and LaMoia.

"Not from us," Boldt repeated.

"We're running out of time, here," LaMoia reminded.

Boldt took a risk. "Let's do it this way. I'll fill in the blanks and you'll stop me when I'm wrong."

Behind them some patrons cheered. Boldt didn't want to know why, but he briefly could imagine it was for him, given the choice he'd just offered Alekseevich.

Alekseevich pursed his lips and nodded slightly. Olson pulled out a narrow pad of notepaper, versions of which were in both LaMoia's and Boldt's coat pockets. Birds of a feather, he thought. LaMoia signaled the waitress, accomplishing what the Russian had failed to do. He ordered a vodka on the rocks for their subject.

Boldt translated what he'd brought in his head as questions into statements, and carefully laid them out like a card dealer turning over cards in a poker game. Both he and LaMoia looked for "tells"—tics or mannerisms indicating the suspect's knowledge of events, or his reluctance or unwillingness to share. Few were practiced enough not to involuntarily reveal something of their inner workings. Alekseevich had a language to overcome, the late hour, the few drinks he'd already consumed. Boldt worked him slowly, focusing almost entirely on Paul Geiser and Danny Foreman. Alekseevich tried to mask his curiosity—he'd clearly been expecting questions about David Hayes.

"Foreman's on Svengrad's payroll," Boldt stated for the man, about halfway into his laundry list.

"No." Alekseevich was working through the vodka a little quickly, a tell that revealed his discomfort.

The answer surprised Boldt. It had seemed the most obvious explanation. "You know this, or you're guessing?" But when Olson shook her head, he realized he'd asked a question, not made a statement.

"Hayes disappearing. You tried Geiser, thinking he was behind it, and got it wrong. Geiser gave you Foreman."

"Yes."

This reminded him of the game Twenty Questions that he'd played as a kid on long car rides with his parents. Thinking of his parents made him think of his sister, and thoughts of his sister made him think of his children. He didn't like doing business this way, but he stayed with it because Olson wasn't objecting. He stated, "Foreman threatened Svengrad. Extorted him for Hayes's return."

"I not know about that," Alekseevich said, breaking away from his monosyllabic answers—an extremely good sign that he was either growing more comfortable with the process or was becoming more drunk.

LaMoia looked ready to say something, thought better of it, and whispered into Boldt's ear. Boldt felt bad about using his friend, about not revealing the bigger game he had planned, but only he and Liz could later be held responsible. He wasn't dragging LaMoia into the consequences of what he had planned. He believed Liz's safety depended on this secret.

"You found Foreman," Boldt stated. "Tonight, I mean."

"Yes. Geiser was persuaded to make a phone call for us. Foreman took the bait."

"Foreman gave you the location of the warehouse—where to find Hayes. And your guys pursued it."

"Yes."

"Who tortured Hayes out at the cabin, if not you?"

"Not me," Alekseevich confirmed. "I don't know who."

"Someone else you work with?"

"No. It would have been me," the man said, indirectly confirming he'd done the others.

Regardless of gaining some clarity, Boldt felt pushed more deeply into the labyrinth rather than finding a clear way out. He then asked the question that LaMoia had posed to him, converting it into a statement. "Paul Geiser is on Svengrad's payroll."

Alekseevich hesitated, looking over at Olson.

She said, "You're dipping into privileged territory, Lieutenant."

"It's not privileged because it's not on the record, Detective."

She nodded back to Alekseevich.

"Perhaps," the Russian said.

"That's not good enough."

"It is best I can do. I have seen this man, Geiser, only but once, out at the Whidbey house." Alekseevich was slowly working away from plain answers, and Olson, to her credit, was making no attempt to stop him.

Boldt asked Olson about the Whidbey house and she informed him this was the Svengrad residence, a palatial estate on the southwest shore of Whidbey Island.

Boldt said, "Geiser was supposed to help get the injunction lifted—get Svengrad's caviar out of federal impound."

The man shrugged. "I do not know."

Olson explained, "Malina happened to see Geiser in a hall over at the U.S. Attorney's Office during a grand jury prep. It was a fluke—a dedicated elevator stopped and opened on the wrong floor. Malina looks out and recognizes Geiser from seeing him at Svengrad's estate. We never connected the dots any further than you just did, assuming the meeting had something to do with the caviar, but we've been careful to shelter ourselves from the prosecuting attorney's office. That's why we're dealing with the U.S. Attorney's Office instead—because of this thing."

This turned Boldt's world upside down. He now believed that for the past several hours he'd had Foreman's and Geiser's roles reversed. None of this fully ruled out that Hayes had been hidden by Foreman as part of a cooperative deal between the state's Bureau of Criminal Investigation and Geiser's office, as Foreman had told Liz. It seemed entirely possible that the two agencies might have discovered Alekseevich's informant status and wanted to protect the "ownership" of the Hayes case by keeping Alekseevich all to themselves. Turf wars could make monsters out of a common investigation.

Even if it proved true that Geiser had taken a bribe, or was still on Svengrad's payroll, it might involve nothing more than working on Hayes's parole and the injunction on the caviar. Svengrad's knuckle man wasn't going to have the answers to these deeper questions. The bottom line was that Boldt could trust neither Foreman nor Geiser. He knew Svengrad was seeking answers to some of the same questions that he had, meaning the race for the money still seemed to be on, which kept Liz squarely in it. This both excited and terrified him.

"Does Svengrad plan to kidnap my wife?" Boldt asked. The big man shrugged, and Boldt accepted the answer, believing Svengrad unlikely to include his subordinates in his long-term plans. It didn't confirm or deny the possibility.

"The comment about my son and his playing piano," Boldt said, distracted from his intended line of questioning. "Is Svengrad willing to play that card? My children? A police officer's children?" Boldt felt a bubble in his throat.

Olson tensed; this was clearly news to her. LaMoia looked unruffled, but Boldt could feel his concern like heat.

"Not me," Alekseevich said. "I not harm children. This man from bank? The one with heart problem? This was not me."

He meant Tony LaRossa and the abduction of LaRossa's family.

Boldt pushed, "But Svengrad is willing to play that card."

Alekseevich stared across the table and took a long sip of the vodka, draining it.

"Answer the question," Olson told him more vehemently than anything she'd said yet.

But Alekseevich already had answered the question, whether she'd picked up on it or not. That cocksure silence of his spoke loud and clear.

"What now?" Alekseevich asked, never breaking eye contact with Boldt.

That was Boldt's question as well.

TWENTY

THE SATURDAY BEFORE THE GALA reception and the ceremonial switchover from WestCorp to MTK proved the longest day of Liz's life. The waiting for the phone to ring; the surveillance/protection by both uniformed and plainclothes SPD officers, some of whom lingered in her living room; the temptation to call Kathy and the kids, versus Lou's determination not to make any contact whatsoever for fear of Svengrad somehow tracking it.

The only break in the day arrived in the form of a briefing. Pahwan Riz, the director of Special Operations, asked for a meeting with Liz and Lou to discuss what was expected of her "in the event" she was contacted. Lou agreed to the meeting, in part because he had to, in part because she was looking to relieve the tedium and monotony of waiting for the phone to ring. But Lou's primary reason for taking the meeting was to gather as much information about Riz's plan as possible in order to thwart it. If the combined efforts of Seattle Police and BCI prevented Svengrad from getting his money wired out, then the video was certain to surface, damaging if not ending both their careers. Quite possibly Miles and Sarah would be put permanently at risk. Lou had to defeat his own people while figuring out a way to protect his family. If he could double-cross Svengrad in the process—so much the better. Whatever Riz planned played into that.

Lou briefed her before the others arrived. "I'm cooking something up."

"I thought so."

"It's complicated."

"It is, isn't it?" She enjoyed the irony, though Lou seemed to miss it.

"It's going against my own guys. You've got that, right?"

Her faced knotted in concern. "You can't do that, Lou. Not for me. Not for anyone."

"The kids?" he inquired, silencing her. "Going against the very people who are about to be in this room, which is why it's important you go along with anything they tell you. It doesn't mean you *will* go along with it, but for now you'll tell them you will."

She nodded, cringing at the idea of his turning against his own team.

"Danny Foreman is not to be trusted. The deeper I look into all this, Danny keeps showing up."

"And he'll be here?"

"I suspect he will."

"I told you he seemed off when he paid me that visit," she said.

"The point is, I don't want us giving anything away, to Danny or any of the others, something they could use later on or something to tip them to my plan, so for now I'm keeping some things from you, and I just wanted to be up front about that."

"So noted."

Lou took in a lungful of air and held it, and she knew this to signal something important about to be said. She felt herself brighten with anticipation.

He said, "But you need to know that John and I took Hayes into custody last night."

She felt faint, unable to speak.

"Private custody. Not downtown. We got him out of a difficult situation, and I'm hoping he'll repay us by cooperating. That's a work in progress."

She clarified, "You got him *out* of a difficult situation. That's what you're saying?"

"However improbable, it's true."

"Private custody? What does that mean?"

"The point is, I'm working on something."

"I never doubted that, Lou. I just regret—"

He interrupted. "It's a long shot. In all honesty, it probably has only a faint chance of succeeding. But for right now, it's all I've got. And it's already in motion."

"In all honesty." She repeated his words with desperation in her voice. Her own lack of honesty had brought all of this upon him. She hated herself at that moment.

To her surprise, a man named Marc O'Brien ran the meeting. She didn't recall having ever met the man, and his attendance reinstalled her sense of violation—that some stranger had, at least in his mind, taken control of her life, was here to dictate to her what had to be done and how to do it. Judging by looks, O'Brien belonged in an Irish pub with a pint in hand to fuel his glowing cheeks and bubble nose. His loud voice supported his demeanor of reckless overconfidence. Here was a man who, on a sinking boat, would announce to anyone who would listen what a great day it was for a swim. His next-in-command, Pahwan Riz, the dark-skinned Malaysian, tracked Liz's every reaction, her every movement with his crisp green eyes, like a cat watching the family dog.

Lou, John LaMoia, and Daphne Matthews all sat stiffly on the same couch together, Matthews in the middle, lined up like Kewpie dolls at the county fair. Maggie, the infant child under Matthews's legal guardianship, slept in a car seat propped up between two chairs in the kitchen, turning the new mother's head that direction whenever an errant sound surfaced. Danny Foreman, looking worse for the wear, two fingers of his left hand bandaged, occupied a needlepoint bench against the wall that fronted the stairs leading to the home's second floor. Unseen up there, a police officer sat near a window keeping watch. Another indignity she could not get used to: the castle keep. Foreman sat forward, resting on thick forearms that pressed into his thighs. He lifted his head every so often looking as if he might speak, but apparently not finding the strength to do so.

She knew that if he'd had his way, Lou would have kept Foreman out of the meeting. But as he'd explained it to her, he couldn't block BCI from sitting in on the briefing, and he didn't have anything more than circumstantial evidence to bring against Foreman, not to mention that one cop charging another cop was fraught with bureaucratic red tape and could not be done without the inclusion of the very highest brass—and Lou wasn't prepared to go that route, given that he was planning to end-run his own department himself.

Riz announced, "The purpose of this meeting is that at some point in the next twenty-four to thirty hours, we expect that the conversion of funds resulting from the merger will necessitate an attempt to move the embezzled seventeen million out of the bank. That will apparently require your participation," he told Liz. "Your cooperation."

O'Brien said, "We believe you will either be contacted or abducted."

He said this loudly, and in a way that to her sounded grossly impersonal. She felt shivers ripple up her arms.

Riz clearly felt the man's insensitivity as well. He lowered his voice, looked directly at Liz, and continued, "We don't know where or when. We don't know how. Our intel is basically nil on this case. All we have is you, Mrs. B., and it's time we laid down some ground rules."

Liz had hoped to sit around as a spectator, a listener, to avoid any direct participation in this meeting, to let Lou do the talking for her. But she felt her mouth move, and out came words. "Yes . . . well . . . I don't know how many of you have ever been on the other end of this kind of surveillance, but I find it claustrophobic, invasive, and oppressive. So the sooner it's over, the better."

Riz and O'Brien ran down a number of possible scenarios for her abduction or participation.

Liz said, "You must be aware that there are at least four other people with security clearance to access the IBM AS/400s."

Pahwan Riz said, "Detective Foreman?"

Danny Foreman came awake, like one of Miles's toys that reacts to sound. Lou had mentioned that Danny had been tortured a second time, but there was no evidence of that. "Liz, BCI has had its eye on those of you with access since the day Hayes was paroled. You and LaRossa are the only two they've contacted, and LaRossa is now in ICU and not an option. That is not to say we aren't paying attention to the others. Of course we are. But the bets are on you." He sagged his head again, the doll back asleep. He sucked down his coffee as if it were juice.

O'Brien said, "Our play is that you're their target. Keep in mind that we are substituting one of our people for you, so there is basically no situation in which we see you in any kind of trouble. But we must take precautions. Our primary concern is what actions we take as a group, and specifically you as an individual, if we in fact experience an ACL. To brief you on the various proactive responses at your disposal."

All Contact Lost. Lou had coached her on some of the abbreviations, all of which she felt sounded childish and unnecessary. The secret codes made it more serious to them but more ludicrous to her—like a bunch of kids up in a tree fort planning a raid. O'Brien had begun the meeting laying out the difficulties of surveillance, of hostage situations, raising the possibility that her surveillance team might lose track of her at some point. The moment he said that, she realized a pawn had no choice but to move where and when the player dictated.

"If I carry one of those tracking boxes, they'll search me and find it, right?" she asked. "I mean, assuming they realize they've got the wrong woman and then somehow get hold of me."

Riz explained that there were other, smaller devices available that could be rigged inside her bra or in a hem, the toe of a shoe, or even her underwear or "on her person," which she took to mean a body cavity, and she felt briefly ill.

Riz added, "With the smaller devices transmission distance is considerably reduced." He made it sound like he was selling her a vacuum cleaner.

"So put one in my clothes. I'm okay with that."

"Fine," Riz said.

Lou met eyes with her, admiring her. She appreciated the gesture, but realized that at that moment he had little idea what she was going through.

"Your options include," O'Brien listed, "your playing by their rules and waiting it out; your attempting to give us some way to locate you; or—"

"Escape," LaMoia said, interrupting.

"Consideration of escape is *not* an option," Matthews said, objecting. "Trying to outrun organized crime single-handedly is simply not an option."

Again, husband and wife met eyes. Wasn't this exactly what Lou was proposing to her? Wasn't this the solution he had planned?

Again words left her mouth. "You're saying it is *not* an option." She made it a statement.

Matthews said delicately, "Thinking about it, focusing on it is not an option. They'll pick up on it. Hostage situations require the abducted individual to loosen the hold of the keepers. One does this by *playing into* whatever it is they've asked of you. By cooperating, not disobeying. You surprise them by your willingness, your eagerness, to cooperate. This has been proven over and over again to be a hostage's most effective way to gain enough physical freedom and emotional detachment to invoke a causal action that either reconnects with surveillance or provides an opportunity for intervention."

"Taking a phone off the hook, for instance," Riz said. "If we suspect a general area you've been taken to, we'll look for that kind of thing: a phone line left open for a minute or more."

O'Brien added, "You can 'accidentally' turn a stereo or television on too loudly. If they've got you in a car, you might bump the emergency flashers, might even turn them off yourself, apologizing."

Riz said, "Activate the rear wiper if it's not raining. Toss litter from a window. All these things are potential helpers."

"But what you don't do," Matthews said, "is try anything too overt: dialing the lieutenant's number, or 911 from a telephone or mobile phone. That would put you at risk, even if you see the opportunity."

"Check that," Riz said, interrupting Matthews. "If you dial 911 from a land line, even if you hang up immediately, we've got you, so don't rule that one out completely. Same with a pay phone, a car phone—a cell phone," he said, glancing at Matthews, "anything you can get your hands on."

Liz took note of the contradiction and sided with Matthews. Riz and O'Brien sounded more like they wanted her to keep the game going than to protect herself.

"Try to stand out of the crowd whenever possible," O'Brien said. "If they've got you moving, and they very well may, then cross on the red lights, jaywalk, use the stairs, avoid the crowds. It's the simple little things that allow us to stay with you better."

"The computers," Foreman said suddenly from his bench. He glanced at Liz. He had told her his and Geiser's intentions—that she wire the money to a government account regardless of what people like Riz told her to do. "Yes!" Riz said. "Should you find yourself logging on to the AS/400, about to gain access, first please type either Miles6 or Sarah4 as your password. The server won't allow you access, but you'll try again, using your correct password, and you'll be in. By doing so, you drop a handkerchief for us to follow."

"A handkerchief?" Liz inquired, not appreciating the analogy. It made her into a Victorian woman trying to garner attention.

"We could tell you more, but we'd have to kill you," a smiling O'Brien joked before thinking. The comment sobered and silenced the room. O'Brien apologized and said, "We believe Hayes possesses some way to erase all record of whatever he has you do while inside the server. If you signal us ahead of time, using Miles6 or Sarah4, it greatly increases our chances of tracing whatever it is you initiate." She fought herself to not look over at Lou. "It has to do with network IP addresses, and things I don't even understand, but White Collar Crime made it clear that they need you to send us the smoke signal if they're to have a chance."

Riz said, "Miles6, Sarah4, spelled exactly as they sound with the numeral following. We thought they'd be easy to remember. You type in either password, and we're piggybacked with you as you go in."

"It's like uncoiling a ball of string as you walk through a maze," Foreman said, lifting his head again and meeting eyes with her. He didn't want her giving them that string to follow. He wanted her doing this his way. Message received.

Liz found herself in a staring contest with Danny.

Matthews broke in. "You need your rest. We're done here."

Not long thereafter, everyone left the house. She and Lou rounded up the coffee mugs.

"So?" he asked.

"Ugh," she said.

Lou put on some music—plaintive jazz—and gently steered her by the elbow to a dead space in the room that offered no clear line of sight through a window, despite all the shades being drawn. He whispered, and it caused her shivers.

"I can't imagine what you're going through. They mean well, for what it's worth."

"Not much," she said.

"Is it possible, what they said about tracking you inside the bank servers?"

"Oh, yes," she replied. "If key tracking is present, then every time I touch a key they'll follow it."

He considered this for a long moment. "Then whatever you do, you mustn't enter those passwords they gave you. You mustn't turn on the key tracking."

"They don't know David," she said, immediately regretting the intimacy that implied on her part.

He glanced up into her eyes. She saw disguised hurt.

She explained, "He's far too sophisticated a programmer to leave any of this up to human error. Yes, anyone using the AS/400 would have to log on to do so, and to move the money out will require routing information and an account number, and it's possible, though not certain, that account data will have to be manually input. But would he allow a key-tracking program to run? Absolutely not. My value to him is that I can get past the physical security to reach the AS/400 *and* I have a password that will allow access into it. But do you think he would allow their software to record whatever account numbers are input? He's smarter than that, Lou. Even if I type one of those passwords, David will have already thought of a way to defeat it. Trust me, they're not in his league, Lou." She added, "I don't mean for that to be hurtful."

"It's good information," he said, though his voice cracked, belying his true emotions.

"Danny gave me this look," she said. "He's still expecting me to transfer this money where he says to transfer it."

"It's not Danny I'm worried about. It's the idea that *whoever* gives you an account number risks your remembering it. By phone, by note, it doesn't matter how it's delivered—it's your recalling it later they can't afford."

"They are typically enormously long strings," she said.

"Doesn't matter," Lou returned. "You're a banker. They can't rule out that you have a head for such numbers. And if you memorize the destination account, the money can then be traced and found, right?"

She nodded, understanding immediately the subtext and why her husband was reluctant to say it aloud. "If I'm around to repeat it," she said.

Lou did not look at her, nor did he speak directly to her comment. Instead, he backed away and mumbled something about needing a cup of tea.

This, she realized, had been his fear all along.

□ □ □

"Are we going to talk about this plan of yours?" she asked, the two of them eating ham sandwiches at the kitchen table. Lou had stayed at the house following the meeting, some-

thing she hadn't expected but found comforting. At first
she'd thought him exhausted and in need of the rest, but
she amended that opinion as he then spent two hours working over a yellow legal pad.

He said, "It's occurred to everyone that you'd be at extreme risk. We know for a fact that my guys will expect
me to insist you use a stand-in. I will demand it, of course.
I have already. They will never, in a million years, believe
I would arrange for you to double-cross them."

"So they'll expect an undercover woman to play my
part, and we'll go along with that."

"We'll go along with it on the surface. Anything else
would be out of character."

"So it's kind of a race," she said.

"If we play it right, that's exactly what it comes down
to, yes. The real Liz beats the fake Liz to the AS/400s."

"And we accomplish that, how?" she added.

"We beat them off the starting line. We deliver the
unexpected—something they didn't plan for. It's not easy
to fool the fooler. Not when they have as many as a dozen
undercover officers watching our every move. But I know
their training. I know the contingencies they plan for. Our
bigger concern is Svengrad. He lost Hayes *and* the software; he lost everything. He knows that you are needed to
accomplish this. It's inevitable that he comes after you. Remember that none of the people here this afternoon, except
LaMoia, knows I have Hayes locked away."

"Gaynes does," she said, playing devil's advocate and
immediately regretting it, for she saw the consternation it
caused.

"She wasn't here for the meeting, and she's on our side
anyway."

She wasn't sure why she corrected him this way, as she so often did. To gain the upper hand? To show him who the clearer thinker was? To be noticed? In the short term it felt good to correct him, but within a few seconds she typically wanted to crawl and hide, knowing her timing was terrible. She apologized to him, saying, "I do that all the time and I'm not sure why."

Lou winced, stung perhaps by her sincerity. "We're going to make it through this."

"You think?"

"Taking him into custody humanized him for me." There was no asking about whom he was speaking. He went on for a moment, talking himself out of any feelings of superiority that his abducting Hayes accounted for, discrediting any moral supremacy—that he worked the side of good and David the side of evil. He was telling her that he'd overcome some hurdle, and she was listening.

She wanted to tell him that he shouldn't risk his career by pulling a sting on his own people, but in many ways it seemed too late for that. If the tape was released, his career and his family would suffer; but if he were caught tricking his own people, he might lose his pension as well. With her actions she had put him squarely into unworkable options, and now she forced him to look for some way out. She told him as much, expressing her remorse as sincerely as possible. She said, "I don't think this kind of thing can be undone using legal pads."

"You'd be surprised. Legal pads come in very handy."

"We're going to joke about this?"

"What choice do we have?"

"A woman is going to take my place out there. You realize the danger we put her in?" she asked, allowing her real anger to surface now. "Never mind all the secret codes that *I* can use to leave crumbs for your people to follow. What about her? What codes is she going to use when these people—very nasty people according to you and yours—realize they've got the wrong Liz Boldt?"

Lou held up the pad of legal paper. She saw inked handwriting and boxes and arrows—a complicated diagram resulting from a conflicted mind. He said, "The best defense is a good offense."

"You can't be oblique right now. I'm not up to it."

"It never gets that far."

"Never gets how far?"

"Your surrogate. I agree. We can't let that happen."

"You can stop it?"

"Timing," he said.

"But they're ready right now. They've got some stand-in ready around the clock to take my place. That's what they said, right? Did I miss something?"

"They're expecting you to receive a call. Everything hinges on them listening in to our land line and both our mobiles. You get the call and a clock starts. A substitution is planned—here at the house, if possible; in the field, if not."

"But how has that changed?" she asked, still puzzled.

"You arranged for the costume to be delivered to my office, did you not?"

"I did." It took her a moment to realize he intended that as his explanation, not a question for her to answer. "The costume," she said.

Lou pointed to the top of his yellow pad and a box there so heavily outlined the ink had smeared. "It all starts with the costume."

She didn't know what that meant, not exactly, but resolved herself to the fact he was now calling the shots. He saw some way out of this, however dim. No matter that she struggled to have faith in him and his yellow pad, she was bound to him body and soul. He ran the early part of the show, and she committed herself to doing exactly as he instructed, even if it struck her as an exercise in futility, which it currently did. The later part of the show, inside the bank, was all hers.

"I'm never going to sleep tonight," she said.

"Yeah," Lou agreed. "I know."

TWENTY-ONE

LIZ WENT TO CHURCH SUNDAY morning, and Boldt went with her both out of a longing to be near her and a desire to protect her. Over her objection, she carried her mobile phone, set to vibrate if called, and the two sat on the aisle so that she could jump up if it rang. Boldt didn't mind the services, appreciated that there were two readers instead of a minister, that the sermon derived from the Bible and an interpretive work, not the pulpit and preaching. The hymns, sung robustly, often ran gooseflesh down his arms, praising love and promising hope. Of all things dear to Boldt, hope was perhaps the greatest. He reflected on his motivations for becoming a cop all those years ago, aware that hope factored into it, a belief in a moral code and the knowledge that someone had to uphold that code. Other cops had brothers who had been shot, sisters raped, homes vandalized, all valid reasons for signing up. But for Boldt it had amounted to something far less visceral: a cause, a calling. The church and its parishioners represented the community he felt he was there to protect. And so the service was filled with irony for him, as the person who needed the most protection was his own wife, and for reasons of adultery and what the church would call sin. In the past few days he had worked his way to a form of understanding that made their time together tolerable. He felt forgiveness a long way off, a firefly at the end of a very long tunnel, but a necessary step toward a full healing between them. Whether he and Liz made it fully back to sharing love or not, there was no abandoning the family.

"What if I'd gotten the call last night?" she asked over a salad at a sandwich shop after church.

"You didn't."

"But if I had?"

He shrugged off the question. "You roll the dice, you take your chances."

"We weren't ready."

"The costume was delivered to my office late Friday," he said. "I checked," he said, when she gave him an inquisitive look. "After we talked last night, I thought I'd better check."

"So why's it so important?" she asked. "The costume? Or aren't you going to tell me?"

"You have enough on your mind."

"That's a lousy excuse."

He stabbed his salad. A little salty for his palate. "Too much anchovy in the dressing."

She eyed him across the table, annoyed by his avoidance. "So we were ready," she asked, adding, "if I'd gotten the call?"

He said, "The complication was no delivery on Sunday. I had to find a way around that. John's gone to help us out. Then again, maybe it won't be you at all. Maybe you're a diversion, nothing more. Maybe Phillip is inside the bank at this very moment making the wire transfer."

"You'd have heard, wouldn't you?" She sounded deeply concerned, and he realized that she was already exhibiting some hostage traits, involving herself emotionally to the point that if someone took her place it registered as disappointment instead of relief.

"I would have," he confirmed, worried about her once again. His concern came in waves, but he noticed a tendency for the troughs to run lower as the minutes ticked on. "If the call had come early, my plan wouldn't have flown," he admitted. By prior arrangement, they both knew what came next. Liz was to throw herself into it, while Special Ops looked on in befuddled confusion. If all went well, for a brief few minutes Daphne Matthews would play his wife. There had been a time when he would have welcomed that thought. He now understood far better the pain such fantasy represented.

"What are you thinking?" she asked. "You've gone silent over there."

For over six years he had kept a secret, and now it seemed there was no room for such artifice. Her past had been stripped off her without choice, dogs tearing at the hem of her clothing until exposed. The process had allowed Boldt to remain sanctimonious, when in fact he had his secrets too. "The woman I slept with . . . the one-night stand when we were separated—"

"I don't begrudge you that," she said, interrupting. "I was running around with David. You were hurt. We've been through this."

"It was Daphne," he said, identifying his partner for the first time. Crushing Liz, judging by the surprised look on her face. She gently placed her fork down onto the edge of her plate, some salad still attached, the dressing now dripping onto the table. Too salty, he thought, as she quietly excused herself from the table and walked toward the rest rooms.

A full ten minutes passed before she returned solemnly to the table, her face and neck glowing red as they did after a hard cry. Boldt had paid. She stood there by the table, never making any move toward the chair. "Ready?" she asked. She turned toward the door before he answered, and he followed, resisting her effort to make him feel bad for telling the truth. In his mind there was a time and a place for everything, and this had been both. He felt he needed to explain Daphne's willingness to go along with this, to put herself and her job at risk; he felt obligated to be as honest with her as she had been with him, and there was just no good time for such revelations. They came when they came, and his had come in a sandwich shop after church and the call for redemption in the beautiful hymns. The other thought on his mind, the one he dared not share with her, was that he might be in jail by the end of the night, and that if he were arrested, the one person he could count on to fight for him was Daphne Matthews, and that Liz should understand the connection they all three shared. The truth could hurt no one. *Our strength is not lessened by giving utterance to truth.* One of the readers had read that line during the service and it had stuck in Boldt's craw as he had realized all the pain she carried for bearing the burden of her truth, while his own truth remained guarded. No more. He had not said this to wound her, despite what she might think. He told her because he had a bad feeling

about the events to come, and he needed to bare all before
their arrival.

She kept to their bedroom for the first few hours of their
return to the house, and he left her there to deal with it.

She ventured out only once, stopped in the doorway,
and said to him, "It's all right. What you did. Telling me,
I mean. It's my problem, not yours."

"If you believe that, we're in trouble."

"If you believe we're not in trouble already, you're fool-
ing yourself," she fired back. "Danny Foreman said I'd get
a call Sunday evening. Tonight. That the call would arrange
for me to pick up David's software, that I'd make the transfer and the money would go to a government account."

Boldt had expected the conversation to remain on his
brief affair with Daphne Matthews—that Liz would make
him pay for that. But now he realized she was looking for
a way out of that morass while at the same time attempting
to remain clear about what was expected of her. He picked
up her lead and explained, "Danny is the one who'll be
making the call. Danny must be the one with the software.
I'm guessing he was the one who ran me on my goose
chase. The Palm Pilot—when he was talking to you—
wireless Internet access. He was following my every move
in the car that night. According to Geiser, there is no deal
between him and Danny Foreman, which means either
Geiser is lying as Danny said he would, or Danny is pulling
a Lone Ranger in order to make these arrests and recover
the money. The third possibility is that Danny's planning
an early retirement by keeping the money for himself. I
don't want to believe that. The one who got burned by
Hayes's disappearance is Svengrad—and he's also the one
with the long reach, the one to watch, which is why he

directed that you would be using his account for the transfer and no one else's."

"But *what* account? Where's the number? He should have given it to me by now."

"He can't. He knows Pahwan would stick some electronic glue onto that account number and that he, Svengrad, would never be free of us. He's too smart for that." Boldt asked, "So the question is: How and when will he get the account number to you?"

"And why has he waited until now?"

Boldt felt a flash of heat pulse through him, as if he'd accidentally grabbed a live wire. Past conversations percolated through him like groundwater rising during a flood. He answered, "Because he knows you aren't in the bank . . . that you aren't anywhere near that server." It hit him so clearly—it explained so much.

"He's watching me? Having me watched?" she said, suddenly looking left to right as if expecting to catch someone staring.

The tumblers fell into place and the truth unlocked for him. He felt an immense sense of relief, wondering at the role of random chance and whether he or Liz would have reached this same place, made this discovery, had he not confessed to her.

He continued by saying, "Listen carefully to what I'm about to tell you."

TWENTY-TWO

SUNDAY AT 5 P.M. BOLDT'S cell phone rang as if he'd set an alarm clock. He and Liz were sitting in the living room, the shades drawn, she on the couch, he in a chair, she pretending to thumb through a catalog, he monitoring the surveillance radio channel via an ear bud. For the past thirty minutes no words had been exchanged, as the clock moved toward the bank reception.

A thirty-year-old female officer, whose name Boldt had already forgotten, remained within earshot at the kitchen table. Liz continued scanning gift items as he answered the call, didn't succumb to the gravity of the moment. Boldt terminated the call and said to her, "There's a taxi out front. The driver's on his way up to the door with a box."

Liz checked her own phone, then glanced up at Boldt before he turned his attention to the kitchen where the officer was already receiving orders over the secure walkie-talkie.

Boldt jumped up and waved Liz into the bedroom and the backup officer out of sight, cradling his handgun behind his back and moving toward the front door. All for show.

Liz knew this taxi's arrival was Lou's doing. He waited for the doorbell to chime, gave it an appropriate pause, and opened the door. The cab driver sounded half Indian, half Arab. "Happy birthday to the Missus," he said. The box was wrapped in a flower-print paper, torn and untaped on one side. The driver explained, "I don't deliver nothing without seeing what's inside. But it's okay. Only clothes. Forty bucks for a five-dollar fare, what the hell?" He added, "There's a note," pointing out the unaddressed white envelope taped to the top.

Boldt stepped back, leaving the door ajar, and told the driver to open the box. "Empty the contents."

"Listen, Mister."

Boldt displayed his shield and repeated himself.

The driver tore off the paper and nervously upended the box. A pile of black and white clothing spilled out. Boldt instructed him to shake out the clothing, which the driver then did. Boldt returned the gun to its holster, tipped the man ten dollars, and attempted to send him away, at which point the driver said he'd been instructed to wait for the fare.

"To take her where?" Boldt inquired.

The man shrugged. "I wasn't told. Listen, you want me to take off—"

"No." Boldt put on his best face of confusion for the sake of the backup officer. He sent the driver to wait in the cab and then pushed the door shut. He held up the first of what turned out to be several oddly shaped pieces of clothing. A nun's habit.

Boldt locked the door, called the Command van and suggested they double-check the cab number to verify it was legitimate. He quickly filled in Riz on the little he knew of the situation, and promised "more to come."

Boldt carried the box and the note into the living room, summoned Liz and the officer, and placed everything on the coffee table. Boldt handed Liz the note that he himself had printed out.

The envelope was not sealed. She slipped out what turned out to be a movie ticket.

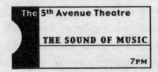

"This is them," she said, again for the sake of the plain-clothes officer.

"Yeah. We can still call this off," he offered, as she sized the clothing.

"They don't gain anything from hurting me as I leave the house. They need me inside the bank. Willing to co-operate."

The plan called for Officer Malone, already dressed identically to Liz by prior arrangement, to switch out and take her place ahead of Liz's arrival at the bank's merger party. There were several contingencies available to accomplish this. At present Malone remained on her stomach in the back of Liz's minivan in the Boldt garage. That could change as needed, but those changes would take time and Boldt had the advantage now. Special Ops had expected a phone call with an account number. They'd gotten much more.

Boldt heard over the radio that the cab was legitimate. He checked the window and confirmed it remained parked at the curb, engine running.

"No minivan," she said.

"Yeah, I know," Boldt said.

"So we'll have to do the switch somewhere else."

"Right," he confirmed, making sure the woman officer overheard all this.

Liz moved into the bedroom and donned the nun's habit over her existing clothing, a smart black cocktail dress, sheer pantyhose, and a pair of low heels. The officer pointed out she'd have more mobility if she lost the heels but that Malone wore the same shoes and so she'd better keep them on. Liz agreed.

Boldt hung up from a cell phone call. "It's a sing-along, like *Rocky Horror*. Costumes. Twenty bucks a seat."

Trying to make light, Liz said, "I'd make a better Maria, don't you think?"

The officer reminded her that her bra contained a tracking device and assured her that they'd never be far away. Husband and wife met eyes—a covert exchange that the officer was not allowed to see.

Liz added a starched white section over her shoulders. Boldt helped secure it in place with Velcro.

Liz donned a Flying Nun headdress. He found it odd that a few pieces of clothing could add so much innocence and virtue. Her face looked peaceful and beautiful, not a strand of hair showing. Even as pale as she'd been lately, next to the stark white fabric her skin looked Italian olive, healthy and vibrant. All lies.

They met eyes in the mirror. Boldt forced a smirk.

"If you're thinking of making a joke, don't."

He grinned and nodded. "You'll be fine."

Boldt answered his cell phone and heard Danny Foreman's voice. Foreman occupied his Cadillac Escalade, parked down the street from the Boldt home, riding alone. Boldt walked into the living room to take the call in private, knowing that at this same moment, Homicide detective Mark Heiman was at On-Sat, keeping track of the location of Foreman and his car. Boldt still didn't trust Foreman despite Hayes having no recollection of who had beaten him.

Foreman asked, "What the hell is going on?"

"Some kind of attempt to spoil our game plan, I imagine." Boldt explained the movie ticket and the nun's costume.

"Does that sound like Svengrad?"

"Hayes, maybe." Boldt put it out there, playing as if he didn't know any better. He wondered if Foreman had returned to the warehouse yet, if he knew Hayes had "escaped." He, Boldt, had to play it as if Hayes were still at large. This juggling act of lying to Foreman, misleading the surveillance team in hopes of springing Liz, tricking the officer assigned to their home by allowing her to hear rehearsed conversations between him and Liz, all took their toll. Playing several roles at once, Boldt felt scattered and schizophrenic.

Liz appeared from the bedroom.

"I don't like it," Foreman said. "What if it's someone else—Geiser, for instance—trying to manipulate Liz for his own gain?"

"Making that kind of suggestion could get you in trouble, Danny. I could accuse you of the same thing." He let that hang there. "Then where would we be?"

He heard Foreman breathing into the phone. Foreman said, "They're going to want her at the reception, not at some three-hour movie. You can't let her make this play."

Boldt had expected a similar argument from Pahwan Riz. The embezzled money had to be wired out ahead of the merger, and the chaos of the VIP reception appeared to offer the best opportunity. A person could argue that Liz should ignore the nun's habit, the movie ticket, and head straight to the reception, due to start at 7:30. But to his credit, Riz, accustomed to the fluidity of a special operation, had so far issued no such directives.

"That's Reece's call, not mine," Boldt told Foreman. "You leave it up to me, Liz stays home tonight, watches reruns, and goes to bed early."

Riz had a good plan all worked out: Malone subbed for Liz during the most exposed part of her itinerary, from the minivan on, in case Liz was abducted. Meanwhile, Liz would be transferred under tight security to the bank—safe once inside and able to access the AS/400, through the security requiring her palm print. It was a plan Boldt could not allow to happen because of the cards Svengrad held.

"Reece has a good plan," Boldt reminded.

"Doesn't include this," Foreman complained.

"We adapt, right, Danny?"

"I'm just saying: I don't like it."

"So noted." Boldt disconnected the call. So far, so good. Riz had not thrown up any roadblocks.

"Miles6, Sarah4," Boldt reminded her as he approached. He didn't want her using these passwords under any circumstances but had to appear otherwise.

THE BODY OF DAVID HAYES   283

He stepped forward to hug her and she whispered into his ear. "Is this going to work?"

"Stay with the plan," Boldt said into her ear.

She kissed him on the cheek. It felt strangely foreign to him. He felt like kissing her back or hugging her, but inexplicably did neither. Instead, he opened the door for her and watched as she walked toward the waiting taxi.

He had calls to make. Arrangements. His complex plan to beat his own people without breaking laws and without being discovered suddenly seemed so fragile, so easily broken. Seeing the taxi drive off, he wished he'd said something more to her, longed for a second chance before sending her off without so much as a dress rehearsal. If Svengrad or Foreman had a plan to abduct Liz, Boldt had just beaten them to it. He'd abducted his own wife by arranging the costume, by buying the ticket to *The Sound of Music* ahead of time. By having it delivered by taxi. However tenuous, he controlled the strings now, though for how long was anyone's guess.

□ □ □

LaMoia felt awkward dressed in his black funeral suit, a white shirt, dark vest, Stewart plaid bow tie, and gray felt hat. With his hair pulled into a small ponytail and tucked down his collar, even his colleagues were unlikely to recognize him—which was, of course, the point.

Fifth Avenue, Seattle's most posh shopping street, was crammed with traffic, the sidewalks overflowing with both the dinner crowd and theatergoers. The 5th Avenue Theatre stood directly across the street from the WestCorp Bank

Center. The Four Seasons Olympic Hotel occupied the opposite corner.

He stood in a line of several hundred people, families, kids, full-bodied coeds in tight, colorful shorts, all dressed from various scenes in the movie. Women in full skirts and high heels—Maria. Men dressed as boys in lederhosen with its *latzbund* and *schlitzfleck*. More nuns than in a convent. But the real shocker was the uniformed Nazis—enough to run a concentration camp. It was as if the film had given an excuse to the white supremacists to play dress-up.

LaMoia was one of only a handful of Max Detweilers, giving him the feeling that he'd chosen the least inspired costume in the bunch. For her part, Matthews, as always, looked astonishingly perfect as a rosy-cheeked Maria, turning more than a few heads as she and LaMoia had found their places in the long line that awaited a slow box office.

The earpiece from his cell phone alerted him to the arrival of Liz Boldt's taxi just west of the theater. Pahwan Riz's team had followed her but were scrambling to get people costumed and on the ground in order to stay with her.

"The Sarge is a genius," LaMoia told Daphne. He pressed his hand to his ear to isolate the voice in the ear bud. "The flying nun just entered the ticket holders' line behind us. Reece is about to blow a valve."

Daphne said, "Get seats near the back. I'll tell her to look for your hat."

"You be careful."

"It's not me they want," Daphne said.

"That's what worries me," he said. "Nothing stupid."

"Agreed."

LaMoia couldn't see over a couple of Nazis ahead of

them. So when they made it inside and Daphne split off toward the women's room, he lost sight of her. Liz Boldt pushed past in her nun's outfit, close enough for him to reach out and touch her.

LaMoia kept his hands to himself.

◻ ◻ ◻

Liz loitered by a trash bin in front of the women's room where a line had formed. The theater's lobby teemed with costumed moviegoers hungry for popcorn and to be seen by friends. The din made it hard to think. Bumped from behind, she turned to face Daphne Matthews, who looked strikingly beautiful in her Maria outfit. She felt her face flare behind the emotions of looking at her husband's former lover, an identity kept secret all these years. The sickening combination of disinfectant, perfume, and hairspray overcame her as they moved into the rest room. A strong waft of marijuana overcame the other odors. She hadn't seen a bathroom so crowded since her high school prom, and all the women dressed as one of three or four characters. She rubbed up against the Baroness, only to see the stubble of beard through the cosmetics. Somewhere in heaven the Von Trapps were as nauseated as she.

Wall-to-wall costumed freaks, Liz realized. Some were on drugs, or boozed up, anything to lower their inhibitions and allow them to croon through the three-hour film, thinking they were Pavarotti or Sills. The volume of talk in the tiled room proved deafening, the air thick with too many conflicting odors.

Again Daphne bumped her from behind. Adrenalized, and mildly claustrophobic, she felt tempted to scream out at the woman. Instead the two pushed into a toilet stall together, and Daphne turned quickly to lock the metal door.

"You," Liz said, not sure why it came out this way.

"He briefed you, didn't he?" Daphne asked.

"Oh, he briefed me all right," Liz said, finding the opportunity impossible to pass up.

Reaching behind for her own zipper, Daphne looked back at Liz curiously. "We should get started."

Liz made no effort to undress, embarrassed beyond belief to have to show her body to "the other woman." She said, "He told me it was you. The affair. The one-night stand."

Daphne looked as if she'd been punched, as if she needed to lean past Liz into the toilet bowl. She said, "Yes . . . well . . . this isn't the time."

"All these years," she said. "Your coming to our house. Always playing so sweet and considerate. How did I miss it?"

"Liz, whatever you two are working through, I'm not part of that. We've got enough going on here without this. Okay? This is designed to buy you time. We're wasting that time."

"It's more insidious than what I went through with David," she said. "You see him every day. Interact with him every single day. How can you do that without thinking about it? I don't think you can. You don't, do you? So you think about it, and you both share it, even though it's years behind you. That's kind of sick for a psychologist, don't you think?" She didn't understand why she clung to this, except that the last thing she wanted to do was disrobe in front of this woman, and engaging her seemed a way to stall. Daphne pulled the dress off her shoulders, revealing first her substantial cleavage and then a white bra and finally the smooth tummy of a woman who had not given birth. Flawless, like something from a magazine, and only then did Liz glimpse the depth of what Lou had gone through to suffer her own affair with David Hayes.

Liz felt herself an awful combination of humiliation, regret, and anger. Her emotions bubbled to the surface. The stall was so small that Daphne switched places with her, passing closely enough that their chests touched. Daphne sat down on the toilet in order to keep the dress from touching the floor, pulled down past her underwear to her knees. A waxed bikini line.

Liz asked that she be allowed to undress in private. Daphne looked at her as if she were crazy and said, "There are fifty women out there, all waiting for a stall. Liz, please . . . now."

"I can't do this."

"Don't be ridiculous."

She wanted to say: *You slept with him. You were naked with him. I've had cancer. I've had two children.* But she understood how petty and trite that would sound—especially aimed at a woman offering to take her place in a dangerous situation and one in which Daphne was to go unmonitored; Daphne was preparing to trick her own colleagues, risking all kinds of future discipline. She said nothing, but stood paralyzed by the situation.

"Undress. Now!" Daphne said sharply.

"That'a girl!" a stranger's voice shouted from an adjacent stall.

Daphne sat down on the toilet in bra, tights, and shoes, working to get the tights off.

Liz turned around and asked Daphne to help with the

Velcro to the various pieces that made up the nun's habit, which Daphne did.

Daphne said, "You can bunch the top of your dress at the waist. The skirt is longer than yours, so you can wear the LBD under it." Little Black Dress.

Liz got the habit off. She felt cold fingers as Daphne unzipped the cocktail dress for her, and helped her half out of it. She would need the dress for the reception. Lou had chosen it in part because it would hide underneath the Maria dress.

"Bras," Daphne reminded.

Liz felt nauseated. She was being asked to bare her chest in front of Daphne as they switched bras in order to move the concealed tracking device. There was nothing left to her chest, wizened by nursing two children, flattened by gravity, corrupted by the starvation of cancer treatment. She turned her back on Daphne and then passed the bra back, wiggling her arm until Daphne claimed it. The one that was handed her was a bigger cup size. She swam in it, and she found this humiliating. Liz reached for some toilet paper mumbling, "This is embarrassing."

Daphne struggled to adjust Liz's bra straps. The undergarment barely contained her breasts, fitting uncomfortably. "Hand me the rest of the habit," she requested.

"I get two dresses. You get none," Liz said, turning now as she stepped into the Maria dress.

"That's about right."

"That thing—a couple Velcros is all to close it. You're going to fall out left and right."

"Luckily, it's dark," Daphne said.

"How can this possibly work?" Liz asked, having trouble with the zipper and once again needing Daphne's help.

"We switch purses—the one thing that identifies you—and I find a seat and watch the movie. The hook is baited. Everyone, our own people included, are watching for a nun leaving the bathroom with your purse. I hide the purse and they'll never confuse me with you. You'll fail to show." Daphne pulled a red-headed wig from her own bag. "We get you into this. You join John near the back. The two of you leave together at intermission. Two people leaving together, not a single. A Maria, not a nun. He walks you out, by which point you're headed for the reception—better late than never. You're in the bank while Special Ops continues sorting through nuns trying to find you. Lou looked at this thing from every way possible. It's not perfect, but it's as close as we're going to get."

"How do I get in the bank? We're assuming the bank is being watched, aren't we?"

"One thing at a time," Daphne said. "John's got that covered."

"That's all you're going to tell me," Liz said, sounding disappointed.

They exchanged purses. Liz placed all kinds of symbolism into this act and thought that as a psychologist Daphne could probably sort through it all, but had no desire to discuss it.

"And if my cell phone rings? If *they* give me instructions that go against this plan of Lou's?"

"He worked this out with you, didn't he?"

Liz felt deflated. He had, in fact, walked her through this a half dozen times, but she'd wanted to hear it again. She now realized the absurdity of this desire, given their current location.

Daphne instructed, "Go out there and find John. That's

all you focus on right now. It's a zoo out there. Find John and follow whatever he says. He's at the back of the theater." She repeated, "The back of the theater."

Liz felt inadequate, ashamed of her behavior over the past few minutes, responsible for people putting themselves at risk—all because of her past. But she could not find it within her heart to thank the woman. She helped Velcro Daphne into the habit. Skin showed, and flashes of underwear.

They transferred the contents of the purses, Liz making sure she retained the two bank IDs she carried—one supplied by Lou—her wallet, lipstick, and mobile phone.

"All set?" Daphne asked. Daphne looked good even with just the oval of her face showing. Jealousy brewed inside her once more.

She nodded.

Daphne added, "For what it's worth: John and I are happy together."

"It's not worth much," Liz said quickly and uncharitably. "But I'm working on it."

"Good." Daphne indicated the stall door, and the two women spilled out into the din and clamor of the rest room, among a dozen competing odors. Women's voices crooned off-key, "The hills are alive . . ."

Daphne joined in at the top of her lungs as if having the time of her life. The back of the habit hung open slightly, exposing her bottom. She never missed a step.

A clear, perfectly pitched voice on top of everything else. Liz thought she might be sick.

She stepped into a world where people lay in wait for her, and this thought terrified her. She wanted to be home. With him. She wanted another chance at whatever it was

they now called their relationship. Marriage? Companion-
ship? Parenting? She pushed away the thought that an organized band of criminals, perfectly willing and capable of
submitting to violence, needed her services first and her
lack of memory second. She held off the thought that Boldt
believed Danny Foreman had turned against them all and
represented an uncontrolled, unchecked piece of the equa-
tion, seemingly willing to take matters into his own hands.
Her feet moved forward steadily as she trained her face to
look to the floor, exposing as little of herself as possible,
containing her new red-headed identity. But she knew even
the most well-trained man would have a hard time keeping
his eyes on her given the busty nun in the loosely attached
habit who split off and headed down an aisle and took a
single seat in the middle of the theater. Daphne Matthews
and her flashing backside had every eye in the lobby. No
doubt, all part of Lou's plan.

Liz pushed her way through the thick crowd, tolerating
the close contact. Her claustrophobia began to work against
her. She hated crowds.

She took up a rhythmic chant in her head, scanning
the seats for sight of John LaMoia: "Only a few more
minutes . . . a few more minutes . . ."

There he was, waving a box of Milk Duds at her, his
arm around the empty chair she would soon occupy, a gor-
geous babe to his right spilling out of her dress while
openly flirting with him: John LaMoia, in heaven. Liz felt
a sense of dread sweep through her, as if a thousand eyes
followed her down the row. She felt those eyes boring into
her, studying her, looking to identify the face beneath the
wig, and she regretted not having used the toilet while
she'd had the chance.

□ □ □

Liz never sang a note. For an hour and a half LaMoia seemed to enjoy himself, an ear bud planted in his left ear as he monitored the surveillance team's radio traffic. He crooned through the songs as if he'd rehearsed the parts, but she saw his eyes tracking the room like a Secret Service agent's. Nothing got past him. He faked a few smiles for her, and she appreciated that, but he felt as nervous as she did. Lou was the only one who knew fully what was going on, and she found her trust in him the only comfort.

Within moments of the intermission announcement, just as the room erupted into applause and people jumped from their seats, throwing the auditorium into chaos, her phone buzzed and tickled her right hand, and she touched La-Moia's shoulder to get his attention.

He nodded, and she answered it, plugging a finger in her left ear.

A low, mechanical, sterile voice said, "It's time." The line disconnected.

She felt all the color drain from her, all warmth. She existed in another realm where all motion slowed around her, and all sound stretched and distorted. LaMoia asked, "What's up?" but her brain barely processed the inquiry.

"It's time," she managed to say.

"What about the phone call?" LaMoia asked, misunderstanding.

"It's time," she repeated, explaining that this had been the message delivered. The room spun. She locked on to the armrests in order to slow the carousel. She wanted the movie back. She didn't want to go anywhere, do anything.

As childish as she knew it to be, she wanted nothing more than to stay right where she was.

LaMoia leaned into her ear. "I'm going to tell the Sarge, but not until we're out of here. This is our chance—this craziness. You gotta get up. We gotta get moving."

"I don't think I can."

"I'll carry you if I have to, but we're outta here."

That got her moving. She stood and followed him out into the throng. LaMoia motioned toward a side exit where a number of people were already lighting cigarettes as they stepped outside. She and LaMoia cut through a row of seats toward these open doors, and as they did she felt the eyes on her once more and the seeds of distrust and fear fought to take root yet again. Up the street the WestCorp Bank Center loomed.

"I don't know that I can do this," she said to LaMoia.

"I don't think you got a choice," he returned. "Hang with me. We're almost there."

But in her heart of hearts she knew this too was just another lie.

They had barely begun.

TWENTY-THREE

BOLDT WORKED THE CASE LIKE a fire juggler with too many torches in the air. He had recused himself from direct participation in Liz's surveillance, surprising no one by declining an offer to take a seat in the Special Ops steam-cleaning van, electing instead to drive himself around and listen in on the radio. Riz warned him politely but directly that he didn't need "any rogue operatives" during his effort to keep Liz safe, and Boldt lied, assuring Riz that he would keep his distance.

He took up a position, parking across the street from the bank building's north entrance, a place that included a view of one of the two entrance/exits to the high-rise's private underground parking facility. His biggest concern remained Svengrad and men like Alekseevich. Into the mix he threw Foreman, whom he knew to be operating solo but whose motives remained unclear, and therefore his danger to Liz difficult to assess. Somewhere out there, Boldt believed Olson and Organized Crime were keeping watch now that Alekseevich's status remained so closely tied to this case and Boldt's decision making.

His job was to trick Special Ops into sitting on a decoy—Daphne Matthews or one of the several dozen other nuns in attendance at the movie—while LaMoia smuggled Liz out of the theater and put her in play. Svengrad had made it perfectly clear that no substitutions were to take place, and as yet, Boldt felt unwilling to challenge the man. The second part of his job was to allow Liz to transfer the money without Danny Foreman messing things up or getting selfish. Ultimately, he had plans beyond this, but early into the chicanery, his focus remained his wife's safe transfer, slipping her past the watchful eyes of Special Ops' "B"—as in "bank"—post, a group of three technicians who currently occupied a *Seattle Post-Intelligencer* panel truck conveniently parked over an open manhole with unseen video trunk lines running into the bank through the floor of the truck. From that truck the three could monitor every surveillance camera in the building, could directly communicate with bank security, and could even listen in over the public address system's microphone during tonight's reception. He knew his one advantage was that unbeknownst to anyone but him and a trusted few, he was working directly with his nemesis, David Hayes. Hayes was the wild card he intended to play to its fullest. As much as Boldt was loath to admit it, Hayes could run circles around all of them.

"Yo!" Boldt heard in his ear after answering his mobile phone. LaMoia informed him that Liz had received a call just after the start of intermission. A synthesized voice again, short and to the point. *Foreman,* Boldt thought, finally beginning to sort out the various roles being played. Assuring Boldt that he and Liz had slipped away successfully, LaMoia concluded by saying, "We're happening."

Translation: They were about to cross the street to the WestCorp Bank Center.

Call-waiting chirped in the phone and Boldt signed off with LaMoia, accepting a call that turned out to be from Heiman at the On-Sat navigation offices. Foreman's Escalade was on the move, heading downtown.

"Interesting timing," Boldt muttered. This too fit into an expected pattern.

He called Gaynes into action. Posing as a waitress, she would now join the reception, a stopgap and final line of defense known only to him. Hayes was to be guarded by Milner, one of LaMoia's trustworthy soldiers. Boldt ended the call, expecting to see his wife at any moment, wondering if his plan could get her into the bank without her being seen or detected and identified by the elaborate electronic surveillance already in place.

He counted on David Hayes to help him, if indirectly. In fact, Liz's survival now depended on him.

□ □ □

In the midst of a light drizzle and traces of ground fog that swirled between the high-rises like smoke from a fire, a darkened figure stalked through the rain toward the west pedestrian entrance to the WestCorp Bank Center shopping complex, a lower-level mall that sat below the bank.

Police radios, quiet for the past several minutes, drew attention to this visitor. The mall stores had all closed at 6 P.M., though access to parking and the tower elevators remained open. Not one pedestrian had entered the shopping complex in the past half hour, raising suspicions as this figure approached.

The "B" unit commander, Dennis Cretchkie, jockeyed his team, directing an undercover wheelchaired officer to enter the facility behind this visitor. Cretchkie called for reports. Off Fifth on University, the Town Car set jammed the Olympic Hotel's U-shaped driveway, the hotel doorman blowing his whistle for taxis stacked along the curb. A small group of white seagulls flashed in the black sky and shrieked noisily overhead. A homeless woman pushed a supermarket cart laden with soggy blankets and aluminum cans uphill, leaning into her effort. A street-cleaning machine lumbered slowly up University, brushes spinning, eliciting the complaint of car horns as it hindered traffic.

The undercover officer in the wheelchair reported that the unidentified pedestrian was a woman carrying an umbrella that obscured her face. As this unidentified subject—"unsub"—approached the west entrance of the underground mall, the cop in the wheelchair worked furiously to intercept her, hoping she might hold the door for him and thereby give him a good look at her face. His effort failed.

□ □ □

Monitoring surveillance activities over the police radio, Boldt sat forward in the front seat of the Crown Vic, the steering wheel pressing into his chest. Every action, every move by Special Ops was crucial to the success or failure of his plan. Boldt was parked with a view of the north side of the block-square complex, with no view of the unidentified woman who had just entered WestCorp Center. With the announcement of her entering the mall, Pahwan Riz, one block east, with a view of the 5th Avenue Theatre, pressured his detectives and operatives in the audience for the exact location of "the mark." *Liz*.

"I want a positive ID," Riz said, "and I want it now."

Damn him, Boldt thought. Riz had always been one of the smarter ones. Boldt phoned Daphne Matthews to warn her that Riz's team was inspecting the patrons more closely in order to obtain a positive ID.

A moment later Matthews said, "I see them. It's Brandy and Klinderhoff, each coming down an aisle." Judging by her suddenly muffled voice, he pictured that she'd bent forward, head to the theater floor. "But it's crazy in here."

"I need at least ten to twenty minutes, Daffy."

He heard a loud cheer and music in the background.

"The purse!" Boldt shouted. "Make sure they see the purse." He knew how a cop's mind worked. The purse would convince either Brandy Schaeffer or Howie Klinderhoff as easily as if either saw Liz's face.

Daphne disconnected the call, and Boldt was left with indelible melodies swimming in his head. He saw a WSDOT Metro bus pull to its stop on Fifth Avenue. The arrival of the bus won the attention of Cretchkie and his "B" unit because it briefly and effectively blocked Cretchkie's view of the complex. An undercover officer was dispatched, though too late. Cretchkie shouted across the radio, "Get the fucking buses off Fourth and Fifth Avenues. All eyes on anyone and everyone coming off that bus!"

Riz cut in, demanding once again that Liz be identified in the film audience.

The umbrella woman entered an elevator and rode it one floor to ground level, where she had to switch elevators in order to continue into the office tower. The wheelchair officer followed on the next elevator car, reporting every few minutes.

The bus pulled away, scattering pedestrians, most of whom stayed on the WestCorp block, requiring Cretchkie to account for them.

In all of the commotion, little if any attention was paid to the homeless woman's abandoned supermarket shopping cart, now canted into the wall just outside the entrance to the bank's underground parking garage.

Boldt fixed upon that shopping cart. A smile crept slowly across his face.

Liz was inside.

□ □ □

Liz struggled to clear her head. During the walk with LaMoia at intermission he directed her across the street and down into a sunken courtyard plaza that fronted a Japanese restaurant. There, she jettisoned Maria's frock, covering her little black dress with a street urchin's Salvation Army wardrobe.

LaMoia indicated a street person's shopping cart packed with aluminum cans and some other junk. It had been secreted into some bushes in the courtyard.

He then smeared her face with some brown base, making her look street dirty. "There's a damp towel in the cart. Use it to clean this off." Lou had planned all this carefully in advance. She found it difficult to hold up under the pressure.

David Hayes had put her here, and the level of her resentment briefly stole all thought and clarity. Despite her usual Christian thinking, she vowed to have some kind of revenge against him. Ultimately, recovering the money would be the revenge, and she steeled herself to make it through the next hour of her life and to put things straight.

When the bus pulled up, at the very minute LaMoia had told her it would, she pushed the junk-laden supermarket cart against the concrete wall and slipped into the shadows of the underground garage, already planning her metamorphosis. She kept only the damp rag. Fatigue took a physical toll on her, leaving her feeling spent—despite the clamor of her heart in her chest.

She headed directly to the glassed-in area that contained the elevators and stairs. It was from this garage that she had first sneaked away to a rendezvous with David Hayes, from this garage that she had left on maternity leave.

As she heard the distant hiss of the bus brakes releasing, she reached into the waiting elevator and tripped the button for the ground floor, then jumped back out of the car. As she pulled open the heavy door to the fire stairs, immediately adjacent to the elevators, she heard the elevator doors slide shut behind her. She stepped inside the stairs and began to undress immediately. She cleaned her face in the reflection of a fire extinguisher box.

Lou believed her sending the elevator up might distract the minimum-wage security team, whose job it was to monitor television screens in a darkened room somewhere in the building. Dressed now in her black cocktail dress, Liz climbed the stairs. The garage stairs deposited her into the main lobby. She still had to pass through security in order to reach the main bank of elevators.

Liz said hello to Dilly, the portly security man with whom she was friends. As she did so, she used Tony

LaRossa's ID card on the turnstile in front of the metal detector through which she would pass. Lou had no doubt that Pahwan Riz had cued security's computers to watch for Liz's entrance to the office building. It was even possible the security computer had been set for a special notification when Liz's ID card entered the system. Lou's gamble that Riz would not have given the same consideration to Tony LaRossa's card paid off. The light turned green, the turnstile moved, and Liz passed her purse to Dilly while she stepped through the metal detector.

Dilly looked shell-shocked to see her. She stepped up to him, physically closer to the man than she'd ever been, and whispered clearly into his ear. "I know you're supposed to report my arrival, Dilly. Believe me, I know *all about* it. And that's a decision you will have to make. But if you do, what happened to Tony LaRossa will happen to me." She kissed him on the cheek, took her purse, and walked away, not looking back.

The elevator typically required the use of an ID card to reach the restricted floors, including the twenty-fifth floor and I.T.'s data processing. For the sake of the reception, that requirement had been overcome by stationing a security guard as an elevator operator to shuttle guests. This came as an unexpected complication. Liz's way around being seen by this security guard was to use the stairs once again, for one reached the stairs before the bank of elevators. She climbed twenty-five floors in less than ten minutes, her heart and lungs burning, her calves aching. Using Tony's security card, she entered the floor at the end of a hall that had been taken over by the caterers. The roar of conversation and the smell of chicken satay greeted her. A moment later she was just another little black dress in a reception with dozens of invited guests.

Lou had taken it on faith that Hayes's software would reach her. She felt less inclined to believe this, knowing David was under watch and believing that without his direct participation the transfer would not happen. But it was Lou's show, and she played her role as directed. In her head an imaginary clock continued counting down the minutes to the corporate switchover.

□ □ □

Boldt called Gaynes on her cell phone and asked her location.

"Heading into the lobby from the shopping area."

"They saw you enter. They put guys on it."

"The mark?" Gaynes asked, meaning Liz.

"She's in."

"Oops," Gaynes said. "Gotta go. Looks like I'm about to be caught."

She disconnected the call before Boldt could remind her that if her cover as a staff waitress for the caterer failed, she should use her police credentials against the bank's rent-a-cops, and that if confronted by Cretchkie or Riz she should pass blame back onto him, Boldt, who in turn would argue that it was his wife, and if he wanted to slip his detective inside the bank then it was his prerogative. It was in fact *not* his prerogative, but he could live with a brief dressing-down from Riz if it came to that.

He encouraged his cell phone to ring, awaiting confirmation that Liz had reached the twenty-fifth floor. Even if the empty-elevator ploy got security's attention, Boldt expected no drastic action to be taken by the bank. No one in his right mind was going to shut down this merger reception as the couple approached their wedding bed.

Boldt put his head back against the headrest, understanding but not quite accepting that he had to wait it out like a director in the wings watching a play.

Then, when the phone did ring, it was only Heiman, reporting from On-Sat. "The Escalade's moving south," the voice said. "Heading through Fremont at the moment. If I had to guess," Heiman said, "I'd say he's still heading downtown."

□ □ □

Having tended once again to her hair and lipstick, centering the strand of pearls she wore around her neck, Liz rounded the corner into the open area of the twenty-fifth floor and immediately spotted Phillip Crenshaw's gray-white mane across the crowded room. She elected to steer clear for the time being. Phillip had been carefully briefed on all aspects of the embezzlement case, by Liz, the police, BCI, and the prosecuting attorney's office. Liz didn't want him seeing her and then making phone calls to check up on her. If they crossed paths, fine; she would tell him in private that she'd been run through what now appeared to be a ruse, but still had not taken possession of the software, nor had she been given the account number—all true.

It surprised her how well the data center transformed for the event. Her staff had done a terrific job. Several transit posters announcing the merger had been placed strategically to hide unsightly workstations. Helium balloons grouped in threes livened up the place. Champagne flowed

as waiters and waitresses circulated. It appeared that most
if not all of the forty to fifty invitees had shown up. Finger-
food-sized crab cakes and cheesy hors d'oeuvres laced the
air and enticed Liz's empty stomach. She recognized any
number of faces and said short hellos to various groups as
she passed, making her way to the registration table
manned by several of her staff. The overall mood was fes-
tive: canned jazz playing and champagne lifting voices into
peals of laughter. A lot of money was being made off this
merger, not the least of which went to the attorneys, a cabal
of suits who hovered near the wine bar like a school of
barracuda.

"Charlotte." Liz smiled at the attractive young woman
behind the welcome desk.

"There you are!" Charlotte bent over and reached below
the table. She handed Liz a name tag that bore a small blue
ribbon, a touch that Liz didn't care for but something Phillip had insisted upon. The ribbon identified Liz as "co-
hostess" and made her feel cheap, as if she were throwing
a Pampered Chef party instead of a reception for a
multibillion-dollar merger. "This came for you."

Charlotte gave her a plain manila envelope. A plain
white label bore her name and nothing more. It was the
right size and shape and thickness for a computer disk.

"How'd you get this?"

"It was messengered to the lobby desk. Dilly sent it up."

"When was this?"

Charlotte heard the concern in Liz's voice and reflected
it. "Just before we got going. A few minutes before eight.
Why?"

Liz backpedaled, sorry she'd suggested there was any

problem. "Oh, no reason." She forced her face to soften. "It's just in time. Thanks." She glanced to her right, where the end of the room was sectioned off by polished steel beams and thick, unbreakable glass, and looked right at one of the twin AS/400s, a black, solid block of computer the size of a washing machine. Behind the server and out of view was a small desk holding a large flat-panel screen and a keyboard. The placement of this workstation intentionally screened the operator in order to prevent any eavesdropping or spying from without. The machine's twin sister sat to the right in a small office of its own. This more private room was where most of the heavy lifting was done by programmers and maintenance. This was Liz's destination. To reach it, she would have to pass through a palm-scanner, as well as an ID reader. She would be under the glare of the overhead lighting, visible to all. She would stick out, given that there was no activity at that far end of the large room. Her entrance to the space would alert security and, in turn, the surveillance team.

The cake had been Lou's idea, his solution to part of this dilemma, and only then did she think to follow up with it, asking Charlotte about its readiness.

"It's here," Charlotte replied. "But we're saving it for *after* the switchover, right?"

That had been Liz's original instruction, but now that had to change for the sake of timing. She could feel Special Ops close on her heels. "The switchover is actually just ceremonial. Phillip . . . Mr. Crenshaw, will throw a switch, yes. But the final exchange of data won't occur until after midnight. Then our servers are off-line for good."

"Right . . ." Charlotte clearly wondered why Liz would explain what she already knew.

"So what can it possibly matter when we serve the cake? The point being that once the switch is thrown, the party peaks, and maybe folks don't stick around for the cake."

"Just admit it, Mrs. Boldt," Charlotte said, nearly stopping Liz's heart. "I know your real reason for changing plans."

Liz felt the color drain out of her face and her hands go cold.

"Choc-o-holic, anyone?" Charlotte cracked up. "Confess your sins, Mrs. Boldt!"

Liz felt nervous laughter escape from her throat. "Caught!" she said, her knees weak and actually trembling. "Me and chocolate! You got me. Let them eat cake."

"How soon?"

"Let's give the hors d'oeuvres another few minutes, and then surprise everyone." Liz kept one eye on the end of the room, and the brightly lit secure office. "And don't forget the candles and the room lights. Phillip wants this to be dramatic."

Charlotte beamed. "I'll tell the caterers."

"I'll do it," Liz said, wanting both the excuse and the opportunity to avoid circulating as much as possible. "If anybody's getting an advance taste of that cake, it's me."

Charlotte grinned, and Liz left before her mouth got her in real trouble. She'd never been a good liar, even through the months of the affair with David. Had Lou not been so consumed at the time, he would have caught on sooner.

The caterers from Wild Ginger had usurped both the galley kitchen and a small conference room across from it, down a hall near the stairs that Liz had climbed only minutes before. Asian odors of pickled ginger and plum and cinnamon thickened with her approach. It took her a minute to locate the woman in charge, a woman with whom she'd had dealings. Their meeting in person was cordial and businesslike. Liz asked that the cake be brought out earlier than originally planned, and the caterer saw no problem with that, asking for five to ten minutes to clear the hors d'oeuvres and to orchestrate the change. Liz said Charlotte would dim the lights when signaled, knowing full well there was no dimming the overhead fluorescents. The entire floor would be briefly dark, the guests' attention fixed on the candles and the cake. This would be the moment Liz needed.

Halfway back down the hall, she stepped into an empty office and pulled out her cell phone. Lou answered right away.

"I'm in. Watch for the lights. Five minutes, maybe ten."

"They're searching the theater. Riz is going to have this figured out soon if he doesn't already. They'll think you were pressured into this, but they'll still expect one of those two passwords from you." *Miles6. Sarah4.* She didn't intend to use either; there would be no alerting Pahwan Riz to the actual transfer. "I've got Bobbie inside as a waitress," Lou continued. "When you're done in there, you need to call me."

He'd stressed this need to call him about a dozen times and it annoyed her that he'd repeat it yet again. "I got that, Lou." She regretted the tone, not knowing herself, hoping that whatever woman she'd become over the past few weeks would not stick.

"Okay." Boldt ended the call.

Liz slipped the mobile phone back into Daphne's purse and spun in the chair, preparing to leave.

"I thought that was you." A deep male voice she recognized before looking up. Danny Foreman blocked the doorway.

"Wouldn't miss my own party," she said.

"Who were you talking to just now?" he asked. "Lou?"

How much did he hear? She couldn't remember what she'd said on her end of the conversation. The manila envelope that contained a disk remained inside the purse. *How much does he know?* "I don't remember your name being on the invitation list," she said.

"Half of Special Ops is looking for you in a movie theater at this very moment."

"Not you."

"Not me. I wanted to make sure we still had our understanding. Protect the state's investment in this investigation."

If the money went anywhere but the Svengrad account, her children weren't safe. She thought that by now Danny Foreman probably understood this as well. She said, "I wonder what Pahwan Riz would think of your being up here. Lou, for that matter. Couldn't just your presence here blow this?"

"I'm here to make sure you get out safely."

That gave her chills. Lou had warned her no one would want her remembering the account numbers. Her thoughts poured out of her before she could stop her mouth. "It's not a government account, *is* it, Danny? Never was. This is about Darlene for you. Injustice. This is something between you and David and this guy Svengrad."

"You're at serious risk once this transfer is made."

"From whom? What's your plan, Danny? How safe am I?"

"You're mistaken, Liz. Horribly mistaken. It *is* a government account. I told you before: We need that money as evidence if we're going to get a conviction. It's as simple as that."

"Simple?" she asked. "Can you actually say that?" She didn't know how to read him. Half in shadow, Danny Foreman wore an intractable expression. "Should I call Lou or Special Ops and thank them for sending you? Should I ask security to call someone to let them know you're here at the reception? How do you want to play this?" She felt the seconds passing by, and her chance to sneak inside the AS/400 room escaping along with it.

"I'm going in with you," he said. "I'll input the account number myself. We wouldn't want your nerves causing you to mistype a number."

This was completely unplanned for. "Wiring the funds requires an account number, an ABA routing number, and a name for the account. It's foolproof, Danny. I won't mistype it."

"I'm going in with you. Look at it this way: In the event of a trial it will protect us all if I witness your actions."

"I'll be lucky to get in there myself, alone. Two of us? No offense, Danny, you're not exactly dressed for the occasion." Of the guests assembled in the room not twenty feet away, half wore tuxedos. Foreman looked as if he'd slept in his clothes for the past week.

"I'm going in there with you."

She looked for some way to circumvent him. It dawned on her then—a possible way to lose Foreman, but she would need a head start. She would also need an alternate plan, the answer to which lay with Lou—Lou, and Bobbie Gaynes, a wild card whose presence here remained unknown to Foreman because it remained unknown to Special Ops as well. "Okay," she said, "you win."

Foreman first looked surprised, then satisfied with himself, until she spoke again.

"Do you know how to tie a bow tie, Danny?"

He frowned, then caught on to the suggestion.

"We've got to get you looking right," she said. "Let me see what I can work out with the caterer. I'm the one who hired her in the first place." She had him cornered and they both knew it.

"I'll come with you," he said.

She wanted to object but didn't feel confident lying to him, fearing he'd see through the lie. She nodded acceptance, her mind working to see a way out of this, Danny Foreman an albatross she could ill afford.

Thinking more clearly than she, he said, "I'll take your cell phone."

She reached into her purse and took hold of the phone, offering it but not yet passing it to him. "Will you? And what will you say to Svengrad when he calls? You need his wire information or you don't have a case against him. Isn't that right?"

"You must have that information by now."

"I do not," she told him, wondering as his face tightened further if she'd given him too much information. This was Lou's world, Danny Foreman's world, not hers. She started her phone back toward her purse but Foreman took it from her.

"All the more reason you need me," he said, pocketing it.

She needed the phone. Special Ops would be watching all calls from and to the bank's phones; she didn't want to be "caught" dialing Lou's cell phone number. She also still expected the call from Svengrad. Not to mention Lou.

"There are security cameras *inside* this room with the servers," Foreman said. "Riz has cameras aimed at both keyboards in case the key-tracking software fails."

Liz realized he was just talking this through. He was right; she'd been briefed on the locations of these cameras as well.

"Lou worked it out, didn't he?" She waited to see what he was getting at.

"LaRossa gave Hayes a way to monitor your security cameras," he said, theorizing. "Svengrad hasn't called you because he knows you're not in the restricted room yet. He's waiting for your move." He paused. "You did or did not use your own ID when you entered tonight?"

Liz had thought her use of Tony LaRossa's ID had been to hide her from Special Ops, not from Svengrad. Only now did she sense that Lou had this second motive in mind as well. She clutched her purse, as Foreman reached for it. She felt an urgent need to protect Lou's plan, whatever it was. "There *is* a security camera in this hall. I *do* know that. You'll be on camera if you come with me. This may take me a minute." She tore herself free from Foreman's grip.

She turned and stepped out, and Foreman followed. Together they walked down the hall to its dead-end fire-stairs door. Liz's mind raced to find a way around this. Foreman remained a half step behind her and to her left. She couldn't turn and outrun him. She needed a break, a way to put even a few seconds between them, seconds in which he would not miss her.

At the galley she introduced Foreman to the caterer as

"a law enforcement officer." Liz explained he needed a cover, and that she'd thought of his taking the place of one of the waiters for just a few minutes.

"He'd need a white shirt and tie," the woman replied.

"I'm aware of that," Liz said. "That's why we're speaking to you."

The woman sized up Foreman like a fashion designer. She said, "Let me talk to Michael. He's about your size."

A few agonizing minutes later Foreman faced a young man carrying a white shirt and bow tie. "We'll use the office," Foreman said, indicating the door down the hall. "Wait here," he said to Liz.

Foreman and the waiter moved down the hall and entered the office to exchange shirts and let Foreman tie the tie. He left the office door ajar to prevent her from slipping past.

Liz winced a smile. The mouse had walked willingly into the trap, all of his own accord.

Liz drew the caterer close and whispered, "When he asks, you tell him you had your back turned and didn't see which way I went."

Before surprise had a chance to fade from the caterer's expression, Liz gently pushed against the stairway door's panic bar, then threw her hip into pushing it open and slipped out. Cool air slapped her face. Her limbs and chest went feverish with adrenaline. At the bottom of these stairs was freedom, and for a moment that temptation weighed on her like gravity.

Before she reached the first landing, she heard a flurry of footsteps from below. Someone—security, probably—was coming up. Coincidence? she wondered. A random security check? Or had LaRossa's ID triggered a full-scale search? If a search, they wouldn't be busting through the front doors of a formal party but using the stairs, as she now heard so clearly. She debated returning to the relative safety of the twenty-fifth floor behind her. The footfalls continued to climb toward her, and at a pace that indicated someone in shape, reinforcing her belief it was a security guard. At last, with nowhere to turn, she stiffened her posture, took hold of the railing, and descended—*walked*—one hand on the rail. She was one of the five most powerful people at WestCorp, and this building belonged to WestCorp—at least for a few more minutes.

Bobbie Gaynes rounded the landing in the black-and-white uniform of the caterers. "Mrs. B.," she said, clearly surprised. "What's wrong?"

"Danny Foreman's up there." She explained her predicament and what she needed from Gaynes, speaking quickly and in a hushed voice.

"Okay then," Gaynes said, when Liz had finished.

"You can't get onto twenty-five without an ID card—from this side, the stairs. It's restricted access."

"So I'll pound until someone opens up," Gaynes said.

"If that doesn't work. . . ." Liz fished into Daphne's purse and passed Gaynes the LaRossa ID, telling her to use it, "But only if no one opens the door for you. And if Danny asks if you saw me . . ."

"Foreman doesn't know me. I'll just be a waitress who sneaked out for a smoke and got locked out." She added, "Hopefully the caterer goes along with that."

The women reached out and grabbed each other's forearm at the same time. It seemed an awkward gesture to Liz, somewhere between a handshake and a hug, but she was grateful for the contact. "Five minutes, tops," Liz reminded.

"Got it." Gaynes bounded up the stairs effortlessly.

Liz turned and hurried down to twenty-four, believing she still had a chance to accomplish the transfer on time. Floor twenty-four lacked the security of the data department immediately above. Liz passed into a darkened corridor, switching on the lights and running through the maze of hallways. Inside, the pounding of her heart counted the passing seconds; the lighting of the cake and the darkening of the room were only minutes away.

□ □ □

When Boldt saw the first set of lights appear in the windows on the twenty-fourth floor, his first thought was housecleaning. But then another string, and a third string illuminated, and the short time between them suggested someone in a hurry, and his blood rushed to his face. It looked as if security were chasing someone. He thought of Gaynes and Liz.

At that same moment, the police-band radio sang with exchanges between the command van and Special Ops officers who had failed to locate Liz inside the theater, frustrated and limited in their effort by the darkness and the audience's penchant for jumping to its feet in spontaneous song. Judging by the growing agitation in Riz's voice, he sensed he'd lost his mark and feared his surveillance had failed, which in turn reflected directly on him and his ability to lead. Riz was a smart, capable cop. Soon he'd be checking with his people already in the bank, those assigned to watch the security monitors. How much longer until Liz was spotted, and what would the repercussions be?

The string of lights now stretched entirely across the twenty-fourth floor. Boldt craned his neck and put his face to the windshield to see.

Unable to tolerate another minute of this, and understanding the need for someone to distract Riz's people from seeing Liz on a security camera, Boldt left his Crown Vic and marched through a light drizzle toward WestCorp Center, well aware that as he did so, he became a target of his own surveillance.

□ □ □

Liz reached the elevator bank on twenty-four and called an elevator, the wait excruciating. She knew that by now Foreman would be frantically searching for her, probably dressed as a waiter and moving through the guests, tray in hand.

Use of the elevator meant risking identification by the security guard operating the car. Her hope, that the car might arrive filled with smokers or late arrivals, that she might meld into the mix, proved too optimistic. The doors opened and she boarded an otherwise empty car—she and the guard. He stared at her, well briefed.

"Yes, it's me," she said, once the doors had closed. The one floor ride would be over quickly.

"I thought so," he said.

"They probably didn't tell you about this part," she said. He said nothing.

"Don't blow it by saying something," she said, just as

the doors came open. She walked out, glancing directly at him once more to show him the strength of her conviction.

As the doors shut behind her, she had no idea if her ruse had worked, but she didn't have the luxury of worrying about it. By the time the guard reported her and the announcement went up the chain, she needed to be sitting in front of the AS/400 making the transfer.

Liz moved through the main door, Charlotte at the table to her right, looking for a tall, African American waiter, so she could steer clear of him.

"Elizabeth Boldt?" a heavily accented voice asked from her left.

She turned to see a big man with a beard and dark, piercing eyes. She lowered her sight to the name tag stuck to his lapel, his name written in a casual cursive, not the calligraphy that her staff had arranged and paid for.

"Yasmani Svengrad," the man introduced himself, extending his hand.

She found herself rooted, frozen in place. She did not offer to shake his hand, and a moment later he lowered his own.

"S&G Imports. We're a private banking customer," he said, naming WestCorp's elite customer program that required seven-figure net worth. Phillip's staff, not hers, had handled the invitations to the private banking customers. "Eight ounces," he said.

"Excuse me?"

"We donated some caviar to tonight's event. Very last-minute. Eight ounces of Beluga. Another eight of Osetra."

This explained his receiving an invitation.

This man who had watched her children, who had threatened to expose the videotape, said, "We have interests in common, you and I." He had yet to take his eyes off her, holding her with that steady stare.

She felt weak, almost faint. Whatever Lou, Foreman, and Riz had thought, none had prepared for this moment. Rather than show her weakness, she fought against the urge to step back, stepping forward instead, nearly touching him. "I share *nothing* in common with you," she said while looking him squarely in the eye.

A grin parted the graying beard and mustache. Svengrad was amused by her, nothing more. "A few minutes of your time is all, Elizabeth." He lowered his head to where she *felt* his voice as it warmed her neck. "I love how you look in satin," he said. Standing erect again, he regained that confident smile. He raised his voice. "Yes, I'd love a tour. Please, lead the way."

Liz caught a signal from Charlotte, who was no longer at the reception desk but standing in the doorway that led back to the hallway where she'd just been with Foreman and the caterer. Charlotte moved her fingers to signal she was about to kill the lights, and Liz nodded, holding up a single finger—one minute—knowing her moment had come.

She walked away and Svengrad followed. They passed through a few knots of conversation until Liz heard her name shouted out. She processed it as Phillip's voice—a summons from the boss. She turned, waved, and quickly pointed toward Charlotte, then tapped her wrist indicating "time." To her relief, this proved enough to stop the man. In her peripheral vision, she picked up Danny Foreman, an empty tray held high and carried in front of him. Without making eye contact, she hurried on, Svengrad following.

She imagined that behind her Foreman was now plowing through the cocktail party to catch up.

With thirty seconds to go, she navigated past a group of workstations, reaching the glass barrier that contained the first of the AS/400s.

She turned in time to see Foreman in his waiter's garb, his bow tie crooked on his long neck, hurrying toward them. Liz's left hand hesitated above the green screen of the palm reader, a book-sized device mounted by the door to the glass room, her own ID card ready in her right. She slipped the edge of the ID card into the card reader.

The lights went out. The guests cooed and turned to face the candle-bright cake that appeared in the doorway at the opposite end of the room. Liz pressed her hand to the screen and watched a small red light turn to green. She heard the *click* of the electronic latch. Svengrad was now pressed up against her, physically contacting her.

"Wait!" Foreman called, still a few steps off.

The room was all ghostly shadows and cutout silhouettes, the only light from EXIT signs and the distant glow of the cake visible in the reflection off the door's security glass. A smaller image appeared behind Foreman's tall silhouette. "Agent Foreman," the female voice said, "Detective Gaynes, SPD. You're interfering with a surveillance op."

Liz used the distraction to pop open the door and slip inside, but with Svengrad immediately behind her and coming through as well. She turned quickly and bumped the man out of the way and hurried to push the door shut. A satisfying *click* rang out just as Foreman turned from Gaynes and lunged for the door. The thick glass muted whatever Foreman said to the detective, but even in the limited light, Liz saw his fury.

Liz hurried to the door of the neighboring server room, got it open, and turned to pull Svengrad through behind her just as the overhead lights switched back on. A dull electric hum filled the room. The server was a brushed, dark gray. It looked much bigger close up than she remembered. She went to work immediately, having no idea how much fuss Danny Foreman might make, how much trouble he might cause her. She dropped the manila envelope on the floor, slipping the optical disk it contained into the server, grateful that such operations required little of the operator. The disk auto-loaded. A few small lights on the server flashed, and Liz intently watched the screen, awaiting its instruction to input the wire information.

> *INPUT*
> *USER ID:*
> *PASSWORD:*

This was her moment. Without her, the server would not permit access. Lou had been clear about how to play this moment, and she rose to what she considered the most important performance of her lifetime.

"Without me, this doesn't happen," she told Svengrad.

"You didn't go to all this trouble just to change your mind."

"The video."

"You'll have it."

"Yes, I will," she said. "And you will have your company back and your passport reauthorized when I do."

"What's this?"

"From my husband. *Quid pro quo*. You understand Latin, Mr. Svengrad? He said to tell you that he talked the government into releasing your product. But he also had INS make your passport invalid for travel outside the country. It all depends on the return of the tape."

"Enter your password," he said.

Lou had stepped her through this carefully, believing the conversation would take place over the phone. In person, she found it much more difficult to say it with conviction.

"Your company and your freedom for that tape," she said. "Your word on it."

"My word," he said. She didn't believe him.

Lou had insisted she bargain with Svengrad, despite her repeated arguments that he held all the cards. "It's complicated," had been Lou's reply, who went on to say he couldn't tell her everything that was in play.

She typed in her user ID, and then her password, which appeared as a series of asterisks.

Svengrad pushed her out of the way and sat down in the chair, and Liz did not attempt to fight him. She told him, "I was going to use whatever account information you gave me. You could have trusted that."

Svengrad watched the screen as various commands were announced and small graphs, indicating loading time, moved like the mercury in a thermometer, marking progress. He said only, "This is better."

One of the loading instructions caught her eye—an account number she recognized—and for the first time she understood what David had done to hide the money. *Brilliant,* she almost said aloud.

Finally the screen they had both awaited presented itself, a preprogrammed menu offering wire transfer options. Svengrad instructed her to stand back from him. He slipped out a piece of paper, pulled the keyboard into his lap, leaning over it, and carefully input the information into the machine. She wondered if he knew about the camera looking down from above, or if his instincts were nothing more than blind luck. Either way, she thought he'd probably used Hayes's know-how to cut off the surveillance. The entire process passed quickly. Liz marveled that all these weeks of agony had culminated in a few keystrokes and no more than a couple minutes of time.

Svengrad hit the ENTER key. The screen hesitated, then delivered a graphic announcing the transfer was complete. "Done," he said, looking at Liz with a triumphant look.

Lou had fed her several lines, making her repeat them carefully, on the off chance Svengrad left the phone line open as he gave her wiring instructions. She said them now. "Yes, well . . . I, for one, never trust David when it comes to his programming." Svengrad's triumph suffered a momentary twitch of concern. "You and I saw that money get wired. For your sake, I hope it goes where you think it's going."

"David Hayes knows better than to cross me."

"Yes," Liz said. "That's exactly what I thought."

The screen indicated the drive was "REFORMATTING." David had programmed the disk to erase itself and all traces of the transaction after the wire transfer was complete.

"Looks like he thought of everything," Liz said, moving to the door ahead of Svengrad, who took a moment too long to come out of the chair. She pushed through to the sister server room and quickly out the secure door back into the office area, Svengrad now right behind her.

Danny Foreman and Gaynes watched them, Danny fuming, but to Liz's surprise, he stepped aside and allowed room for them to pass. Gaynes, who held Danny by the elbow, never took her eyes off Foreman. Lou had explained to Liz that Danny's motivations were in question, and it seemed possible that in these few minutes, Gaynes had given him a choice of options.

Liz had nothing to say to Danny Foreman. She wanted her children back home and, at the very least, the semblance of an ordinary life returned. She wanted out of this party, out of this building, and nothing more than to be home in bed, though she knew it could not possibly be that simple for her.

Gaynes said, "Whatever you did in there ... Security crashed. Special Ops is on their way up. Foreman and I are going to try the stairs. You, Mr. Svengrad, I would suggest should return to the party. You try to leave now, they'll question you. Mrs. B., it's you they're after, I'm afraid. It helps us all if you can delay them a little."

Liz nodded. The group broke up as Phillip approached.

"Mr. Svengrad," the CEO said in his best host voice. He didn't look comfortable all of a sudden. "I see you've met Elizabeth!"

"Yes," Svengrad said. "She was just explaining some of the complications of the switchover to me," he said, eyeing Liz. "Quite impressive."

Phillip eyed Liz and looked into the server room. There was no telling what might become of her when suspicions and the inevitable interviews began. Phillip stepped closer to Liz, throwing an arm around her. "Hell of a party, Liz. Well done." He looked at Svengrad. "You have any more questions, Mr. Svengrad, why don't you address them to me."

At that moment, four undercover detectives rushed from an elevator, turning the heads of many in attendance.

Liz felt choked with emotion when she saw Lou among them, his eyes searching the room and finding her. He then registered Svengrad's presence as well and a triumphant look overcame him. Proud. Defiant.

"What's this?" Phillip asked, looking suspiciously at Liz.

"This . . . ," Liz said. "This is my husband."

TWENTY-FOUR

LIZ AND BOLDT STOOD INSIDE the front door of their home, LaMoia's Jetta parked and running at the curb. It was five in the morning, a pale hinting of the sunrise rimmed the horizon. They'd both been up all night, she in debriefings with Special Ops, Boldt writing a report that was mostly lies.

"I told them exactly how David did it," Liz explained. "He split the money into tens of thousands of tiny amounts—a few cents, a few dollars—and tacked those amounts onto trades as Securities and Exchange Commission fees. It worked because the SEC account is one of only a very few accounts that we don't audit unless the government files a complaint. David kept the funds moving through the system, these tiny amounts charged as SEC trading fees, impossible for us to connect or follow. Only the software knew where that money was on any given day. My guess is that at the end of the quarter, just as the SEC fee funds were about to be wired to Washington, the seventeen million was collected into the SEC fee account we hold for the government, giving David a chance to 'find' it"—she drew the quotes—"and wire it out. It would be safe there for a few weeks, a few months, even years. He got locked up, and it just stayed in the system, looping around, impossible for our auditors to identify. The merger meant our SEC account would be closed, the balance paid—all this happens invisibly and automatically each quarter, the government being paid what it's owed—but the merger forced him to wire the money out or lose it forever. The government would have eventually reported the overage, and maybe then we'd have finally figured it out."

Boldt said, "They could only grab the seventeen million four times a year."

"I'm guessing. Yes. He wouldn't have wanted it to be lumped together for very long, nor very often. Auditors *might* have spotted that, though even that's doubtful. The whole purpose was to keep it moving."

"And no one reported the incorrect SEC charges on their statements?"

"How many investors are going to question a few cents more on an SEC trading fee that's a charge they probably don't pay attention to anyway? He did the smart thing: He hid that money out in the open." She changed the subject, asking, "What do you do if he doesn't give you the tape?"

"John has one of his wild ideas. He's been studying terrorist technologies for the past two weeks and, typical of him, has 'borrowed' a device."

"You'll be careful."

It was a sentiment impossible for her not to express, but Boldt wished she hadn't. He didn't want to think of this upcoming meeting as dangerous, though he knew otherwise. Judging by Svengrad's tone of voice, he had already been hit with the surprise. Boldt's mission was to deflect and redirect the blame.

"It's more ridiculous than dangerous," he said of La-Moia's idea.

"You'll have backup?"

"Speaking the lingo now?"

"I'm a fast learner," she said, "and don't avoid the question."

"Not officially, no," he told her honestly. "That would mean answering all sorts of questions at some point, questions you and I don't want to answer."

"Forget that," she said. "I'd rather answer questions, pay a fine, go to jail, than be stupid about this."

"John will be there. Outside. He'll call for backup if needed. It's a meeting is all," he said, trying to reassure her. "We expected this." He corrected himself, "*I* expected this."

"It's not worth it, Lou."

"It *is*," he said. "It's very much worth it."

"Not if you're at risk."

"It's not like that. Honestly. If I thought it was, I wouldn't do this. He's not going to arrange a meeting if he plans on torturing me; his goons are going to bust in here and do it. He has questions. That's all."

"We gave him his money. He should be happy."

"Absolutely," Boldt said, trying to keep the lie out of his eyes. "Maybe he wants to thank me."

She leveled a look onto him, and he knew then that she knew. He saw the first twinges of realization sink into her. "What did you do?" She closed her eyes, then looked at him fiercely. "You couldn't leave well enough alone, could you?"

The trouble with marriage was that all that familiarity, the years of arguments and discussions, of practical jokes and conspiracies, meant that one's barriers became invisible to the spouse, easily penetrated. Liz looked through him and read his thoughts effortlessly.

"Oh, my God," she said. "You conned a con man? Lou? Speak to me!"

"I followed my conscience on this one."

"It was all *done*, Lou. We *did* it. Over! The children," she pleaded, as either her concern or her anger glassed her eyes.

"Exactly," Boldt said. "I'm not saying I did anything, but if I did, I did it for the children. *No lies,* right?" This had been their mutual agreement going into parenthood, to lead by example. The comment struck deeper, as he knew it would. They'd been living nothing but lies for too long, and for him this was a fresh start instead of a continuation.

He kissed her good-bye without saying anything more. He had no sense that he was heading into anything more dangerous than on any other day of work. A meeting was all. She accompanied him to the front door. An unmarked police car still watched the house. Boldt hoped this meeting with Svengrad might end the need for such precautions.

She touched him once lightly on the arm as he opened the door. The tenderness of that gesture cut him to his core and he felt emotions ripple through him. He had explanations for everything he'd done, for what he was about to do, but they would have to go unspoken. He hoped they might go unspoken for a very long time. He smiled at her and let her shut the door behind him.

"Drive," he said, and LaMoia pulled the Jetta away from the curb and out onto the street.

Boldt looked into the empty backseat.

"It's in the trunk," LaMoia said. "Thing's about the size of a microwave oven."

Boldt shook his head.

LaMoia said, "I'm telling you, Sarge, it works great."

"Forget it, okay?"

"No way! You gotta let me do this. If nothing else we put this guy back into the Stone Age. Every computer, every phone, every disk, every *tape,* zeroed."

He'd explained it to Boldt in trying to sell him on the idea. The box in the car's trunk emitted an electromagnetic pulse, essentially a blast of radio waves that rearranged any magnetic charge. The military had been developing the technology for years—first discovered as a side effect of an atomic blast, a pulse of energy that, while not radioactive, interrupted and defeated anything with a memory chip. The technology remained fairly bulky and heavy, still too conspicuous to be smuggled onto an airplane, though this and other uses were believed possible prospects for terrorists down the road.

"I think we'll do this the old-fashioned way," Boldt said. "Leave James Bond for the movies." He added, "I'm going to talk to him. That's all."

"He'll never give you back that tape."

"Probably not."

"All I do is plug the thing in and turn it on. It uses the wiring in the building like a huge antenna. The pulse—a radio wave—goes down that wiring, and like an antenna, anything within fifteen to twenty feet of any wall, that means anything plugged in or not, is zapped. Bam! Erased. Zeroed. It's fucking phenomenal. Cell phones, pagers, calculators. In your pocket. In a chair. Even inside a *safe.*

Refrigerators have memory chips in them. Did you know that?"

"I think we'll leave his refrigerators alone this time."

"No matter what he tells you, he's going to keep a copy of the tape. You said so yourself. Then he's got his finger on you. He *owns* you, Sarge."

Boldt shot his sergeant a look. He didn't like this talked about in that way.

"This thing will erase it. It's magnetic. Anything and everything in that building gets erased. Doesn't matter where it is. Zap! Fried tomatoes."

"We'll do this my way," Boldt said.

"That's fine, Sarge. But if I find an outside outlet, I'm popping the trunk and plugging this thing in. My suggestion is: Leave your cell phone in the car."

Boldt knew he meant well, and initially he'd even supported the idea because the effectiveness of the technology sounded convincing. But if the contraption worked—and he was beginning to think it might—he thought it unwise to be meeting with Svengrad when tragedy struck. He explained this to LaMoia and saw the man's enthusiasm sink.

LaMoia dropped Boldt off outside the corrugated steel warehouse and wished him luck. Boldt did, in fact, carry his cell phone, and it was set to dial LaMoia's phone with two pushes of the same button. Boldt would hold his hand on that phone in his coat pocket, ready to call the cavalry if needed. Although LaMoia's instructions were to call for backup and to wait until it arrived, Boldt knew he'd never wait. That was fine with him.

Yasmani Svengrad sat behind his desk in the office area built into the refrigerated warehouse space. Boldt saw two other guys, one of them Alekseevich, who looked a shade paler than when Boldt had last seen him. Neither man made so much as a gesture that might telegraph their prior introduction. Boldt had been searched, his weapon and his cell phone temporarily confiscated, his plan to signal LaMoia disrupted. The magazine had been removed from his weapon, which now sat useless next to his phone at the far corner of the large desk. Boldt kept his eye on the phone. If he dived for it, he might be able to get the signal off.

Boldt sat down in a chair this time, not waiting for an invitation.

"Where is it?" Svengrad asked. He'd trimmed his beard recently, possibly for the reception, now less than twenty-four hours behind them.

"Where is what?" One of any cop's most practiced skills was the art of lying. Interrogations required hours of playing straight-faced to the most challenging situation. Boldt knew he excelled at such subterfuge, confident that he could go one-on-one with the most heinous murderer. For all his experience as a military man, Yasmani Svengrad was out of his league.

"You do not want to play such games."

Boldt knew he was supposed to feel the chill of such a statement, but it struck him as amusing instead. He allowed nothing to be revealed from his expression. He couldn't be sure Svengrad wouldn't conceal a tape recorder to later try to use to extort him, so he had to tiptoe around outright admission. Then again, LaMoia's machine would erase such tapes as well. "Still looking for that money. Is that it?"

"I wired that money out of the bank myself," Svengrad said, at which point Boldt knew no tape recorders were operating. He felt free to talk openly now.

"I know that."

"Where is it?"

"You're the one who wired it. You just said so yourself."

"The police intercepted it. That was not part of our agreement."

"If we'd intercepted it, you'd be wearing orange coveralls. It would be front-page news, *and* I would know about it. But you know that as well, so I've got to think that the first thing—the first *name*—that popped into my head also popped into your head."

Svengrad opened a desk drawer and placed a black videotape on the blotter in front of him. "We had an agreement," he said, sliding the tape toward Boldt, who didn't believe the gesture for a moment.

"This, and how many more copies?"

"The only copy."

"I don't believe that."

Svengrad shrugged. "Suit yourself."

"What is it you want?"

"No," Svengrad said. "It's what *you* want." He met eyes with Boldt, glanced over to make sure the office door was closed, and said softly, "I'll give you Alekseevich. Physical evidence, also. You give me immunity, I'll even give you a witness to the tortures."

This was an unexpected and exceptional offer, but Boldt showed nothing of his surprise. He eyed the videotape, wondering if it could possibly be the only remaining copy. "And in return?"

"His location. Hayes. Anything you know about where he is. That, and if you have him, then you call off the dogs for a few minutes. Send them out for coffee."

"You think he did this to you again? Intercepted the wire

transfer? Would he do that? He's not stupid. And even if he did, do you think he's anywhere any of us could find him?" Boldt allowed a grin. "He did it again?"

Svengrad was not amused. "You know where he is."

Boldt shook his head.

"You have him in custody. Why else did you lock up Foreman? Hayes is cooperating with you."

"Foreman is being held by Treasury for questioning, nothing more. No charges have been filed. In the end they'll determine he has done no wrong. A little overeager is all. Clearing this case took him over. He beat the tar out of Hayes to get to the truth, and then tried to cover his tracks. It happens."

Svengrad wore a look of contempt. "I'd hoped we could help each other." He placed his hand on the videotape and drew it back toward himself.

"Let me ask around."

"It's the original tape," Svengrad said, picking up on Boldt's line of sight.

Boldt knew that already. The neatly typed surveillance title on the spine of the videocassette told him as much. "I thought you were giving it to me. The prior agreement."

"It's still possible, but you will have to do this other thing for me." Boldt suspected this would go on the rest of his career. The tease, the request for another favor. Again he considered LaMoia's device.

"How would Alekseevich be handled?" he inquired, offering Svengrad the first glimmer of hope.

"However you want. We'd let you know where to find him. You'd pick him up. I'd deny any accusations. I'd need the letter of immunity beforehand."

That was never going to happen, but Boldt nodded as

if it might. The identity of the government snitch would remain protected. "I can make some inquiries."

"A location for Hayes is all I need. One phone call."

Boldt retrieved his weapon and cell phone and left. He walked out to LaMoia's Jetta through a light mist and sat down into the passenger seat.

"So?"

"Blackmail. He wants Hayes. The wire never reached his account."

"Imagine that," LaMoia said, knowing Boldt had arranged this, had kidnapped Hayes from the warehouse in order to accomplish this.

"It's only the two of us. You understand that."

"Three of us. You have to include Hayes."

Boldt nodded. "Yeah," he said. "For a minute there, I debated giving him up. He offered me Alekseevich in return."

"A lot of good that would do us," LaMoia said, as angry and frustrated about the protection surrounding Alekseevich as Boldt.

"He was incredibly calm about it," Boldt said. "I thought he'd be much angrier. Violent, even."

"That's good. That means he hasn't connected it to you or Liz."

"He's going to use the tape," Boldt said. "I sat there, and I looked in his eyes, and I knew that he'd take me down at the first opportunity. He wants to believe Hayes did this to him, but he's not one hundred percent convinced, I don't think. He'll burn us, just to get back at me in case I had anything to do with it."

"It was a hell of a stroke, Sarge, manipulating him to input that account number *himself*."

"It's the only thing saving us. He can convince himself that Liz didn't cross him because he typed in those numbers himself."

"And who else but Hayes could intercept that wire?" LaMoia said, admiration for his lieutenant in his voice.

"Right."

"I found an outlet," LaMoia said. "There are a couple on the west side of the building. Do me a favor and go home and spend a night with your family. Don't do anything on this until tomorrow."

"You can't take this kind of risk alone, John."

"Message received. Just go home and sleep on it, would you?" He added, "Listen, if I do this, the Sturgeon General will be sure it was Hayes. You know he will."

"The grand jury will sit Thursday. Alekseevich testifies. A week or two from now and Svengrad's in lockup."

"So take a vacation."

"I don't want you doing this alone."

"I heard you the first time. So?"

"So," Boldt said, after a moment of thought, "I'm coming with you."

□ □ □

"What's going on?" Liz asked from the warm side of the bed.

Boldt, in the familiar act of dressing into street clothes in the dark, said, "I'll be back within the hour."

"Are you going to tell me?" she asked in a groggy voice.

"No," he said. "Better if I don't. Better that you could answer questions honestly."

"Questions from whom?"

"Internal Investigations." That silenced her for a moment.

"I'm sorry," she said, sensing her own role in whatever it was he had planned.

"Me too," he said. "But maybe this is the end of it."

"If only," she said. "Is it dangerous?"

"I don't think so. Not particularly."

"It's not worth it if it is."

He stood over her at the side of the bed. He could just make out her face in the gray light that leaked around the perimeter of the window blinds. "You never woke up," he said. "Never noticed me missing from the bed."

"If you're trying to scare me, it's working."

He left the room, stopping in the kitchen to make a traveling cup of tea.

LaMoia's Jetta was parked behind an art supply store in Ballard, as planned.

"Yo," the detective said, as Boldt slipped into the passenger seat. LaMoia looked like it was twelve noon.

They drove to within a hundred yards of Svengrad's warehouse in complete silence. Then LaMoia pulled over and withdrew a "drop gun" from the glove compartment. Not SPD issue, and if shots were thrown, it wouldn't be traceable to LaMoia.

"I don't like the look of that," Boldt said.

"Get over it."

"You're nervous."

"I have *no idea* what that thing in the trunk is going to do. What I do know is that I'm not parking anywhere near that warehouse because cars these days are all about computer chips, and that thing fries computer chips. So here's the deal: You're the wheel man. You drop me off, wait exactly two minutes, and return to pick me up. I can't keep a phone or radio on me, the thing will fry them too, so it's all about timing. You hear shots fired, I'd appreciate some backup."

"You've got the roles reversed," Boldt said. "If anyone's putting himself at risk, that would be me."

"I got briefed on the operation of this thing," LaMoia said. "Besides, you're technically challenged operating a toaster, for Christ's sake."

"Two minutes," Boldt said. He came around the car. LaMoia popped the trunk so that it was already open, and Boldt drove them toward the warehouse.

He glided the car into position, LaMoia directing him with hand signals. LaMoia flew out the passenger door, lifted the trunk, then left it unlatched as he slapped the car to signal Boldt's retreat.

As Boldt pulled away, he saw LaMoia struggling with what appeared to be a very heavy metal box. It looked like a miniature window-mounted air conditioning unit. Three blocks away he reversed the Jetta so it aimed back toward the unseen warehouse. One eye tracked the second hand on his wristwatch while he divided his attention, focused on the darkened street before him.

All at once, Boldt heard a loud explosion, and his foot went to the accelerator faster than conscious thought. He removed his weapon and laid it in his lap as he drove at a breakneck speed down the rough, potholed roadway. He caught sight of the orange glow in the sky and the smudged black plume of smoke billowing from what turned out to be a phone pole. An electric transformer on the pole was afire, raining viscous drops of flame down onto the crusted blacktop below like some medieval cauldron.

Boldt saw LaMoia by the side of the building, embracing the bulky steel device in both arms. The car rocked as LaMoia deposited the device into the trunk. The detective hurried around to the passenger side and said, "Go," although he was only partially inside.

Boldt hit the accelerator hard, and the Jetta raced off. No sign of any trouble behind them, as both men strained toward their respective door-mounted mirrors.

"Shit!" LaMoia said. He was sweating and breathless. "Little kink they're going to have to work out. I hit the button and that transformer blew like it was part of the plan."

"So it worked," Boldt said, somewhat astonished.

"Apparently so."

"The transformer. That could help us. Whatever happened in that warehouse, maybe it gets blamed on the transformer's problems."

"You think it's designed to do that?" LaMoia asked, suddenly beaming behind a smile. "Yeah, I suppose that's possible," he said. "Power company gets blamed for it. I like that. That's what they get for raising our bills every six months."

Only then did it fully dawn on Boldt that the master videotape of his wife's indiscretions was now erased, and that at the same time Svengrad's import company had been dealt a serious setback, losing all their business data.

He heard sirens behind them, responding to the burning transformer.

"Thing scared the shit out of me when it blew like that,"

LaMoia said, reliving the moment. He was twisted around in his seat trying to get a look toward the fire. But he gave up and came back around, facing the windshield.

"Definitely not something we want terrorists to have." He explained himself, saying, "The way I see it, I was just doing a little homework."

"John LaMoia, the good student," Boldt suggested. "Why doesn't that work for me?"

"Give it a rest, Sarge."

As Boldt drove, the sun brightened the eastern horizon. Boldt would be in bed before it was fully dawn.

"Thank you, John." Said to the windshield, but as sincerely as he could make it.

"I love shit like that. Blowing stuff up. Setting shit on fire. My pleasure, Sarge, believe me." LaMoia chuckled to himself. "Besides, what are friends for?"

□ □ □

Boldt searched the papers the following morning for any mention of an unexplained power outage in south Ballard. He found a paragraph about the transformer fire. He'd been placed on administrative leave pending a full review of the Special Ops at the theater and WestCorp Center. Pahwan Riz and Marc O'Brien were too experienced not to recognize internal interference when they saw it. Proving it would be next to impossible, given the loyalty of Daphne, John, and Bobbie Gaynes. Boldt would ride it out, as he'd ridden out other challenges in the past.

Danny Foreman was taking early retirement, no charges filed.

Liz returned from a meeting at the bank that Tuesday

afternoon, Boldt having gassed up the car and packed it for the drive to Wenatchee. They were to pick up the kids there and keep driving. Sun Valley. Yellowstone, with the tourists gone. They would loop around on one of the most beautiful highways in the country, on the western border of Montana, and on up to Coeur d'Alene, where they'd spend most of the next week doing nothing. Boldt didn't know how it would go; he wasn't great at doing nothing.

Liz was quiet for the early part of the drive. She'd climbed in with a stack of papers, her purse, and a newspaper.

"What's going on?" he asked.

"I'm not going to be offered a contract with MTK."

"You've been *fired*?" This news hit Boldt in the center of his chest. Not only did Liz love the job, but she'd been one of the top five officers in the bank. There'd never been any question of her being worked into the merger.

"The tape, maybe," she said. "You think?"

Again, he felt the wind knocked out of him. "No?"

"Or maybe Danny got me in trouble trying to save himself."

"I would have heard about that," Boldt said, though he wasn't so sure all of a sudden. "Fired?"

"Phillip doesn't trust me—that's at the bottom of it. Nor should he! I'll get a good letter. I keep the pension. It's an honorable discharge," she said, trying to make light of it.

He knew how devastated she had to be, and admired her for her display of courage. "I seriously doubt it was the tape," he said. Then asked, "Are you okay with this?"

"No. But I am ready for a change. Consulting, maybe. More time at home afternoons." She added philosophically, "You never fully undo something like this. If there's one overriding lesson, for me anyway, it's about the repercussions of our actions. Maybe there's some closure now. I've carried this—we've *both* carried this—for a long time. It would be nice to get it behind us."

Boldt glanced into the rearview mirror, the road receding behind them, and he nearly mentioned the symbolism to her but thought better of it. He kept it to himself. He hoped Svengrad would be jailed over tax evasion, but he wasn't sure he'd ever stop looking over his shoulder. Svengrad had a long reach. He kept this to himself as well.

Liz was quiet for a few minutes, looking out her window as if the sights there were new to her. Then she reached down and unfolded the newspaper and opened it, fingering through to the business section. "Did you read this morning's paper?"

He had, but he claimed not to have. Nothing got past her.

She turned it over to below the fold. "Tell me about this."

Boldt kept driving, eyes on the road.

"An adoption agency, an inner-city soccer program. Was I supposed to miss this?"

He adjusted the rearview mirror, still saying nothing.

"Six million dollars in anonymous donations between the two. How much longer until another eleven in similar donations makes the news?" She said, "You must have forced David to do it, because this isn't like him."

"We negotiated certain conditions to his receiving protection, it's true. Testimony on Danny's behalf is part of it. Danny wasn't trying to make himself rich; he was trying to clear a case that no one else cared about. He went about it the wrong way, but Hayes overheard some important statements that Danny made—some, while beating him. Geiser will roll on Svengrad. It'll come down like a house of cards."

"You didn't rescue him to save him," she said, figuring some of it out on the fly. "You needed him to intercept the wire for you."

"You make adjustments as you go."

"All seventeen to nonprofits?"

"Let's just say that KPLU will be playing jazz for a long, long time." He switched on the radio. Oscar Peterson. He felt Liz staring at him, could hear her mind churning as she debated what to say, what to ask. Finally, she just sighed, opened the paper, and began reading. "The adoption agency was a nice touch," she said. "It's the one Beth and Tony used."

"Yeah," Boldt allowed. "I thought that sounded familiar."

"You're never going to admit this," she said, "even to me?"

"When the statute of limitations has run out, we'll talk."

"Seven more years together," she said. "I like the sound of that."

"Me too," Boldt admitted, taking the wheel firmly in hand and changing lanes.

TWENTY-FIVE

BOLDT HAD NOT FELT THIS nervous since the birth of their first child, who now sat inside the room behind them. They'd flown down as a family. Liz's sister's kid, in her last year of graduate work at UC Berkeley, had offered to take Sarah to the Exploratorium, leaving Boldt and his wife on an uncomfortable wooden bench in a hallway that reminded the lieutenant of waiting outside a courtroom.

Liz had busied herself with projects since leaving the bank. The garage was spanking clean. When she offered to index his jazz albums he knew it was time she found work again. For his part, he was back at work, though staying behind his desk. He'd even booked himself back into the Joke's on You, playing jazz piano during Happy Hour. He felt at peace each evening from five until seven.

From the room behind them they heard Miles's inspired piano playing. Boldt recognized the song: a Monk ballad the boy had picked up from Boldt by ear.

It had been difficult, the past month. They had not made love yet, and he wondered if that was going to happen, or if they were doomed to one of those marriages of living together but not fully loving together. He didn't want that.

She asked, "Do you think—"

"Yes," he interrupted, knowing as only a husband can know, that this question had to do with the child on the other side of the wall. The kids were the sinew that bound the muscle of the marriage. That muscle kept growing stronger with exercise. "They're going to tell us he's unusually gifted, and it's going to be left to us to accelerate that talent or let him develop like any kid his age." She nodded. "He knows it all intuitively, Liz. I've never seen anything like it."

"Our little Mozart."

"It's going to mean tough choices," he said. "Financially. Sending him away."

"They don't have to be tough," she said. "We'll just listen for what's right."

He wanted badly to reach down and take her hand just then, but something stopped him. It struck him as too sentimental, or maybe an act of forgiveness that he couldn't yet afford.

They heard singing from the other side of that wall. A pure, golden voice right on pitch. "Amazing," he said.

"We'll work it out," she said. "You trust that, don't you?"

This was a much larger question than she let on.

"I do," he said, the words indelibly reminding him of the original vows they had made to each other.

"I'd like to hold your hand," he admitted.

"Then why don't you?" She offered him hers.

"I don't know," he said, still unable to take hers up.

"Well, we'll start there," she said, placing her hand back into her lap.

The music grew behind them, the clear voice penetrating through the wall, and they both turned to face each other at the same instant. The song pushing through the wall was "Edelweiss" from *The Sound of Music,* his son's voice so pure and simple.

Boldt caught himself humming along.

If You Loved *The Body of David Hayes*,
Be Sure to Catch Ridley Pearson's Newest Thriller,
Cut and Run,
Coming in April 2005 from Hyperion.

An excerpt, the Prologue and Chapter 1, follows.

PROLOGUE

─────────────

SIX YEARS EARLIER

The forty-first day was their last together.

Roland Larson was holed up in a truck stop's pay phone, half-mad from guarding her round-the-clock while denied any privacy with her whatsoever. He resorted to calling her on the phone. He'd slipped her his cell phone, and now dialed his own number to find her breathless as she whispered from her hardened bedroom, the aft cabin of the bus, not thirty yards away.

"I can't stand this," she said.

He found himself aroused by the hoarse, coarse sound of her. Forty-one days, under every conceivable pressure, and this the first complaint he'd heard from her.

"Us, or the situation?" he asked.

Hope Stevens had been moved on three separate occasions: first, to a wilderness cabin on Michigan's Upper Peninsula, the kind of place Larson could see himself retiring to someday, a lethargic life so different from the one he lived; then she'd been moved to a nearly abandoned Air Force base in Montana, the desolation reminding him of a penitentiary, a place he knew well; and finally, into a private coach, a customized diesel bus that Treasury had confiscated from a forgotten rock band, its interior complete with neon-trim lighting and mirrored tables. Painted on three sides as a purple and black sunrise, the coach comfortably slept six and converted to club seating by day. Three deputies, including Larson, two drivers, and the witness traveled together—one of only a handful of times in the U.S. Marshals Service's long history of witness protection that a "moving target" policy had been adopted. The last had been aboard a sleeper train in the mid-'70s.

Ironically, the more attempts made upon her life, the more importance and significance Hope Stevens gained in the eyes of her government. It wasn't for her keen understanding of computers that they guarded her, nor for her fine looks or sharp tongue (when she did bother to speak); it was instead for a few cells and chemicals inside her skull and the memory trapped there, living now like a dog under the front porch, cowering with a bone of truth in its jaws.

The problem for Roland Larson was that the longer he guarded her, the more he cared for her—cared intensely—a situation unforgivable and intolerable in the eyes of his superiors and one that, if discovered, could have him transferred to some far outpost of government service, like North Dakota or Buffalo. But the few private moments shared with her overwhelmed any sensibility in Larson.

After just seventeen days of protection, the Michigan cabin had gone up in flames—arson; in the resulting firefight, a shadowy ballet in the flashes of orange light from the mighty blaze, two deputy marshals had been injured.

When, at the Montana Air Force base, mention of "persons unknown" had been intercepted by some geek in an

NSA cubicle, the marshals had been instructed to move Hope yet again. Larson wasn't much for running away from a faceless enemy, but he knew well enough to follow orders and so he did.

As a former technical consultant to an industry probe of fraudulent insurance practices, Hope had connected a string of assisted-care facilities to millions of dollars in wrongful charges. The names she'd eventually given Justice—Donny and Pop Romero and, by inference, the young scion of the crime family, Ricardo Romero—were well known to federal law enforcement's Organized Crime Unit. The Romeros, notorious for inventive white collar crime on an enormous scale, also played rough and dirty when required, the arson and the shoot-out at the lake a case in point. Hope's value to Justice was not only her initial discovery of insurance fraud—a scheme involving billing Medicare long after the patient was dead—but, more important, her interception of a series of e-mails sent to and from the Romeros that proved to be murder-for-hire contracts. Five executives of the same health care consortium that had called for the probe, all referred to in the correspondence as whistle-blowers whose actions threatened the Romeros, had later been found brutally murdered, the victims of so-called Serbian Spas—laundry bleach enemas that burned the victim from the inside out over a period of several hours, their families tied up and forced to watch their prolonged deaths.

Intended perhaps to implicate the Russian mob, these horrific tactics did nothing of the sort. The FBI had immediately placed the Romeros onto their Most Wanted list and their two remaining witnesses, Hope Stevens and an unnamed accountant, had been placed in protective custody.

The e–mails had been electronically destroyed; they existed now only in Hope's memory. Government prosecutors believed a jury would convict based primarily on her testimony. And so they sequestered her on the garish bus, never allowing her off, never risking her being seen in public, and never stopping the bus for more than fuel or supplies. The strategy had kept her alive for the past ten days and left everyone on board with a bad case of cabin fever. Discussions had begun to once again relocate her, this time, to a "static," or fixed, location, probably a federal facility, quite possibly a short stint inside an unused wing at a federal penitentiary, or in an ICU at a city hospital. They had myriad tricks up their sleeves if left to their own devices. They seldom were.

"Isn't there something you can do?" Hope asked. "Order us to stop at a motel, and arrange for you to guard my room? There has to be something."

"I'm only guessing here," Larson answered, "but I think a few of the guys might see through that tactic." He caught his reflection in the polished metal surrounding the pay phone's keypad. No one was going to call him pretty, although they had as a child. He'd grown into something too big for pretty, too hard for handsome, like a puppy growing into its feet. Pedigree be damned.

She sputtered on the other end, not quite her trademark laugh but a valiant effort.

He said, "You could make like a heart attack, and I could give you mouth-to-mouth."

A little more authentic this time.

At the cabin, and then again at the Air Force base, they'd managed to find moments together, though not the moment both of them longed for, one he repeatedly daydreamed about. But once onto the bus, they'd barely shared a glance. A phone call was as much as they were going to get.

"It's probably better this way," she said. "Right?"

"No. It's decidedly worse."

"As soon as I testify . . . as soon as that's over with . . . they'll put me into the program and that will be that. Right? We should have never started this, Lars."

Her testimony against Donny Romero—the fraud case— would come first. The capital murder charges were likely still a long way from prosecution—a year or two—but he knew better than to mention it. One didn't talk about the future with a protected witness, the reality far harsher, the adjustment far more difficult than they understood. In practice, breaking off all contact with one's former life proved traumatic, invariably more difficult than the witness imagined.

"Seriously?" he asked. "Because I don't see it that way at all. I wouldn't trade one minute with you for something else."

"You're hopeless."

"I'm hope*ful*," he said, an intentional play on her name that he immediately congratulated himself for, though no doubt one she'd heard before.

His feeling for her had come on like a force of nature, as unavoidable and inexplicable. Together, they communicated well; she accepted teasing in the face of all the madness; they fit. And when you found that, you held on to it.

Nearly ten minutes had passed since he'd left the bus. Members of his small squad would be wondering why the delay. Ostensibly, he'd left the bus to settle the bill—with cash, *always cash*—but ten minutes was pushing it.

"My gut tells me we'll work this out somehow," he lied. He couldn't see them ending this now—not before they tested the boundaries. He'd attended the seminars on avoiding emotional attachment with the witness. Brother bonding with the male witnesses was as dangerous as what he and Hope had stumbled into. It screwed up everything, risked everything, and he well knew it. It could not possibly have a happy ending. Still, he encouraged her to stay with him while he looked for some way around it all, a way that he suspected wasn't there. At this moment, after what they'd been through together, letting her go was not an option.

"Lars," she spoke, yet again in a hushed whisper, the crisp sibilance rolling off the *s* and causing a ripple of gooseflesh down his left side. It snaked into his groin and lodged there. But rerouted by a synapse, it suddenly sparked across a gate in his brain that translated it differently, albeit a beat too late: This was nothing short of the sound of panic.

"Hope?"

"Oh, my God."

The line went dead.

The bus.

Larson dropped the receiver and ran, losing his balance as he took a corner too quickly on wet tile, ignoring the yellow sandwich board written in Spanish and English with an icon of a pail and mop and a splash of water. He went down hard. He scrambled to his feet, knocked over a corn chip display, and hurried out the truck stop's main door, the cashier's cry of complaint consumed by the high-pitched whine of highway traffic.

"Rolo?" This came from Trill Hampton, a member of his squad, a fellow deputy marshal. Approaching footfalls of shoes slapping blacktop came on fast. Larson's running had sent a signal. Hampton was in full stride, already reaching for his piece.

Larson's arrival into sunlight temporarily blinded him. They'd stopped at far too many truck stops over the past ten days for him to immediately recall the layout of this one. They'd parked out here somewhere. A spike of fear insinuated itself as he considered the possibility that the entire bus had been hijacked, for he didn't see it anywhere.

But then, as Hampton caught up to him and edged left, and the two of them moved around the building, Larson spotted the rows of diesel pumps and the bus where they'd parked it, wedged amid a long line of eighteen-wheel tractor-trailers.

Hampton walked gracefully, even at double time.

Leading at a slight jog, Larson assessed the bus from a distance, seeing no indication of trouble and wondering if he'd misinterpreted Hope's distress.

"What's up?" Hampton asked, not a sheen of sweat on his black skin.

He wasn't about to confess to phoning the witness from the truck stop.

"A bad *feeling*?" Hampton questioned. "Since when?"

He had a flat, wide nose, too big for his face, and a square, cleft chin that reminded Larson of a black Kirk Douglas.

Larson wasn't exactly the touchy-feely type; Hampton saw through that.

Larson sought some plausible explanation for Hope hanging up on him. He seized upon the first thing he saw. "Why isn't Benny stretching his legs?" The older of their two drivers had been complaining to anyone who would listen about a bad case of hemorrhoids. Larson saw Benny through the windshield, sitting behind the wheel.

"Yeah, so?"

They drew closer. Benny not only still occupied his driver's seat, but his head was angled and tilted somewhat awkwardly toward his shoulder, as if dozing. This, too, seemed incongruous, as Benny rarely slept, much less napped.

"Rolo?" Hampton said cautiously. Now he, too, had sensed a problem with Benny. Hampton and Larson went back several years. Hampton had come out of one of New Haven's worst neighborhoods, had won a wrestling scholarship to a blue blazer prep school, and had gone on to graduate from Rice University. He'd wanted to be a professional sports agent, but had become a U.S. marshal as an interim job, at the urging of an uncle. He'd never left the Service.

"Radio Stubby," Larson instructed.

Hampton attempted to raise Stubblefield, the third marshal, who remained inside the bus, but won only silence.

"Shit!" Hampton said, increasing his stride. The man could cover ground when he wanted to.

The two were twenty feet away from the bus now, Larson adjusting his approach in order to come from more of an angle to avoid being seen, his handgun, a Glock, carefully screened.

He instructed Hampton: "Hang back. Take cover. Lethal force if required."

"Got it." Hampton broke away from Larson, hurrying toward the adjacent tractor-trailer and taking a position that allowed him to use it as cover.

Larson found the bus door closed—standard procedure. Benny would typically open it for him as he approached, but that didn't happen, sounding a secondary alarm in Larson's head. He slipped his hand into the front pocket of his jeans, searching amid a wad of cash receipts for the cool, metallic feel of keys—the duplicate set to the bus that, as supervising deputy, Larson kept on his person.

Benny remained motionless, not responding; Stubby not answering a radio call. But who could storm a bus through its only door—a *locked* door, at that—and overcome two drivers and a deputy marshal?

Larson heard thumping from inside. Banging. Just as he turned the key, out of the corner of his eye he caught sight of a state police car parked beyond the diesel pumps and he thought: *Benny would open the door for a uniform.*

As Larson opened the door and entered, the banging stopped abruptly. Larson both tasted and smelled the bitter air and knew its source from experience: a stun grenade—an explosive device that uses air pressure to blow out eardrums and sinuses and render the suspects temporarily deaf and semiconscious.

The narrow stairs that ascended to the driver prevented him from seeing into the main body of the bus. He saw only Benny, whose shirt held a red waterfall of spilled blood down the front. Larson's first assessment was that the man's nose was bleeding—typical with stun grenades. But then he saw a precise line below his jaw, like a surgical incision. His open eyes and frozen stare cinched it: Benny was dead.

Weapon still in hand, Larson kept low and climbed the bus stairs, ready for contact. The banging he'd heard had been someone attempting to breach the hardened door to Hope's cabin. He saw Stubby, unconscious or dead, on the left side, behind a collapsible table. Clancy, the other driver, sat upright in a padded captain's chair opposite Stubby, his head tilted back. A game of gin rummy between them had ended abruptly. No blood or ligature marks on Clancy.

No sign of a state trooper either, the aisle empty, a sleeping cabin on either side.

One of Stubby's golf clubs lay broken in front of the rear cabin's door, which appeared intact and suggested Hope remained safe, a source of great relief. The intruder had been trying to use a club to pry the door open.

There was only one key to that door, hidden in a Hide A Key in the rear engine bay. Larson edged forward.

He went down hard as a strong hand gripped his ankle and pulled from behind. The gun hit the carpet and bounced loose. The wind knocked out of him, Larson reeled.

The intruder was a stringy guy with frog-tongue reactions. He seized Larson's hair from behind and pulled. But Larson rolled left and the razor blade, intended for his throat, missed and caught the front of his right shoulder instead. Larson broke loose, dived forward, and grabbed the gun. He spun and squeezed off three rounds. Two went into the mirrored ceiling, raining down cubes of tempered glass, and blinding him in a silver snow.

A crushing force caught Larson in the jaw, snapping his head back. He inadvertently let go of the gun for a second time. The intruder had fallen onto him, and Larson realized he'd hit him with one of the three shots. Larson grabbed for the man and felt fabric rip.

A uniform. Larson fought back, the wounded man keeping him from the gun. Larson bucked him off, but his cut shoulder caused his arm to flap around uselessly, refusing all of Larson's instructions. Tangled up with the man, Larson drove his left elbow back and felt the crunch of soft bone and tissue, like an eggshell breaking.

He then heard a series of quick footfalls and looked in time to see the intruder hurry off the bus.

Landing out on the parking lot's pavement, the uniformed man's voice shouted, "Someone call for help!"

Larson came to his knees. His head swooned. He looked around for his gun through blurry eyes.

□ □ □

Hampton saw the slender state trooper throw his hands in the air as he called for help. He was bleeding. The man sank to his knees in front of the door to the bus.

Hampton held his weapon extended and stepped out from behind the tractor-trailer. "Hands behind your head," he called out, not feeling great holding a gun on a man in uniform.

As the trooper sat up, Hampton saw a yellow-white muzzle flash. He took the first round in the thigh, driven back by the impact and losing his balance. He sprawled back onto the hot blacktop, rocking his head to the right and watching the suspect run off. He fired two rounds from his side.

□ □ □

As Larson dragged himself toward the front of the bus, he tried to lock down anything he remembered about the intruder: thin and wiry; strong; the uniform; a scar. He focused on the scar. The lines of pink, beaded skin crossed, forming a stylized infinity sign on the inside of his forearm. Larson's vision filled with a purple fringe, the dark, throbbing color coming at him from all sides. His shoulder was cut badly. Sticky down to his waist. He felt faint. Sounds echoed. Again he smelled the tangy air, laced with black powder and sulfur. Bitter with blood. His stomach retched. He felt as if he were being pushed and held underwater—dark water—by a strong, determined hand. He resisted, but felt himself going. Deeper.

His last conscious thought was more of a vision: not an infinity sign at all, but two triangles facing inward, touching, point-to-point.

Like a bow tie.

CHAPTER ONE

THE PRESENT

Of all things, Larson thought he recognized her laugh. Here, where he least expected it. It carried like a shot, well past his ears and spilling down into the audience where it ran into a waterfall of others—though none exactly like it— and broke to pieces before the footlights and spots that made the dust in the air look like snow. It might as well have lodged in his chest, the way it stole his breath.

He'd started the day perfectly, the way he wished he could start every day, busting his body into a sweat while pulling on twin sticks of composite carbon painted on the scoop in a diagonal of rich burgundy and black, the owner's college colors no doubt, driving the borrowed scull through swirls of no-see-ums and gnats so thick he clenched his teeth to filter them out, the occasional dragonfly darting swiftly alongside as if challenging him to a race. He'd been up before the birds, and would be done—put away and showered, Creve Coeur Lake behind him—before the rush-hour traffic made the city's famous arch stand still.

He'd taken in the play on a whim, calling the box office

to see if there were any singles available, a guilty pleasure he wouldn't have told anyone about if he hadn't engaged the receptionist, Lokisha, in a discussion of Shakespeare on the way out the door.

The fact was that in over five years of secretly searching for Hope at Shakespeare festivals and performances—in places as far away as Ashland, Oregon, and Cedar City, Utah—he'd become passionate about the Bard himself: the violence, the romance, the lies and deceptions, the cunning, the manipulation, the *symmetry* of the plays. It had never occurred to him that he might find her here in his own backyard. The belief in coincidence had been trained out of Larson in the way a dog could be made to lie by the dinner table and not look up to beg.

He'd felt his BlackBerry purr silently at his side several times over the past ten minutes, but it was after hours and it did that for any incoming e-mail, spam or legitimate, and he wasn't about to bother the people sitting next to him by lighting up a pale blue electronic screen in his lap while they tried to remain firmly in the sixteenth century. The intermission was fast approaching. He'd check e-mail and messages then.

This city was the last place—the absolute last place—he might have expected to hear her laugh: a combination of wild monkey and a Slinky going down a set of stairs. Even almost six years later he would have known her musical cackle anywhere. But St. Louis, in the Fox Theatre? Not on your life. Not on hers, either.

But it was Shakespeare, which he knew to be in her blood. If he were to find her, it would be at a performance like this—and so a part of him was tempted, even convinced, that he'd finally found her.

The balcony. He imagined her selecting a seat that offered the strategic advantage of elevation, because that was just the kind of thing he'd taught her.

Onstage, Benedick, having dived into a horse trough, addressed the audience, his black leather riding pants and billowing shirtsleeves leaking water. Another volley of laughter rippled through the crowd, and there it was again. Larson felt like a birder identifying a particular species solely by its song.

He was no longer laughing along with the others. Instead, driven by curiosity, he was turned and straining to look up into the balcony.

Being too large for the closely crowded seats, his temperature spiked and his skin prickled. Or was that the possibility running through him? He represented Hope's past, her former self. Would she want that as badly as he did? Had she somehow found out about his transfer? Through all his training, coincidence nipped at his heels. Baffled, unsure what to do, he stayed in his seat.

The Fox Theatre, a renovated throwback to a bygone era, dwarfed its audience. Its combination of art deco, gilded Asian, quasi-Egyptian splendor, with anachronistic icons, like a twenty-foot-tall cross-legged Buddha, lit in a garish purple light, looked intentionally overwhelming. Despite the vastness of the hall, Larson felt impossible to miss. At well over six feet, and with shoulders that impeded both the theater-goers on either side of him, he would stick out if he stood. It seemed doubtful she might spot him, might recognize him from the back at such a distance, but he hoped she would. He glanced around once more, amused and concerned, intrigued and feeling foolish, his muscles tense. His shoulder ached, as it had ached for the past six years every time a storm drew near. He'd carried the same badge all these years, though now his credentials wallet showed a different title, Larson having been reassigned, along with Hampton and Stubblefield, to the Marshals Service's elite Fugitive Apprehension Task Force. Part bounty hunter, part bloodhound, part con man and actor, FATF marshals pursued escaped convicts and wanted felons in an effort to return them to their predetermined incarceration.

If she spotted him before he spotted her, what would come of it? Larson wondered. Would she fight through the crowd to be in his arms? Would she run? Again he put his own training onto her, deciding for her that she'd selected an aisle seat near an exit. She'd probably make for that exit rather than risk running into him.

He'd lost all track of the play. The audience erupted in laughter, and he'd missed the joke. He continued to imagine various ways this could possibly be her, but none made sense. Not here. Not St. Louis. Not unless she, too, were looking for him.

Six years. It seemed alternately to him like both a matter of days and a lifetime. What would he say to her? Her to him? Would she even care?

Larson wiped his damp palms on the thighs of his ⋯s. Again, a wave of laughter washed over the crowd. ⋯s time, something different: her distinctive laugh was ⋯r a part of it. Larson turned again in his seat, scan-⋯ious exits. No sign of Hope, but slightly behind him, a pair of men in dark suits stood with an usher, both dutifully scanning the crowd.

In an audience of twenty-five hundred, there were plenty of men wearing suits—but none quite like these two. Conservative haircuts, thick builds. The big guy looked all too familiar. Federal agents, like himself. Though not like him at all. FBI maybe, or ATF, or even Missouri boys, working for the governor. A WITSEC deputy? The federal witness security and protection service was now a separate entity, but had recently been part of the Marshals Service.

Larson knew many of those guys, but not all. These two, WITSEC? He doubted it.

He might have thought they were looking for Hope, but the big one looked right at him and locked on. This man somehow knew the row, the seat—he knew where to find Larson. Cocking his head, the agent directed Larson to meet up with them. Larson held off acknowledging while he thought long and hard about how to play this, the earlier buzzing of his BlackBerry now more persistent in his memory.

As with Hope's laugh, two deputy marshals, or agents, materializing at the Fox was anything but coincidence.

He felt tempted to check the BlackBerry but didn't want to leave his head down that long. The big guy's posture and the way he bit his lower lip revealed a gnawing anxiety, a nagging unrest. This wasn't a social call.

A nearby woman wore too much perfume. He'd been struggling with it through the performance, driven to distraction. Only now did he find it nauseating.

The audience laughed uproariously.

Larson chanced a last strained look toward the balcony, then gave it up.

Hope didn't miss anything. Whether she'd seen Larson or not, she'd likely have spotted the suits by now, and therefore was already well on her way to gone.

Intermission arrived with a wave of crushing applause. The stage fell dark. By the time the houselights came up, Larson had already slipped past four sets of knees, avoided a handbag, and laid his big hand on a stranger's shoulder.

Hope would now head in the opposite direction from the two agents; she would quickly put as much distance between herself and the theater as possible. Seek cover. Avoid public space. She would never look back and would not hurry, no matter how desperate she believed her situation. Her walk would be controlled, yet deceptively swift, her demeanor casual though determined. She would never return to the theater again, no matter what the show. If he were to catch her, he would have to run; and if he ran, the two bloodhounds were sure to follow; and if they followed, and if he led them to her, then he'd prove himself a traitor to her.

Stuck. Larson tested the agents' purpose by mixing himself into the throng and making for the opposite exit. But his head traveled a full head above most, like a parade float.

As expected, the two immediately followed, rudely pushing open a route to attempt to intersect Larson's path. Larson got caught in a snag of people as a wheelchair blocked the aisle. He cut through a now-empty row, working away from the men. Copies of *Playbill* littered the floor. He took the right flank and pressed on toward an interior door where people mingled looking lost.

Out of habit, he tested his skills, scanning the crowd for any woman wearing a headscarf or a hat, any woman making quickly for the main lobby and the doors beyond. He didn't spot her, and all the better. He had no desire to get her tangled up with these two.

Someone shouted and he knew it was for him. Adrenaline pricked his nerves. His stomach turned with the mixture of human sweat, cologne, and perfume. He pushed on to his left, his swollen bladder taking him down a long, wide set of elegant stairs as he joined a phalanx of men eager for urinals. He heard his name called out and cringed. It reminded him, not favorably, of being singled out by a coach, or the school principal.

He hazarded a look: The big one with the leather face and edgy disposition was following him, the younger one immediately on his heels.

He stopped on the stairs, and the current of impatient men streamed around him. He addressed his two pursuers as they drew closer, the face of the more senior of them revealing his surprise that Larson would allow himself to be caught.

"Gimme a minute of privacy," Larson said as he continued down, determined to appear unruffled.

Reaching the basement level, he entered a cavernous anteroom that held only a mirror, a small wooden table, and twin tapestry chairs that looked to be from a museum. Beyond this anteroom was the actual bathroom, about the size of a soccer field. Sinks straight ahead. To his left, a room of stalls; to his right a roomful of old porcelain urinals—there must have been thirty or forty of them. Built into the wall and floor, and so obviously antiques, the urinals looked surprisingly beautiful to him.

Larson took his place in line and emptied his bladder. One of the great pleasures in life.

"We need to talk." The same low voice, now directly behind him. The big one had followed him down. Junior Mint was no doubt standing sentry at the top of the stairs, ensuring that Larson didn't slip out.

"And I need to pee," Larson said, not looking back, but the magic of the moment spoiled.

A hand fell firmly onto his shoulder.

"Fuck off!" Larson shrugged and wrenched himself forward, dislodging the grip. Thankfully the man stepped back and let him finish. As he washed his hands he saw two images of the big pain in the ass in the cracked mirror.

"That was unnecessary," Larson cautioned. He wanted to establish some rules.

The agent said, "We were told you could be slippery. To respect that in you. That's why the hardball."

The guy at the next sink over stopped washing and eavesdropped on them.

"You trying to butter me up?" Larson asked. "You've got a funny way of doing that."

"I'm trying to get a message to you."

Larson had to stare down the man at the adjacent sink to get him to leave.

"So, deliver it."

"Here?"

Larson turned and faced the man, Larson taller by several inches. "Here."

Seen close up, this other guy's face carried an unintentional intensity—something, somewhere, was very, very wrong.

The man cupped his hand and leaned in toward Larson, who did nothing to block him, as his own hands were now engaged with a paper towel. The guy's breath felt warm against Larson's neck, causing a shiver as he said, "I was told to tell you that we've lost Uncle Leo."

Larson dumped the towel into the bin and heard himself mumble, "Oh, shit."